"Connie Rinehold's fertile imagination reworks a sad, lovely legend into a romantic's delight. If you believe in fate and happy endings, *Forever and a Day* is the story for you."

—Kasey Michaels, author of *The Homecoming*

"YOU DON'T EXIST. I MADE YOU UP. I DID. YOU'RE A DREAM."

He smoothed tendrils away from her face, lifting and kissing the ends before spreading them on the pillow.

Her heart jumped, then lay quivering in her chest.

"Midnight eyes with the sparkle of starlight in their depths." He pressed a kiss to one closed lid, then the other.

She felt it. Oh, dear heaven, she felt it—a dry press of warm lips, a lingering, and then nothing.

"Skin fair as the petals of a morning rose, creamy fair with a touch of dawn pink on your cheeks, and a mouth that curves upward, as if your spirit smiles even when you do not." His lips caressed each cheek in turn and slid down to her mouth, brushing the corners, skimming his tongue over the rest, and then nothing.

She reached for his mouth, reached for more of the sweet intoxication of his scent, his taste. But she could not reach far enough or high enough. Her eyes opened slowly, and her lips parted as she saw him above her. . . .

"In *Forever and a Day*, Ms. Rinehold spins sparkling words into a tale of enchantment."

—Joan Hohl, author of *Another Spring*

EXTRAORDINARY ACCLAIM FOR
CONNIE RINEHOLD
AND HER WONDERFUL PREVIOUS NOVELS

UNSPOKEN VOWS

"This is one for you who have a treasure trove of keepers! On par with the formidable Celeste De Blasis' *The Proud Breed.*"

—*Heartland Critiques*

"CONNIE RINEHOLD'S BEST WORK YET. The story is filled with passion and depth. It was an excellent read and I enjoyed it tremendously."

—Heather Graham, author of *Runaway*

"Reaches right down inside to touch your soul."

—Kathe Robin for *Romantic Times*

"RIVETING, SEDUCTIVE AND DEEPLY SATISFYING. I savored every word."

—Virginia Henley, author of *Enslaved*

LETTERS FROM A STRANGER

"AN EMOTIONALLY COMPELLING TALE . . . warm, thoughtful, and tender."

—*Romantic Times*

"Connie Rinehold wields her pen like a master swordsman in *Letters from a Stranger*. A poignant story of today, one that shouldn't be missed."

—*Rendezvous*

MORE THAN JUST A NIGHT

"With vivid characterizations and Connie Rinehold's flair, *More Than Just a Night* is a compelling tale of romance and suspense."

—Catherine Hart, author of *Tempest*

"I WAS CAPTIVATED FROM THE FIRST PAGE TO THE LAST by the powerful and compelling love story, and held spellbound by Ms. Rinehold's rich, expressive prose and depth of emotion. *More Than Just a Night* is alive with all the raw passion and emotion of the West."

—Kathe Robin for *Romantic Times*

CONNIE RINEHOLD

FOREVER AND A DAY

A DELL BOOK

Published by
Dell Publishing
a division of
Bantam Doubleday Dell Publishing Group, Inc.
1540 Broadway
New York, New York 10036

ISBN: 0-440-21359-2

Printed in the United States of America

Published simultaneously in Canada

February 1996

10 9 8 7 6 5 4 3 2 1

OPM

Dedication

To my mother, Glenna English—the best
there is.

To Morgan Kane—for painting so well what I
see in my imagination.
I love my covers, every one!

To Marjorie Braman—for many reasons, but
most of all for being a good editor.

To Meryl Sawyer, Maggie Osborne, and Jo Ann
DeLazzari—you're terrific!

To the new members of my family:
Daughter-in-law Sydney Elsner Rinehold—for
your big heart and sweet nature.
Son-in-law Joe Viera—for always knowing when
I need bizarre jokes and big hugs.
Grandson Joey—for joy.

And to Erica Winkler—surprise!

With special thanks to:
Francie Stark and Virginia Rifkin—there is not enough paper for me to list the reasons why.
Damaris Rowland and Steven Axelrod—you know why.
The Pikes Peak Romance Writers and Colorado Romance Writers—for support.

Then her finger moved in the moonlight,
Her musket shattered the moonlight,
Shattered her breast in the moonlight and warned him—
with her death.

The Highwayman—*Alfred Noyes*

PROLOGUE

The five sisters of Fate clustered around the fire, transfixed by the scenes taking form in the blaze, shocked by their inability to manipulate the earthly drama to suit themselves. Clotho sat at one of many spinning wheels, her hands guiding filaments of color into a fraying strand on the wheel. Ilithyia stood beside her, while Atropos hovered nearby, her shears poised to sever the strand. Lachesis knelt before the hearth, her eyes glazed with horror. Nemesis stared at the tableau of a single musket shot and the courageous act of a human they all favored—Bess, sweet, timid Bess, who knew nothing of the cruelty of man . . . until now.

Bess . . . standing tied to her bedpost, the musket of one of her redcoat guards tied beneath her shattered breast, her finger still curled around the trigger . . .

Bess, slumped against her bindings, praying that the man she loved had heard the shot and taken warning, then closing her eyes as the hoofbeats of his horse faded, carrying him away . . . Bess, smiling in relief as she breathed her last.

Bess, whose thread of life broke before Atropos could sever it cleanly.

Atropos lowered her hand, the shears snipping uselessly at her side. "It isn't time," she whispered in disbelief. "The girl has defied us."

"We must see what lies ahead—quickly, before more harm is done," Nemesis said and waved her hand over the blaze.

Time scrolled forward, to the break of dawn, to Dante listening as the tale spread through the village of how Bess had died to warn him of the redcoats' trap, and then to the bright gold of noon and Dante riding back toward the inn, with his rapier drawn, his outrage an eerie howl that seemed to go on forever.

"He cannot go back to the inn. He cannot!" Ilithyia, the goddess of childbirth, cried.

They gazed at the fire, at the highwayman galloping down the road, his fist raised, his howl of fury reaching them with such force that it echoed in the room.

Another figure ran out into the night—the tall yet frail figure of Tim, ostler at the inn owned by Bess's father. Tim, who had the body of a man and the mind of a baby. Tim, who loved Dante as a friend and Bess as a woman.

Tim, whose simple mind had not comprehended the consequences of betraying them both to the redcoats. He'd only understood that Dante wanted to take Bess away from him. Away where he could not see her, brush her hand, receive her smiles, breathe in the scent of roses when she passed by him.

And now Bess was dead and Tim ran into the line of fire to save the only other person who had treated him with kindness and friendship.

Again there were musket shots as bursts of fire reached out from the windows of Bess's chamber and a hail of musket balls struck Tim, felling him in the path of Dante's horse. Dante reined in hard at the sight of the poor half-wit lying in dust and blood. His horse reared high. More shots exploded in the air. More balls knocked Dante from his saddle.

He lay by the side of the road, by the rosebush he had planted for Bess not so very long ago. His hand lifted toward a bloom withering on its stem, but he could not reach it.

Atropos stepped forward and poised her shears over the strands winding on the spindle.

''No, it is not his time either.'' Nemesis laid her hand on her sister's arm, staying her from severing the life of the man whose blood watered the roots of a rosebush by the side of the road. ''His time or not, he is dying,'' Atropos snapped. ''We must gain control—''

''I'll find you, Bess,'' Dante choked. ''Neither heaven nor hell will have me until I do . . . I swear . . .''

''No,'' Clotho moaned as his thread frayed, with only a single strand clinging to her hand, a wispy fiber of spirit refusing to release its hold on life. ''He defies us even now.'' She pointed to the fire, to the image of Dante walking toward a river limned by a waning moon, its black waters churning as if its spume would reach out and pluck the unwary from solid ground.

On the opposite shore, light flickered and grew brighter.

"It is her . . . Bess," Ilithyia said hoarsely and pointed to the woman standing across the waters, her black hair flying in a gusty breeze, her hands reaching toward the man she had loved more than her own life. "She is waiting for him. . . ."

A figure shrouded in cloak and hood stood on the shore, one hand outstretched to collect coins from the beings lined up to enter a boat bobbing in the water.

Dante took a coin from beneath his tongue and showed it to the ferryman.

Clotho caught her breath as a mist rose from Dante's body, a shadow of luminous mist assuming his form as it separated from him and rose upward to hover among the clouds, apart from its earthly host.

As one, the sisters gasped as the specter drifted away on the midnight breeze.

The ferryman shook his head and barred Dante's entrance to the boat.

Atropos shrank back from the scene in the flames. "How can Charon turn away a soul?"

"You heard him: 'Neither heaven nor hell will have me.'" Lachesis, the giver of good fortune, said. "Dante's soul is lost to the winds and must be redeemed before he can cross over."

"Such fools humans are to think they can dictate their own destinies," Atropos spat.

"A fool?" Clotho said. "He has cheated death."

"He has chosen his own fate," Nemesis said, "and now he must suffer the consequences."

"He was such a beautiful, wondrous child." Ilithyia nodded toward the spinner. "And the thread of

life Clotho spun for him is equally wondrous in its strength and texture.''

Clotho stared down at the fragile strand clinging to a thicker, stronger thread. A thread whose transparent core was blended with strong nubs the blue-black color of Dante's hair, the moonsilver that matched his eyes, the claret and buff of the clothing he favored.

''But he is no longer a child,'' Ilithyia said and pointed at the image of Dante standing on the empty beach in the darkness, reaching out to the woman waiting on the far shore. Bess, too, reached out, her body straining forward, as if she could bridge the gap between one world and the next. The clouds parted over the moon, and a chain of light streamed over the inky water between man and woman, linking them, binding their destinies.

''See what he has become,'' Atropos sneered, ''and remember that because of him, Bess's thread broke too soon.''

''Hush, Atropos,'' Lachesis said. ''He is truly in our hands now, for none other will have him while his soul wanders in the ether.''

Clotho reached for the torn ends of Bess's life and held them next to Dante's. ''If I am careful I might pick up their threads again and continue, but it will take much time and all the skill I possess.'' She turned to Nemesis the Inevitable, punisher of those who broke the laws of nature and protector of those who lived in harmony with the universe. ''What say you, sister?''

Nemesis studied the threads of the man and woman, turning them over and twining them in her fingers. ''We have no choice. Bess will wait on that shore forever with no hope of peace unless we allow her to return in another time, another place.'' She smiled grimly. ''But do take your time, Clotho, in re-weaving the filaments together, and spin out Dante's thread in neutral colors until it can be interwoven with Bess's.''

Ilithyia gazed at the fire. ''A pity he cannot begin life anew like Bess.''

''Impossible,'' Nemesis said. ''Instead, Dante will wait as Bess waited for him night after night. And he will be trapped within the boundaries of his transgressions, riding the same road night after night and year after year, waiting for his spirit to return to his body . . . waiting for Bess to live again.''

''Time without meaning, and existence without life will be just punishment for his carelessness,'' Atropos said.

Lachesis knelt in front of the hearth and reached into the flames, seeming to touch the beautiful face of the man. ''May he find all that he has lost . . . sometime . . . somewhere.''

PART ONE

Renewal

She twisted her hands behind her; but all the knots held good!
The Highwayman—*Alfred Noyes*

1

Wyoming—1878

So few possessions with which to begin a new life, Betina mused as she shoved her single packed bag beneath her bed, then stared out at the expanse of night outside her window. Mountains rose about her home, both shelter and barrier to the outside world. A world she hadn't seen beyond Cheyenne and Laramie, and had only heard about from the guests who frequented her father's guest ranch. A world of people and places separated by great bodies of land and water.

Such vastness to cross alone with nothing to guide her but the knowledge gleaned from books and the idle talk indulged around an evening fire.

"You can't go off to a foreign country by yourself," her father had said.

"Yes, I can," Betina responded. "I am long past my majority and free to do as I wish."

"Wait until you're married and let Tim take you on a Grand Tour if that's what you want." Her father nodded as if the matter were settled. "I'll arrange for a solicitor in London to sell the property for you."

Of course it made sense, yet she hadn't felt particularly sensible when she'd received notification that she'd inherited a posting inn in England from a distant relative. An inn that apparently had been abandoned a century ago, though ownership was passed down from one generation of the Wells family to the next.

Immediate visions of dark moors and sheer cliffs towering over a foaming sea filled her imagination. Her family and friends didn't understand why she wanted to go. They didn't think she could manage such a journey with only Phineas, the retired foreman who had been like a grandfather to her, for company and protection.

But then, her family and friends didn't believe she could do anything at all except live the life already planned for her.

She couldn't blame them really. From the day of her birth she'd been called slow-witted or simple-minded. Kinder souls described her as being fey. She suspected that her parents had looked upon their infant daughter, who was far too quiet and unfocused to be normal, and feared that the descriptions were right. But then she had progressed through childhood, sitting up, walking, and talking at all the proper times. To this day they expounded on how easily she had learned to read and write—with amazing comprehension, they said—as if they needed to remind themselves of her quick mind whenever she fixed them with a particularly vague look or tossed and whimpered in her bed with the same dream night after night.

A dream that had first come to her with her menses—of a phantom rider galloping toward her on an unfamiliar road, the moonlight a luminous thread behind him, tethering him to earth, holding him just out of her reach.

She hadn't told her family what the dream was, nor that it both frightened and excited her at the same time, that she awakened with tears of frustration because she'd tried so hard to see his face, to touch him. They wouldn't understand that the place in her dream seemed familiar to her though it bore no resemblance to the craggy, snowcapped mountains and gnarled landscapes of Wyoming. They wouldn't understand that the dream seemed more real to her than the world she inhabited, just as they didn't understand her.

Only Phineas understood her. He spent hours spinning tales for her of faraway places and distant lives. At other times he shared long silences with her, nodding from time to time as if they were actually conversing. He said that she was simply absentminded.

She'd liked that explanation for her frequent journeys into herself, for the way her view of the world always seemed slightly out of focus, as if she were observing it all through wavy glass. And though she was always aware of what went on around her, she felt as if a part of her mind stood apart . . . watching . . . waiting . . . searching . . . for something.

She wished she knew what it was.

Betina sighed and turned away from the window. The packet of papers she'd taken from her father's desk lay on her bed next to her reticule. She'd felt an uncommon anger at him for assuming that he would keep them for her, that he would control her inheritance, and that she would naturally want him to do so.

With her inheritance had come a profound sense of freedom and a restlessness to journey beyond the small world fashioned by others for her comfort. She didn't want to walk down the aisle on her father's arm only to be handed over into Tim's care.

The newly appointed foreman of the guest ranch and son of her father's banker, Tim was both quiet and strong. Quiet enough to be comfortable with Betina's silences, and strong enough to take care of and protect the small empire she would inherit someday.

She loved Tim—for the childhood they'd shared, for his steady presence daring anyone to see her as anything but a desirable woman, for his faith in her when he'd insisted that her father bequeath his wealth solely to her without the usual provisions that it be controlled by his future son-in-law. Most of all, she loved him for encouraging her to go to England if she must. For all that, she wanted him to have a good wife. She wanted him to be happy.

But she wasn't entirely sure that she was the one most capable of giving him all he deserved from life. She wasn't sure she wanted to be the right one for Tim.

She knew that she didn't want Tim to show her the world.

She wanted to discover it for herself.

For that she needed money, courage, and a head start on her way to England.

Her heart leapt into her throat as someone knocked on her door, then opened it before she could grant permission to enter.

Her mother walked in and quietly shut the door behind her. Dear Mama, who went through the motions of honoring Betina's privacy, yet never gave her time to enforce it. Etta Wells would be horrified if her daughter actually pointed out the oversight. But Betina wasn't in the habit of horrifying anyone, even in such a small way.

"I suggest you hide that before your father realizes it's missing from his desk," Etta said, nodding toward the packet. "I've always found a pocket sewn into the underside of my petticoat to be an excellent hiding place."

Betina could only open her mouth and stare. Her mother, the oh-so-gracious and biddable wife of Jacob Wells, host of wealthy Europeans and Easterners—and on occasion royalty—hid things in her petticoats? "Why?" Betina asked.

"I've had occasion to squirrel away a secret or two over the years." Etta smiled as she produced several squares of muslin, needle, and thread from the pocket of her dressing gown. Mama had pockets in everything she owned, and they were usually full. "A woman needs to have her own hiding places for the private bits and pieces of her life." As she spoke she sat in a chair and threaded her needle. "Take off your petticoat . . . and give me the one you've packed. We haven't much time to get you ready for your journey."

Panic rose thick and suffocating in Betina's throat as she instinctively fumbled with the tapes at her waist and stepped out of the undergarment. Mama knew. But how could she? She had never defied her parents' wishes before. "Am I going on a journey?" she said carefully.

Etta took the petticoat, turned it inside out, and began attaching one of the hemmed squares with small, even stitches. "You're going to leave at first light after your father and our newest guests leave for the hunting trip I suggested. They're quite excited about seeking prey without benefit of dogs and buglers and bush-beaters. At this time of year they will have to go far to find game and are planning on being gone for two weeks." She shook her head. "I still can't get used to the idea that men will pay so much to stay at a guest ranch, hunt animals they have no intention of eating, and sleep around a campfire. 'Getting a taste of the primitive life,' they call it. If they want primitive they should race winter across the mountains in a prairie schooner with a barrel of stale water and nothing but a handful of grass to wipe their lily-white . . . well, never mind. Give me your other petticoats please. I hope you had the sense to pack a woolen one as well as your muslins. The baron that arrived yesterday tells me England can be quite damp and chilly, particularly in the north."

For the first time in her life Betina's mind didn't wander as her mother indulged in lengthy dialogue. She stared at Etta, her panic dissolving into flutters of excitement. Mama *did* know, and she was sewing pockets into her petticoats—private places in which to hide her secrets.

Still, Betina was wary. She couldn't remember a day in her twenty-one years when Mama had gone against Papa. Nor could she remember a time when her parents hadn't always been within reach. They had loved her, given her everything she could possibly need or want, taught her about the dangers of the outside world, and protected her from them with single-minded devotion.

She was so sheltered that she wasn't entirely convinced that any dangers existed aside from the brawls in Cheyenne and the predators that came down from the mountains. None of that frightened her. The rowdies in town treated her with all the respect her father demanded, and the one time she had seen a mountain lion had been more interesting than threatening. She'd stared at the cat, studying its bared teeth and mangy coat, taking in every detail. The cat had lost interest in her and wandered off long before she'd lost interest in it.

She'd kept the incident to herself, knowing that if she told, her father would have insisted on sending one of the hands to guard her even when she went to the necessary.

"I haven't all night, Betina," Etta said. "And you must get some rest before you leave." Folding the finished garment, she looked up at Betina with raised brows. "And don't tell me you've changed your mind. I won't have it."

"You want me to go, Mama?"

"No. I want to keep you close where I can protect you and love you and—" Again, Etta shook her head firmly, as if to dislodge the sentiment. "You have to pick up your own life, spin it out in your way, whether your father and I like it or not." Sighing, Etta reached under the bed and pulled out Betina's valise. "You're not our baby girl anymore, and we can't continue to treat you as if you are," she said as she found Betina's petticoats, smiled that one was indeed woolen, and again began stitching pockets into them. "To tell the truth, I'm ready to have my husband all to myself. We began with strong passions and big dreams, you know. The passion produced you, and too many years of hard work gave us our dream in this guest ranch. I'd like to have the freedom to enjoy it with your father." Closing her eyes, she leaned her head against the chair. ‘‘I'm tired of fighting him over you. I would very much like to have his attention once in a while.’’ She opened her eyes and met Betina's gaze. ‘‘I would very much like for you to learn independence, so that you and I can both enjoy your adulthood.’’

Betina sank onto the edge of the bed. Of course she'd heard Mama argue with Papa over the years, more so since she had begun to change from child into woman. But it had never occurred to her that Mama had felt neglected or hurt because of Papa's protectiveness.

Betina tilted her head as she gazed at her mother, seeing her in an entirely new way. ‘‘It never occurred to me that you weren't happy, Mama,’’ she said softly. ‘‘I thought—’’

‘‘You thought that being the mother of Jacob's daughter was enough for me?’’ Etta asked with a catch in her voice.

‘‘I'm *your* daughter too.’’

Etta nodded. ‘‘I gave birth to you, but your father took you over before I knew what had happened. By then it was too late. I've felt more like your nurse and governess than your mother. . . . I've felt like an outsider.’’

Stricken, Betina could only sit rooted by her own realization of guilt. She knew what it was like to be an outsider, feeling out of time and place and trying to touch something that was beyond her reach. She should have recognized it, that expression she'd seen on her own face when she'd looked in the mirror. It was so clear on Mama's face and in her voice that Betina could feel it wrapping around her, suffocating her, blinding her to everything but her own need.

She didn't know what to say. Mama wouldn't want sympathy or apologies. It occurred to her then that maybe Mama wanted the same thing she'd wanted for most of her life—understanding. "Mama," she said as she picked up the finished petticoats and laid them in her bag, "is that why you carry on conversations as if you don't expect anyone to answer you? Because Papa and I were close and you felt left out?"

Etta smiled sadly. "I shouldn't have stood back and let it happen. But it did my heart good to see Jacob be such a devoted father. Most men think that their job is done once their seed is planted. They're too busy doing 'man things' like being strong and capable and protective. They forget how to be loving."

Sighing, Betina pushed the bag back under her bed, then straightened. "Not Papa," she said wryly. "He needs to learn how to spread love out more. Sometimes I feel as if I'll drown if he doesn't let me go."

"He worries about you."

"I know, Mama. I worry too," Betina whispered. "What if I *am* simpleminded and unable to cope, as everyone says?" There, it was said. She'd finally admitted that the opinions of others had nurtured the doubts within herself, doubts that kept her close to her family's love and protection, where no one ridiculed her behind indulgent smiles or shook their heads in pity.

"You have a fine mind, Betina. You are simply quiet and watchful, and that can be a very good thing. I suspect you see more than the rest of us." Knotting the thread, Etta bit it off and folded the last petticoat and draped it over the arm of her chair. "As for being afraid—I'm glad to hear it. A little healthy fear can be the best kind of protection."

A fine mind . . . see more . . . Betina knew that her mother meant what she said. Mama never minced words or cut the truth with the kindness of a fib.

She realized then that Mama, like Phineas, wanted her to act her age and treated her accordingly. "But Papa—"

"Your father can do nothing to stop you," Etta said firmly. "You're twenty-one and sound in both mind and body. He knows that even though he'd rather you didn't."

Etta rose and crossed over to sit beside Betina. "When your father returns from the hunting trip he will find a note that I have taken you to San Francisco 'to satisfy your urge to travel.' The note will also be an invitation for him to join us there. I think a whole continent and an ocean will put enough space between you."

"He'll be furious with you."

"Probably," Etta said. "But he'll get over it. Never doubt that he loves me, Betina. A marriage with love can have a stronger hold on a man than a grown child who doesn't need coddling anymore."

"Do you think you can keep him in San Francisco for a while, Mama?"

"I still have my looks and my figure, and . . . well, never mind about that."

Betina hid her smile at her mother's sudden flush of embarrassment. "Remember when I was thirteen and my monthly came?"

Clearing her throat, Etta nodded as she fiddled with her collar.

"I was so frightened, and you held me on your lap and explained what it was and why and what would come later . . . with a man. Then you took me to help the wife of one of the hands birth her baby."

"It was a good day for us," Etta said, her eyes misting.

"A day for doing 'woman things.' " Betina leaned over and kissed her mother's cheek. "Thank you, Mama, for making me feel grown up even when I wasn't."

Etta wrapped her arms around Betina for a long moment of silent support and comfort. Then she scooted back to fish a wallet from her pocket. "I've been saving this since the day you were born—a special gift from me to you. There's three thousand dollars in here and a letter of credit drawn on your inheritance from my father . . . enough, I should think, to keep you for a good while." She laid the wallet in Betina's lap then grasped her shoulders, holding her at arm's length. "I'm pushing you out of the nest, my darling. Something is waiting for you out there, and it's long past time that you found it. After you do, come back to us as the woman you were meant to be."

A memory crept like mist through Betina's mind, of a phantom on horseback riding in her dreams . . . plucking a rose from a lone bush . . . tucking it into her hair. A dream so real and vivid that she could smell the rose, feel the excitement of his rakish smile, believe in the enchantment of stolen moments and romantic promises. "Something is waiting . . ." she mused, then shivered in fear and in hope at the prospect.

Etta stood and took a handkerchief from her pocket to blot at her eyes. "Yes," she said. "Something is always waiting for each of us."

I'll come to thee by moonlight, though hell should bar the way.
The Highwayman—*Alfred Noyes*

2

Northern England—1878

"Farewell, my friend," Dante whispered as he smoothed the mound of earth covering the body of his horse. How many did that make? he wondered. Nine? Ten? How many had he buried wherever they had dropped, then marked the place with a plank for a gravestone? It was only fitting to honor his mounts in such a way. Only fitting to commemorate the only consorts he'd had in the last century.

He envied them for their ability to age and die. He envied—and sometimes hated—them for escaping life with such clean finality.

Escape. How badly Dante craved whatever release the Fates would grant him, yet he was trapped at the scene of his crimes, imprisoned by a curse of his own making. He knew what he was and why. There was only one question left unanswered.

How long? How long must he exist as neither man nor ghost? How long would he be denied the sharp urgency of hunger and the gritty desperation of thirst, the warm lethargy of satiation and the ease of answered need? How long would he exist in a soulless body that never aged nor suffered pain while his mind dwelled on the agonies of the past?

He knelt to pat the earth more solidly around the plank. ''Nothing will stir tonight,'' he said as if the gelding still stood beside him, nuzzling him with the warm breath of life on his neck. Tonight the old road would be as empty as the inn, leaving him with nothing but memories of past glories, nothing but endless visions of betrayal and loss.

Nothing.

The phantom rode only when he did, joining him for a gallop down the road leading toward the inn, making him feel as if he were truly alive, reminding him of the exhilaration of the chase, the challenge of trying to rob the Fates of their power over him, the hope that he might finally capture his soul and either become mortal once more or be destroyed at last. It mattered not which, for he knew that without his spirit, he could neither live nor die.

But it would not happen tonight. He would not feel as if he could almost touch the other part of himself, almost reach him for a few exhilarating moments. Moments when he almost felt complete.

And with each rising of the sun he would suffer the utter despair of knowing that no one waited for him, that there was no one with whom to share the sunshine, no one to hear his pleas for oblivion.

He was weary of the loneliness and desolation, weary of the hollowness within himself. He was weary of the guilt.

Bess had died to save him. Bess, who had loved him with an innocent devotion that had made him feel strong, invincible . . . worthy. She had gazed upon him with stars in her eyes and kissed him with the only sweetness he had ever known. She had trusted him as a man like him should never be trusted.

Bess had loved him, and she'd proven it with her life.

And he had loved her, his foolish princess in her tower, his sweet and beautiful angel who leaned out her window, her ebony braid falling over the sill for him to kiss. He hadn't known until she was gone that he hadn't loved her enough. He hadn't realized that he'd merely fed off her love, taking it into himself to nourish his dreams, to sustain his belief that he could be so much more than he was.

He had used her, stealing kisses and leaving promises in return. He had destroyed her.

And then he had ridden the old road one more time to mock his enemies, the bold highwayman in his claret velvet coat and tan breeches, his cocked hat and high black boots, laughing an ugly laugh and shouting curses at the sky. He would have died then and perhaps found redemption in his own doom if his soul had not forsaken him. But no, he'd had to vow that he would not rest until he found Bess again; he'd had to forbid his soul to enter whatever realm awaited him. A flamboyant gesture to be sure, he thought bitterly. A gesture delivered with his usual arrogance in a voice loud enough for all the powers above—and below—to hear, to condemn himself to the edges of existence, where sounds were distant and hollow, where he saw all that was real through a mist and only his memories were sharp and clear.

"How long, damn you?" he shouted to the sky, knowing he would not be heard nor answered except by the sound of his own anguish echoing over the empty moor and rebounding from the silent copse of trees surrounding the deserted inn.

Everything around him was as much a shell as he was—the inn where he had once seen hearts being filled with warmth and life, souls being replenished with smiles and laughter, people sharing love and sorrow and dreams.

People. Tomorrow he would walk among them, endure their fear of him as he searched the village for a new mount. And not one of them would understand the absurdity of a man who could not die having to suffer the inconvenience of replacing his all too mortal horse.

Tomorrow, if the Fates were in a generous mood, he might even find a nag worthy of a phantom. He stared up at the sky as if he could see the sisters among the clouds of Olympus. He'd trusted them to favor him. Women always had. But instead they'd wielded his dying words like weapons and held his hope for release like a carrot in front of him, a reward that was always beyond his reach.

"How long?" he whispered as he walked toward the lone rosebush by the side of the road. A bush he had planted for Bess, a gift she could look upon from her chamber window and breathe in the scent of flowers carried on the evening breeze. But the bush existed without life, a solid presence that never changed, never grew, never bloomed . . . forsaken by life and death alike. . . .

Like him—a body without a soul, a heart without a purpose, a mind that knew nothing of what lay beyond the boundaries of his own private hell.

How long would he remember the power of Bess's smile as he'd risen in his saddle to tuck a bud into the love knot plaited into her hair? How long would he dream of her shadowy form standing on the shore of a black river, her hair blowing in the wind, her hand outstretched toward him?

As long as Bess's exile from life.

The answer was a sigh on the spring wind, a rustle in the trees growing on either side of the road, a quickening inside him that felt like awareness stirring after a winter's silence. But he refused to listen. He dared not believe that she was indeed exiled and would return to him, that he would be granted the opportunity to . . . what? Appease his conscience by loving her as she deserved? Redeem himself by becoming the hero she had thought him? Or again destroy her by taking too much and giving too little?

Silver twilight bled into the blood-red horizon of a dying day, casting all that surrounded him in an ethereal glow. He stared at the rising moon—a robber's moon that would shed just enough light to guide a highwayman to his prey, yet not enough to illuminate his path of escape through the trees.

But there was no longer any prey.

And he had no one to escape but himself.

They had tied her up to attention with many a sniggering jest . . .

The Highwayman—*Alfred Noyes*

3

"There's no room for you here," the woman said, her gaze on Phineas as she stood in the doorway of the small inn, barring their way inside. Not once had she spoken directly to Betina or met her gaze.

"Be there another place to board?" Phineas asked the woman.

"Never mind, Phineas," Betina said with a calm that threatened to drain her. "We'll get supplies of food and some household necessities and go on to my property tonight. I'm anxious to see it."

"You'll be staying there then?" the woman asked, seeming oddly pleased as her gaze skidded away from Betina to again rest on Phineas.

"We must hurry," Betina said, ignoring the woman. "It's late and we'd best get back on the road before we lose all the light.'' The woman gaped as Betina turned on her heel and walked away with a slow, measured tread though her knees refused to bend and every step jarred.

She'd never known how devastating rejection could be until she'd encountered that of the villagers and farmers who were to be her neighbors.

Breathing deeply and barely managing to compose herself, she forced her gaze to find and linger on each of the villagers scattered singly and in whispering groups along the main thoroughfare, hovering near doorways as if the need for escape might be imminent.

Escape from her.

It had been the same when they had stopped at a posting house for their midday meal and later when they'd paused at a farmhouse to ask directions to her property. Each time she'd been forced to retreat into the depths of the coach her London solicitor had provided, just so Phineas could pry information from the natives. When they'd arrived at the village an hour ago they'd seen the farmer riding his white horse from shop to cottage to produce stall, talking rapidly and frantically waving his arms. He'd paled and slunk away when he'd seen the coach and Betina staring at him from the window. Evidently he'd taken a shortcut into town for the sole purpose of warning his neighbors about her arrival.

Of course she'd become accustomed to being avoided at home, but the people there were friends and family who loved her, or at least cared about her. They didn't attempt conversation with her because they knew she rarely paid attention as her mind wandered along her own trails of thought. They shook their heads and whispered about her, but it was with a sort of benevolent pity that hurt at the time but did not maim.

The people here were strangers to her, yet they saw something in her that provoked more than pity or even wariness. None appeared surprised to see her—a stranger—in their midst, yet it seemed as if they feared her. And in their fear she saw her own—that she wasn't normal, that Mama and Papa believed she was because they had to, that Tim believed it because she was pretty and made few demands and simply because he wanted to. Because they knew that in spite of her oddities she was kind and gentle and harmless.

She hadn't realized until now that she had wanted to go out in the world so she could know that she would be accepted anywhere as she was at home. To prove to herself that she wasn't really so different from others and that she didn't have to depend on others to protect her from the harsh realities of life.

Pride had not been something she'd contemplated until now, when humiliation cut deeply rather than simply bruising her. She found it now and used it with a fierce determination to hold up her head as she reached the coach and turned to wait for Phineas to catch up with her.

"I'll take ye on out to the inn and come back for what we need," he said as he took her elbow to help her into the coach.

"No." She clamped her mouth shut on a rising note of panic and bent to grope in her reticule for the pouch of money she periodically replenished from her petticoat pockets for traveling expenses. Finding it, she raised her head, deliberately blurring her view of the townspeople as she swallowed and held out the pouch.

"No. Get everything we need for at least a week. I'll wait here."

"A week, missy? Ye sure?"

She smiled for the benefit of their avid audience. "Do you want to come back any sooner than you have to, Phineas? I certainly don't."

"Can't fault ye for that," he said as he took the pouch. "They be a spooky lot, for sure."

"It appears that they think I'm the spook," she said, unable to hide the catch in her voice.

"I'll help ye in then, missy. Ye stay put, ye hear?"

Something snapped inside her at the subtle warning in his voice. Suddenly she was angrier than she'd ever been in her life. Angry enough to defy her own fear as well as that of the villagers. "I'll manage, Phineas. Right now I've a need to stretch a while longer before I sit down again. You go on before the shops close."

He smiled at her and nodded his head in the way he had when he approved of something she said or did, then turned toward the produce stalls and food shops.

The moment he disappeared into the butcher shop she felt his absence, felt the utter loneliness of standing on a street littered with strangers who stared at her and muttered among themselves while making signs as if they were warding off the evil eye. Such bravery she had when Phineas was beside her, she thought with bitter self-mockery. Why couldn't she have simply surrendered to the dark safety of the coach like the coward she was? Still, she'd managed to traverse the territories and states of America, cross the Atlantic and the length of England without suffering a single qualm. She certainly should be able to manage a show of courage for a minute or two.

Again she glanced around, willing the villagers to meet her gaze, to see her smile and realize that she was no different from them.

No one did. The closest she came to eye contact was two women whispering and shooting furtive glances her way.

Concentrating on the details of the village itself, she focused on an alley between a tailor's shop and a small cottage—the tailor's home, she presumed—and saw a darker shape among the late-afternoon shadows. She squinted and made out the form of a man leaning negligently against the stone wall of the cottage, his head cocked as if he were listening to the two women.

A shiver crawled up her spine as she realized he was staring at her . . . directly at her, without fear. And in that brief moment she imagined that his eyes were light, like pale blue ice, cutting through the darkness, seeing through her.

"That's her," a farmer's wife said, pointing to a coach layered with the grime of a long journey. "Rides in grand as you please and says she'll stay at her inn. Can you imagine it? *Her* inn, she says. Someone ought to tell her it belongs to none but the highwayman. Someone ought to tell her—"

"I won't be telling her a thing," the woman's companion said as she peered at the coach. "Did you see her? She's the one, I tell you, black hair and all, and come back from the netherworld to finish things with *him*."

Dante knew from the way the woman said it that she was referring to himself. *Him,* who haunted the old deserted post road leading out to the equally deserted inn. *Him,* whose name was invoked to terrorize strangers and frighten small children into behaving. *Him,* a shell of a man, a cursed being who was denied even the companionship of his own shadow.

He leaned back against the stone wall in an alley, hiding and waiting until the last minute so he could fool himself into believing they weren't right, that he was simply a mortal man seeking the society of others. And a fool he was. A hundred years should have been adequate time for him to learn that, like gossip, legends could be twisted into something ugly if told often enough.

He'd heard it all in the last century, and still it was agony to hear frightened whispers rather than conversation, to know that they spoke *of* him rather than *to* him.

Once . . . *ah, God* . . . once he had been their hero, making fools of the wealthy as he robbed them, eluding capture with taunting laughter and flamboyant antics, sharing his increasing wealth with the tenant farmers and shopkeepers when rents and taxes came due, then robbing the collectors as they rode away with their pockets bulging and their coaches riding lower with the burden of overfed bodies and overblown conceits. What a grand joke it had been to help others without relinquishing so much as a ha'penny of his own loot.

Once the villagers and tenant farmers had made of him a legend to be shared and expanded and celebrated.

Now they feared him.

Why couldn't they see him for what he was—a pathetic fool with a century behind him and a future that stretched into infinity, promising neither life nor death?

The two women shifted their baskets and turned to more fully see the coach parked across the street.

"Who'd have thought someone would come to claim the inn after so long?"

"It's *her*, I tell you, come to claim more than the inn. She'll be after *him,* I'll warrant."

Claim the inn? Dante realized what they meant then. It hadn't occurred to him that they had been talking about *his* inn. His mouth slanted in a derisive half-smile. His *haunt* would be a more appropriate term. He glanced at the coach, his eyes narrowed to make out the woman silhouetted by the glare of the sun lowering behind her. A woman, indeed, he mused, with her small stature and soft, soft curves, her refined profile and stiff posture. . . .

A woman who dared to claim the inn.

Not bloody likely.

Uncaring who he frightened, he stepped from the shadows and onto the cobbled walk.

The two gossips screeched and scattered, their broad hips jiggling as they ran toward the safety of their homes.

Something stirred in the air, like a collective gasp, as the man stepped into the light, still holding Betina's gaze. Yet she noted nothing about him except the shadows of him, in a closely cropped beard and deeply set eyes, in the planes of a strong face and stronger body, as if his features were blurred and he weren't quite complete. But the longer she stared at him, the more ridiculous her thoughts seemed. He was simply a man. Only a flesh and blood man whose expression showed nothing but a clenched jaw and tight mouth.

He appeared angry and she wondered why.

Activity fluttered up and down the street—doors slamming, feet running, mothers calling their children.

Betina blinked and saw empty space where the man had been. Not looking further, she climbed into the coach with undignified haste, uncaring if her ankles showed as she lifted her skirts or if her hat fell off as her head bumped the top of the doorway. Still, she glanced back over her shoulder at the hat lying on the ground beside the coach. It was her favorite, worn especially for the occasion of driving out to her property for the first time. Somehow it had seemed important that she arrive at the inn looking her very best, even if no one was there to see her. Now it didn't matter. Only escape from the morbid scrutiny of the villagers mattered. Only hiding from the penetrating gaze of the man mattered.

She settled against the squabs and smoothed her skirts, willing her hands to stop trembling and her thoughts to take a more rational course.

With the street empty of villagers and their morbid curiosity, and the walk across the way unoccupied by *him*, it was easy to tell herself that he was only a man. A man who had simply looked at her, nothing more. Of course his stare hadn't been malevolent or sinister. He'd merely been interested, curious.

Hadn't she wished for someone to act as if they saw her instead of turning away from her in fear and whispering about her behind their hands?

She raised her hand to trace the shape of her face—her eyes and ears, nose and mouth and chin and the rusty-black hair that she'd woven into a chignon at the back of her neck—assuring herself that she hadn't suddenly grown a third eye or a longer nose. She was as she'd always been—a smallish, well-proportioned woman with pleasant features and an abundance of self-doubt. A woman who was neither ugly nor frightening.

Betina peered out of the window as a man rode past, the clatter of his horse's hooves on the cobbles disturbing the uncommon stillness in the village. She recognized him as the farmer who had raced into town ahead of her and Phineas. Red-faced and winded from his gallop from house to house, he dismounted and glanced about, apparently only now noticing the lack of activity around him.

Another man stepped out from the shade of the smithy's open-fronted shed and pointed to the big stallion. He held out a handful of coins as if he was preparing to bargain for the horse. That normalcy soothed her as she focused on the men and the animal in question, linking the incident to home and how Papa and Tim never allowed anything to interfere with the serious business of buying and selling livestock. At least there were two people in this town that had more important things to do than treat her as if she were the devil's familiar. . . .

Suddenly, she recognized the tall, lean body and ice-cold eyes.

It was *him.*

Dante smiled as the horse lifted its head and pranced while its owner held the reins too tightly. The nag had spirit and was too fine for the likes of the dairyman. Better yet, it was white. A ghostly, mottled white. A fitting mount for a phantom.

Before the man could take a step away from him, Dante cut him off, not bothering with pleasantries that would not be appreciated. ''Name your price for the horse.''

The man turned as pale as his mount. ''Lord save me,'' he muttered and shoved the reins at Dante.

''Name your price,'' Dante repeated.

''Take it,'' the dairyman said. ''Just leave me and mine be.''

''A noble steed for the price of a promise. Fair enough,'' Dante said as he deliberately dropped several coins on the ground, and turned to the stallion that stomped and tried to back away. Dante smiled and crooned to the beast as he scratched its head between its ears, then pressed his forehead against its forehead, closing his eyes for a moment and continuing to whisper in a singsong cadence. The horse quieted and whuffled and nodded its great head as if it were agreeing with him, and Dante knew the animal was his. It had been this way with animals and women and poor halfwits when he'd been truly alive. Now only the animals responded to his charm.

He mounted the horse and turned it toward the post road. For effect, he paused at the edge of the village and pulled on the reins, commanding the horse to turn and dance in place. From behind windows and doors he saw faces peek out at him, then hastily back away, out of sight. The few people left on the street turned and ran for shelter, their mouths working, Dante knew, in mumbled incantations against evil.

A short barrel of a man of indeterminate age left the baker's and stood on the walk, watching Dante as if he knew him. And for a brief, jolting moment a sense of familiarity shot through Dante. But then it scattered and disappeared as if it hadn't been. He turned to gaze ahead, denying that he'd felt anything at all.

As he rode past, the woman in the coach leaned forward in her seat, her hand gripping the edge of the window, her head tipped to one side, her lips parted in an attitude of surprise. . . .

Surprise rather than fear.

Everything about her seemed fresh and clean, with her fair skin that bloomed with a soft blush of rose on her high cheekbones, her wide eyes and dark brows that arched and curved like the wings of a falcon drifting on currents of air. And for that moment he felt an odd quickening as he stared at the points of her upper lip, the full sensuality of her lower one, the natural upward curve of the corners. . . .

He pulled back on the reins and the horse reared up, its front legs pawing the air as Dante held the woman's gaze, captivated by the innocence in her countenance, the fascination of her stare.

He'd succumbed to such innocence as hers once before . . . and he'd destroyed it with unkept promises and selfish love.

The horse planted its feet on the ground and stood with its head held proudly high. Dante's mouth slanted in a mocking smile. He swept his cocked hat from his head with a flourish, held it to his chest, and bowed in her direction.

Her face paled with fear.

It was a start.

A cloud of dust billowed around him as he gave a deep-throated laugh and urged the stallion into a reckless gallop away from the village.

His derisive laughter echoed in the air as if it came from a deep and rocky pit, a sound eerie in its hollowness.

Betina couldn't move, couldn't take her gaze from the man disappearing down the road. Fear held her captive as surely as the fantasy that visited her in the dark of night. A fantasy who always swept off his hat, always held it to his heart like a silent pledge as he rode out of her sleep in the moment before dawn touched the sky with color and light.

"That's a fine horse," Phineas said.

The phantom of her night dreams rode a fine white horse dappled with palest gray, as if it were part real and part mist.

"A fine-looking man too." Phineas opened the door to set several cloth bags of supplies on the floor at her feet.

Yes, fine-looking . . . and sinister, with his dark beard and deeply set eyes that seemed to see right through her. A man, she reminded herself . . . not a vision. Betina blinked and focused on the place where man and rearing horse had seemed about to take flight into the clouds. Nothing was there—not even a grain of dust in the air—and if Phineas hadn't commented, she would have wondered whether she'd seen anything at all.

Silence hung thick and oppressive around her. Doors and shutters were closed and the town looked as if it had been abandoned except for the occasional face peeking from a corner of a window and the fresh produce still set out in front of a farmer's stall. A basket lay on its side in the street, its contents scattered on the cobbles, and the blacksmith's bellows were smoking where they had been abandoned half in, half out of the smithy's still burning fire. Everywhere she looked she saw the clutter of haste—a bonnet crumpled on the ground, a precious egg cracked and spilling its meat beside the gate of a cottage—as if a plague had descended and the citizens had fled danger without regard to possessions. As if they had sacrificed material concerns for the preservation of their lives.

She released her breath and straightened. The stillness around her seemed even more macabre as the rim of the sun touched the horizon, spreading a crimson glow on the underside of clouds moving in from the sea. "Can we go now?" she asked.

"Mayhap we should before they call the vicar to cast us out," Phineas said and retrieved her hat and handed it to her before climbing up onto the driver's box.

The coach rolled from cobbled street to dirt road with a thump of the wheels. Thatched roofs and civilized dwellings gave way to a wide moor shadowed with peat bogs and brushed with heather that glistened like amethysts in the twilight.

A half-moon rose as they left the rumpled lavender moor to enter a portal of trees that marked the beginning of her land. Something quickened inside her as she stared at the road, so desolate and unearthly in the luminous silver light of evening. There was a stillness in the air, a sense of waiting in the trees that bowed over the road like grieving old men, their branches meeting overhead in an attitude of some odd ritual dance. In the lantern light their branches and leaves appeared stiff and brittle and dull—more gray than green. Nothing seemed to flower here as it did on the color-splashed moor.

Nothing but the gloom of despair.

Dante found his old hiding place by the side of the road and urged the horse into a dense stand of trees. Here the moonlight streamed over the packed earth of the road, revealing anything that approached, be it of this world or the next.

He cocked his head at the distant sound of wheels creaking over the track. He saw nothing through the mist that crept over the ground, yet the sound persisted—wheels turning, hooves plodding, invading his domain. . . .

So the woman thought she would claim the inn, did she?

She would lodge there, would she?

Dante thought not. No one trespassed on this parcel of the world that was both his prison and his refuge. It belonged to him, a monument to the memories that were all he had left of mortal existence save the shell of his body and a mind that saw no further than yesterday.

Memories of Bess and what he had done to her.

Again he laughed, and the sound became a howl to summon the moon.

Tonight, the highwayman would chase more than his soul.

For the road lay bare in the moonlight;
Blank and bare in the moonlight;
And the blood of her veins in the moonlight
throbbed to her love's refrain.
The Highwayman—*Alfred Noyes*

4

The shadows of the trees seemed to reach inside the coach, brushing over Betina, touching her with a deep, pervasive sadness. Mist crept along the ground and rose in plumes around the coach, its tendrils climbing up the closed windows and sliding away again.

The coach lurched to a stop and she heard Phineas crack the whip and urge the team on, but the coach only rocked and swayed and slid backward as if it were mired in mud.

"Sit tight, missy," Phineas called as she opened the window. "I've some planks to slide under the wheels. We'll be free soon enough."

She gazed out at the trees separated by moonlight and leaned forward, perching on the edge of her seat as a shadow moved beneath an ancient oak, an apparition that seemed to rise from the mist that clung to the ground . . . a man standing so still and watchful that he seemed a part of the shadows, his pale-silver eyes seeming to reflect rather than see. A breeze disturbed the leaves above him and a shaft of light fell on his face.

Something fluttered and tightened in her chest—both fear and fascination as she stared at him, at his strong features sharply defined by twilight and shadows, at the mocking smile on his finely molded mouth framed by a closely cropped beard and mustache.

It was *him*, the man she'd seen in the village.

So, she had come.

Dante saw the woman lean forward in her seat, stare at him in startled recognition and then a dawning fear. Good. He was well-practiced in cultivating fear, and she looked to be an easy subject. Easy enough, he'd warrant, to run away before another night fell over his domain.

A shame really. It had been a long time since he'd met a challenge worthy of his talents.

Dante watched the old man struggle to slide short planks beneath the wheels of the coach. It would take some effort, for the coach had sunk into a deep pothole and it had rained heavily the night before. He'd tested the mud himself and known that a lumbering vehicle could not find purchase in such muck.

The ever-present mist and last night's rain served him well tonight.

His horse grumbled and backed away, jerking on the reins as clouds drifted across the moon, creating ethereal patterns of ebony and silver on the ground. Dante cupped his hand over its muzzle, silencing the stallion though its hooves lifted and fell in a mincing, skittish dance.

Dante smiled. Even his horse was spooked. It was indeed a perfect night for a haunting.

Across the road, mist undulated on the ground like a live thing awakening . . . tendrils of evening fog winding upward, taking the transparent form of a man and horse, a man with *his* face, *his* body, and a steed of white mottled with pale silver.

Dante's lips moved, yet he could utter no sound. It was too early for their usual chase down the road, and somehow Dante knew that it was the woman who had lured his soul from the vapor. The woman. A perfect lure.

It was ideal—he and his soul working in harmony to drive out the intruders. He willed the woman to turn her head, to see what he saw, to panic and run. . . .

To provide him with the opportunity to at last capture his spirit and claim true life or final death.

His fingers tightened on the reins and he tried to turn to mount his horse, but the mist held him fast and he could do nothing but watch as the shadow part of himself rode forward, the ghostly mount beneath him bunching its hindquarters, lifting its forelegs . . . leaping high toward the coach.

Surely he was only a wraith conjured from her imagination. Surely it was the place with its brooding veils of mist playing tricks on her. Betina blinked her eyes and pinched her arm, hoping she would not feel it, that she was asleep and again dreaming of the phantom who both beguiled and terrified her. Her arm stung from the dig of her nails and her eyes focused. He was still there, standing beneath the tree, a man of shadow and frost, savagely beautiful and fiercely intent as he stared at something beyond the coach.

Betina tore her gaze away from him, turned her head to follow his gaze.

A column rose from the shimmering fog, taking shape as it drifted toward her. She glanced at the man beneath the tree, then back to the phantom rising from the mist, two visions of the same man, one solid, one luminous and transparent—two parts of the same whole, yet separate.

She couldn't breathe, and her heart seemed to stop beating. Her body could not move and she felt strangely languid . . . accepting . . .

Accepting that the specter of man and horse was galloping toward her, leaping in a graceful arc, permeating the coach itself . . . passing through her. She felt it—a surge of warmth, a soft caress like a breath inside her, a whisper that was sensation rather than sound . . . a whisper that felt like a promise.

And then, sudden cold . . . unbearable loneliness . . . unutterable grief, as the luminous vapor slid out of her, away from her.

No! It was a soundless cry trapped within Dante as the spirit leapt through the opposite side of the coach, man and rider losing form and scattering on the evening breeze, his soul lost to him as it had been lost for a hundred years.

Dante sank to his knees, his body reeling with sensations he'd experienced for less than a moment—a touch of warmth, the drift of womanly scent, the sound of her gasp and then a sigh, the richness of seeing her through the eyes of a man who was truly alive. Sensations that stunned him with their sudden appearance and tortured him with their equally sudden absence, leaving him as empty as the inn, with no fire in the hearth and no laughter in the air.

He was nothing but a shell of flesh and bone, bereft of soul and spirit. He was dead and trapped in the pretense of living, cursed to think yet not feel, to need and to be denied, to chase his soul night after night with no hope of becoming whole.

A soul that had touched *her*, become a part of *her* for the space of a breath. *Her*, the woman who had mingled with the part of himself he had lost.

Why her?

The land grew silent, and even the clouds seemed to pause in their journey, as if reproaching him for asking a question to which the answer was obvious. He felt the beginnings of hope awaken within him, stretching with the possibility of salvation from his wretched existence, but he ruthlessly denied it.

He had learned to fear hope a long time ago.

Lurching to his feet, he stumbled through the forest, dragging his horse behind him as he raised his voice in a bellow of rage that seemed to last for a hundred years.

A deep, anguished howl echoed in the stillness—a primeval sound of torment and rage that seemed to come from within Betina as well as without, calling to her and finding an answer in the longing that cried out in her soul, the unfamiliar desire that quickened and warmed her body with need.

She gasped and panted and thought her heart would explode in her chest. Tears streamed from her eyes, and her sobs seemed as hollow and tortured as the cry of the man who'd stood watching her from the side of the road.

With trembling hands and frantic sobs she fumbled to open the window, to call Phineas's name. Swiping the tears from her cheeks, she pushed on the door and lunged out of the coach, finding nothing to ease her way to the ground. Her foot slipped in the mud of the pothole; her knee collapsed and she pitched forward.

"Whoa, missy." Grabbing her arm, Phineas kept her from landing face-first in the muck. "What are ye about in such a hurry?"

"Did you see him, Phineas? Did you hear it?"

"No one to see out here, missy," he said lightly, though he glanced at her sharply.

"He . . . it . . . looked like a ghost." Even as she said it she shook her head, denying it, refusing to believe what she'd felt, what she'd seen and heard. "It was . . . they were . . ." She shook her head, unable to describe what could not be.

"Ye look like a ghost yourself," Phineas said. "Mayhap ye fell asleep and had one of your dreams."

The chill grew worse, numbing her fear of the man she'd seen, replacing it with the sharp bite of Phineas's remark. She wrapped her arms around her middle, tightly, holding herself steady while the world suddenly shifted beneath her. "You too, Phineas?" she said, knowing she hadn't quite masked the pain, terrified that her dream had replaced reality, that her mind had slipped into itself for good. "You think I'm—"

"Two posts short of a fence?" he supplied as he wrapped her cloak more securely around her and lifted her into the driver's box, then climbed up beside her and twisted around to turn up the wicks on the lanterns hanging on either side of the seat. "Last I heard, dreaming is a natural part of living. It's one part of ye telling the other part what might be. Ye just started listening sooner than most. To my way of thinking, that makes ye smarter than the rest of us.'' He twisted around to glance back the way they had come. ''I think there are a lot of dreams talking here. Listen good, missy, and ye'll find what ye're looking for.''

Phineas clucked to the horses and cracked the whip in the air, and the coach lunged forward over the planks and onto dry ground.

''Wait, Phineas, the planks,'' she said, grasping at any semblance of normalcy she could find. It unsettled her to think that, in one day, the commonplace had become unusual.

''We'll leave them,'' Phineas said, driving on. ''Appears to me that hole doesn't dry out too often, and I don't expect anyone will come along and steal them.''

She shivered and wrapped her cloak more tightly about herself. The road was unkempt, the surrounding woods silent, the sky patched with clouds that seemed to hang low and still, though she could feel a cold breeze cutting through her. ''It doesn't look as if anyone has come here in a very long time,'' she said, startled that she'd voiced her thought aloud.

''Ye going to ask why, missy?''

After the way the villagers had reacted to her, and after seeing men made of mist and shadow, she was afraid to ask. Yet Phineas groped in his pocket for his pipe and clamped it between his teeth. She'd never known him to conduct a conversation without his pipe. Whether she asked or not, she knew he was going to tell her.

''The baker liked to talk,'' Phineas said. ''Told me some history ye might find interesting.''

History . . . like that she'd read in books. History explained through logic and reason things that otherwise seemed impossible, like who invented the steam engine and hot-air balloons that mingled with the clouds, like the extraordinary acts of heroes and the evil doings of villains. History was real, believable.

With smooth, absent motions, Phineas used one hand to pack his pipe with tobacco, then shifted it to the side of his mouth nearest her. Mechanically, she reached into her reticule for matches, struck one, and expertly held it over the bowl as he drew on the stem until a soft, fragrant cloud of smoke puffed upward.

''Will your history explain why those people treated me like a pariah?'' she asked.

''Mayhap,'' Phineas said.

''All right, I'm listening,'' she said on a sigh. At least if Phineas was talking she wouldn't be as likely to dwell on things she couldn't explain. And she felt safe with the lanterns glowing brightly around them, enclosing the coach, moving with it, a circle of light separating them from the mist and the darkness.

Phineas nodded and puffed, as he always did before launching into one of his tales. ''His name was Dante de Vere, and he was a highwayman a long time ago—about a hundred years or so—who loved Bess, the innkeeper's daughter. Her papa was like yours, caring so much for her that he sent her away to school so she'd be refined enough to find a decent husband, like the local squire or the vicar. But she loved the outlaw and planned to run away to the colonies with him when he had enough money.'' He paused to pull on his pipe and exhale several times. ''He rode right up to her window every night before his raids, and someone watched—twas the ostler, y'see, a poor half-wit who couldn't think like other folk. But he could feel sure enough, and what he felt was love for Bess and rage at Dante—his friend—who wanted to take her away. He turned Dante in to the redcoats.'' Phineas glanced over at her as if he were searching her expression, then directed his gaze toward the road once more. ''They came to the inn—your inn—and tied Bess to the bed-post with a musket beside her and pointing up at her chest to keep her quiet. When she heard her highway-man coming up the lane, she managed to get her finger on the trigger and fire. The shot warned away her man the way she wanted, and it killed her. Funny thing though: She had to know she'd die—no way she couldn't—and still she be doing the deed with a smile on her face.''

Sorrow filled Betina like a cold breath. *Bess had known she would die . . . and she had smiled.* She had given her life for his freedom . . . and she had smiled. It didn't make sense. ''What happened to him . . . Dante . . . the highwayman?'' she asked as an image of the man she'd seen raced across her mind followed by a drift of mist.

''He rode off but came back the next day after he heard what she'd done. They got him too, but he never died.''

Frowning at his choice of words, Betina turned to look at Phineas. ''What did he do?''

''He never died,'' Phineas repeated, then clamped down hard on the stem of his pipe.

The shivers renewed and doubled themselves and she shook so violently, she thought she might fall from the high seat.

"To this day they say he dwells in the gardener's cottage of the crumbling manor house down the road a ways."

"What of the people who live in the manor?"

"Well, Bess's papa had plans for her to wed the squire, and he were willing enough being that she was both comely and quiet. After she died, the squire went off with a rich widow to live in the city and left the place to rot." He plucked the pipe from his mouth and tapped the bowl against the side of the driver's box. Sparks scattered behind them as the coach rolled on. "The highwayman has no one to say him yea or nay as to where he dwells or what he does. So Dante rides like a demon over the road, following the same path night after night as he whistles a tune and shouts promises to the dead. Tis his soul he chases down the road, they say. And tis Bess he waits for . . . Bess, with black hair and eyes, almost like yours."

Betina couldn't comment. She could do nothing but listen to Phineas and hear the words "like yours" echo over and over in her mind as the memory of an unearthly howl of rage and yearning haunted her memory.

Pausing, Phineas stared ahead, as if he, too, heard something, then continued. "Her papa boarded everything up and went to the colonies. He wouldn't sell the place—said it was Bess's monument—and after a while no one came near it. I expect he found a wife and had more children. Looks like the cousin who left ye the inn would be coming from his new family. Mayhap it's been passed down from one generation to the next and ain't no one ever claimed it till now."

Something caught and twisted in Betina's chest as Phineas ended the grim chronicle of a daring hero and an innocent maid, of high adventure and bitter betrayal, of tragic loss and tormented spirits. An enduring legend that drove the villagers to make hasty signs to ward off the evil eye and cross the street to avoid brushing her skirts for fear of being cursed themselves—all because she had black eyes and long black hair. All because she had some resemblance to their tragic heroine of the past. All because she had no fear of taking up temporary residence at the inn where it had all happened.

She concentrated on the villagers' superstition rather than the causes behind it. She wouldn't give credence to their belief in such things. Dreamer though she was, she knew that her imaginings weren't real, that superstition was nonsense fostered by idle minds. "And that's why the villagers fear me?" she asked.

"Can't say it's all fear, missy. They be waiting, y'see. Waiting for their Bess to come back and make things right."

"But they wouldn't give us lodging—"

"They want ye here to end things. Ye can't do it from the town."

"What am *I* supposed to end?" she asked, irritation rising in her voice.

"They say the highwayman is waiting for Bess to come back," Phineas said as he tucked his pipe away. "They say his soul won't return to him until Bess does."

"Bess. Not me."

She felt Phineas's faded brown gaze on her, a penetrating scrutiny that she'd always interpreted as understanding of what lay beneath her faraway looks and distracted thoughts. But now her thoughts were clear and full of arguments against the absurdity of the villagers' behavior. "Nothing you've told me explains why they turned me out, but seem to welcome you."

"I don't be a part of their legend, missy. Ain't nothing going to be settled or finished by me. Tis only ye that has the power to do that, or so they be believing."

She didn't like that answer at all. And it was as absurd as the rest of it. She'd barely begun living her own life. How could she possibly be the key to resolving someone else's? "It's only a legend," she said firmly.

"And where do ye think legends come from?" Phineas asked.

"It's all superstition and Shakespearean drama," she stated. "I can't believe that it really happened."

"Can't ye now?" Phineas asked in the purring brogue that hadn't given way to a western drawl in the twenty-odd years that he had worked for her father. "And why not? Seems an honest tale to me."

"Honest, Phineas? With a woman who kills herself to save her true love?"

"Don't ye be thinking a woman—or man—could love that much, missy?"

"What is the point?" Betina replied. "If she is dead, what good is her love to him?" She frowned at that as she pondered her own question and wondered why it mattered, why it seemed to have some personal significance. Shaking her head, she discarded the thought and formed a question she doubted Phineas could answer. "And what of the phantom who supposedly chases his soul on this very road night after night?"

"What of him?"

"The notion is too foolish for even my fertile imagination, Phineas." Yet, even as she doubted the validity of what amounted to a yarn spun from imaginary floss, it seemed as real to her as this land of mystical traditions and dark history . . . a place Betina had seen in her dreams. A place that lent itself well to dark tales of forbidden love and tragic endings with its green fields and heathered moors, thatched cottages and stone castles, its misty air and ancient, crumbling walls.

She'd grown complacent in her new freedom. The farther she'd traveled from home and family, the clearer her thoughts had become, perhaps because, she told herself, there was no Papa to think for her, to make her life easy and safe and pleasant. Mama wasn't with her to pull her to earth when her fantasies began to take flight. There was no Tim to assure her that she was normal and beautiful and worthy of being loved by someone besides her family.

Since she'd left home her mind had been focused on her surroundings. Not once had she caught herself woolgathering or exploring a thought completely at odds with what was going on around her.

Until now.

Now she'd seen a man and imagined she knew him, and if Phineas were to be believed, she'd seen his soul and felt its touch.

"What did ye see back there, missy?"

The answer was a drift of awareness in her mind, a memory of warmth and a soft caress inside her, a whisper that was sensation rather than sound . . . a whisper that felt like a promise. . . .

"A dream . . . I saw a dream," she said, and in a way, she thought it might be true.

"Mayhap ye did," Phineas said enigmatically, as if he'd heard her thoughts and understood them. His voice was a whisper in the dark, seeming disembodied as he spoke again. "Neither man nor ghost, he is flesh and blood, with eyes as silver as the glow of a cold and barren moon . . . as cold as his heart . . . as barren as the place where his spirit once thrived."

Inexplicable fear jumped in her throat at Phineas's words, at the way he said them in a quiet, musing voice. "You did see him," she whispered, and held her breath for his reply.

"Didn't say that."

"But—"

"Twas what I heard in the village."

The chill grew harsh and biting, and the night suddenly seemed thick and suffocating. Whether Phineas had seen the man and the phantom or heard it in the village, the description was too accurate to dismiss. She had only now heard the legend, yet she had seen the embodiment of it, felt the presence of it.

It could not be, yet it was.

"Missy, whatever ye saw or didn't see, whatever is lies or truth, doesn't change a thing," Phineas said as he shifted back in his seat and pulled the brake. "Ye're here for a reason, and it's right in front of ye."

As always, Phineas's logic was inarguable and welcome, giving her ordinary things to think about and a purpose to pursue. Turning her head, she closed her eyes, then opened them again, forcing herself to think only of what she knew was real, to focus on what she could touch, to see only what was ahead.

Steeply roofed and flat-faced, the inn stood three stories high in the center of a clearing, a neglected monument to the past, the building itself enduring while the boards that covered all the windows but one were rotting away, defying man's attempt to seal off memories of sorrow and loss. In the creases and mortar of its weathered stone and timber walls she saw character lines, as if it were alive and had simply grown old while sleeping . . . waiting for someone to care enough to awaken the memories it had once spawned beneath its slate roof.

Her gaze riveted on the gabled windows of the third floor, Betina descended from the driver's box, barely aware that Phineas had grasped her around the waist and lowered her to the ground. Acknowledging his help with a distracted smile, she turned to walk toward the building, bemused by its familiarity to her, captivated by a sudden vision of how it had once looked with a well-tended vegetable garden and pruned shrubbery, freshly painted timbers and sparkling clean windows.

As Phineas held a lantern from the coach high, she stepped up to the door and yanked on a rotting board nailed over the small window set into the upper half. A splinter pierced her palm, but she ignored it as she rubbed away a circle of grime and peered through the glass.

"It be too dark to see, missy. Mayhap we should go inside."

She nodded and reached for another board, which crumbled away from the rusty nails holding it in place. They all did, as she and Phineas touched one, then another on the door and one of the ground-floor windows, only to have them turn to splinters and dust in their hands. The door opened easily, swinging inward on remarkably silent hinges.

Aromas greeted them as they entered—of a meal just completed and tobacco lingering in the air, of lye soap and lemon oil, of human sweat and perfume. Yet all was silent and empty.

The common room was clean and free of cobwebs, as if men had been bellied up to the counter and meat had been spitted over a fire in the inglenook mere minutes before. To the right of the door was a sitting room, the upholstery of the settee and chairs worn, yet possessing a luster that was not dulled by dust, and there was an indentation in the seat of a large tapestry-covered chair as if it had only recently been vacated. An open book lay facedown on a table beside a teacup and saucer.

It looked as if it had only closed down for the night and its occupants might be asleep in the chambers upstairs, as if a hundred years hadn't passed since its abandonment.

She felt the silent presence of Phineas beside her, so patient and calm, as if nothing were out of place . . . or out of time, as if all was as it should be.

Absently, she wandered around, picking up the teacup, then helping Phineas put away their food in the spotless kitchen. She found the root cellar with ease and next to that a store of wines and ales, and carried up a bottle of wine for their supper.

She commented on nothing—not the vegetables that looked fresh nor the brew that hadn't gone flat, not the pan full of soapy water in the kitchen nor the windows that looked clean and clear from the inside, though she knew they were coated with grime outside. The tables in the common room had been scrubbed clean, and ashes in the grate spoke of banked fires to ward off the chill of a spring evening that had lasted for a century. Perhaps someone had been here to clean, she speculated, though she knew better. No one from the surrounding countryside would come here, and all entrances had still been barred, but for the single window on the third floor.

"It's all a mite peculiar," Phineas commented as he sliced ham and cheese and bread and set it on the heavy table made of thick boards. "Ye be scared by all this?"

"I suppose I should be," she mused as she sat down. If the legend Phineas had told her was to be believed, lives had ended here, lives that continued on somehow, waiting for completion. But as she sat nibbling at her meal in the large, square kitchen, she felt only the weight of melancholy pressing down on her for the tragedy that had interrupted those lives. She remembered the man by the side of the road, and the phantom whose touch inside her still lingered with warmth and yearning. And from the moment she'd entered the inn, she'd felt a sense of homecoming, of belonging, as if she'd just left it a few moments before. "I *should* be frightened," she repeated. "But I don't think I am."

"Then what do ye be thinking?" he asked as he gave her a sideways glance.

She breathed deeply and glanced around, feeling the past enfold her with a sense of rightness and peace. "I think that the spirits here are friendly," she said softly, and in that moment she thought she could believe every word of the legend Phineas had told her, could accept the truth of things that could not be.

Almost.

Phineas nodded in what seemed like satisfaction, and even that didn't seem strange to her.

"The family quarters are on the third floor, I think," she said as she and Phineas finished their supper. I'll take the rooms at the west end."

Phineas cocked his head and gave her a long, probing look. "I lit a fire up there and left a kettle of hot water near the basin. I'll be sleeping on the second floor near the stairs. Ye go on. I'll be staying up a while yet."

She smiled at him, knowing he chose his room for the sake of propriety and to be on guard should anyone steal inside to rob them. She didn't ask how he'd guessed her choice of rooms. She only wanted to know what it would be like to sleep beneath her own roof, free from the cloying protectiveness of her parents and the kindly yet patronizing attitudes of their friends. "All right. Good night, Phineas," she said, and carrying her glass of wine with her, found her way to the third-floor chambers with the angled ceilings and deep dormer windows.

Here, too, all was clean and undisturbed. The bed was high and narrow, with a feather tick that smelled as if it had been freshly aired. Muslin curtains hung at the windows and fresh wood was stacked by the hearth. A bureau with worn spots in the finish occupied one wall, and next to it was a sturdy brass-bound trunk. Lifting the lid, she gasped at the delicate fabrics and exquisite workmanship of frothy gowns in vibrant colors—all folded and wrapped in tissue paper and looking as if they were brand-new. A trousseau perhaps? Why else would they still be packed rather than hanging in the wardrobe that leaned against another wall?

Curious, she opened the doors of the freestanding closet and examined the simple cotton dresses and petticoats—the perfect wardrobe for a country girl living above an inn. The drawers slid open easily to reveal old-fashioned chemises and underdrawers, woolen stockings and ribbons, muslin and flannel nightdresses with delicate embroidery around the high collars and ruffled sleeves—all worn but in good repair.

Tracing the stitchery with her fingers, Betina marveled at the fineness of the work, the softness of the fabric. Without thought, she undressed and washed, then shook out a nightdress from the drawer, slipped it on over her head, and covered it with a faded rose velvet robe she found hanging in the wardrobe.

Everything fit her perfectly—the inn, the room, the clothing.

She curled up on the cushions arranged in the window seat and took a sip of wine, then set the glass on the sill and rested her cheek on her knees. She stared out at the ribbon of moonlight marking the highway that rose and dipped over the moor, the silver-lace glow that fell through the trees surrounding the yard, the single shaft of ethereal light angling down on a lone rosebush standing at the place where the road turned into the yard. It was a strange place for a bush that more properly belonged in a cultivated garden. Stranger still was its lack of blooms and the odd reddish color of the leaves, though it was obviously alive.

There were so many strange things in this land, yet they drew her, filling her with a sense of purpose and direction, as if every moment in her life had been leading her to here . . . now.

She studied the centuries-old stone stable and outbuildings as she again thought of the man who'd watched her and the phantom who'd touched her—separate, yet in her mind, bound to one another somehow . . . a man and his soul.

Dante de Vere.

The name was a melodic slide in her mind, with sounds both hard and gentle, sounds that seemed both noble and dangerous. The man, the phantom, the mist, and the name—it was all the stuff of daydreams and fairy tales, of a love so strong and so right it transcended death and time and the coldness of reason.

Tonight, as the moon sailed across cloudy skies and the rest of the world seemed a century away, she could accept all that had happened, all that she'd felt. No one was here to question her visions. No one was here to tell her what she should do or think or feel.

It was hers, everything she saw, everything she felt, phantoms and all.

And as her eyes drifted shut in sleep, Betina felt as if she had arrived at both the end and the beginning of her life.

Back he spurred like a madman, shrieking a curse to the sky . . .

The Highwayman—*Alfred Noyes*

5

"It is done," Clotho said as she leaned back in her chair and flexed her fingers. "Bess's threads are once more joined, and I have repaired Dante's." She glanced over at her four sisters clustered around the fire. "Have they felt it yet?"

Ilithyia shifted to give Clotho a view of Betina in the flames. "Bess's mind is open, accepting of the strangeness around her."

Atropos snorted. "For now. She will be frightened enough once the shock and weariness wear off."

Lachesis waved her hand and the scene shifted to Dante, crashing through the woods in search of his horse. "He does not yet understand. All he thinks about is capturing his soul."

"And so he shall," Nemesis said as she turned to study the threads and run her fingers over the rough

places where they had been mended. "Soon he will understand what is happening."

"And what of Bess?" Clotho asked.

"She has been asleep for a long time," Nemesis said. "It will take time, and even when she does comprehend, the decision will be hers. We have little power over the human heart."

"Bess's thread is strong and vital," Lachesis said as she reached over to touch the strand. "She will not make life easy for him, I think."

"She is timid," Atropos snapped, "and she has always been a foolish dreamer, seeing life as she would have it rather than how it is."

"It makes no difference," Ilithyia said. "They have defied us and taken destiny into their own hands. We can do little for them except add what color and strength we can to their threads."

Lachesis sighed. "But must Dante suffer more?"

"His thread did not break completely," Clotho reminded her. "He is bound to the moment when the strands separated."

"And he must return to that moment," Nemesis said firmly. "He must slip into the past and bring it into the present, or Clotho's efforts are for naught. The thread will not hold and he will be trapped as he is now . . . forever."

"He must live through it again," Ilithyia affirmed. "Or he will not live at all."

Atropos smiled in satisfaction. "It is a small enough price for a second chance."

He whistled a tune to the window, and who
should be waiting there
But the landlord's black-eyed daughter,
Bess, the landlord's daughter,
Plaiting a dark red love-knot into her long black hair.
The Highwayman—*Alfred Noyes*

6

Betina recognized the melody mingling with the sigh of wind in the trees and thought stars would sound like that, if they could sing.

She raised her head from her knees to gaze out the window, searching the darkness for a familiar shadow, the twinkle of a rapier in the moonlight, the flash of a roguish grin against a closely bearded face.

He was there, in the mist below her, his hand reaching up as his foot raised to the trellis that climbed to the top of the window below.

Throwing open the sash, she waited for him to reach her, yet he couldn't; her room was too high. She leaned out and extended her hand, felt the brush of his fingertips against hers, and wanted more.

Her hair fell over the sill, the curl at the end of her braid touching his hand, winding around it in the only caress she could give him. And he kissed the strands and brushed them across his lips, breathing in the scent she wore for him.

"I have no rose for you," he said, and it was a deep, purring whisper.

"It doesn't matter," she said. "The bush will bloom again."

"Will it?" he asked, and the mist spiraled upward, reaching for him, seeming to drag him back.

"It's alive."

"It exists," he said as he drifted down the trellis, "but that does not mean it is alive." The mist curled around him, enfolding him like a shroud, then scattering on the night wind.

"Don't go," Betina cried as she opened her eyes and pressed her hand against the closed window. She stared out at the yard, searching for him, seeing nothing . . . not even mist. Lifting her hand to her hair, she felt the tangles and curls that fell to below her waist. . . .

It was not braided. She hadn't worn braids since she was a child.

It had been a dream . . . only a dream.

Dante rolled to his side, awakened by the nudge of his horse's nose on his cheek. It had returned to him, thank the Fates. At least those fickle sisters still granted him some favors.

A subtle change in light filtered through the trees as the moon reached its zenith, washing out his memory of black, silky hair and the fragrance of rose petals. He lay where he'd fallen earlier, where he'd beat his fists on the ground, hoping to feel the pain or the cold or the prick of nettles beneath him. But sleep had overcome him with visions of the past, of her voice and her hand reaching for him from her window.

He never slept. He never dreamed.

Until the woman came, and his soul touched her, betraying him once again.

"Why?" he whispered as he turned fully onto his back to stare up at the moon. Was his soul so lonely that it could be easily fooled by black hair and dark eyes?

The woman was not Bess. The woman was older, more defiant. Bess never would have lifted her chin and defied the cruelty of the villagers. His meek and modest Bess would have never accepted a man's touch as the woman in the coach had accepted and sighed over the touch of his soul inside her. Never would Bess have leaned so far out her window to reach him.

Bess was dead.

He levered himself upward to his hands and knees, then rose to his feet, shaking his head to clear it of the sleep that seemed like a drug, the dream that seemed like reality. Only a dream.

Yet only the living dreamed. . . .

It's alive.

It exists.

He snarled at the memory of his dream, at the truth of the words. The woman at the inn was alive. *He* merely existed.

Until he reclaimed his soul.

He gathered the reins in his hand, mounted his horse, and leaned over to run his hands over its neck and withers, feeling the strength and power of its muscles already bunched to take flight.

Tonight the phantom would ride after all. With such a fine mount beneath him, he might capture what he had lost.

The night shimmered with silver light and mist. Nothing stirred—neither breeze nor beast nor clouds in the sky. Moonbeams glowed through the portal of trees, illuminating the road and abandoning all that surrounded it in darkness. Though there was no wind to disturb them, the subtle shadows cast on the dirt passage by brittle leaves and gnarled branches shifted and swayed as if they had been summoned by spirits to dance in some mystical rite.

Unable to sleep in a strange bed, Betina had been drawn back to the window by the incandescent glow of light and the nearly full glass of wine on the sill that might ease her way into dreams.

She discovered that she needed neither wine nor sleep to dream in this place.

The longer Betina sat at the window and stared at the moonlight streaming through the arch of old and withered trees, the more she felt as if she were the woman waiting for a dashing highwayman to ride toward her, then pause to pluck a rose from the now barren bush. She could almost hear the *tlot, tlot, tlot* of his horse's hooves as it pranced into the yard, delivering its rider to the spot just beneath her window, could almost hear the masculine voice of her lover whispering a promise to her as he plucked the thorns from the rose and tucked the blossom into the love knot at the bottom of her braid.

Her eyes closed at the vision, the dream . . . the useless wishing for such love. Yet she continued to see the tableau, to feel the fear and hopelessness as it must have been on that night a century past. . . .

The soldiers marched into the inn, took the landlord's daughter, and tied her to her bedpost in full view of the window, a musket bound to the length of her body, its muzzle pressing into her breast. She struggled against her bonds and sobbed in anguish to realize all was lost. She inched her finger down and down, the ropes scraping her flesh as she found the trigger and waited . . . waited . . . knowing what she must do—

Tlot. Tlot. Tlot . . .

She listened to the familiar sound . . . the pause . . . the rhythmic dance of hooves, and bade a silent farewell to the man who was her breath, her heart, her soul. Staring out at the ribbon of moonlight, she pulled the trigger, felt the jolt and the fire, the shattering of her heart and her hope, as the beat of his horse faded into the night, away from her . . . dying sounds of his freedom as he rode to safety, taking her future with him.

She stood waiting on the far shore of a dark river.

And she saw him return, saw him shake his fist at the window as his stallion pawed the air, heard him shout a curse in the air. The explosion of powder and ball shattered the stillness as it tore into him, knocking him from his saddle. He lay in the road, his blood watering the rosebush as he whispered a vow to the sky.

"Wait for me, Bess. I'll come for you, and neither heaven nor hell will bar my way. . . ."

The promise was like a soft wind reaching out to her across the river of death, and she knew that he would keep his word. . . .

Sometime . . . somewhere.

Betina gasped and opened her eyes. It seemed so real . . . shockingly, frighteningly real, as if it was a memory rather than a fantasy. The darkness inside the inn closed around her, holding her a captive audience to the eerie shine of moonlight on mist outside. Even the shadows seemed alive as they drifted together and then apart, taking shape and moving until she thought they weren't shadows at all, but a man and horse galloping down the road.

The road wound ahead of Dante, canopied by trees and oddly glowing with a silvery mist. And at the end a shadow loomed, the old inn standing desolate in a deserted yard, its windows dark, like eyes with no life burning within them.

Tlot. Tlot. Tlot. The hooves of his horse echoed in the deathly silence as he rode toward the center of his existence—the rosebush growing by the side of the road, its leaves rusty red, like blood, its stems barren of blooms even though it was late spring. The place where he had died only to survive in a living hell.

The scene ahead of him shifted, strands of color spinning and blurring around him, past him, and then it settled again, familiar as the memories that haunted him. Yet it was different somehow, as if the memories had become real . . . as if time had curled back on itself and he was in the past again.

The windows of the abandoned inn were bright and welcoming, and voices raised in laughter and ribald song thrust into the silence . . . and then a single shot.

He jerked his gaze to the upstairs window. A shadow slumped behind the lace curtain and then the windows darkened, and he was once again enshrouded in silence and desolation. A sense of grief passed through him, leaving behind unutterable anguish, inexpressible fury.

His horse reared and minced backward, but he held his seat as the mist swirled around him and sinister clouds bearded the face of the moon—

Tlot. Tlot. Tlot. He turned his head at the sound and saw a vision of man and horse riding toward him at full gallop . . . chasing him. It couldn't be, not at this early hour of the night. Yet he knew it was, knew that the shape of his pursuer exactly fit the void inside him. What was this? A trick to further torment him?

With a feral snarl, Dante spurred his mount. He would not wait patiently to be passed by or to have his soul scatter and drift away from him before he could reach it, touch it. He'd had enough of such cruel games.

The rider gained on him, mist and shadow rather than flesh and bone. The vision streamed into formlessness as it drew abreast of Dante, tendrils reaching for him, enveloping him, warming him as he could not remember being warmed, soaking into him and filling him with life, becoming a part of him . . .

Making him whole.

Again the scene shifted, like one tapestry sliding away to reveal another.

An arrow of flame reached out from the upstairs window of the building, then another and another. The report of musket fire sounded muffled, as if it had traveled a hundred years through time. Yet his body jerked, once, twice . . . a dozen times, and pain tore through his shoulder and his side, his thigh and the side of his head. His horse lurched from beneath him and ran into the trees. He lay still in the dust, and he knew that he was dying . . .

Again.

Or perhaps time *had* circled in on itself and he was dying still. Dying from shots fired a century past, reaching for him through time itself.

And again the world spun around him and the mist swirled, then scattered on a gusty breeze, like a spirit shattering and drifting away.

But it was mist . . . only mist.

How ironic, he thought, that his soul had caught him rather than the other way around. He stared at the rosebush, his mouth curved in a smile as he waited for the end to come, welcoming the release that would surely, finally, be his.

Pain. It burned through his body as the air chilled his flesh. It was night, he realized, with the moon hanging low in a cloudy sky, its light a thin ribbon along the road surrounded by woods. He tasted dirt, and his vision was clouded by something that ran into his eyes. Blood. His blood, watering the roots of a rosebush that did not bloom. He had not died.

Ah, God, he had relived the past, been shot with the same powder and ball, yet still he lived.

Desolation. He felt it as a tangible presence in his soul as he stared at the old stone building that lay neglected and decaying on the post road ahead of him like a body no one cared to bury.

Waiting. Someone was waiting for him, yet he could not imagine who might do such an extraordinary thing. There was only his horse standing at the edge of the inn grazing on wild grass. A horse he hadn't yet bothered to name.

Sorrow. It sat in his mind like dust collected in an abandoned room as he struggled to his feet and staggered across the yard to test the boards nailed over the windows. They gave way easily with a creak of rotting wood and rusting iron. He peered through the glass, searching for signs of life, seeing nothing he hadn't seen before—the inn as it had always been, untouched by time, as if it, too, were waiting.

Emptiness. It echoed inside him like memories of past glories and forgotten pleasures as he tried the door and found it locked and barred. Had he imagined the woman and her old guardian?

He limped and lurched from one window to another, slipping in his own blood, then righting himself as he wondered why he suddenly wanted so badly to live. It was there, inside him, a voice shouting above the chaos of time and memories that crowded together in his mind like a mob without purpose or direction. A voice that hadn't been there for a long time. The voice of hope.

Shaking his head, he leaned against a tree and stared at an upper-story window that had escaped being barred. His body grew chill and numb; sweat broke out on his forehead and ran down his face. His knees began to buckle and he hugged the trunk of the tree and rested his cheek on the back of his hand—

A light appeared in the upper window . . . and a shadow. A soft, woman's shadow that glided past with delicacy and grace, a long mane of curling hair floating about her form as she brushed it in long, weary strokes.

He fell to his knees in the dirt and extended his arm toward the window. "Bess!" he called, but it was weak and gasping and she couldn't possibly hear.

The shadow remained at the window, unmoving . . . silent.

With the last of his strength he tried to whistle, but it had been too long and he barely remembered the tune. The notes faltered, yet it seemed important that he keep trying. Lowering his head, he concentrated on catching his breath, on forming the notes and using the last of his strength to make them reach the woman standing in the window.

It came to her again—the melody she'd heard before, yet this time it was clear rather than a whisper of sound, clear and faltering at first, then steady and in tune before it ended abruptly like an interrupted sentence.

It was real.

Betina picked up the candle she'd lit in her restlessness and blew out the flame, closing her eyes for a moment before squinting into the darkness outside. And it was dark, without mist or moonlight to frame the shadows. Too dark to see much of anything. She hoped there would be nothing to see. . . .

She frowned and wondered where the mist had gone so suddenly.

With that thought the waning moon reappeared, angling a single shaft downward through a break in the trees to fall on a shadow in the yard.

The shadow moved, and she saw that it was a man as he raised his head and then slumped over in the dirt.

A man . . . where it was said no man would venture . . .

Except *him*.

She backed away from the window, yet her gaze remained fixed. Fear crept in on her thoughts even as her heart told her to call for Phineas, to run outside and help someone so obviously in distress. Of course fear was a healthy thing in the territories, a weapon, her father had said. But when danger came to her home in Wyoming, the fear was always a hard thrust of panic and a loud voice of caution, not this sinister, lurking presence that warned her away altogether.

Away from what? she reasoned. A man who could not even hold up his head?

Perhaps not a man at all.

The voice was an insidious hiss, spreading the poison of fear, surrounding her, smothering her.

She shook her head and forced her feet to move, one step then another toward the door.

Foolish girl.

It was true; she knew it was, yet she couldn't stop herself from reaching for the latch, pulling the door open. "Phineas," she called as she ran into the hall and down the stairs. "Phineas!"

She ran full tilt into Phineas's solid form. "Here now, missy. What be the trouble?"

Her breath whooshed out and she realized she'd been holding it as she ran. "Outside . . ." she gasped. "A man . . . hurt . . . I think."

Phineas nodded as if there was no surprise in her announcement and took her arm to steady her.

"Your gun, Phineas. You should get—"

"No need for that, I'll warrant." He picked up a lantern with his other hand and hustled her down the stairs.

As she stumbled along beside him, across the great room and out the door, she thought she should question his certainty. Though no one at home would withhold aid from a man in need, they would not be so foolish as to approach a stranger—wounded or not—without adequate protection.

But the air that struck her as she stepped outside was thick and salty from the sea roaring against the cliff not so far away, and a pervasive chill soaked into her. This was not Wyoming, and the only outlaws roaming here were phantoms with neither substance nor life.

Instinct took over as she approached the figure lying so still in the dirt, his only sign of life a faint moan and then a thready stream of words.

''Bess . . . I'm coming . . . almost there . . . Bess . . . make it up to you . . .''

He repeated it over and over, a chant that chilled her more than the air—

''Ye hold the light, missy, while I get him inside,'' Phineas said as he shoved the lantern into her hands and bent over the man. ''We be needing bandages and the medicine kit your mother packed for ye.''

Betina stared at the bloodstains spreading over the man's claret velvet coat and buff breeches, the bruises forming and swelling on his beautiful face, the dust that looked like powder in his neat beard.

It was *him*—the man she'd seen in the village and by the side of the road. The man who had visited her dreams. *Him* . . . the phantom who had climbed the trellis by her window to kiss the ends of her hair. But he lay in the dirt, bleeding and moaning in pain. . . .

A mortal man after all.

The thought seemed a mockery, bringing her no measure of calm, no sense of safety. The trees stood about the yard, dark as another shade of night, brooding and seeming to lean over them even more, watching and waiting and clinging to the most fragile threads of life.

He opened his eyes as Phineas levered him into a sitting position. "Let me go, damn you."

"Ye be going nowhere, laddie," Phineas said calmly.

The man squinted up into Phineas's square face. "Nowhere . . . already there . . . a century . . . a bloody cen—"

Phineas heaved the man over his shoulder. "Now ye be keeping your ravings to yourself, else ye scare the missy."

Betina was already scared. So scared she couldn't move or think in any rational pattern. Scared enough to tell Phineas to toss the man over his horse and send him away before she heard any more of his ravings. Too much had happened for her to believe that the man spoke out of delirium. She'd run out of logical explanations for what she'd experienced in the last few hours.

She'd run out of reasons to defend her sanity.

"Run ahead and open the door for me, missy," Phineas said, and his voice sounded far away.

Silently, Betina turned and held the lantern high as she led the way back into the inn.

Where was he? *Why* was he?

The soundless questions roamed through his thoughts as he awakened to mellow candlelight and the scent of clean bed linens, the comfort of a feather mattress and soft pillow, the heat of a fire blazing in the grate. He turned his head and winced with the feel of a hot knife scoring his temple and caught his breath at the weakness that sat on him like a stone.

He focused on a ribbon laying on the chest across the room—as bright and shiny-new as it had been the day Bess had bought it from a traveling merchant, as bright and shiny-new as the night he'd pulled the shutters from her window and climbed inside to take whatever memories he might find of Bess. He'd found the ribbon laying exactly where it was now, and it had been enough of a keepsake, for he had never seen his Bess without a red ribbon tied in a love knot at the end of her braid. A ribbon he'd carried in his pocket ever since.

He had no pockets now. He wore nothing but his skin and, he realized, a few score stitches that pulled tightly over his wounds. Wounds that had not mysteriously disappeared, but scored his mind with an awareness of throbbing, burning pain.

He'd forgotten what pain was like.

Pain . . . wounds . . . his blood flowing out of him . . .

The past circling in on itself like a dog chasing its tail.

It had happened again.

And still he was alive.

Alive.

He blinked as a clink reached him, musical almost, stunningly clear in the silence. Clearer than he could remember hearing anything in a very long while. And then he realized that the mist was gone from his vision and the world around him had sharp edges and colors with depth and richness, as if even they were alive.

He was alive.

Another clink caught his attention and he felt his mouth quirk at the beauty and whimsy of it. He squinted into the brighter light beyond the doorway, adjusting to the details of form and movement. A soft, rounded form . . . rustling fabric . . . a profile of alabaster flesh and refined bones . . . a sweep of dark lashes and a fall of ebony hair oddly touched with rich glimmers of deep crimson, like a flame reaching out from the darkness.

It was her.

She bent over a table, pouring tea into a cup, her motion creating the music of sterling on porcelain that seemed so new to him and so infinitely exquisite. She turned toward him and paused as her gaze met his, staring at him with wide, questioning eyes. Midnight eyes with the sparkle of starlight in their depths.

Eyes that were questioning and wary as she continued to stare at him as if she were woolgathering and he was simply in the path of her thoughts and she really didn't see him at all.

He returned her stare, searching for familiarity and finding it in her face that was both strong and delicate, in her skin that was fair as the petals of a morning rose, creamy fair with a touch of dawn pink on her cheeks, in her mouth that curved upward at the corners regardless of her expression.

She caught her breath and her body gave a small jerk as if she only now realized that she was staring at him . . . that he was staring back. She frowned and shook her head, and he realized that she saw him as a stranger, that his presence in her life startled her.

He knew then that she didn't know him, that her memories were simple ones of the here and now. Yet in her eyes he saw the restlessness of a soul that had dreamed for a hundred years.

A soul that was frightened by its awakening.

He knew who she was and why she was here.

And he knew that he loved her.

Then look for me by moonlight,
Watch for me by moonlight,
I'll come to thee by moonlight . . .
The Highwayman—*Alfred Noyes*

7

His gaze on her was like a touch as she continued to make tea, waiting as long as she could before turning to him, going to him, seeing again the face that haunted her day and night.

It had been eight days since Phineas had carried him inside and laid him on a table in the great room to cut away his out-of-date clothing and remove from his body a dozen balls that had been ammunition in old flintlock muskets. Eight days of watching over him, of studying his face, of listening to him call her "Bess." Eight days of touching him while she changed his bandages and bathed his body, admiring in spite of herself the fine way in which he was made with long, lean lines and hard muscle.

And every moment that she was with him she reminded herself that he was real and solid and it had been her wayward imagination that transformed him into the phantom of her dreams. And then she told herself that he didn't seem familiar to her and that she sat with him and fretted over him as she would any wounded man . . . that she would have held his hand through the night and wept for fear that he might die no matter who he was.

At times she almost believed herself.

She'd refused to think about how he'd come to be shot on the road leading up to the inn when she'd heard no gunfire, or why he fit so perfectly the description of the rogue outlaw of the legend Phineas had related to her. She denied that the sight of him, the feel of his flesh as she bathed him and changed his bandages stirred up her body while her mind dwelled on thoughts of midnight whispers and slow, provocative caresses beneath soft sheets. . . .

She couldn't stop thinking of how he called her "Bess," even when he seemed lucid.

It was so much easier to accept what had happened, just as she had accepted the strangeness of the inn and her sense that it had been waiting for her.

As they had since the night he'd stumbled into the yard, such thoughts pricked her with anxiety and panic, but she brushed them away. *He* was the one who had kept the inn clean. Or better yet, *he* had been living here all along rather than in the gardener's cottage of the manor house. Of course—such a reasonable explanation! And the man was no phantom, but fevered flesh and blood seeping from a dozen wounds. Of course, he'd been attacked too far away for her to hear the shots, and he hadn't fallen from his horse until it had brought him here. Of course Phineas had been right;

the man had been raving. She was not the lunatic. *He* was.

There could be no other explanation.

Unable to delay any longer, she filled a cup with tea and carried it into the bedroom.

He reached out for her, wanting to touch her fair skin, trace the lines of her delicate face, feel the warmth he could only imagine with a room and a doorway between them. But there was a sting and burn in his shoulder and midsection that went bone-deep and he could not move further for the linen tightly binding his wounds. His leg, too, felt tight and confined and the muscle ached persistently.

She said nothing as she came to him, the cup and saucer in her hand. She smelled of roses. Her hair was unbound, as if she had paused in her brushing to make the tea, and she wore a velvet dressing gown with a paisley shawl over her shoulders.

Was it cold? he wondered and concentrated on his body beneath the covers, testing it for sensation. Suddenly, his teeth began to chatter. Cold. He could not recall when last he was cold . . . or hot . . . or anything at all.

Leaning over him, she slid her arm beneath his shoulders and eased him up, then held the cup to his lips. "Drink," she ordered softly.

His teeth stopped chattering and his shivers calmed with the warmth of her touch, with her nearness that soothed and reassured him as she sat down beside him and held him closer, supporting his head on her shoulder. He felt weak, so damnably weak—

"It will ease your fever and calm the pain," she said.

Hot liquid trickled into his mouth and down his throat. It tasted vile, and smelled worse.

Taste and smell. Those, too, were forgotten sensations, though he seemed to recognize them easily enough.

"Drink all of it, please," she said in that sweet voice that sounded like the murmur of angels. And she'd said "please" so politely, as if he were a guest come to call in the afternoon.

He drank deeply of the tea and her presence, her touch, absorbing it. He'd known her and loved her before, yet he'd never been so close to her, never held her or been held by her, never shared more with her than promises and hopelessness. Reaching up, he took a strand of her hair between his thumb and forefinger, feeling the silkiness of it, inhaling her scent as he raised it to his lips and felt it curl into him. Ah, God, but it had been so long since he'd dared to hope for more than the most innocuous touch from her.

It was well worth living for.

The cup clattered in its saucer and both fell to the floor as she gasped and jerked to her feet. She stared at him, her gaze wide and distant, her hand covering her mouth and her body stiff, as if she were being held hostage by an unseen force.

"What is it?" he asked in a dry, rusted voice. He swallowed and tried again. "What do you see that is so frightening?"

She shook her head and backed away from him.

"Am I such a bad patient?" he asked softly, afraid to further alarm her.

Turning, she began to straighten the room, putting distance between them in the guise of picking up soiled bandages and adjusting the curtain over the window.

The distance was in her voice, too, as if her thoughts had dismissed him and ventured elsewhere. "You've been shot—many times." She breathed deeply and clasped her hands at her waist, stilling their trembles. "Phineas and I removed the bullets—balls, actually, from old guns, muskets I think. I'm sorry, but you will be scarred."

She was babbling, spilling out words to cover nervousness. Bess had never chattered, though she had often slipped into the same attitude of preoccupation when she'd been agitated or troubled. "Phineas—the old man?" he asked, deciding not to trouble her more for the moment.

"Yes, Phineas," she said in that vacant way that was so poignantly familiar to him. "Your horse saved you, I think," she said as she picked up the fallen cup and saucer. "He must have brought you a good distance, since we didn't hear any shots. . . ."

He barely heard her as his thoughts drifted from past to present and back again. *Balls. Old guns . . . muskets. The interior of the inn as it had been so long ago, never changing . . . as he had never changed.* But this time she'd been at her window, his Bess, waiting for him. And she was here—had been here—taking care of him, sitting beside his bed, holding his hand and weeping. He closed his eyes as he remembered struggling into consciousness from time to time and seeing her, feeling her presence even when she was across the room. He would fall back into the darkness then, a floating, peaceful descent because he knew she was with him, a part of the world once more.

Bess—returned to him. Life—returned to him. His soul—a part of him once more.

Bess . . . loving him . . . waiting for him night after night in the light of a robber's moon . . . loving him and believing he would take her away to a land of adventure and freedom. . . .

Bess . . . her heart shattered by a musket ball. Bess . . . dying to save him—

His body jerked and his eyes snapped open as horror bathed him in a cold sweat. She was still standing over him, the empty cup in her hand. "It happened again . . . the past reaching out for me . . . shots finding me from a century ago . . . but not touching you . . . as it should have been . . . all as it should be . . . you . . . alive. . . ."

Her hand over her mouth, she shook her head and backed away from him, her eyes wide with horror.

He reached out and grasped the skirt of her robe as he stared up at her. "You shouldn't have done it, Bess. You should have let them kill me the first time. Then we'd both be free. . . ."

A bizarre sense of memory washed over Betina, drowning her as she listened to him, to words that made sense to her though they shouldn't. For a fleeting moment she felt as if she were seeing what he spoke of, living it, as if she'd lived it before.

Shock numbed her as she heard the shots in her mind. Her body jerked as if it had suffered the impact of a shot and her chest felt as if it were exploding; a deathly cold seemed to flow through her veins.

Death . . . it felt like death, and she wondered how she knew and why she accepted it so calmly.

She looked down at his hand, grasping her robe so tightly even though he was losing his grip on consciousness, his eyes closed, his breathing slow and steady, his face relaxed. And it was the sight of his hand, clenched around the velvet as if he would hold her there, that broke the spell his words had cast upon her.

Anger vanquished the lassitude she'd experienced as he'd spoken. Anger that she would be duped so easily into believing she was a part of the legend, believing even for an instant that she knew exactly what he referred to, that she'd experienced it and her memory held the images, the sensations. She felt as if she were being pulled into a vortex, held by forces she neither saw nor understood, forces that would tear apart her life and her future and make them into something else. She had to fight it. She had to hold on to herself and not fall prey to the imaginings of others—

"Bess . . . wait for me . . . I'll find you. . . ."

His voice startled her and her gaze darted to him, seeing that he was still asleep and living a dream . . . or a nightmare.

". . . though heaven or hell should bar the way . . . I'll find you. . . ."

She tried to pull away as his voice trailed into incoherent mumbles. But even now his grasp on her robe was strong. She stood beside the bed, afraid to wake him by prying his fingers open or yanking the cloth away from him.

So afraid . . .

She took a step back, then another. Her robe pulled but did not come free from his hold.

Free. The hysteria grew until she thought it would burst in her chest. . . . *should have let them kill me . . . first time. Then we'd both be free. The first time . . . first time . . .*

She heard it over and over again, and her mind was filled with fear rather than questions. Fear because she didn't have any questions and knew that she should. Fear of the knowledge that seemed layered in her thoughts, waiting to be peeled back and exposed. Fear of the man himself, of the yearning she felt for him, of the sensations that were a riot inside her.

His eyes opened suddenly and he stared at her, mesmerizing her with that glittering silver-blue gaze that seemed to penetrate her to the core. "You came back. You waited for a hundred years and you came back. Ah, Bess, you humble me with your love."

With clammy and trembling hands, she untied the sash of the robe and shrugged it off, letting it fall to the floor around her feet, but before she'd taken a step, he began to toss his head back and forth on the pillow and mumble in his febrile sleep.

"Bess . . . blow out your candle or they will see us."

Transfixed, she stood with her feet tangled in her robe. The room seemed to darken, and mist seeped in through the fireplace and the slivers of space where the window joined the walls, bathing the room in a quicksilver glow where the man seemed like a pale shadow on the bed.

"I can wait no longer for you, Bess."

As he spoke his voice grew stronger, and her mind whispered in response. *"It's too soon, Dante. Papa—"*

Again she shook her head, denying she heard herself speak though her mouth did not move and she uttered no sound. She could not move nor breathe nor cry out in protest. More images took possession of her and became her while he spoke and she answered from the depths of her mind.

"Will you live your entire life for your papa?" he spat the word out as if it were bitter.

"He wants me to be happy. In time he will understand that—"

"Time," he scoffed. "You delude yourself. Time will not change his mind. Nor will all the gold in the country . . . if I should live long enough to steal it all."

"Don't."

"Don't what, Bess? Don't talk about my occupation? Don't mention how I have gathered a fortune to lay at your feet? Don't remind you that I am an outlaw with a price on my head?"

"I don't want your fortune."

"Look around you, love. Your papa is a prosperous man. You've every comfort. Would you be happy married to a poor man who has no skills beyond a certain charm with the ladies and the recklessness to rob their husbands?"

"I would live anywhere with you."

"But not in the foreseeable future, and not anywhere away from here."

"Dante, I love you. What must I do to prove it?"

"A ship leaves England soon for the colonies. Pack only what you cannot part with. If I do not come for you at dawn, then watch for me tomorrow night. We will be far away before you are missed."

"I can't just leave. It would hurt Papa so. I am all he has."

"I am on borrowed time, Bess. We leave tomorrow or not at all."

"Dante—"

He fell silent and his restless movements stilled as the mist seemed to reverse itself, disappearing as abruptly as it had appeared.

Feeling as if she had just awakened, Betina blinked at the light from the candles and glanced around the room, seeing nothing unusual, hearing nothing but the labored sound of her own breathing. Yet it had all been so clear—his words, and the frightened whispers in her mind. She'd felt it all—the desperation, the love, the panic when the voices fell silent.

Whoever . . . whatever . . . this man was, he was not like other men, with his quicksilver eyes looking at her as if he knew her, and his deep, whispering voice that beguiled her into believing she belonged in his hallucinations.

How easy it had been to pretend he was simply a stranger in need of aid, to send her thoughts along distant paths where the sight of him was like the mountains at home: shadows on the horizon that did not hinder or intrude. It was her only talent, picking up the threads of a fantasy or story that lingered in her imagination to relieve the tedium of chores or to escape the hurt inflicted by friends who perceived her as different and treated her accordingly. Only Phineas cut through the haze of her thoughts with his musical brogue and colorful stories, both real and imagined.

She bit back a burst of hysterical laughter. Perhaps everyone was right and she was different. Or perhaps she was mad. Normal people did not see mist as having form and dimension, much less passing through their bodies with a touch of warmth and tenderness. Normal people did not dream of phantoms, then imagine they had come to life.

Leaning over, she pressed her forefinger against his hand, then drew away at the hot, dry feel of his flesh.

Phantoms did not become feverish and mumble in their sleep. "Bess . . . wait for me . . . I'll come for you. . . ." He reached out for her again.

She pressed her hands over her ears and stumbled in the folds of her robe as she ran through the door into the parlor that connected the sickroom to the bedchamber Phineas occupied.

The small, private parlor was empty and cold, and she heard Phineas's snores in the next room. She raised her hand to knock, then lowered it again. Phineas had been up the night before taking his turn at watching over their guest, and he'd cut wood for most of the day.

What could she say to explain waking him in the middle of the night? That a man riddled with bullet holes and raving with fever had terrified her? What was there to fear? Words? The man certainly couldn't lift himself off the bed to physically harm her. And if he could, she'd know what to do. Papa and Phineas had seen to that by the time she'd reached the age of ten. Once Papa had taken to his bed for a whole day after a practice session with her on the proper use of a lady's knee in an altercation.

Her mind might be a bit removed from everyday life at times, but her reflexes were excellent.

She wandered to the door of the sickroom and leaned against the frame as she studied her patient, confirming that he was indeed mortal and helpless. His mouth was turned up in a smile and his eyelids twitched as if he saw something even in sleep. It was a wonderful smile, tender and peaceful and . . . endearing.

He really was handsome, with high cheekbones, straight nose, and high forehead strongly defined in his lean face. His mouth was thin yet well formed, and his eyes . . . oh, dear heaven, his eyes were almost pure silver with a soft sheen that looked like the mist at twilight. She would never forget them, never forget the age and weariness she'd seen in them the first time he'd looked at her.

But in his sleep he appeared harmless enough, even with his roguishly pointed eyebrows and the widow's peak that swept back in thick, ebony waves away from his face. With his mustache trimmed to grow into the beard that closely followed the lines of his square jaw and blunt chin, he looked like a proper rogue . . . or an outlaw. . . .

No! She rubbed her arms and backed away from the door. She would not allow herself to think of that, she told herself as she paced the sitting room. She was too old to get caught up in such fairy tales. And he was not the man in her dreams. *Her* phantom hadn't had a face that she could see, until this man had mocked her in the village and stared so rudely at her from the side of the road.

She'd simply assigned his face to her fantasy. And why not? she reasoned as she made yet another circuit of the room. It was a good face for a spirit who inhabited such provocative dreams.

Curling up in the upholstered chair by the fire, she tucked her feet beneath her nightgown and leaned her head back. Other people thought with reason rather than imagination. In the last eight days she had succeeded at it with some effort. She could do it again, and again, until it became a habit, like brushing her hair or responding to idle chatter with noncommittal phrases when a pause occurred.

She rubbed her temples with her fingertips. She would do it. She had to, for she was becoming thoroughly annoyed at having to constantly remind herself that she lived in a normal world with normal people who did not turn to mist and haunt the highway for a hundred years.

And she was completely put out with the story of a woman who had been so foolish as to kill herself out of love for a man who did not deserve such sentiment, much less the gesture it inspired. If he had been worthy of her love, the need to warn him never would have arisen in the first place. He would have long since given up his lawlessness to ease her mind—a much more practical sacrifice as far as Betina was concerned.

There! She nodded her head in satisfaction at such reasoning, assured that when she made the effort she could be as sensible and clear-thinking as the next woman. Wasn't that one reason she had come here—to escape the tedium and frustration of her sheltered life, to learn independence, and to fill her mind with the concerns of running her own life and making her own decisions? She'd done quite well for herself on the journey. She'd even faced the villagers' hostility and fear with defiance. Heavens, she had made any number of important decisions since leaving home. She was independent, blast it, and no mysterious stranger who wore out-of-date clothing and rambled on about a silly girl who couldn't make up her mind was going to send her into a decline. She would manage this.

And maybe—just maybe—she would become so alert and practical-minded that the phantom would desert her dreams.

* * *

Betina whimpered and rolled her head from side to side. Gasping at the pain cramping her neck, she opened her eyes and slowly eased her head upright, stifling a cry at the muscles that were tight and burning from the awkward angle she'd slept in all night. She tried to ease her feet out from under her, but they were completely numb and cold. Then she smiled at the realization that she'd slept deeply for hours and only darkness had inhabited her mind.

She hadn't dreamed.

"Hold still, missy," Phineas said from behind her as his large, blunt fingers began to knead her neck and shoulders, easing her head up at the same time. "Ye should be knowing better than to fall asleep in the chair. And where might your robe be? I don't be needing two invalids on me hands." He walked around the side of the chair and tossed a woolen throw over her. "Warm up now before ye get up. There's tea on the table beside ye."

"Thank you, Phineas," she sighed.

"I don't suppose ye be knowing how our guest fares."

"Um . . . he woke up for a while."

"And did he tell ye his name?"

Dante, came the unbidden thought. She'd heard the name before, in the legend Phineas had told her, and because it was unusual and fresh in her mind it had slipped into her fantasies. Pleased that her newfound rationality hadn't deserted her, she shook her head. "I didn't ask."

"He might have kin that should be told of his plight."

Kin. Of course. He might even have a wife or a lover named Bess. It was a common enough name.

''He'll probably be awake for a longer time today, Phineas. You can ask him.''

''Can't,'' Phineas said. ''We be needing supplies from town.''

''I'll go,'' she said quickly.

''Can't. How would ye be driving the coach, missy? Besides, the folk there won't sell to ye. To their way of thinking, ye belong here. They be that anxious to know what turn their legend will take next, and would most likely deliver you to the crossroads tied to a rail.''

''Surely they're not that ridiculous in their superstitions.''

''Ye be knowing better than most how folk hold to their stories to ease the troubles of living day to day.''

She lurched to her feet, irritated that Phineas would so readily remind her of what she was trying so hard to change. ''Well, I certainly wish that you were the focus of their legend rather than me.''

''I be too old for such,'' he said, and his expression was eloquent with sorrow. ''Tis for the young to be dreaming dreams and wishing for the moon.''

''All right, Phineas, you go then,'' she said softly, unwilling to disturb whatever memories he saw just then.

''I be sorry, missy, that ye be so plagued by what ye don't ken. Ye've been cooped up here a mite long.''

''Yes, well, I should be used to being ignored and receiving odd looks. I just didn't expect to experience it so far from home.'' Knowing she sounded churlish, she ducked her head, retreated from the parlor, and climbed the stairs to her room.

* * *

Dante awakened to full awareness of himself—of the warmth of his flesh, the gnawing hunger in his belly, the persistent ache of healing wounds.

It was true. It had happened. He was again mortal.

Bess was here.

Bess . . . older and more beautiful in her maturity, more courageous in spite of her apparent fear, more defiant and independent than before. Bess, the same yet not, as if her soul had been born into a new life while he had existed in the old one for a hundred years, without a soul, without sensation, without the weaknesses that both plagued and gave pleasure in life.

What new intrigue did the Fates weave now? Was he to find Bess again, love her as a woman rather than a girl, only to lose her? Were they doomed to recreate their lives as they'd been before, meet the same end as before?

Or was it a second chance?

He didn't give a bloody rip what the Fates decreed, as long as it was either life or death rather than something in between.

He glanced out the window, seeing clearly the treetops with their lifeless foliage and petrified bark against a sunny sky, and hearing just as clearly the neigh of a horse in the yard below. Metal clinked, and it took him a moment to identify the sound of a team being harnessed to a coach, the creak of wheels as it rolled slowly through the dirt yard then picked up speed on the road. It had been so long since he'd been concerned with such things.

A second chance . . .

Whether it was intended or not, that was exactly what he had. He'd cheated those fickle sisters once, and he would do it again if he had to.

But this time, he would do it right.

Nearer he came and nearer!
Her face was like a light!
The Highwayman—*Alfred Noyes*

8

I can do this. I can do this. I can . . . Betina chanted to the rhythm of the rolling coach wheels as Phineas drove away from the inn, farther and farther away from her, until the only sound she heard inside the inn was her own voice. Alone. She was alone with *him*, and even the weakness and the wounds of the man lying in the bedchamber below hers offered her no sense of safety.

But safety from what exactly? She tried and tried, yet couldn't find a logical answer. All she knew was that last night she'd suddenly felt as if she were walking through her dreams rather than the world around her.

The mirror in front of her reflected her image, clothed in a dress she'd worn a hundred times before, yet the woman she saw seemed to have been altered in some indefinable way, as if she were someone she might have seen once upon a time but couldn't quite place.

Panic clutched at her suddenly, a vise of fear that held her still, barely breathing as she stared at her hands, her forefinger holding a half-knot in a red satin ribbon.

She had braided her hair.

She never wore braids. They gave her a headache.

With desperate little sobs she tore out the ribbon and raked her fingers through her hair, pulling it harshly, separating the sections and tearing out strands in her haste. Wrapping her arms around her middle, she bent over, trying to catch her breath, trying to convince herself that she'd done it to keep it out of her eyes, done it because the dampness of the climate set it into so many curls she looked as if she were all hair.

She could have pulled it back and tied it at her neck. . . .

Deliberately she envisioned all the coifs she had worn and experimented with in the last few years after she'd come to care about such things. Playing with her hair, or sitting quietly while her mother wound and pinned and wrapped it, had always been so relaxing, a lovely way to daydream as Mama chattered on about this and that.

Oh Mama, I wish I'd listened. I wish you were here to tell me that everything is all right, that I am as I've always been.

She straightened and reached for her brush, taking a stroke for every panting breath, pulling it through her hair in every which way, then slowing as her heartbeat calmed and an image came to her of home and Mama, her pockets bulging with bits and pieces of her life as she spoke without expecting an answer, and of Papa checking on her a dozen times a day to make sure his little marmot was still safe and happy.

Little marmot . . . She smiled at that. Papa had always called her that in private, saying that she was like the cute little prairie dogs that stood so still on their mounds, watching the world go by and crawling into their burrows when it came too close.

How badly she needed to hear Papa's incessant warnings and advice rather than the whistling that drifted to her from the room below.

He was awake.

He'd be hungry and thirsty, and it was time to check his bandages.

The sooner it was done . . . the sooner he healed . . . the sooner he would leave.

She gathered her hair into one long hank and tied it into a loose knot halfway down, then flipped it over her shoulder to hang down her back. There. Now she looked more like herself, she thought, as she glanced in the mirror to make sure all her buttons were fastened and her skirt had not caught on her petticoats.

The whistling trailed off, leaving the house silent. Maybe he'd fallen asleep again and she wouldn't have to speak with him or look into his eyes, that seemed like light passing through her.

She took a deep breath and left her room, making a slow, measured descent on the stairs, crossing the second-floor landing, and continuing on down to the kitchen. If he was well enough to whistle he was well enough to wait until she had a cup of coffee and a piece of bread.

He began a new tune, a jaunty melody that skipped through the air, the notes rising and falling like little girls jumping rope.

Her foot began to tap as she poured the coffee Phineas had made into a thick stoneware mug and added sugar and cream. Phineas may not have lost his accent, but he had wholeheartedly embraced the western notion that good coffee was thick as mud, black as sin, and hotter than hell itself.

A smile tugged the corners of her mouth upward as the tune picked up in tempo and flowed into an intricate flow of notes. He really was quite good at that. And, she realized, the whistling was doing what her efforts at logic had not: It convinced her that he was just like any other man and it was a lovely spring day and the legend of the highwayman and the landlord's daughter was fading in her memory.

She set another mug on a tray and filled it with mild tea flavored with the mint leaves she'd found in a box next to the tea leaves. Toast. Toast would be good for a convalescent. It was time for him to have solid food. Having a hearty appetite herself, she could imagine how weary he might be of broth and tea.

Humming under her breath, she picked up the tray, climbed the stairs to the second floor, and used her hip to push open the door.

The whistling stopped abruptly in midnote.

She halted in the middle of the room, her smile fading as he stared at her, his lips still pursed slightly as if he, too, were afraid to make a move.

"Bess . . . the tray," he warned, and his voice struck a shocking chord in her, as if he'd spoken to her in just that way before.

Her hand shook and a finger of toast fell to the floor. She leveled the tray just as the tea began to slosh over the side of the mug, and set it on a table by the bed. "My name is not Bess," she informed him briskly, hoping she sounded like her mother and her voice did not quiver with the sudden chill that ran through her.

"No?" he said as if he were humoring her. "What is it then?"

She turned her head and gasped.

"What is it?" he repeated.

"Your hair," she said and backed away, out of his reach.

He lifted his hand, wincing at the motion, and felt a few strands. "It appears to be intact," he said reasonably.

"It's changed . . . last night it was all black." *So black it shone blue in the light,* she added silently. "At least I think it was." She shook her head and narrowed her eyes on him to study the color as she tried to recall. "Has it always been like this?" she asked, more to herself than to him.

"I wouldn't know," he said, his own eyes narrowing. "Like what?"

Midnight dark woven with moonbeams. "Um . . . silver . . . it has silver in it."

"Has it?"

She clenched her fists. "Tell me—has it always been like this?" She prayed he would say yes. Then she could accept that in her usual absentminded way she hadn't paid as much attention to his appearance as she'd thought. There was comfort in that, a refuge of sorts in her shortcomings.

But he sighed and looked at the wall bordering his bed as he raked his hand through his hair. "I haven't looked into a mirror in a very long time," he said, and it sounded like an admission of guilt.

"Why not?"

"I live alone and have only myself to please. . . ." His voice trailed off as he frowned and flexed his fingers and began to bend his wrist and make shapes on the wall with his movements.

How odd.

Her natural curiosity overcame her uneasiness. "What are you doing?"

"I have a shadow," he said softly, then turned to her with a jubilant grin. "Bess! I have a shadow!"

It was so absurd, she couldn't stop herself from stepping closer to him and raising her own hand and making a shape on the wall. "We all do," she said inanely and felt like a child playing games.

"We all do," he repeated and his grin drooped into another frown. "I'd forgotten." He moved his hand and their shadows drew closer together.

Of their own accord, her fingers opened as if to receive his. Her stomach fluttered as he watched her face, his gaze brooding, penetrating, like the mist that had passed through her in the coach.

In the shadows on the wall his fingers opened and laced with hers, interlocking parts mingling, joining.

The flutter became heat inside her, and her hand felt his touch though she was out of his reach. She jerked her arm down, slicing the air and feeling the coolness of it, the emptiness of it. He, too, lowered his arm, slowly, and his mouth slanted in a smile that held no pleasure. "You shouldn't be frightened of me," he said. "You know I won't hurt you."

His statement was one more absurdity on a pile of absurdities—the final one that toppled the stack, sparking an anger that smoked and fired between one moment and the next and launched her into a tirade as she clenched her fists harder and leaned toward him. "I think," she said between pants of outrage, "that you had best worry about my hurting *you* while you lay helpless in that bed . . . *my* bed, I might add. *You* hurt *me*? I come from Wyoming, where we fight Indians and cattle rustlers and . . . and . . . desperadoes. I have a gun and I know how to use it, and if you don't behave like a proper guest in my inn, I will give you a personal demonstration." She tried to catch her breath, but every fear and bogeyman she'd imagined since coming here were lighting fuses in her mind.

"What is lacking in my behavior?" he asked, and the amused arch of his brows was all it took to set off the explosions.

She stuck out her forefinger, pointing at him. "You haven't told me your name."

"If you recall, I've been indisposed."

"Tell me now," she demanded, suddenly anxious for the information while she was feeling strong and capable and brave.

"Dante de Vere, at your service, Miss . . . ?"

Dante de Vere. Of course she'd known he would call himself that. For all his peculiarities there was intelligence in his eyes, and one like him would be thorough in his guises. "Dante? What kind of name is that?"

"One I stumbled upon, Miss . . . ?"

"Dante." She shuddered and trembled with the anger that obliterated every other emotion. "You're mad, and I'm sure you've escaped from . . . from . . ."

"Bedlam," he said.

"Yes, Bedlam."

"So you think I'm insane."

She nodded vigorously. "Among other things. Why else would you wear outmoded clothing and ride around howling at the moon and terrorizing the natives into believing you're the embodiment of their legend?" She sighed heavily and caught her breath and swallowed as her trembles eased. It made sense. So much sense that she was furious with herself for not thinking of it sooner. "You all but stole your horse from that poor farmer," she sputtered, then clamped her mouth shut. Not with her dying breath would she admit how he had terrified her.

"I left him more than adequate compensation. Rest assured he picked up the coins after I was out of sight."

"You bullied him."

"He expected it. They all do and would be disappointed if I did not oblige."

"You are insane."

"I am realistic and take advantage of what I cannot change. Their legends are sacred to them and their only defense against boredom. Far be it from me to deprive them of the only interesting dinner conversation they're likely to have."

"So you are the one they call the phantom highwayman. And you took the name of a dead man to convince them."

"It is my name, Bess."

"Don't call me that. I am not Bess. And you know very well that you are not Dante de Vere."

"You know very well that I am."

"You're mad," she said as she inched her way toward the door. "Fool the villagers if you like, but don't try it on me. I have too much sense to be taken in by superstitious gibberish."

She scooted her hand along the wall and breathed a sigh of relief as her fingers reached empty space.

"Then why are you leaving?"

She jerked her hand down to her side and lifted her chin. "I am going to get my gun." Taking the final step, she edged around the door frame and slipped into the hall.

"Will you be back?"

Without turning to face him again, she nodded. "To change your dressings."

"With a gun in your hand?"

"I'll use a very large pair of scissors for that," she said with what she thought was a sufficiently threatening tone, and then ran down the stairs to the kitchen and slammed the door shut, propping a chair against it to fortify her sanctuary.

Panting, she sank onto one of the chairs at the plank table. What had she done? Oh, dear heaven, how could she have been so foolish as to confront him? Clearly he was dangerous. He had to be. Why else would someone have shot him? Actually, more than one someone had to have shot him to put so many holes in him from one-shot muskets.

She buried her face in her arms crossed on the table. She should have played along with him, pretended that she suspected nothing, that she'd noticed nothing untoward in his dress, his manner, or his name.

Dante . . .

Oh, dear God, this couldn't be happening.

How strange it all was. Absently, Dante held up his hand and watched the play of darkness on the wall as his memory recounted the scene with his hostess.

Hostess. That alone brought a wry smile to his mouth. Even that was strange, the working of muscles in his face that had been idle for so long. Yet Bess had always inspired a smile, whether in exasperation or indulgence or genuine amusement.

Bess, who had met him every night through the portal of her window because they could not meet where they could be observed, particularly by her father. Yet the old man had left—for the village, he presumed—without any apparent concern for Bess's safety. It felt peculiar to be alone in a room with her, feeling warmth from the same fire, smelling the same odors of food and wood smoke, sharing the same shaft of sunlight. Their time together had been of stolen moments and soft whispers, of dreams never realized and yearnings that had to be satisfied with a simple touch of hands, a brush of lips over the curl at the end of her braid.

He had no doubt that the woman was Bess. She had the same innocence, the same timidity, the same wide-eyed look of a child in a woman's face. Yet she had changed too. The Bess he remembered had not been so outspoken, nor so amusing and impulsive and plucky. Bess would have cowered rather than spoken of defending herself with a gun. She would have trusted without question that no one to whom she'd shown kindness would harm her.

No wonder he hadn't recognized her in the village.

She had matured. Her soul had learned. Bess, the timid child-woman, was now simply a woman possessed of a charming naïveté and reckless courage.

A century ago he had loved Bess, indulged her, wanted to protect her.

Now, in spite of the absurdity of her diatribe, he respected her as well.

Wincing, he turned to his side and raised up, supporting himself with one arm while reaching for the mug with the other hand. Vague memories of the last few days teased him, of Bess sliding her arm beneath his shoulders and helping him raise up enough to drink one concoction or another, of the scent of roses mingling with beef broth or weak tea and the sound of her voice as she urged him to open his mouth, to swallow . . . of the soft fullness of her as she supported his head against her breast while he drank.

Her accent was different too, a smooth drawl rather than the clipped way she'd learned to speak in the boarding school her father had insisted she attend.

This Bess, he sensed, was just as well educated, yet her manner was less reserved and more liberal in expression. Her soul had obviously traveled far to find where it belonged, just as his had waited for what seemed like forever and a day to reclaim its life.

He took an experimental sip of tea and felt a jolt in his throat at the familiar taste of mint.

Bess had always had a fondness for mint in her tea.

He lay back on the pillow and frowned up at the ceiling, thinking of Bess, the way she was now, and the things she had said. They were here, where they had both made pledges to one another. Here, where nothing had changed and their vows hung in the air like the mist and gloom of abandoned lives. Here, where it had all ended—the innocent love, the enticement of hope, the promise of more.

Here, where it had all begun again.

Her eyes grew wide for a moment; she drew one last deep breath.
The Highwayman—*Alfred Noyes*

9

So much for new beginnings.

Betina sighed as she brewed a fresh pot of tea, delaying as long as she could the moment when she would have to return to the man upstairs and dress his wounds. It was easier to think of him in such abstract terms rather than by a name that evoked excitement and anxiety and a dread of something she could not name.

Yet deep inside her thoughts, knowledge blinked and tried to awaken. Knowledge she did not want and could not accept.

She couldn't be wrong about the man who played with his shadow like a baby discovering the various parts of himself and took the name of a legend and appeared in her dreams as if he belonged there. A phantom indeed. He bled and burned with fever and moaned in pain. He was a very mortal man and a lunatic besides. He had to be.

And she was alone in the house with him, feeling more timid and scattered than ever before. Alone with him, her insides trembling like startled butterflies every time he looked at her, touched her. She called the sensation fear, but knew it was something else—something like excitement, anticipation, awareness . . .

Desire.

The tea was done, but she didn't want another cup. She'd already had three and she thought she might float up the stairs if she drank another. Not for anything would she venture outside to the necessary with *him* so close and Phineas too far away to protect her. It would be too much like her childhood fear of being caught in the outhouse with her bloomers down during an Indian raid. She clamped her hand over her mouth as a giggle escaped her, a high, frantic sound in the stillness of the inn, eerie in its solitude.

Control. She had to get control of herself or she, too, would go mad.

Cocking her head, she listened for sounds from the sickroom. Nothing. Was he playing with his shadow again? Or had he fallen asleep?

She frowned and listened harder. Surely he hadn't had a relapse?

But, no, he couldn't have taken a turn for the worse—not when his color had improved and his voice had been so strong and sure, his mind so sharp and quick. A mind that was as warped as the boards that had been nailed over the windows for a hundred years.

No. He had to be all right. Most likely he was entertaining himself with his toes.

Another sigh stuck in her throat, of frustration and anger. Frustration over such an obviously strong and healthy man giving in to absurd delusions. Anger with herself for halfway believing in those delusions. She wished she was as empty-headed as everyone thought her to be. Anything was better than having a head stuffed with nonsense.

She was beginning to think that freedom was highly overrated, if it existed at all. How badly she wanted to go home, where she would be safely cloistered within her father's protectiveness and her mother's routines. But she couldn't even do that. Not after all her pleas for independence and the first show of courage she'd ever been brave enough to make. Not after what her mother had told her about needing a little freedom of her own.

She hoped Mama was enjoying her freedom, and Papa too. Someone should. *She* certainly didn't feel free. Here she felt imprisoned by the visions that haunted her sleep—visions that seemed more like memories that couldn't possibly belong to her. Visions of a man who called her "Bess" and touched her as if she belonged to him. And heaven help her, when he touched her she felt as if she *did* belong to him, body and soul.

It was too much. Even a woman with uncommon strength of purpose and unflinching courage would flee such circumstances. There would be no disgrace in returning home. None at all. Perhaps in a few months or a year she could tour another part of the world . . . someplace with which she felt no sense of connection. A tropical island perhaps, where there would be no mist, no trees and bushes that were alive yet seemed dead . . . or sleeping—

A *thunk* sounded overhead, then a crash.

Panic dug sharp claws into her chest as Betina picked up her skirts and ran up the stairs.

Remembering that the man who called himself Dante was demented, she halted abruptly in the doorway and peered into the room as she tried to catch her breath. The mug she'd brought him earlier lay on its side on the floor beside the tray. Reassured that they were the victims of the crash she'd heard, she took one step inside and forced herself to look at him.

He lay on his back, his chest heaving with exertion, his uninjured leg bent over the side of the bed as if he'd made an effort to rise.

"I can't seem to get up," he said between gulps of air.

So much for her fear of him, she thought. The lunatic was too weak to inflict harm on anyone but himself.

She clicked her tongue as she'd heard her mother do when dealing with a stubborn—or foolish—man, and briskly strode into the room and bent to pick up the tray and mug.

"Bess," he said, still breathless. "Will you—"

She rounded on him. "I am not Bess. My name is Betina . . . Miss Wells to you, and I expect you to address me as such." She heard the fury in her voice, felt it in the pressure behind her eyes and the way her blood seemed to throb rather than flow in her veins. Fury that he saw someone else in her face and form, and fury because she wanted so desperately for him to see *her*, because it hurt her to know that he didn't. Fury because she didn't understand why it should be so important to her.

"Betina." He smiled as he repeated her name in a low, musing voice, then again with a soundless move of his lips, as if he were tasting it, savoring it. "Close enough, I think."

She clenched her fists against the urge to slap the satisfaction from his expression. "And what was Bess's surname?" she asked, not at all sure she wanted to hear it.

"Wells," he replied gently.

She threw up her hands. "Well, of course it was Wells. She is—was—a distant relative on my father's side. Maybe I even look a little like her . . . like she did. Family traits are passed on from generation to generation. Maybe you saw a painting of her once and became obsessed with it. Maybe *you're* a descendant of the highwayman." Proud of her spontaneous logic and warming to the subject, she continued. "Maybe you're just terribly lonely and absentminded and use your fantasies for company." *Like me,* she added silently, relieved that she had stopped before revealing so much about herself.

"He has no descendants . . . yet," he said.

"Yet? *Yet?* Well, if he were still alive—and he is not—he would be far too old to undertake such a task now. There is a man in Wyoming—an Indian—who claims to be well over a hundred years old."

"What is Wyoming?" he asked and winced as he attempted to ease his leg back onto the mattress.

Instinctively she rushed to help him, placing her hands under his calf and lifting his leg slowly. "It's a territory in America," she explained, convinced that it was perfectly reasonable that he did not know about her home. Not everyone in the world would be aware of the territories, and it hadn't been so long ago that it was part of the Colorado Territory.

"America? You mean the colonies?"

"No, I mean the United States of America."

"The rebels won? Impossible. Our forces were far superior—"

"Your forces were idiots wearing their red coats and marching in formation and announcing their presence with their drum beating and flag waving."

"Your rebels have no clothes and no weapons. They fight like street urchins."

"Street urchins with minds of their own. The redcoats fought like puppets."

"Yes, I see what you mean. I'm actually rather pleased that the rebels won. The world needs a free country . . . it is free, isn't it? There was talk of a democracy."

A chill crawled up her spine. What was she doing, talking with him about times long past, as if those times were a part of *her* past? What was wrong with her that she had walked right into the conversation as if it were perfectly normal? "Where have you been?" The words escaped her before she knew what she was doing.

"Here," he said simply.

Well, that explained it. *Here* was a backward little place tucked far away from the rest of the world. *Here* the natives lived as if *now* was the past. Who could blame Dante for being a product of his surroundings? After all, she had certainly fallen in with the opinions the people at home had of her, behaving as she was expected to behave and even encouraging some of their beliefs to escape the boredom of their concerns—

"Wyoming . . . where is it exactly?"

"In the western territories that are not yet states," she replied with a bright smile. Now that she understood why he was so odd, all she had to do was humor him.

"States. Are they like counties or duchies?"

"They are states," she said patiently, as if he were a small child learning his letters. "Independently governed yet working with the federal government as parts of a whole."

"Does everyone have a vote?"

"Well, of course they do. In Wyoming even women vote."

"You've developed a fine wit."

"I am not being witty. . . . Women have the vote and can serve on juries and can own their own property."

"I knew democracy sounded too good to be efficient," he muttered. "Women with the vote. America must be in chaos."

"America is growing and prospering and reaches from the Atlantic Ocean to the Pacific." Proud that she was participating in such a discussion and enjoying it, she crossed her arms and smiled smugly. "And we not only won the Revolution, but we trounced the British again in the War of Eighteen Twelve."

He regarded her thoughtfully as the silence stretched between them.

Fidgeting under his stare, she wished she knew how to continue their argument. While they were talking of history and politics she could focus on his peculiarities rather than the breadth of his shoulders, and the muscles so well-defined in his chest, and the length of his legs outlined beneath the sheet. She could lose herself in the subject rather than in the brooding intensity of his silver eyes and the deep cadence of his voice and the smooth slide of his accent. She could—

"So America is a strong country."

She shook herself free of disturbing thoughts and tore her gaze from his strongly carved mouth. "Yes."

"And a man can be free there."

"Of course."

"You make it sound vast and open and full of opportunity."

"It is."

He smiled at her then, and it seemed warm and caressing and familiar. "Ah, Bess, I was right. A place where the only title a man carries is Mister and an outlaw can become an honest citizen." His mouth slanted wryly. "And where even a woman can vote and hold her own property. We *can* be happy there."

The chill was back, racing instead of crawling up her back, freezing her with the dread that plagued her with no warning and no explanation. "Will you stop this?" she said, struggling not to scream at him. "There is no 'we' and I am not Bess."

"Bess—"

"No more." She sliced the air with her hand. "Don't talk to me anymore. Not a word."

"Are you so afraid of the truth?"

The truth. She was beginning to question whether she even knew what truth was. Summoning the vacant look she used so effectively at home, she fixed her gaze on him, deliberately blurring his features until he looked like mist. He could not do this to her. She would not allow it. "If I am to take care of you properly and with true Christian spirit, you will kindly refrain from constantly reminding me of your derangement. Otherwise, I will be convinced that I would be doing you a kindness to allow you to escape your misery.'' She ran out of breath at the end and inhaled sharply.

''I escaped it the moment you appeared in the window of your bedchamber.''

It rocked her, that simple, softly voiced statement, rocked her until her stomach churned and her knees felt weak and liquid, and a thrill of pleasure fluttered in her chest. This would not do. ''All right. Fine,'' she said flatly, fighting to maintain her composure. ''Nurture your fantasies. Wallow in them if you like. But tell me this: If you are over a century old why are you not gnarled and riddled with rheumatism? Why have you survived such a brutal attack? Surely at such an advanced age you would be too weak to—''

''I have lived twenty-nine years.''

''What happened to the other hundred?''

''Nothing . . . nothing at all,'' he said, and his voice sounded hollow with despair.

''I see. Then your madness comes and goes depending upon your convenience.'' *There*, she thought with satisfaction. He couldn't possibly argue with that.

''I waited . . . a hundred years I waited . . . for you, Bess.''

Something warm and tranquil spread through her, like an affirmation she'd been waiting to hear. She didn't like it, not one bit. ''I'm warning you—call me by that name one more time and I will leave you to rot in that bed.''

''Even that is preferable to existing in a void,'' he said. ''At least now I *can* rot.''

''Then please do so at once,'' she said and turned toward the door.

''Betina . . . Miss Wells,'' he called, and the desperation she heard unraveled her short-lived determination to tour France—immediately. Or maybe Russia or Italy. She didn't have to return home. She could have a Grand Tour—

"Please."

Warily she faced him, all thoughts of escape deserting her at the look of profound sadness in his eyes.

"You're right. I am lonely. Please don't go . . . please . . . tell me about your country . . . about freedom and opportunity." This time his smile was strained and tight. "And my bandages do need changing."

Without a word or a thought in the name of prudence, she walked toward him, answering the need he'd expressed as if she could do nothing else. She'd been right; he'd just admitted as much. He was lonely and occupied himself with flights of fantasy. . . .

Like her.

So much for carrying out her threats.

He sighed deeply and seemed to sag into the mattress at her capitulation. "You said that the muskets used to shoot me were old. What do they use for weapons now?"

She pulled a long pair of shears from her pocket and began to snip at the knot holding the bandage on his arm. "Revolvers and shotguns and rifles."

"What are they?"

Frowning, she glanced at him, then returned her attention to her work. Strange as it sounded, it seemed an honest question. "Revolvers have six chambers for bullets, which revolve as the gun is fired. Shotguns have large barrels that spray shot in a wide pattern. Rifles are long guns that use bullets instead of powder and ball, shoot great distances, and can be fired a number of times before reloading."

"Will I know this new world at all?" he asked, and it was a hollow sound in the room.

"I suppose that America—or any place away from here—would seem strange to someone who has lived here all his life, just as this place seems strange to me."

"Is it really strange to you?" he asked with a tentative note in his voice.

She glanced at him suspiciously, but found nothing in his expression. Nothing at all. "I have spent my life in America, first in San Francisco and then Wyoming. In both places progress is welcomed and used to improve our lives. Even your countrymen come to my father's guest ranch to explore and to learn. Of course this place is strange to me."

"What is a guest ranch?"

One by one, she unwrapped the old bandages and examined each wound, checking for infection or poor healing, but he appeared disgustingly healthy in spite of his weakness, the still-red scars only adding to his roguish countenance. All he needed was a saber and feathered hat.

"Um . . . a guest ranch," she repeated, orienting herself to the conversation. "It's quite unique—my father's invention actually. We already had settled there, and when Papa knew the railroad was coming he gambled on the possibility that rich men would follow."

"A man with foresight," Dante mused.

She nodded briskly. "He learned everything he needed to know about the hotel business and put it to good use."

"Tell me what it is like—this invention of your father's."

Only too glad to comply, Betina launched into the same speech she'd heard a hundred—a thousand—times before. "Instead of being strictly a working ranch, it is a working ranch that operates something like a hotel. We offer luxurious accommodations in the main lodge and rustic cabins for the more adventurous visitors. Our guests help with or merely observe the chores, the roundups, and the cattle drives . . . whatever they wish." She continued to speak as she cleaned his wounds and fanned them dry, then closely studied the stitches she'd taken in the deeper ones. "The stitches need to come out," she said and reached for a needle to slide under the threads and lift them. "Some of our guests come for the hunting or to explore the wilderness. Others come because they suffer poor health and benefit from our clean air and dry climate. Still others think to become rich by investing in their own ranches."

"Your guests pay to work?" He winced as she snipped a stitch and pulled it from his flesh.

"They pay for the novelty of the experience. Most of them play at working for a few days, then give in to the luxury Papa provides and allow the help to wait on them." She ran her finger over each scar, feeling for thread she might have missed and reluctant to put distance between them. His flesh was warm, resilient, and his muscles twitched and his breathing became harsh and jerky every time she touched him.

So did hers. She liked touching him and wanted to do more. She wanted to smooth her hands over his chest, feel the firmness of him, see his flat nipples pucker even more in response to her. A sudden vision of his hands doing the same to her stalled her heartbeat and made her breath lurch, and her body reacted as if vision had become reality.

He was silent and she lifted her gaze to his, staring at him as he stared at her. Her lips parted and the room seemed to close around them in an intimate embrace.

His hand skimmed over her arm, up to her shoulder and her neck, and then his thumb rubbed lightly over her lips, pausing in the center as she closed them slightly, kissing him, tasting him. He pressed his thumb inside her mouth—just a little—and lifted his other hand to her cheek, tracing the shape of it, spreading over the side of her face and around the back of her neck, urging her to lower her head, drawing her closer and closer to his mouth, his gaze like smoldering ash on hers.

He paused with their lips so close, not quite meeting, their breaths mingling and her breasts grazing his chest as her heart skipped about in excitement.

She'd dreamed of this, of the desire that came to life so suddenly and ached sweetly in every part of her, of him seducing her and caressing her in ways she could only imagine—

She jerked backward away from him, panting as if she'd been running, still staring at him, unable to break that link with him. No. She had not dreamed of *him*. Never had she felt such need, and never had she felt such an immediate rush of warmth between her thighs. Not even for her phantom, who hinted and promised with his ghostly caresses and the whispers that were merely that—no words that she could fathom, no meanings that were clear.

Until now.

His hand slid away from her face and down her neck and shoulder and arm to close around her wrist, as if he expected her to leave him and he would hold her there.

She thought she should pull away, but she couldn't. It felt too good being near him, too right. But suddenly she felt awkward and unsure under his gaze and glanced away, searching for some way to recover herself.

"Tell me more about your guest ranch," he ordered softly, as if he sensed that the silence increased her discomfort and confusion and he sought to reassure her.

He succeeded, giving her something solid on which to focus. Mama. Papa. A whole world beyond this room.

She arched her back and stared at the window, wishing she could see home through the glass. "When Papa began the Wishing Well Ranch," she said in a faltering voice that grew stronger with every word and thought, "everyone laughed at him. Now he's a very rich man and only slightly less famous among the European aristocrats than the Cheyenne Club. Even rich businessmen from New York and Boston and Philadelphia come and pay for the privilege of getting their hands dirty."

"Wishing Well Ranch?" So quietly he spoke, and it was comforting and comfortable to respond to such a simple query.

"Papa let me name it. I was only ten when Papa moved us to Wyoming," she muttered.

"*Papa* must be an indulgent man," he said with a hard edge of bitterness to his voice. "It doesn't sound like the name of something that would appeal to men."

Heat rose in her cheeks at his tone. Pride stiffened her back and gave firmness to her voice as she pulled her arm free from his hold. The spell was gone, sensations scattered inside her like mist dissolving into small wisps, desire only a tingle on her flesh. She didn't know what had happened and wasn't willing to question it. "The name doesn't have to appeal to them when we provide the diversion they crave. Besides, most men simply call it the Wells Ranch."

He sighed and looked away, as if he, too, were suddenly uncomfortable. "A ranch is like a farm then?"

She dropped the old bandages into the basin and wiped her hands on her apron. "I suppose, except that we grow cattle and horses along with crops of corn and grain and hay. Papa says that if the cattle market should falter 'as surely it must,' " she quoted in a deeper voice, "then we will still have our guests to keep the ranch alive. He says that entertainment is entertainment and never goes out of fashion."

"Your father is not only a visionary but a shrewd man as well."

"Yes." She blinked her eyes and rose. She didn't want to talk about home anymore. It seemed too far away and too unreal to her now. And leaving there to follow an ill-conceived notion of independence seemed incredibly foolish. She did, however, want to leave Dante. At least she told herself that she should. "Your injuries are healing nicely. I think they will do better now without bandages." Walking toward the door, she paused in the threshold. "I'll have Phineas help you walk around. Please don't try to do it by yourself again."

This time she succeeded in escaping the room that always seemed too small and the man who always seemed too sure of his beliefs and of her, of who she was . . . what she was.

She was his Bess. Dante was sure of it. He saw so many parts of his memories in her—the hair, still so long and thick and gently curled, the mouth that always had an upward curve at the corners, the big, dark eyes that always had a look of vague surprise in them. Her manner, too, was Bess's, with a natural innocence and the constant air of distraction that made her seem fey and so very, very young.

Too young to be so old. Somehow he knew that her soul had grown older, wiser, while his had not. She knew and understood the new, more complicated world she lived in, while he felt trapped in the past by his ignorance of the present.

More than her soul had matured. She was truly a woman now, with insights and intelligence and a wide streak of independence that he'd longed for his timid Bess to have. And her body . . . ah, God, her body was more curved than he remembered—small enough to sharpen his protective instincts, and shapely enough to awaken parts of his body that hadn't known sensation for a century.

A woman worth waiting for.

A woman he wanted as he had never wanted Bess. The simple caress of her tongue on his thumb had stirred him as Bess never had, provoking him to press her for more when he knew it was too soon and he was too weak. . . .

His eyelids refused to remain open, and his mouth began to feel as if it were stuffed with cotton. He felt boneless, weightless, drifting with random thoughts, and then just drifting in one direction while the pain he'd had all morning drifted in another. He frowned and tried to concentrate.

He knew this feeling. Panic nudged but couldn't gain entrance into his thoughts. Only a blurred uneasiness penetrated the fog that seemed to surround him, and carry him deeper into blackness.

Was it happening again? Had he been given life only to lose it again?

"No, damn you," he said, but it came out a bare whisper, the words slurring together. "You cannot play with my mortality as if it were a ball to be tossed about. . . ." The whisper trailed off into silence, as numbness swept over him like a dark, impenetrable cloud. An image of Bess floated across his mind and he grasped it, holding it against the threat of oblivion.

Bess . . . Betina . . . *she* had done this to him . . . drugged him . . . he was sure of it. The tea had an odd flavor.

He would awaken to feel and hear and smell and see. He would continue to live in her world. She feared him—what he said and what she refused to remember.

The girl had become a woman, provocative and demure, wise and naive, brave and yet in some ways still a coward. . . .

He smiled and allowed sleep to spirit him away.

He'd a French-cocked hat on his forehead, a bunch of lace at his chin,
A coat of claret velvet, and breeches of brown doe-skin;
They fitted with never a wrinkle: his boots were up to his thigh!

The Highwayman—*Alfred Noyes*

10

"I'd not thought ye such a coward," Phineas said as he chewed on a crusty slab of dark bread. "The man be weak enough without ye dosing him with laudanum when he don't be needing it."

I needed it! she wanted to shout. But how could she explain to Phineas how much Dante confused her with his crazy talk and seductive eyes? How could she tell him that since they had taken Dante in, peculiar visions intruded into her mind and she imagined herself conversing with Dante as if she'd known him for a long time? That she experienced sensations in her body she'd never known before? Or that she felt as if another person had come to life inside her, someone she knew yet didn't know, someone who was like her, yet not—

someone who was enthralled by Dante's touch and wanted more. Phineas couldn't possibly understand—not when she didn't understand it herself—that she somehow knew that the only time she'd have any peace was when Dante slept too deeply to dream.

It was all too absurd for words.

"Ye be having nothing to say for yourself, missy?"

"I'm not a child, Phineas, to have to explain my every move."

"I wasn't thinking so until now," Phineas said as he calmly spooned a second helping of stew onto his plate. "But ye never deliberately did anything that might hurt another before."

Stung by such an accusation, she stared at her old friend and swallowed a bite that suddenly seemed like a dry rock in her mouth.

He kept on eating as if he hadn't said anything at all hurtful.

She had to defend herself. "Phineas, he was raving and I judged him in need of rest."

"If he was with fever, there were other means to ease him."

"I didn't say he was with fever," she said quietly.

Phineas set his spoon on the plate and gave her a direct look. "What do ye be saying?"

"He told me that his name is Dante," she blurted. "He thinks that America is still thirteen colonies of the crown, and he knows nothing of revolvers and rifles and shotguns." There. It was said. Phineas could make of it what he would. Picking up her glass, she drained the wine and sat back in her chair.

His bushy brows drawn together in a frown, Phineas, too, sat back, watching her as he had when she was a child and he was searching for a thread of sense in her chatter. He'd usually found it, or at the very least accepted her musings to be as important as she thought them.

But then, she thought miserably, dragons and fairies and even a phantom riding through a maiden's dreams were far easier to comprehend than a man who fancied himself the embodiment of a legend, not to mention the odd sense she had that her dreams had come to life.

"He calls himself Dante de Vere, Phineas," she said slowly, willing Phineas to grasp the significance of the name.

His frown still in place, Phineas nodded. "Not a common name in these parts, I'll warrant."

"Or any other parts," Betina agreed, careful not to say too much, to let Phineas draw his own conclusions.

"His clothes were a mite queer."

A coat of claret velvet and brown doeskin breeches, a white shirt embellished with lace at the cuffs and neck, and high black boots . . . a French cocked hat . . . all at least a century out of date. "Yes . . . queer," she replied. She'd given them little thought since she and Phineas had cut them from Dante's body and burned them. Of course she'd noticed them in the village that first day and later when he'd stood on the side of the road, but she'd been fascinated with the man himself rather than the clothes he wore—

Wood scraped against wood as Phineas pushed his chair back and stood. "He'll be sleeping a good long while, I'm thinking," he said as he carried plates and cutlery to the counter.

"Yes," she said, still distracted by the memory of the out-of-date finery that fit his tall, muscular frame as if it were a part of him.

"Then I'll be taking one of the horses and riding into the village to have a game of chess with the blacksmith."

"What?" She blinked up at him. "No. You can't."

Phineas put his plate in the basin used to wash dishes. "I be missing my nightly games, missy . . . and the smith is good enough at it to occupy an hour or so."

She glanced down at her hands and bit her lip to keep from arguing with Phineas. He did love his chess, and she played an appalling game. The minute she saw the carved figures and touched their polished surfaces, she began to imagine queens and knights and pawns and bishops as they might have been once upon a time, slaying dragons and falling in love and—

"He's a mite talkative, but since I haven't heard his tales before I don't mind listening."

"Who?" She blinked again.

"The blacksmith. He's good with a tale and only passing fair at chess," Phineas said patiently.

Comprehension dawned as she stared up at Phineas. He was going into the village to learn more about Dante. She could ask him to stay, or she could wait for him to return with enough information to either set her mind at ease or convince her that her mind was indeed absent and beyond recall. "Oh, yes . . . I know you like to hear new stories." She ran her finger around the edge of her glass. "Does he gossip too?"

"Mayhap."

"Well . . . enjoy your game. I'll read . . . or something." And she would pray that Dante did not wake until it was Phineas's turn to sit with him.

"Are ye so afraid, missy?" he asked as he poured hot water into the basin from a large kettle heating over the fireplace.

"I don't know, Phineas. I don't know anything anymore."

"There's naught to fret over. What is can't be changed."

"Why not?"

"Because it already is. The time for changing was before now."

She hated it when he spoke like this, making sense without explaining a thing, making it sound like absolute truth. It never failed to give her a headache. She looked up at him, letting him see the plea in her eyes. "Don't go, Phineas. Please. I . . . I'm not interested in more stories or gossip."

"Ye don't want to be hearing it, y'mean."

"Yes. That's exactly what I mean. I don't want to hear any more foolishness."

"All right, missy. I'll not go. Mayhap it's best to learn the truth in your own good time."

"There is no truth beyond the obvious, Phineas." Abruptly she rose from her chair, turned toward the basin, and plunged her hands into the soapy water. She felt his gnarled and callused finger beneath her chin, gently forcing her head up, compelling her to meet his gaze.

"Remember that when ye be staring it in the face."

"You believe it, don't you?" she asked, sick with horror at the realization. "You think the legend—all of it—is true."

He shook his head. "Don't know yet. But when ye see things and feel them and think them, ye have to believe they might be true."

"Even when you know they can't possibly be true?" She heard the whisper of fear in her voice and jerked her head away to look down at the wet cutlery in her hands.

"Just because ye can't explain a thing doesn't mean it's not possible, missy." Phineas began drying the dishes with a square of linen. "It just means that it hasn't happened to you before."

"I don't like that answer, Phineas," she said as she rinsed the last plate and handed it to him. "I'm going for a walk while it's still light outside." Draping her apron over a chair, she grabbed an old shawl that hung on a hook by the door and stepped outside.

Sunset brushed fire across the horizon and gilded the treetops in liquid gold light. The road wound away from the inn, a serpentine shadow disappearing into the oblivion of mist rolling in from the coast. Disappearing into forever. Nothing moved nor made a sound. Nothing changed, not even the light as time passed and she walked along the dirt track. Light that fell on the lone rosebush and cast shimmering red on the grayish leaves and buds that never opened.

She wrapped the shawl around her shoulders and pulled it close across her chest as the dormant trees seemed to close in on her, enfolding her in whatever enchantment held them apart from life. It almost seemed possible that this small parcel of the world had been sleeping under some witch's spell, that she had happened into a fairy tale and become a part of it. . . .

That time had indeed stood still for a hundred years.

She shoved the thought away and stopped by the rosebush, staring down at it, transfixed by the ruby glow and the thorns that were black in the shade of the leaves. Leaning over, she brushed one fingertip over a leaf, felt it move beneath her touch, following the movement of her hand, leaning into it as if clinging to her life and warmth. The scent of roses drifted upward, sweet yet faded and musty, like the old quilts her mother packed away with dried flower petals because she couldn't bear to part with them.

She knelt in the dirt and cupped a fragile bud with her hands, feeling how brittle and dry it was, feeling sudden tears fall from her eyes onto the unopened flower as sadness crept over her like the mist, enclosing her and the bush in an ethereal shroud. The scent grew stronger, fresher, intoxicating her, holding her with a memory she'd never had until now.

She'd done this before—knelt beside the bush and cried into its flowers. Cried for the man she loved yet didn't have the courage to follow. Cried in fear of what he was and what she felt and what she would have to do to hold him.

"Come with me, Bess. There's a place away from here that is so large and uncluttered, you can see tomorrow over the next rise. A place where what a man does is more important than what he is."

It had been perfect and magical the way he rode up to the inn and whistled a pretty tune beneath her chamber window, the way he kissed her hair as if she were Rapunzel sequestered in her tower, waiting for him to spirit her away. It had been the best of her maiden's dreams coming true—a man to love her, a man to love with a feeling so profound it filled her until she could nurture nothing else in her heart, hold noth-

ing else in her thoughts, dream of nothing else, waking or sleeping. . . .

Until he had pressed her for more.

"Bess, come with me. Marry me. . . ."

She saw it then—his strength and purpose. He was a man with dreams of his own. She could not live out her life waiting for him to ride up to her window and kiss her hair. She could not love him as he needed to be loved, could not give, nor accept as much as he wanted.

She loved the dream of him with all the innocence of youth. She was afraid to love the man with all the passion of a woman. Afraid he would swallow her up with his courage and daring and grand plans for the future. Afraid to become a woman before she was ready.

And she'd watered the bush with her tears, knowing he would come one more time and she would send him away. Knowing that magic would never again touch her dreams.

Betina shivered with dread and foreboding and felt her tears turn to ice on her cheeks. The memory ended, slipping away as the mist ebbed, tides of the past abandoning her to the mysteries of the present.

She looked down as something stirred between her hands, petal soft and resilient with life. It couldn't be. The bush was stiff, its leaves still rusty gray, its buds still brittle with no signs of growth or life. Crying out, she snatched her hands away and lurched to her feet and stumbled backward. Her gaze darted to the trees that stood bent and brooding over the road, where light had changed from gold to silver with the setting of the sun and the mist mingled with the heather on the moor beyond.

She opened her hand and stared at the bud that she'd torn from its stem. Stared as she spread her fingers and watched the deep-red petals of a perfect rose drift to the ground and turn to dust, as if it had never existed at all.

Dazed, she walked back to the inn, seeing the past so perfectly preserved within a coven of trees and mist, wood and plaster . . . and the memories that had moved into her mind as surely as she had moved into Bess's room.

All of it was like the rose—life waiting to be awakened. . . .

By you, Betina. The voice was only a murmur in her thoughts, yet she heard it clearly and, for a fleeting moment, grasped its meaning before it drifted away.

She climbed the stairs and entered her room, closing the door behind her with a soft *click.* The window drew her, beckoning her with the darkness outside, mocking her with a ribbon of moonlight streaming on an empty road. She searched the shadows among the trees and stared at the land beyond. No phantom rose from the misty moor to ride toward her window. No hoofbeats disturbed the night. Closing her eyes, she recalled an image of the rose that had bloomed with life for such a short time, yet no other memories haunted her thoughts.

She sighed and turned toward the bed. She was so very tired. . . .

Too tired to worry about strange voices in her head. Too tired to dream.

"She heard us," Lachesis whispered.

"And then promptly shut out our voices," Atropos said. "She fights us still."

''And what would you do?'' Lachesis retorted impatiently. ''Accept without question?''

''She is not the same as she was,'' Nemesis reminded. ''The world has a stronger grip on her than before. She is older now. Her soul has learned much.''

''She is still a fool.''

''Not so much as others would have her believe. She journeyed back to her beginnings, did she not?''

''In ignorance. It is not the same thing.''

''And what would you have us do—tell her everything and then tell her what to do?'' Ilithyia asked. ''You know these humans. They are stubborn and will do things their own way even when they already know the outcome.''

''Then what good are we?'' Clotho cried. ''Why do I toil so to mend their futures?''

''Clotho . . .'' Nemesis bent over and picked up a thin and frayed strand the color of sunrise. ''Did you perchance drop this while you were reweaving Bess's future?''

Clotho covered her mouth with her hand as she stared at the thread in horror.

''I see that you did,'' Nemesis said gently. ''Perhaps this is why Bess's understanding is not complete?''

Clotho nodded miserably.

''Can you work it in, sister?'' Ilithyia asked.

With trembling hand, Clotho took the thread and examined it. ''I think so, but it broke away from the skein and the mending will be flawed. I . . . don't know if there is a length missing or not.''

''Wonderful,'' Atropos spat. ''Now we must guide the girl as if she were blind in memory and spirit.''

She waved her hand at the skeins awaiting their attention. "As if we have nothing else to do."

"Hush, Atropos," Lachesis said. "Judging from your bitter disposition, I think you could stand a rest."

"What do you expect? You would be bitter, too, if all you did was wait for the right moment to sever the threads Clotho works so hard to create. I do not get to spin fine threads of many colors. No, I snip away and turn it all to nothing." Atropos glared at a mound of threads cut from the wheel. Threads that had lost their color and beauty . . . because of her actions.

Lachesis embraced her sour sister. "Not this time, Atropos. Don't you see? You have helped Clotho, as we all have, holding the threads of life and love and spirit while she wove them together again. Your shears will not touch them for a very long time."

"My shears did not touch them last time either, but that did not stop them from choosing their own fate."

Nemesis patted Clotho's shoulder. "Continue, Clotho. We are all caught up in the drama these mortals play. I would not have it ended until it is finished."

"Nor I," Ilithyia agreed. "We have waited long and Clotho has toiled hard to renew these lives."

"Renewal," Atropos murmured thoughtfully as a rare smile cracked her dour expression. "I like the sound of it. . . ."

And he tapped with his whip on the shutters, but all was locked and barred. . . .

The Highwayman—*Alfred Noyes*

11

The sound of approaching footsteps reached Dante through the fog of drugged sleep, calling to him with the anticipation of companionship.

It was a sweet sound, devoid of loneliness and despair, full of hope and promise.

Bess . . . He couldn't wait to see her again, to bandy words with her, to look at her—just look—and absorb her presence. It had been so long, and she filled him as his soul filled him, the mere sight of her sustaining him as food never could.

He stared at the door in expectation, gathering his thoughts from where they'd fallen into stupor . . . how long ago? The room was dark, and only moonlight dusted the treetops outside the window Bess had left open.

No, he corrected. Not Bess, but Betina. Betina Wells. Different yet the same.

Different, as the world was different. All that she had told him suddenly thrust into his mind. Would he recognize any of it? He tried to imagine how it would look, how it would be, but he could not envision even such simple things as revolvers and shotguns and rifles. And freedom. Bess—*Betina*—had spoken of it as if it were a God-given right.

Women had the vote. Surely God had nothing to do with that.

The door creaked open and a shadow backlit by a light in the hall loomed in the threshold. Dante squinted as his vision adjusted and recognized Phineas, the old man who had carried him so easily into the inn, then gave orders to both himself and the woman as if he found wounded bodies in his yard every day or two.

Phineas, not Betina. Stifling his disappointment—damn, but he felt like a boy unable to control the pangs of first love—he eased his body into a sitting position, finding it easier every time he tried it. "I'm awake," Dante said, afraid the man would leave again.

Phineas reached down to pick something up and light spilled into the room as he straightened and held a lantern high. "Do ye play chess?" he asked.

Chess. Men still played chess. That, at least, remained the same.

"I would welcome a game," Dante replied. Pressure built behind his eyes, and burning moisture blurred his vision. A game, with another human being—such a small thing, taken for granted by those who belonged in the world. Under the guise of shielding his eyes from the light that grew brighter as Phineas walked across the room, he wiped them with his forearm. Tears. Men were not supposed to display such weakness, yet it felt good. It felt mortal.

"The missy don't be knowing if ye be a dream or a madman," Phineas said as he laid out the board and carved wood pieces on the bedside table.

"Doesn't she?" Dante murmured, distracted by the familiar figures of dragons and knights and ancient castles. One night he and Bess had arranged this very set on her windowsill and he had tried to teach her to play. "Why aren't you playing with . . . ah . . . 'the missy'? Doesn't she know how?"

Phineas snorted. "She knows the game well enough. But after a time her mind wanders."

"I see." Smiling, Dante fingered his queen, feeling the places where the detail had been worn smooth by many hands, as he recalled how Bess had moved the pieces about as if she were directing them through her own private imaginings. They hadn't played again.

"Do ye now?" Pulling up a chair, Phineas sat across from Dante and immediately made his first move. "She's a pretty girl, and I'm wondering if you see more than that."

Shifting onto his side, Dante studied the board and moved his piece. "What would you have me see, old man?"

"Ain't old enough for ye to call me such," Phineas grumbled. "And if ye be sane and have a keen eye, ye'd be seeing that she is a creature of whimsy."

"Her manner suggests the opposite," Dante said carefully. "She expended a great deal of energy trying to explain my . . . oddities."

"Oddities be they?"

"She thinks so."

"The missy be trying too hard to think like other folk. She don't ken that being different is naught to be ashamed of. Or that her mind be as sharp as the next, only it—" Phineas frowned at Dante's move and studied the board.

"Only it cuts in a slightly different direction?" Dante supplied.

His head jerked up and Phineas pinned Dante with a penetrating stare. "Ye see it then?"

"Her logic is more circuitous than linear."

"Ye be using some fine words, boy. A man might think ye had a fancy education."

Dante nodded. "In a hand-me-down sort of fashion."

Sitting back, Phineas planted his open palms on the top of his thighs. "I've no patience for such meandering about a subject."

Amused, Dante arched his brows. "It's your move."

"Aye, that it is." Phineas placed a knight. "I be wanting to know about ye. . . . Your move."

"And what do you want to hear? A neat little tale that makes sense, or the truth?"

"Too late for tales. Ye can't top the ones I heard in the town."

"No, I can't." Dante claimed a piece. "Perhaps you should ask direct questions."

"Mmmm. Ye be of high birth?"

"My mother was a French noblewoman, my father a stable hand."

"French . . . check." Phineas grinned in satisfaction at making such a move so early in the game. "How do ye come to be here and speaking the Queen's English?"

"My mother's family was rather disturbed that she conceived the child of a servant. They banished her to a cousin's care here in England. He was the local squire."

"And?"

"And the cousin died. His heir arrived, allowed her to have her child, then offered her lifetime security if she would act as governess to his son. Hence, I benefited from the same education and picked up the speech patterns of those who had the time to cultivate their pretensions. As I grew older I was put to work with the gardener . . . a pity really, since *my* lofty pretensions suited me quite well to the butler's post."

"Ye would have smashed the master's nose within an hour, I'll warrant."

"No doubt."

"So how did ye come by such fine clothes?"

"I stole them from the master, and later was able to purchase my own."

"And mayhap a horse from the master's stable?"

"That too." Dante neatly trapped Phineas's king as he delivered the unvarnished truth. "Checkmate. How else does one run down coaches on the highways?" He rolled to his back and turned his head to meet Phineas's gaze. "Your move again."

"Ye've kept in practice."

"At chess, after a fashion. At larceny—not recently. As you know, there is little activity on the old post road."

"Ain't none that I can see . . . not since we scraped ye off the ground and brought ye inside."

"That is because I am inside. If I were fit, and you and Miss Wells hadn't arrived, I would still be terrorizing the citizens with my nightly rides."

"How long since there be someone to rob?"

"Ah . . . there it is, a question to challenge my verity," Dante said as he crossed his arms behind his head, winced at the stretch of torn muscles, and sighed as the pain subsided.

"Depends on whether ye be an honest man or not."

"An honest man," Dante chuckled. "I suppose that is a matter of perspective. I have been known as a thief and a scoundrel, among other things, but I have never been accused of being a liar."

"How long then?"

Again Dante met Phineas's gaze and crooked his mouth in a wry smile. "It has been close to a hundred years since I relieved the privileged of both pride and possessions."

Phineas cleared his throat. "Ye might be a bit out of practice after such a long time."

The simple comment, delivered as if they were speaking of a paltry six months or merely five years, caught Dante by surprise. "What—no outrage that I would try to twit you, old man? Or are you secretly planning to have me carried off to the nearest asylum while I sleep?"

"Can't see any reason for it."

Impatient at Phineas's lack of reaction, Dante narrowed his eyes, searching for some telltale sign that he was, at the very least, being humored. "The 'missy' can. Isn't that why you're here? To confirm her opinions of the state of my sanity and put her mind at rest with prompt and decisive action?"

"The missy be good at imagining things and letting her thoughts take the long way around a subject.

She also be good at hiding from what she don't want to face.''

''I take it she learned those traits from you,'' Dante said with a hint of sarcasm. ''You've yet to come right out and speak your mind.''

Abruptly, Phineas began to set each chess piece in the separate compartments of a wooden chest and place the board on top. ''Didn't expect ye to be so forthcoming,'' he muttered. ''Thought I might have to ease ye into talking plain.''

''I have no reason to lie, since I can neither prove nor disprove my claims.''

''The proof is in the seeing.''

Again Dante was caught unaware by Phineas's easy acceptance of what he'd heard. ''What would you like to see? Shall I walk through a wall or take flight around the room? I'm sorry I have no document to prove the date of my birth.''

''Ye needn't be so testy,'' Phineas said. ''I see enough to think your mind is sound. If that be the case, then you're either what and who ye say ye are or I be the crazy one to still be believing in miracles.''

''Miracles?'' Dante scoffed. ''You think this is a miracle?'' It seemed even more incredible—no, absurd—to say it aloud. To call it a miracle was beyond Dante's comprehension. ''Miracles are supposed to be good, old man. Curses are another thing entirely.''

''Aye, but when a curse is broken ye have a miracle.''

Dante studied Phineas's expression, searching for signs that the old man was simply keeping him occupied until the sheriff arrived to take him away. ''You actually believe what I've told you?''

"Ain't sure anyone but ye will ever know for certain. But it be my way of thinking that a mind can conceive a thing only if the possibility exists in the first place."

Dante frowned and stared at the shadow of his body cast on the wall by the lantern light. "A philosopher," he mused. "You're a bloody philosopher."

"Mayhap, in my own way."

Raising his arm, Dante clenched and relaxed his fist, manipulating the image on the wall. "You know, I haven't had a shadow since my soul and I parted company," he said, testing Phineas further. "In the last day or so I've wondered why it would return only when my soul did."

Phineas shrugged. "Could be because without that part of yourself ye have no human substance, though your body be solid enough. And if ye don't be having substance, ye don't be having a shadow either."

"Or it could be that we're both mad as hatters." Dante lowered his arm and sighed. "I suppose only time will tell."

"The only thing time will tell is what kind of man ye be now."

"Ah, yes, I almost forgot. You're here to discern the nature of my character, are you not?" Dante turned his head and nodded at the ornately carved box that held worn images of mythical dragons and knights and stately queens. "That was just a ruse."

"I wanted a game," Phineas said. "Ye play with cunning and foresight."

"Thank you," Dante said, amused in spite of himself. "I could say the same about you."

"I lost."

"That remains to be seen, I think. But if you take much longer to make your move, I will expire of boredom." He met Phineas's gaze. "Why don't you save us both time by warning me away from your 'missy'?"

"She ain't *my* anything. She belongs to herself and I'd see it continue that way."

"I forgot," Dante said drolly. "You come from a place that encourages such thought. She told me about women's rights."

"Ain't nothing to do with suffrage," Phineas said patiently. "The missy has always been on her own. She be different from others, y'see, and folk never took her into their lives nor let her have one of her own."

"What of her family . . . her parents?" Dante asked, though he knew the answer. His Bess had been different too.

Phineas reached into his pocket and pulled out a pipe and tobacco pouch. "Oh, they love her right enough, but her papa sees her as a baby and treats her like one. The missy let him because he didn't expect nothing from her except that she be his sweet little girl to be protected and taken care of." As he spoke he packed the bowl with tobacco, lit a taper from the lantern flame, and held it to the pipe. "For all his cosseting of her, he don't know a thing about her."

A wry smile pulled at Dante's mouth. He remembered it so well—how Bess's father had sheltered her and treated her as if she were made of fragile crystal rather than flesh and blood. "He gave her the best of everything and directed her life as if she were not capable of independent thought," he said thoughtfully.

"Twas like that," Phineas agreed. "And her intended does the same."

The statement didn't surprise Dante, but it chilled him. Bess had also been promised to another—a fine, upstanding country squire, and the same man with whom Dante had shared lessons. Unfortunately for the poor besotted fellow, Bess had barely known he was alive.

"And her father chose this man for her," Dante stated.

"After a fashion. The missy has known him most of her life and she cares for him, but she don't be feeling no grand passion for him." Phineas paused to puff on his pipe. "Her beau is a good enough man, but he don't know her either. Him and her papa both think the same way—that the missy is quiet and sweet and submissive. That it's her nature to be that way."

"Odd, but I didn't see that when she threatened me with a gun and then told me to rot 'at once,' " he quoted.

"Did she now?" Phineas grinned around the pipe stem clamped between his teeth. "She never bothered before. Her papa and Tim don't understand it ain't sweetness that keeps her quiet. She just slips away from them into a world of her own making to escape the one they create for her." He fixed Dante with a hard stare. "Ye seem to have no trouble keeping her interested in this one."

"No . . ." Dante's voice trailed off as he recalled the night before Bess had left to stay with a cousin in the city, where she could learn all the airs and graces of a refined young lady. She'd been so young and frightened as emotion had spilled from her voice, touching him with the magic of learning that he was loved for the first time in his life. . . .

Dante cleared his throat and jerked his thoughts from the past. ''What of her mother?'' he asked. Bess's mother had died in childbirth, yet Phineas had mentioned a mother.

''The missy's papa is a strong man who don't be entertaining no opinions but his own. If the missus said a contrary word he would humor her and then do what pleased him. Once in a while she'd get in a word or two though.'' Smoke billowed and wreathed around Phineas's head as he spoke. ''The missy's mama gave up trying to wedge in between Betina and her papa, until the missy was ready to go off on her own. Twas her that helped me and the missy sneak away.''

''She wanted her daughter gone?''

''She wanted her daughter free,'' Phineas corrected. ''She loves the girl mightily and wants her to settle into the world in her own way.'' Rising, he picked up the box and the lantern and glanced down at Dante. ''I be wanting the same for the missy and wouldn't take kindly to anyone trying to make her fit where she don't belong or where she won't be happy.''

''Is that why you helped her escape?''

''Aye. Tis time she found her own way in life. Ain't no need for anyone to be telling her what that way is. She'll find it soon enough, I'll warrant.''

''I haven't such power,'' Dante said. ''She indeed has a mind of her own.''

''Where you're concerned, I be thinking otherwise,'' Phineas said and fixed him with a hard and steady gaze. ''I be thinking that ye can bring thoughts to her mind and feelings to her . . . to the rest of her just by looking at her. Tis the nature of men and women and the urges God gave them to get ideas across without saying a word.''

Dante shifted uncomfortably at Phineas's penetrating scrutiny and all-too-knowing perceptions. Recollections of that morning stirred in his mind and his body—of Betina leaning over him, accepting his silent urging to come closer, her breasts firm against his chest, her mouth a breath away from his, her gaze locked with his as if nothing and no one else existed. Her eyes had been soft and dazed as if she were under a spell, or perhaps caught within a memory. She'd moved toward him as if she were in a trance. And he'd ignored all that, wanting her any way he could have her, wanting *her* as she was now rather than as he remembered her to be.

"I see that ye be disturbed by the truth," Phineas said.

Disturbed? Dante thought. Yes, he was disturbed. The old man was right. He'd thought Bess had returned to him, and in a way she had, but only as a small part of another woman. Only her sweet spirit and vague manner. The rest was uniquely Betina, a person in her own right. A person who was more than Bess ever could have been, a sensual creature whose body responded to his with complete and artless honesty. Betina inspired in him carnal thoughts that had seemed almost obscene in relation to Bess.

The realization jolted him. He had loved Bess, the girl who would forever remain a girl, loved her ethereal beauty and sweet innocence. But he had that quickly, that completely, fallen *in* love with Betina, the woman—

"What's meant to be will be," Phineas said, cutting into his thoughts. "But I won't be having ye take advantage of the missy's romantic notions and pushing her before she's ready."

Dante nodded. "Warning taken, old man."

"Them be just words. I'll be looking for proof in the way ye be acting with her." Turning, Phineas ambled out the door, a cloud of smoke drifting in his wake.

Darkness filled the room, yet Dante didn't notice as he heard Phineas's words echo over and over again in his thoughts. *Tis time she found her own way in life.* The old man had put into words what Dante had thought once upon a time. He'd also thought that Bess's way followed the same path as his. But she hadn't been ready to explore life. The Bess he'd known so long ago never would have been ready.

But the woman who had left her home and family and betrothed was another story altogether. . . .

Her betrothed. Tim. A name that struck a chord in Dante. Never would he forget the ostler for whom he'd felt genuine fondness and a brotherly instinct for protection. Nor would he forget the sight of his poor simpleminded friend running into his path to warn him of danger, of his body being struck down by shots meant for Dante. He'd grieved for Tim in those few seconds before he'd felt the impact of the shots.

But that Tim was dead, and the man Phineas spoke of was someone else entirely. This Tim was—had to be—a man of strong character and impressive consequence for Betina's father to approve his suit. Yet if this man was important to Miss Betina Wells, she would not have left him so impetuously with only an old man and a gun for protection. He smiled with amusement. Precious good the gun would do her when she hadn't the sense to keep it on her person. Apparently women had been given the vote in America to pacify them into accepting their fathers' dictates on other issues, like choosing a husband. No doubt their votes were cast aside the moment they weren't looking.

For some reason the thought disturbed him.

Bess—Betina—might not know her way in the world, but he'd bet his soul that she knew her own mind well enough to search until she found it. He had no doubt that she valued freedom. Wasn't that what Bess had wanted all those years ago—the right to make her own decisions without influence from her father or from himself? But her decision had and always would have been to remain at the inn, pretending that the world extended only as far as she could see. For that privilege she had forsaken her love for him.

And then she'd sacrificed her life to save his.

To give *him* freedom.

He stared out the window at the moonlight that streamed over the road, an eternal thread linking him to the past and leading him into the future. Once he'd thought he knew what he wanted. He'd loved Bess's innocence and air of distraction that demanded so little of him beyond flowers and pretty words. He'd loved the magic of loving and being loved. He'd nourished the dream without realizing that once fulfilled it would be more than wishing and wanting.

It would be a part of the world and of life, where magic survived reality only in wistful memories, like the rosebush that neither aged nor bloomed.

Like a man cursed by the Fates because he dared to spin his own magic with a recklessly uttered vow.

What Bess had done so long ago was real and honest, acknowledging with her death the love that she hadn't had the courage to give in life.

All he had done was rob himself of his own destiny.

Until now.

Until now he had given no thought to what renewed mortality might mean to him, to what he would do with it. The world awaited him, yet he wondered if it would welcome or shun him for his ignorance of time and place. Would he be a stranger to the ways of men ruled by earthly concerns of progress and science?

Would Betina love him? Or as she denied the memories that came to her in dreams, would she also deny the awareness that was like a spell in the air between them?

He'd lived in the netherworld too long to deny the power of magic and dreams. He'd suffered loneliness long enough to know that magic, like love, could imprison as well as enchant and that dreams, like freedom, could delude as well as promise.

He'd been such an arrogant rakehell all those years ago. Arrogant and reckless and so cocksure of his invincibility. He'd never bothered to ask questions or to think beyond the exhilaration of the chase, the intoxication of besting his betters, the wild rush of seeking out the forbidden to claim a tender caress, a sweet kiss, a precious declaration of love.

Now he had a sobering awareness of how vulnerable he was to mortality and danger and heartbreak. And he had even more sobering questions—about the world outside his sanctuary, about the new ways of men, about Betina Wells and the courage that seemed to surprise even her.

She'd come here—to him, though she would deny that—against all protests, against all the fear he sensed in her. She had learned to reach out for what she wanted, to claim it.

He'd learned nothing in a hundred years, yet in the space of one day he'd discovered something worth living for. Betina was all that he had lost and more. The pluck that spiced her sweetness exhilarated him. Her beauty intoxicated him. The spirited wit that slipped past her preoccupation brought him the heady rush of discovery.

In her, he saw a woman and knew that he loved her.

Nothing else seemed to matter.

He stared at the darkness and knew for the first time in forever that it wouldn't last more than one night at a time.

Part Two

Remembrance

Nearer he came and nearer!
The Highwayman—*Alfred Noyes*

12

The nights seemed like forever to Betina, with wakeful imaginings and restless longings replacing her dreams. Three days passed and ran together without more than the briefest encounters with Dante. Only the mystery of him occupied her time and her thoughts, and she found it all too easy to drift with the days, an observer rather than a participant.

Phineas had declared Dante fit enough to be alone at night and took care of him during the day, using his superior strength to help Dante walk and regain his health. Judging from the amount of time Phineas spent with him, Betina suspected that they had become friends. The chess set had been moved permanently to the second-floor suite.

She wandered aimlessly around the inn, touching this and examining that as she wondered about the people who had lived here. How many times had *he* walked through the rooms, sat at one of the tables to drink a tankard of ale and exchange banter with the other customers? Had he ever climbed the stairs to Bess's room, to stroke her and kiss her and make love to her in the bed where she herself now slept?

The scene ran through her imagination. His long, beautiful body—naked and sleek with muscles and perspiration—moving over hers, their bare legs entwined, their mouths sealed together as their bodies were sealed one within the other, muffling their sighs and moans of pleasure. The vision failed her then, for that was all she knew of the act, all she'd seen when her phantom called on her in her dreams.

She closed her eyes and leaned against a wall as she felt the heat and quickening of response, the stirring of sensation, the throb of sudden need that prompted her to cross her arms tightly over her breasts.

"Curses," she muttered as she stepped outside to take one of her frequent afternoon walks over the moor. The Dante she knew had not been in the common room nor had he been upstairs making love to Bess. The inn had been boarded up for a hundred years.

Yet today her wayward mind persisted in imagining otherwise, playing out the legend over and over again, using herself and Dante as the players.

She checked the position of the sun, dismayed to find that only embers remained of the day. Still, she doubted if she would be missed before she walked to the ramparts and back. Following the sound of the sea crashing against rocky cliffs, she found the narrow little path she'd already begun to wear in the ground from her restless pacing along the elevated coast.

She breathed deeply and thought she'd never get enough of the tang of salt sea air or the dustless wind that lifted her hair, sifting through it in a wild caress. Nor would she ever find a scent as fresh and clean as the heather that carpeted the moor, the stems and tiny flowers swaying in the ever-present breeze like fairies dancing.

She paused at the end of her little trail and turned, studying the single straight line of trampled-down grass and heather. Extending fifty yards or so, it seemed a pitifully short mark for her to have made after traveling so far from home. A mark that began and ended exactly nowhere.

And what, she asked herself, was she doing about it besides wearing the track into a shallow pit along the edge of the moor? Clenching her fists, she walked backward, stopping every few steps to ruffle the growth packed down by her feet and blur the boundaries of the path.

The sun dipped into the sea, leaving a thin, shimmering streak of gold along the horizon as Betina finished. Again she studied the path and nodded in satisfaction. There. Already, clumps of vegetation stood upright and waved in the breeze. The wind and mist would fluff up the rest in time, obliterating the evidence of her indecision and cowardice.

Carefully, she picked her way over the moor, disturbing as little as possible. Ahead, the trees surrounding her land darkened into shadowed patterns of black flocking against a twilight-silvered sky. She hated this part of her otherwise-pleasant outings, dreaded leaving the sound and smell of the sea, the color and life and open spaces of the moor to enter the dismal woodland, which seemed more like a crypt than a pastoral setting.

It was too much like stepping into another world where nothing changed and even nature held her breath as she passed.

But light glimmered in the windows of the inn and smoke billowed sluggishly from the chimneys. A whinny and the restless stamping of hooves reached her from the stables.

Those windows were alight because of her. Fires burned in the grates because of her. The inn was hers. Dante and, yes, even Phineas were there as her guests rather than the other way around. Yet she was the one who felt like the outsider.

She grimaced at the musty air and took one step and then another and another beneath the canopy of trees, her gaze focused on the stone-and-timbered building. She hadn't journeyed across two countries and an ocean to spend her time in restless wandering and idle thought.

A mirthless laugh escaped her. She'd come here to be independent . . . to search for a new life. Her *own* life rather than one sustained and governed by others. She'd been so tired of being an outsider, loved and indulged in spite of how she was rather than because of what she was. And in spite of her parents' obvious love for her she'd always felt as if she didn't belong, as if she'd been found under a cabbage leaf rather than born into the family. In England, she'd reasoned, she would be taken at face value—a landowner, a woman of means. No one would know her well enough to judge her. No one would care enough to patronize her.

Yet here she was, judged and shunned because of the color of her hair and eyes and the place she now called home. Even her independence was bought with money earned and saved by her mother. What a pity she couldn't appreciate the irony of it all.

Abruptly, she stilled in the middle of the road and narrowed her eyes on the lighted second-floor window. There was the real irony. She'd come in search of a new life only to find a man who insisted that she had yet to complete an old one.

Something is waiting for you, Mama had said, and Betina had thought of adventure and discovery. She had adventured all right—in the luxurious confines of a passenger ship and later from behind the windows of a grand coach and in the private parlors of the best inns on the highways of a foreign land. And she had discovered a place that could not seem to live, yet refused to die.

She'd discovered a man whose familiarity made her fear her dreams. A man whose penetrating gaze and knowing smile made her feel like a woman.

The woman you were meant to be . . . How simple it had sounded when Mama said it the night before she'd sent Betina away. Everything was simple in familiar and protected surroundings. So simple when there were others to take care of her while she dreamed her life away.

She sank onto the ground at the side of the road, thinking hard. That was what she had to do—think and think and think. No one else could sharpen her thoughts. No one else could make decisions for her. No one else could make her the woman she was meant to be . . . whoever or whatever that was.

If only Mama had given her a hint.

Absently, she plucked a leaf from the rosebush beside her shoulder and traced its serrated edges, the veins running through it, the short stub where it had broken away from the bush. Every morning she'd looked out her window as she dressed, hoping to see roses. Every afternoon she breathed deeply as she passed the bush, hoping to smell something other than must and age. But, the rosebush remained as it was, unchanging, barren of color and scent, until she wondered if she had only imagined the single bloom she'd held in her hands.

Surely she was not meant to always be muzzy-headed and unaware, to always drift in a transparent realm of fantasies rather than walk with certain steps through the life she'd been given. Surely she could find her absent mind when she needed it. She'd done it before—just three days ago when she'd spoken with Dante and reasoned out the strangeness of his behavior. In fact, she'd done it quite well.

And then, as soon as she'd been relieved of responsibility, she'd allowed her mind to wander away from herself. She'd escaped to a small trail that began and ended exactly nowhere so she could pretend that life had not changed so very much and that the man who disturbed and confused her did not exist.

Dante again, she thought in disgust. He was everywhere, in her mind, invading her life, intruding on her private reflections—no, her phantom with Dante's face—tapping on her thoughts as surely as he tapped on her window in her dreams. With every reminder of him she felt a breathless excitement, a yearning to know more of him, to hear his voice, to know his touch. Those at least were a woman's sensations, a woman's needs. Mama had told her so, and since she'd never really experienced such things before, she would have to take Mama's word for it.

But why Dante? Why not Tim with whom she'd shared a childhood and who could share her life and her home with perfect ease? Dante knew nothing of the outside world; he didn't even know about guns and rifles and the outcome of the American Revolution or the War of 1812. He was as backward as the villagers, not only believing their silly legend, but expanding upon it as if it were a tangible piece of continuing history.

And now he was trying to make her a part of his delusions. Worse, he was trying to convince her that she was responsible for the legend in the first place.

Disgusted, she dropped the leaf and brushed off her hands.

"I'm glad to see you at least had the sense to wear your shawl," a deep voice said from across the road. Dante's voice.

Startled, she scooted back on her bottom and groped around her for a rock, a log, a branch—anything with which to defend herself.

A shadow stepped out from the shelter of trees, his form hunched to one side and distorted by the slant of moonlight that fell in dapples over the ground and obscured his face like a mask. He moved closer, with his head tilted and his gait uneven from the crutch Phineas had carved from a fallen branch. His pants stopped short above his ankles and gaped at his waist between the braces that held up his trousers and kept his too wide and too short shirt from riding up his torso.

Was this the man she had been so frightened of?

A gust of laughter escaped her. "You look like an overgrown gnome," she said and laughed again, forgetting that she sat leaning back on her hands and with her knees upraised.

"I imagine I do. I certainly feel like one—all twisted about and knobby with lost weight." He smiled and hobbled across the road to stand in front of her and glanced ruefully down at his attire. "And I am a beggardly gnome at that."

Her laughter trailed off as he stared down at her, his beautiful mouth stretched in a smile that showed straight white teeth, his moonstone eyes that seemed to see too much. She hadn't noticed that he'd lost weight, but then she hadn't seen anything but his blood and wounds at first. Now all she saw were lean cords of hard muscle and a brooding depth in his eyes.

Yes, this was the man she feared . . . and desired.

And he was outside again, prowling about the night.

Straightening, she drew her knees together and wrapped her arms around her legs. "I see that Phineas lent you some of his clothes."

"Yes . . . until he can gather my own from my cottage." Without invitation, he eased himself down beside her, using the crutch for balance, then laid the roughly carved wood alongside his injured leg. "I'm rather fascinated by this new fashion," he said as he fingered the faded blue denim of his pants.

She had a sudden, piercing urge to place her hand beside his, to caress his thigh, to explore the smoothness and hardness of him, to lean closer and inhale more deeply his scent. "Um . . . they're called Levi's," she said and tried to shift away from the press of his thigh against her hip. The brush of muslin against denim sounded like a whisper in the dark, seductive and threatening all at once.

The evening suddenly seemed warm, the darkness close and intimate.

He leaned toward her slightly and plucked the leaf from her skirt, then turned it over and over in his hand. "It's green," he said.

"Well, of course it's . . ." Her voice trailed off as she bit her bottom lip and realized that there was no "of course" about it. Every tree and fern and blade of grass in the isolated woodland was stiff and faded as old things were when time robbed them of brightness and resilience.

Yet the leaf was a deep, rich green and it had been supple in her hand like the rose. . . .

She snatched it away from him and dropped it on the ground. It turned to dust, like the rose.

"Renewal," Dante murmured, and his voice trembled a little as if he'd been moved in some way. "You've brought life with you, Betina."

She, too, felt a trembling, like something awakening inside her, stretching and growing and filling her. Panic. It was panic that froze her in place and shortened her breath and gripped her chest as her heart fluttered like wings trying to take flight. "No." She cringed at the high squeak she heard in her voice. She swallowed and tried again. "I didn't do this. It's the rain or the season or the sunlight or—"

"Hush, Betina." He wrapped his arm around her and drew her close, urging her head to rest in the crook between his neck and shoulder, holding her, his hand stroking her hair, his heart beating as unsteadily as hers.

"I didn't do it," she sobbed and clutched his waist, feeling his solid strength and reassuring warmth, forgetting that she thought him mad and dangerous, forgetting that she'd vowed not to let him touch her again, remembering that only with him did life flow so hotly through her veins. Only with him did she feel real. ''How could I?'' she asked and wondered whether she referred to the rosebush or her response to him.

''This bush has neither grown nor bloomed in a century . . . nothing here has grown or shown color.''

''Yes it has,'' she blurted, then wrenched her face away to stare blindly at the trees across the road. She hadn't meant to say that, hadn't wanted anyone to know what had happened when she'd cried into a barely formed bud. If he'd called her ''Bess'' she might have been on her guard, but he'd spoken her name so easily, as if he recognized and accepted that she was a different person.

''Look around you, Betina,'' he said with a weary sigh. ''Look at the ground. Not a leaf has fallen from a tree. Neither squirrel nor bird has foraged here.'' He shook his head. ''The place exists, yet it's not living.'' His voice thickened and wavered. ''Except for the leaf you touched, I have seen little of color here for too long.'' He stared down at the ground and poked his finger into the tiny pile of dust that had been a leaf only moments before.

She closed her eyes and swallowed. She didn't have to look to know what he said was true. Once, a man in her father's employ had been kicked in the head by a horse and fallen into what the doctor had called a catatonic state. It was like that here—life without vitality.

His hand cradled her chin, forcing her head up, forcing her to meet his quicksilver gaze. ''Am I the only one to see the stagnation here, the endless winter sleep of the woodland? Am I the only one who has seen the interior of the inn remain as it was when time stopped?'' His fingers tightened on her cheeks. ''Swear to me that you don't see what I see, and I'll believe I am a bedlamite.'' He glanced around and above them, then back at her, his expression fierce and pleading all at once. ''*Swear,* damn you.''

She opened her mouth and tried to do as he asked, to swear that she saw a fertile woodland rather than a dormant one, that the inn had been layered in dust and cobwebs, but the words stuck in her throat. There was too much anguish in his voice, too much fear in his eyes. She couldn't add to it with a denial of the truth. ''I can't.''

His hold on her eased as he searched her expression. ''No, you can't, can you?'' He exhaled. His features softened in relief, and his low chuckle sounded more like a sob. ''You can't even lie . . . and you wanted to, didn't you?''

''Yes, I wanted to lie,'' she admitted in a whisper.

''It didn't frighten you when you saw it. You didn't even want to question it,'' he stated in an equally quiet voice.

''No,'' she said, and it was barely a breath of sound as she watched him, held by his eyes, by the movement of his mouth as he spoke.

''No,'' he repeated. ''Because you believe the legend is true. Because in spite of the gloom and near death of the place, it was familiar to you.'' His voice was a slow, mesmerizing melody, with lyrics that compelled her to be calm and accepting. ''You knew that it had been waiting for you . . . that you belonged here.''

She lowered her gaze and closed her eyes. She couldn't reply, couldn't admit that she believed in anything but her own confusion. And then it didn't matter, because she felt nothing but the slow, gentle circles of his thumb on her cheek, saw nothing but stark loneliness in his eyes, knew nothing but a need to comfort him in some way. “Where did the rosebush come from?” she asked, wanting to hear the soothing cadence of his voice again.

His hand spread over one side of her face and trailed downward until only his fingertips touched the line of her jaw. Then, releasing her, he leaned back on his elbows and stared up at the moon, his mouth slanted in that mocking way he had. “A young gardener who worked at the manor house planted it for Bess on the day she went away to London to learn the female arts with her cousins. It was barely a stripling then, so the gardener felt confident in telling her—quite dramatically—that it would not bloom until she returned.”

“Oh,” Betina said, unaccountably disappointed. “I thought that the highwayman might have planted it for her.”

“He did.” Dante picked up the edge of her skirt and idly rubbed it between his fingers. “While she was away, her father informed the gardener that he was not good enough for his daughter and he should stay away from her. With all the reckless and witless reasoning of youth, the young man took to the highway, gathering wealth so that he might become worthy of the girl he loved.”

Caught up in the soothing timbre of his voice and the soft breeze that drifted over her, Betina, too, leaned back on her elbows and gazed up at the stars studding the deep-indigo sky. When he spoke of the legend like this it seemed a harmless tale of other people and other lives. She could almost see the story unfold in the shapes of gossamer clouds casting pale shadows against the night, almost feel the pain of loving without hope. "Did the bush bloom when she came home?"

"It thrived and bloomed before that, but immersed as he was in the romance of his declaration, the young man would pluck the buds late at night when his raids were done. When Bess returned home he allowed it to grow its own way, and she believed it did so because of her." He turned his head. "Would you have believed such a thing?"

"I think I would have tried very hard to believe it . . . if I loved him."

"She did not have to try, Betina." He shifted onto his side and gazed at the fabric he still worried between his fingers. "She had a sweet nature, a trusting heart, and her head was full of star stuff."

Star stuff. The words slipped through her, a wisp of familiarity, a touch of memory she could not quite grasp. "Was she . . . absentminded?" *Like me?* she added silently.

"She was not aware of the world as it was, but only as she wished it to be. Everything frightened her. She had a heart too timid and a mind too innocent for a complex world such as this. It was almost as if she weren't quite complete."

"Perhaps you don't give her enough credit," she said through the ache in her throat, not understanding why she should feel such grief for someone she'd never known.

"She had the spirit of an angel and was not meant for this world. I think she knew that." He propped up his head with his hand. "A rose can survive in neither a bed of weeds, nor an inhospitable climate." He swept his free hand in an arc, indicating the woodland that slept around them. "It can only rest and gather strength until it finds a better time to flower."

Betina sighed as shafts of moonlight fell through the trees, surrounding them like curtains of silver gauze, enclosing them in a world apart from any other. A world where magic was the only language, the heart was the only sovereign, and time was measured by moments of sharing. And in that moment, she knew Dante as she'd known no one else. "A rose bloomed three nights ago," she whispered. "A beautiful red rose."

She fell back as he raised up over her and his hand clutched her shoulder, his eyes narrowed and his expression tight as he watched her. "Do you mock the madman, Betina?"

She tried to raise herself, but he held her down with his body angled across hers. "I didn't mean to tell you."

"Have a care to know your facts when you lie," he said harshly as his fingers tightened in a painful grip.

Suddenly she was angry too, as she glared up at him. "Unlike you, I do not tell tall tales," she said and pushed at his chest with both hands.

Losing his balance, Dante fell back with a grimace of pain. He lay on his back, his chest heaving as he tried to regain his breath. His face was ghostly pale in the moonlight and his eyes squeezed shut. "Damn," he rasped over and over again as he pounded the ground with his fist.

Betina slowly slid backward, wanting to get away before his strength returned.

His eyes shot open and his hand shot out to grasp her wrist. "No," he said in a stronger voice. "You will not run from me again."

"I'll call for Phineas," she threatened as she tried to twist her arm from his hold, but for a man who trembled in pain he was surprisingly strong.

"You'll do nothing until you give me some answers."

"Answers to what? You have accused me of lying. I fail to see what I could tell you that you would believe."

He inhaled deeply then released it as he pulled her down closer to him, so that it was she who lay across him with his hands gripping her waist. "For God's sake, have pity and tell me the truth," he said, and his countenance was both desperate and hopeful.

The moon sailed behind a cloud, casting his face in shadow, and only his eyes showed light and clear in the darkness. Just then he looked like the phantom she'd imagined standing beneath a tree the night she'd arrived . . . the phantom whose face she'd seen in her dreams. But she felt Dante as she'd never felt the phantom—the hard planes of his body beneath hers, the rise and fall of his chest against her breasts, the beat of his heart that seemed to echo in her ears as his arms closed around her. She could not move, could not struggle, and wasn't sure she wanted to. Though his hold on her waist was firm it was not brutal, and though he seemed as ferocious as the howl she'd heard that first night, she sensed that he would not hurt her, that his need was greater than any fear she might have. A need for more than answers as she felt him grow rigid against her belly and heard him stifle a groan.

"Tell me, Betina. Tell me of the rose that bloomed."

"It bloomed, and when I dropped it, it turned to dust," she said, breathless at the need that swelled inside her until there was room for little else.

"All of it, Betina." As before, he cupped her chin and urged her to look at him, to be held in thrall by the intensity of his gaze, the raw emotion in his voice. "I must know."

His desperation held her spellbound, compelling her to forget herself and ease his mind. Why it mattered, she didn't know and didn't care. Anticipation and urgency were like frantic throbs inside her. Her breasts tingled. Her cotton dress seemed as nothing as he tensed beneath her, and she thought she could feel every movement of every muscle in his legs and stomach and chest. "I was holding the bud between my hands and . . . crying. When I looked down I held a full blossom in my hands," she said quickly, not wanting to talk, not caring about the rosebush or anything else, but the desire that filled her. "I tore it away from the bush and dropped it. It . . . it turned to dust . . . like the leaf."

"You said it was red?"

"Yes." She ran her tongue over her lips and wished he would forget the blasted rose, wished he would be quiet and kiss her.

"You're sure?" he said and caressed her cheek with the back of his hand, then smoothed her hair away from her face.

She nodded.

"The roses were pink when I planted them," he said, and it sounded as if it came from a distance.

His statement was like an unexpected blow, stunning her into silence as her body continued to tremble, and she vaguely remembered the faintest touch of pink on the outside edges of the petals, as if the deeper color had bled over the rose—

"The highwayman was shot here and fouled the ground with his blood. The bush stopped growing then." His voice was husky and choked, and his eyes were full of wonder as he stared up at her. "And then you brought it back to life with your tears."

"Stop, please stop," she pleaded, then buried her face in the hollow between his neck and shoulder. "I don't want to hear anymore. I don't care about the roses or the past. I don't care. . . ."

His arms wrapped around her back and held her still against his body, his breath warm on her ear as he soothed her with soft words and gentle caresses. "You're so frightened, Betina. As frightened as I was as I chased my soul night after night, neither feeling, nor growing old, nor knowing any human pleasure. I wanted to believe I'd gone daft, but I was denied the escape of lunacy."

She felt the words vibrating in his chest and wanted to stop him, but she could only lay against him, absorbing his warmth, his touch, the rightness of being held by him. The rightness of believing him when nothing he said made sense. She closed her eyes and gave herself over to the enchantment that seemed to wrap around her, as mist crept over the ground and enveloped them with the scent of roses kissed by dew. No one else—nothing else—existed but Dante and her and the mist and the sweet sense of destiny guiding her along a path overgrown by time.

"Look at me," Dante ordered softly.

Opening her eyes, she raised her head and saw him through the luminous vapor. He was the embodiment of her dream, visiting her in the flesh. It was magic being held and feeling more alive than she'd ever imagined. She was bewitched by the sensations in her body, by need stronger than anything she'd ever known, by *him*, as she willingly lowered her head to meet his kiss, to open her mouth to his demanding exploration, to touch his hair and his face and his shoulders. . . .

To believe he was real. This was real. Only this.

She was warm . . . so warm. She didn't know where her heartbeat ended and his began. The magic penetrated her like the mist, filling her with the brush of butterfly wings in the pit of her belly, the languor of warm honey in her veins, the sweet anticipation of feeling more and more with each kiss, every touch. . . .

The precious sense of being so much more than she was.

He bathed her lips with his tongue and groaned against her cheek as his hands sifted through her hair, skimmed lightly over her neck and down her back. She arched against him and her legs moved restlessly, insistently over his. His thigh jerked and he moaned. . . .

And fell still.

She raised her head, saw him gazing bleakly at the stars as the mist receded.

"Immortality would serve me well just now," he said wryly and again smoothed her hair back as if he could not touch it enough.

She heard the strain in his voice and frowned at the tight line of his mouth, the recoiling of his shaft beneath her, yet she didn't comprehend.

"I would take you here in moonlight and mist if I could, Betina Wells. But my body protests such exertion."

It was too explicit for her to misunderstand. And it was too brash for her to ignore. She felt like a fool, writhing over him like a tart, lying with him on the ground by the side of the road as if she had neither modesty nor morals, begging him to "take her" with every movement she made. Desire fled and mortification took its place. She pulled away and struggled to her feet, feeling all arms-and-legs awkward as she nearly lost her balance trying to find something to grasp besides Dante, and her arm brushed the rosebush and caught the wicked point of a thorn. But she ignored the sting of the scratch and the precarious footing she had with the bush behind her and Dante sprawled in front of her. She glared down at him with what she hoped was a frigid expression. "I am not yours to 'take.' "

He winced. "A poor choice of words."

"Yes, and one that will get you into trouble if you venture out of this backwater." She yanked her skirt free of the rosebush and sidestepped out of his reach.

He caught the hem of her dress and tugged. "A poor choice, Betina, but also a common one. I see no reason for offense."

"Then I suggest you acquaint yourself with the more enlightened aspects of modern society instead of perpetuating old superstitions among the natives."

"And I suggest that you enlighten me forthwith so I will avoid such blunders in the future," he snapped.

"I have some literature written by esteemed suffragists in my country. They are far more eloquent than I on the rights of women," she snapped back. It was beyond her why he was so irritated when she was the one who'd been insulted. She would not admit that her own actions were far more insulting to herself than Dante's "poor choice" of words.

"What in bloody hell is a suffragist?" he nearly shouted.

"A woman who teaches other women—and men, if that is possible—that females are *not* chattel and have more than sufficient intellect to manage *their* own property, voice *their* opinions in government, and exercise *free will* regarding when and where they *wish* to give men any part of their lives, *including their bodies.*"

"Good God," he said, his voice as bemused as his expression.

"I'm quite certain that God is far more 'enlightened' and far less arrogant than his male creations. After all, Adam could not get along without a woman to care for him, and God had the insight to know that men would not have the fortitude to bear children." Deciding that retreat was in order while Dante's mouth hung agape, she swished her skirt and executed a satisfyingly indignant flounce away from him.

Even the tug and sound of her skirt ripping could not induce her to halt. Pretending she did not hear the fabric tear nor feel the draft on her pantalooned backside—oh, why hadn't she worn a petticoat?—she strode across the yard, pushed past Phineas, and headed straight for the stairs. Dear heaven, Phineas had been standing in the doorway. What had he seen?

With her foot on the first step she glanced back at Phineas, determined not to quail in the face of her indignity. Neither would she acknowledge his frown as his gaze rebounded from her torn skirt to the yard and back again. "I suggest, Phineas, that you leave Mr. de Vere where he lies. Perhaps he will take root and become as paralyzed as the rest of the vegetation."

As soon as Phineas glanced back outside she dashed up to her room and waited for mortification to reassert itself. But the more she thought about it, the more she felt only a sense of triumph and accomplishment. So many times she'd heard other women deliver clever and stinging setdowns to their male counterparts. Even Mama had done it to Papa or an obnoxious guest, though her delivery was so subtle they rarely realized they'd been bested until they'd had time to think about it.

She'd done rather well, she thought as she tore away the remains of her gown and rifled through her drawers for a clean nightdress. Yes, indeed, she'd sounded quite clever considering she'd never stood up to anyone in her life . . . considering her heart had still been palpitating and her breath had not quite caught up with her from the rush of pleasure Dante's mouth and his hands and the suggestive bulge in his Levi's evoked.

The nightdress trailing onto the floor from her fingers, she nodded to herself in the mirror and thought that Mama would have been proud of her. Actually, she decided, it was more important that, for the first time in her life, she was proud of herself.

"We are all caught up in the drama these mortals play. I would not have it ended until it is finished."

—Nemesis the Inevitable

13

"It is done," Clotho said, as she leaned back in her chair and moved her head from side to side. "The mending is complete, and all the threads for Dante and Betina are now new . . . except for the filaments of memory I retrieved from the past and added to Betina's thread. I only hope it is enough."

"Memory threads," Atropos grumbled as she, too, took a place by the fire. "There was good reason why the elders decreed that memories should begin with each incarnation of a soul. Add too much and the mortals tangle their threads and make more work for us to no purpose. Too little memory and half-wits that they are, they inevitably repeat their own histories. Is it any wonder I find working with them so tedious?"

"What is done is done," Ilithyia soothed as she knelt before the hearth with her sisters. "The past has

been linked to the present and renewed. Now we can look to the future and see if the other will take his place."

"We shall know in time," Nemesis said and waved a hand over the fire. The images of Dante and Betina faded and were replaced by those of buildings nestled among the mountains of Wyoming. A man drove his buggy at breakneck speed through the iron gates and beneath a high, arched sign that read: WISHING WELL RANCH. JACOB WELLS, PROPRIETOR. *Near the corral, a young man of refined looks and impressive stature separated from a group of ranch hands and headed toward the crescent-shaped drive fronting the main building.*

Ilithyia frowned. "I wish we had paid more attention to Tim rather than focusing only on Betina and Dante. He caught us by surprise last time."

Lachesis peered into the fire. "Would that we knew his thoughts."

"We can only observe," Nemesis reminded her. "To intrude into the minds of mortals is forbidden."

"It would make no difference," Atropos sniffed. "Tim's mind has walls of stone. We have never been able to discern what goes on behind them."

"Tim has grown strong," Lachesis observed. "And is not easily cowed."

"As it should be when old threads are strengthened with new ones," Clotho said. "I took great care with him."

"We shall soon see," Nemesis murmured. "Cease your prattle, sisters, and attend the flames before the humans again take fate into their own hands without our guidance."

* * *

Jacob Wells drew the buggy to a halt in the drive, leapt from his seat, and tossed the reins at a stable hand as he glared at his manager walking across the yard. "Tim! I need you. Now!" he barked as he took the steps two at a time up to the double doors that were the main entrance to the house.

The young man he'd shouted at paused at the buggy to help a woman down from her seat and escort her into the house. "What's going on?" he asked.

The woman smiled sadly. "He is angry with me."

"Were you so extravagant on your shopping trip to San Francisco, Etta?"

"There was no shopping trip," Jacob Wells roared as they followed him into the foyer and down the hall to his darkly paneled office. Without breaking his stride Jacob went straight for the cabinet set beneath the window behind his desk, poured himself a glass of whiskey, and tossed it down quickly. He glared at Tim. "Don't you want to know where your fiancée is?"

Unperturbed by Jacob's temper, Tim met his gaze squarely. "Where is Betina?"

"In goddamn England," Jacob roared louder and pounded the top of his desk with his fist. "With goddamn Phineas."

Tim slipped one hand into his trouser pocket and leaned his shoulder against the mantel.

"Jacob, I think Tim and I could use a drink as well," Etta said.

Scowling, Jacob filled two more glasses and grudgingly carried them to his wife and Tim before transferring the decanter to his desk and splashing a double shot into his tumbler.

"Don't you have anything to say, boy?" Jacob barked.

"What can I say?" Tim asked, his expression unrevealing. "Betina and Etta left together, so it follows that Etta let Betina go."

"Hell, yes, she let Betina go. Arranged the whole thing and sent our daughter off with her blessings, then kept me busy in San Francisco for the last month." He downed his whiskey in one swallow and poured himself another. "Probably gave Betina the money she's been squirreling away."

Etta raised her brows. "You know about that?"

"Do I know about that?" he asked the ceiling. "Dammit, Etta, of course I know. It's a piss-poor state of affairs when you and Betina defy me with my own money."

"It was my money," she corrected.

"Only because I made it a goddamn point to leave coins in the cushions and give you more than you needed to run the house."

"Thank you, Jacob," she said serenely.

Tim's unfathomable gaze rebounded from one to the other.

"Don't change the subject!" Jacob boomed loud enough to shake the rafters. "You bamboozled me into meeting you in San Francisco and fooled me into believing you'd left Betina with her cousins in Stockton."

"It wasn't difficult, Jacob. And if you weren't concerned about Betina being in Stockton without us, why should you worry about her being in England? You know Phineas won't let anything happen to her."

"You lied to me, dammit! All that talk about a honeymoon, and I swallowed it whole. Seven weeks Betina has been gone, while I followed you around like a randy bull." Flushing, he stared down at his drink and cleared his throat.

"It was a lovely time, Jacob," Etta said softly. "We should do it more often."

Tim shifted against the mantel and sipped his drink as if he were enjoying a quiet moment after the evening meal, politely observing Etta and Jacob as if they were performers in an entertainment they occasionally provided for their guests.

"What the hell are you smiling about, boy?" Liquid sloshed on a stack of papers as Jacob slammed his glass down on the desk.

"You and Etta should go away together more often," Tim said. "She looks radiant."

"Thank you, Tim," Etta said with a regal nod of her head.

"What the hell is the matter with you?" Jacob raked his hand through his thick mane of silver hair. "It's your fiancée who's traipsing around a foreign country with an old man who indulges any crazy whim she might have."

"Etta's right, Jacob. Phineas won't let anything happen to her," Tim said reasonably. "Actually, I think it might be for the best that Betina went now. She's been restless lately, and some time in a strange place ought to cure that. For all we know she's already on her way home."

"I know she's not," Jacob said and raked his hand through his hair again. "I wired that solicitor in London. She took off for that broken-down place she inherited, and as far as he knows she's still there. As far as he knows," he sneered. "Isn't anybody worried about her?"

"You manage that quite nicely without help, Jacob," Etta said dryly. "Betina is a grown woman. It's past time for her to learn to think and live like one."

"The hell she's a grown woman! All her life we've had to watch her stumble around because her head was in the clouds. Remember last summer when she ran into a fence because she was woolgathering? Damn near broke her neck." He met his wife's gaze with a bleak one of his own. "I'm scared shitless, Etta."

"I know you're scared, Jacob. I worry about Betina too," Etta said. "But there will come a day when we won't be around to protect her anymore. Isn't it better to prepare her for that?"

"Prepare? She's going to marry Tim. The ranch will be hers," Jacob shouted. "A strong husband and plenty of money will be all the protection she'll need."

"Did it ever occur to you that if no one was dogging her heels all the time, she just might be able to take care of herself?" Etta shouted back as she rose and glared at her husband.

"No, it did not!" Jacob ground out as he leaned toward Etta, his fists clenched at his sides. "And I'm not going to argue about this. Pack my bags. I'm going after her."

"If you do, I won't be here when you return," Etta said quietly.

Tim glanced from Etta to Jacob.

Jacob snorted. "Don't give me that bull, woman."

"It's not bull, Jacob. I made this decision some time ago."

"What decision? That you'd try to blackmail me?" Jacob shook his head. "It won't wash. You can't make it alone either."

"Can't I? Have you forgotten that I traveled to San Francisco alone and stayed there alone for almost a month while you were chasing down Bighorn sheep in the mountains? Or have you forgotten that I ran our homestead alone while you were off fighting a war? Did you ever—*ever*—think of all the time you spent with *our* daughter while I made decisions and entertained *our* guests?'' She turned away from him, and her voice lowered to a sound of resignation. ''Seems to me I've always been alone.''

Jacob's head jerked back as if he'd been struck, and his shoulders sagged. Backing up, he groped for the edge of the desk, feeling his way around it, and slumped into his chair, a man stunned by his wife's show of strength and shattered by the truth.

Etta picked up her glass, drained it, then met Tim's frowning gaze. ''Tim, I love my husband and I would really hate to leave him. Still, I can see that he won't rest well until he knows Betina is safe. The reasonable solution seems to be for you to go to England.''

With a thoughtful frown, Tim stared down at his drink.

''Tim,'' Etta said, her voice edged with impatience. ''I'd like an answer, please.''

''We have a full house, Etta,'' Tim said. ''And reservations are made through the fall.''

''We'll manage just fine. It might be that Betina would welcome a familiar face,'' she coaxed. ''Better that it be her fiancé rather than her parents.''

Staring down into the whiskey he swirled in his glass, Tim grimaced. ''She told me she was going, Etta, and asked me not to interfere. I agreed.''

''You agreed, boy?'' Jacob asked hoarsely. ''Why?''

''Because I knew she'd be safe with Phineas . . . and I made some inquiries about the inn. It's isolated except for a village that's still in the last century. The people there are harmless, and I decided it would be a good idea to be reasonable.''

''And you thought she would come crawling back to you after trying to manage on her own and failing,'' Etta said, her eyes narrowed.

Tim shrugged. ''She had a wild hair, Etta. It's better that she get rid of it now than after we're married.''

''I see,'' Etta said, shaking her head in disgust. ''I shouldn't be surprised by the utter arrogance of men, but I still am on occasion.''

''What's gotten into you, Etta?'' Jacob asked.

''Age, Jacob,'' she snapped. ''I'm getting old, and I want a life of my own—preferably with my husband. And when it's over I want to know that my daughter will be able to stand on her own two feet and meet the world head on.''

''She can't. You know that.''

''Do you think I should know it simply because you've told me often enough?'' Etta said. ''I'm beginning to think Phineas and I are the only ones who have bothered to take a good hard look at Betina. Her head isn't in the clouds, Jacob. It's merely lazy from disuse.''

''What the hell does that mean?''

''It means that as long as you and Tim made her decisions for her and took care of her, she didn't have to do it herself. Now she does, and if I know anything I know that she is fast becoming twice the woman I am . . . and make no mistake, Jacob Wells, I'm one hell of a woman.'' She rounded on Tim. ''Now, are you going to England or do I take up residence in Denver?''

Tim's hands clenched around his glass. ''I'll pack.''

Etta nodded in satisfaction and smiled in grim amusement. "I thought you might say that." With that, she left the room and gently shut the door behind her.

"Jesus," Jacob muttered. "Twenty-five years I've been married to that woman and I never saw her like this. What happened?"

"You'd better worry about what will happen if I don't get my ass on the next train out of Cheyenne," Tim said. "I'd rather eat cow pies than tangle with her."

"Jesus." Jacob sat at his desk, staring at the room as if he no longer recognized his world nor the young man he'd approved of to "care" for his daughter.

Tim walked from the office, a troubled frown on his face and a tense urgency in his step.

Collectively, the sisters of Fate sighed in relief.

"Etta is a woman after my own heart," Atropos said. "It is to be hoped that her daughter has the same strength."

"She does. It would be better to hope that she learns to employ it well," Ilithyia said.

Clotho resumed work at her spinning wheel. "There is only so much we can do."

"Yes," Nemesis agreed. "Betina and Dante have a penchant for defying our efforts, as does Tim. I wish we knew more of his mind."

"We never have known," Atropos said as she began to sharpen her shears. "A displaced grain of sand can change the face of the world; so the actions of one such as him can alter the future, as we have learned."

"It will not be so easy for them this time," Lachesis murmured. "We have worked hard to ensure it."

"We always work hard," Atropos said as she oiled her shears. "Dante and Betina have proven that our best is not always good enough."

"It has to be enough," Ilithyia whispered. "It just has to be."

When the moon is a ghostly galleon tossed upon cloudy seas,
When the road is a ribbon of moonlight over the purple moor . . .

The Highwayman—*Alfred Noyes*

14

He came to her again . . . and again.

Every time Betina closed her eyes and began to drift into slumber, he was there, his tall imposing body sprawled in the chair by the window, his face somber as he regarded her over steepled fingers. Yet when she opened her eyes she saw nothing but the luminous darkness left behind by a waning moon, nothing but the memory of Dante soothing her fear, Dante holding her in anger and kissing her in passion, Dante desolate as he spoke of the legend and the rosebush, shaken by her revelation that a flower had bloomed.

Dante, making her believe . . .

She clutched the counterpane up to her chin and squeezed her eyes shut. She'd always believed in magic, but only in her imagination. She believed in her phantom, too, but only in her dreams. Only in her maiden's ideals of love and happily-ever-after.

No! No! No! she repeated over and over again as he appeared, a wavering vision of strength and patience walking slowly toward her, his high boots making no sound on the polished wood floor, his claret velvet coat and doeskin breeches making not a rustle in the silence, the light of the moon hung so low in the sky lengthening his shadow in front of him.

"Bess! I have a shadow!"

"We all do."

"We all do . . . I'd forgotten."

With a sob she banished the memory and willed the phantom from her dreams.

He did not go, but sat on the edge of her bed, his hip pressing against hers, though she did not feel it. And if she could not feel it, then he couldn't be there, she reasoned. "It's a dream. A silly dream—"

"No, not a dream," he said, and his deep voice seemed to echo in every part of her.

"A *very* silly dream," she insisted.

"A memory, Bess. One you refuse to acknowledge." His hand opened over her head and untied her netted snood, pulled it free, and dropped it on the floor, then returned to her hair and sifted through the strands.

Her eyes were closed, yet she saw it all. She knew he touched her, yet only felt an odd sensation of something warm passing through her. She jerked her head away, yet was afraid to open her eyes and look again, afraid that if she did she might see too much. "You don't exist. I made you up. I did. You're a dream."

"Ebony hair touched with glimmers of deep crimson," he said softly as he smoothed tendrils away from her face, lifting and kissing the ends before spreading them on the pillow.

Her heart jumped, then lay quivering in her chest.

"Midnight eyes with the sparkle of starlight in their depths." He pressed a kiss to one closed lid, then the other.

She felt it. Oh, dear heaven, she felt it—a dry press of warm lips, a lingering, and then nothing.

"Skin fair as the petals of a morning rose, creamy fair with a touch of dawn pink on your cheeks, and your mouth that curves upward, as if your spirit smiles even when you do not." His lips caressed each cheek in turn and slid down to her mouth, brushing the corners, skimming his tongue over the rest, and then nothing.

She reached for his mouth, reached for more of the sweet intoxication of his scent, his taste. But she could not reach far enough or high enough. Her eyes opened slowly, and her lips parted as she saw him above her, felt the hard press of his hip against hers, grasped his arm that was angled over her, trying to draw him closer.

He sat at her side, watching her through moon-silver eyes touched with morning blue. She saw him, felt him, yet did not question how it could be or why. She trembled as she saw the shadow of him laying across her, and traced the outline with fingers that tingled at the sensation of touching something alive. He was more than her phantom, more than a dream.

He was fantasy and tangible presence. He was dark desire and mesmerizing seduction. In that moment, in the darkness and silence of night, he was a memory and a hope she could not define.

"Bess once said that I was a wish that could never come true," he said.

"Are you?"

"A wish is a pale thing, Betina, a thing of dreams. I would have more from you than that."

"I know of little else than wishes," she replied sadly.

He shook his head. "Only if you want nothing else, Betina. It is your choice whether to expect more or accept less." He smiled then, but his eyes held only sorrow and regret.

"How can one expect magic?" she asked. "It is but a dream."

"Is it?" He held his open hand over her and only the shadow of it touched her, yet she felt it moving over her body, felt the quickening in the pit of her belly and the warmth of flesh on flesh, felt each stroke as his fingers moved above her breasts, her neck, her face.

And magic drifted in the air—a mist becoming a part of her, a shimmer rippling around her, the scent of fresh roses intoxicating her. Magic touching her as his hand lowered to her, grazing her face with the backs of his fingers, caressing her midriff and stomach through the sheer lawn of her gown. Magic whispering to her with his voice.

"Is it a dream, Betina?"

She felt him as he lay over her and opened his mouth over hers, as she breathed in the scent of him, as he slid down her body and circled her breasts with his tongue. She cried out at the tug of his lips and the rub of fabric on her nipples, trembled as hot pleasure rushed through her to the pit of her belly and gathered between her legs, arched upward with shock and anticipation as his hand moved lower to stroke her there, gently, then deeply, insistently, demanding her frantic sobs and urgent response.

The moon disappeared and the night deepened as he rose above her, an ebony shadow in the iridescent mist, lowering slowly, a weightless phantom molding himself to her, sinking into her, through her, becoming part of her, passing through her, and mingling with her soul. . . .

And then he drifted away from her with the mist, becoming part of it as he had been a part of her for that sighing pause in time, disappearing as it faded into nothing, leaving only a shimmer of star stuff floating in the air.

"Oh, my," Lachesis sighed as she stared transfixed at the scene in the fire. Beside her Ilithyia knelt on the floor, her eyes wide, her breath as labored as those who writhed on the bed in Betina's chamber. Nemesis sat in a rocking chair, watching the tableau with a small smile. Atropos stood beside the hearth, her fists clenched, her lips parted, her body swaying as if in a trance.

"This was not woven into their threads," Clotho whispered thickly and licked her lips.

"No?" Nemesis asked. "Do you know the nature of the filaments you think so pretty?"

Clotho held up the threads she spun simultaneously and picked out a translucent strand that shimmered with all the colors of the aurora from which it came at the beginning of time. "This? I have used it before."

"Yes," Ilithyia said without taking her gaze from the fire. "Do you not remember whose lives you spun with it?"

"Of course I remember. Who could forget Lancelot and Guinevere, Anthony and Cleopatra. . . . Oh, yes . . . I see."

"These two are so beautiful together," Lachesis sighed. "Have a care that the fragile strands do not tangle and break this time, please. I would have their ending be happier than the others."

They were silent for a moment as phantom became mist drifting over Betina, enveloping her, permeating her very being.

"Clotho has used a light oil of rose to strengthen the filaments," Nemesis said, caressing the arms of her chair as if they were flesh.

Atropos took a deep breath and turned sharply away from the fire to restlessly pace the width of the room. "Mortals," she grumbled. "Even when they sleep they are depraved."

Nemesis glanced from Atropos to the scene in the flames and back again. "We must find her a reckless young immortal to ease her frustrations."

"Or perhaps a centaur," Ilithyia said.

"Why not send her on a sabbatical to earth?" Clotho suggested. "A man like Dante—"

Lachesis frowned. "You would corrupt him so? Has he not suffered enough?"

"I would sooner tie these threads into a Gordian knot," Clotho said.

"We jest," Nemesis soothed. "An unkind thing to do at our sister's expense."

Ilithyia turned back to the fire, to the vision of Betina arching upward, welcoming her lover, absorbing him, yet unaware that she held only shadow and mist. "I am more concerned for those two. Will they be all right?"

Atropos snorted as she glanced at the scene in Betina's room and clenched her hands again.

"It is out of my hands," Clotho said sadly. "The threads will spin in their own way now. All I can do is try to guide them."

"Then guide them well, sister," Atropos said as the mist in Betina's room rose and billowed and disappeared.

Nemesis arched her brows. "You change your mind, Atropos?"

"I merely concede to the inevitable." Atropos bowed to her sister, then drew up to her full stiff-backed height, in full possession of herself once more. "You have made your decision clear, and I tire of such"—she waved her hand in the general direction of the fireplace—"such dubious entertainment."

"I had hoped you would acknowledge that mortals such as Dante and Bess—Betina—deserve a second chance," Lachesis said as she snapped her fingers and the scene in the fire shifted to Dante moving restlessly in his own bed. "There are too few mortals who believe in magic."

"I acknowledge weariness only," Atropos snapped and strode toward her chamber. "Good night, sisters. I pray you grow warts for your voyeurism."

Ilithyia chuckled behind her hand.

Clotho left her chair at the spinning wheel and stood before the hearth.

"Definitely a centaur," Nemesis said. "What are you about, Clotho?"

Reaching for a small bottle attached to her embroidered leather girdle, Clotho pulled the stopper and poured granules into her hand. "I tire of hoarding this with no purpose."

"You cannot mean to part with it?" Atropos said from the threshold.

"Only a little . . . enough to perhaps help them remember that beauty is possible, even in a world of mortals." She placed her hand in the fire and spilled the iridescent grains into the flames.

Ilithyia picked up a basket and scooped up a handful of rose petals—petals of deep red tinged with pink. "I plucked these from the bush before they fell, hoping to find some use for them. Perhaps they will remind Betina of the magic of love."

"Ha!" Atropos said. "Humans lack such imagination."

"Most humans," Ilithyia said. "But these two are special." She sprinkled the petals into the fire to mingle with Clotho's aurora dust.

And the petals and dust drifted into the window of an old inn to dance in the air above the form of a sleeping woman and settle on the shoulders of a man awakening in the room below.

Dante shuddered and sat bolt upright in his bed, his eyes wide, his mind fogged by the remains of a dream. The sheet slipped to his waist, and air cooled his sweat-slicked chest. His heart slowed to a steady thump and he inhaled deeply, feeling as if he hadn't drawn a full breath since his vision of Betina lying in her bed and whimpering as mist slid over her body.

His limbs quivered as if he'd been there, a part of the mist, caressing her, sinking into her as she responded to his mouth, his hands, as she spread her legs and arched up to meet him. . . .

Yet it hadn't been him, flesh and bone, but the shadow part of him that mingled with the vapor while he slept . . . while Betina dreamed of his eyes, his face, his body, of him loving her until she cried out and stardust fell around them.

Shifting to his side, he reached to the table and fumbled for the sticks Phineas called matches, struck one, and winced at the sudden flare of light as he held it to the lantern wick.

His hands trembled as he saw a single long, black hair twined through his fingers. Her hair, conforming to the curve of his hand.

The scent of roses and desire clung to his body. Betina's scent.

And as he moved, motes floated around him, twinkling with all the colors of the rainbow.

It could not be, he told himself. It had been a dream. He hadn't been in her room, in her bed . . . in her.

Sweat broke out on his forehead as he threw back the sheet and looked down to study his body. His nipples were puckered as if they'd been teased by a woman's hand. His manhood glistened with moisture as it lay in repose against his thigh . . .

Spent from passion.

He groaned and rested his head in his hands at the memory of sensation, provocative and intoxicating, at the experience that had been more than a dream . . . so much more.

It couldn't have been real. Surely he'd know if it was.

He became conscious of the dampness on the sheet beneath him and shook his head ruefully. He hadn't left his bed at all, but had indulged in the kind of fantasy he'd thought he'd outgrown long ago. A fantasy with tangible results.

A dream. He'd had a bloody adolescent wet dream, accomplishing in sleep what he had not been able to do with Betina earlier that night. Disgusted with himself, he rolled to the other side of the bed and pulled the sheet up over his waist.

Was this his fate—to never know fulfillment except that which he gave himself when his guard was down? If so, it was a damn fine joke that mocked his one attempt at sensitivity and honor.

He'd loved Bess from the first moment he'd laid eyes on her all those long years ago. Not once had another female turned his head nor compromised his fidelity to her. Not once had he given in to the urges that required no tender feelings nor noble sentiments. Bess had been pure and clean and he'd wanted to be the same—for her.

Harboring the romantic notions of youth and exercising the restraint of a true paragon of virtue, he'd waited for Bess . . . saved himself for her. At the time he'd thought himself a sterling fellow for his grand gesture of patience. He and Bess would come together in innocence. They would learn together, discover the physical expression of love together.

With her talk of equality between men and women, Betina would no doubt appreciate the irony, even if he did not. For if she had shared the same dream with him this night, they would come together as equals in bed, knowing the textures and taste and scent of one another without their mortal bodies ever having mingled so intimately.

And they would come together. Betina's responses to his kisses by the side of the road were proof enough that she was a sensual and *aware* woman rather than the angelic girl Bess had been. Proof enough that she wanted him as much as he wanted her.

That she desired him far more than Bess had.

If the Fates had not meant them to be reunited, they would not have sent her back to him.

He and Betina would finish what had begun so long ago.

Ignoring the niggle of doubt trailing behind that thought, he pulled the pillow over his head and laughed at his idiocy. Even in his thoughts he tiptoed about the subject of sex, shying away from the explicit terms other men tossed about to prove their worldliness.

He was a daring highwayman, a dashing rogue, a seductive scoundrel. Women had sighed over tales of his reckless charm and the engaging smile below his mask, his polished manners and mischievous winks as he relieved their persons of baubles and their men of pride.

Even Bess had not been immune to the romance of it all.

And neither was Betina. A more timid woman would have run from here as fast as her coach could bump over the rutted road. A more pragmatic one would have called the redcoats to cart him off forthwith.

Would she be as enchanted if she knew the truth? he wondered. Which truth would prove him more daft in her eyes? That he was in fact one hundred and twenty-nine years old?

Or that he was still a bloody frigging virgin?

One kiss, my bonny sweetheart, I'm after a prize tonight. . . .
The Highwayman—*Alfred Noyes*

15

Betina awakened to dawn and a vague sense of alarm. She lay still, her gaze sliding around the room searching for the source of her disquiet. Motes floated in the air, glittering like crystal dust in the shafts of pastel sunlight glowing through her window. White clouds gamboled in the sky, skipping from treetop to treetop like mythical beings frolicking in the magical beauty of a summer day. A bird sang in the distance, and she thought she smelled roses.

Her breath caught in her throat as she remembered . . .

Roses and magic and star stuff.

She caught her bottom lip between her teeth and closed her eyes. She'd been dreaming again. A vivid, sensual fantasy that filled her being even in memory.

A vision of a phantom of shadow and passion moving over her. A phantom with Dante's face, Dante's voice, touching her, loving her beneath a blanket of mist.

She became aware of how she lay flat on her back, her legs open, her gown damp and clinging between them. Her breasts throbbed with remembered sensation, and her body felt warm, languid.

She opened her eyes cautiously and peered left and right. Her net snood lay on the bed beside her hand, and her hair was spread on the pillow above her head. A rose petal fell from her fingers as she lifted her hand.

A red rose petal tinged with pink around the edges.

She swallowed and moved her hands over the mattress on either side of her, searching, gathering what they found. She stared in fascinated horror as she raised her arm and opened her fingers and more petals fell over her. Petals glistening with grains of glimmering crystal dust.

Star stuff.

Frantically, she glanced around the room and gasped as her gaze passed over then returned to the chair angled in the corner, to the indentation in the cushion of the seat, as if someone had sat there recently. And on the floor in front of the chair a small rug was rumpled, as if someone had stretched out his legs as he sat, his feet pushing the woven cotton away.

Her hands pressed to her mouth, she scooted from the bed and stood on trembling legs. A shower of rose petals and glitter fell from her gown.

With a cry, she stumbled from the room and down the stairs, pausing at the landing to look out the window that faced the road. Her hands flat against the glass, she stared at the rosebush, then turned away.

Nothing bloomed on stems covered with petrified buds and rusty gray-green leaves.

It hadn't changed.

She refused to wonder where the petals came from as she ran into the second-floor parlor and pushed open the door to Dante's room. It swung shut behind her, catching the hem of her gown. Yanking it free, she marched to the bed, grasped the sheet, and flung it back.

She backed up a step and wrapped her arms around her middle as her gaze swept over his body. Never had he seemed so imposing as he did now, lying naked on his bed, his shoulders appearing even broader with his muscled arms outflung and his neck corded with tension. His chest was deep and plated with more muscle that tapered into his lean waist and flat belly, which had a silky line of hair down the center, pointing downward to the manhood she had felt swelling against her as they lay in the moonlight—the manhood she'd wanted so desperately to feel inside her.

Desire renewed and redoubled as she stared at him, at that part of him that even now was growing rigid and *huge*, as if it responded to her gaze alone. A fire began to burn low inside her and her breasts swelled, their centers tightening. Even the brush of her gown against them sent sparks of sensation showering through her. She studied his long legs, spread wide, his thighs and calves so hard and strong, but her gaze returned to his shaft, which angled up and away from his body, and she imagined how it would feel thrusting into her. . . .

Sunlight beamed in through the part of the curtains and glistened on Dante's smooth flesh, and seemed to twinkle in the arrow of hair. . . .

Her gaze traveled upward as she held herself more tightly and bit back a moan at the rose petals and glittering dust sprinkled over his body, over the bed, in his hair and even his eyebrows.

He opened his eyes, his gaze unwavering as it met hers, his hand steady as he reached for hers and drew her near. "You dreamed of me in the night."

"Was it a dream?" she croaked as her gaze was drawn to his unclothed form, to the beauty and power of it.

He covered his midsection with the sheet and pulled her down to sit beside him as the phantom had sat beside her on her bed. His other hand raised to her hair and came away with a petal held between his fingers. "I know little of the difference between dreams and reality these past hundred years, Betina." He trailed the petal across his lips and it billowed with his breath. "I only know what I see and what I feel, and that to think a thing makes it possible."

"Phineas said that." She heard the quiver in her voice, the confusion and fear.

"A wise man, Phineas," Dante said, and he stroked the petal over her arm and hand and between her fingers. "I have dreamed of you for a long time, Betina, yet had no hope of seeing you again. Still, you are here, and I feel my soul filling me with the life I thought I had lost."

"You could not have dreamed of me. You never saw me before . . . before—"

"Hush, Betina." He pressed his fingers to her mouth. "We have shared dreams for a long time, I think. Will you deny it?"

She closed her eyes, yet his image remained in her mind, an image of sorrow and need and hope. And there was nothing she could say to the man or the memory of him within her, for to do so would be to accept more than she could comprehend.

"You are still so timid, love," he whispered. "Yet you are right in a way. I dreamed of you while seeing Bess. Only now do I begin to see far more than my memories of her and my fantasies of what might have been. Can you not see more also? Can you not feel more?"

Barely breathing and unwilling to move away from him, she opened her eyes. *More.* Oh, yes, she saw more, felt more. She saw a man who spoke of unearthly matters and made her believe though she should not. A man who cast spells on her with a word, a touch, a simple thought in the depths of night. A man who fascinated and seduced her and made her feel complete.

He wrapped his hand around the back of her neck and urged her head down as he raised up, pausing when only a sliver of air separated their mouths. "I can only come to you as a phantom until you can come to me as a woman in love, Betina. I can only kiss you if you are willing to cross the distance to reach me." He moved no closer and asked for nothing as he held her with a gentle grip, watched her without expression.

She knew she could easily withdraw from him without harm or threat. She knew he would let her go. But there was magic in his stillness, in the silence surrounding them except for the song of a single bird, in the warmth of his breath mingling with hers, in the enchantment that sparkled in the air. Her lips parted, and she lowered her head that scant distance, meeting his kiss, sighing into his mouth as he eased backward, taking her with him to lie across him, her breasts pressed against his chest, her arms sliding beneath his, her hands caressing his back.

Desire throbbed to the beat of her heart. Anticipation filled her with heat and ran rampant through her veins. A need she had only known in her dreams drowned her thoughts and pooled in her belly. Urgency shortened her breath and thumped in her chest as his mouth rubbed softly over hers, teasing and caressing and drawing away over and over again.

She knew his mouth, knew the scent and taste of him, yet it was all stronger, more intoxicating than the night before . . . more than any night before. His body was firm and hard and warm—not mist and shadows at all. And the air was filled with golden light—not star stuff and dreams.

Dante framed her face as he had when they lay beside the rosebush and held her away from him, held her so she could see only his eyes filled with question, his mouth bracketed by strain as he studied her face. "Is this a dream, Betina?" he rasped.

She shook her head, too frightened to speak, too wary of her emotions to acknowledge them. She had not been afraid of her dreams until they'd become real. She'd loved her phantom when she'd thought him of her own making. But he lay before her now, a man of strong passions and stronger determination. A man who had existed between life and death for a century, waiting for the woman he loved.

She lurched to her feet and backed away, unable to deny the love she saw in his eyes, unable to deny an impossible truth.

Turning, she ran for the door.

It was not a dream. It never had been a dream.

. . . and the hours crawled by like years . . .
The Highwayman—*Alfred Noyes*

16

Dante had known the moment Betina accepted the truth. He saw it in her eyes as they widened with the shock of realization, in the sway of her body as if she'd been struck by the truth and fought to remain upright, in the panic with which she'd run from the room, her face pale and her lips pressed tightly together. But he hadn't thought she would run from him.

He should have known better.

Bleakly, he stared up at the ceiling and acknowledged how truly insane all this would seem to anyone who had not lost his soul and been doomed to chase after it for a hundred years. And like the jackanapes he was, he had pressed her with wild tales of curses and old lives being renewed, expecting her to swallow it whole, to remember him and fall into his arms without a single misgiving. He'd taken it for granted that she would love him as she always had.

Obviously he had assumed too much.

But, why shouldn't he have? He had accepted a great deal more over the years. He'd not run the moment he'd realized the truth. He still loved her despite the changes in her appearance and manner. He still loved her and wanted her even if she didn't look the same, act the same.

Obviously the Fates were not finished with him yet. It wasn't enough that he had been imprisoned at the scene of his crimes for far longer than a lifetime. They weren't satisfied with such a lenient sentence. They would have his pride, too, as they ran him through his paces as if he were a horse or a dog. He rubbed his hands down his face as he wondered what tricks he was expected to perform.

And then he wondered if Betina was to be dangled before him and then snatched away. She was betrothed, though he found it difficult to take that seriously. Betina certainly didn't dwell on it and use it—as most women would—as an excuse when retreating from a passionate encounter with another man. In fact she'd only mentioned her fiancé once in passing—not a good sign for the poor sod, but an excellent indication that she could be claimed by a man who would not be so foolish as to let her venture away from him.

"I'm not yours to take." Betina had said it with so much pride in her bearing, and so much uncertainty in her voice, as if she knew it would require very little to convince her otherwise. It was an opportunity he couldn't resist, a challenge he couldn't refuse.

Betina was his, and he would prove it.

He sat up and swung his legs over the side of the bed, wincing at the jab of pain in his thigh then promptly forgetting it as his mind took another turn. Born and raised into the modern world, Betina was naturally a product of her time. She spoke of women voting and holding office and serving on juries. She'd come across the sea with only an old man for a chaperone. She'd spoken of freedom as if it were the grail found on the shores of America. For all he knew of it, women might be the ones—God forbid—to do the courting and the proposing of . . . whatever.

He should have realized that the world would change, that he was the one who did not fit.

But that was nothing new. Being the bastard son of a governess, educated as well as any aristocrat yet trained to be the gardener of a country squire, was not exactly *de rigueur.* Yet he had conformed to whatever mold he found convenient at any given time, able to play the gentleman or the bumpkin at will. It was part of his charm and the reason for his success in his chosen occupation. Who would bother to suspect a laborer with grime under his fingernails when the notorious highwayman was clearly a man of breeding and elevated social graces?

He rose to his feet and strode to the window with a stiff, uneven gait.

Betina had been brought to him by time and circumstance and, yes, by the Fates who so mercilessly wove his life—and Betina's—into patterns of their own design. But they had given him something else as well. He had a future now, a second chance. He had choices and a will free to explore the possibilities denied him for so long.

Betina or Bess, old soul or young, she was still essentially the same person—a dreamer who used her air of preoccupation as a weapon against what she did not understand . . . or didn't want to accept.

And she was his.

It was the only possibility he would consider.

Dante followed the tantalizing smell of coffee and fresh-baked bread to the kitchen and found Phineas sitting at the table with a plate of eggs, ham, and some odd-looking potatoes in front of him. Across the planks another plate was heaped high with steaming food.

"Eat," Phineas ordered, then bent to his breakfast.

Dante glanced around the spacious room as he pulled out a chair and sat down.

"She's out walking."

"A little early, isn't it?" Dante had watched Betina walk down the road every afternoon and return just before the day's end. It was why he'd been waiting for her yesterday eve. She'd been late returning and he'd been seized with a sudden, jolting fear that she was gone again.

"She be troubled."

"Ah." Eyeing the potatoes, Dante poked them with his fork. "Do you know why?"

"I be looking at the trouble fiddling with his potatoes like he's been fiddling with the missy. They're just fried with onion in bacon drippings. They won't bite ye." Phineas took a bite of egg, chewed, and swallowed before he continued. "The missy, on the other hand, will if ye push her too far."

Spearing the smallest slice of potato he could find, Dante raised his fork to his mouth and sniffed. "Odd, but I have the impression that she wouldn't harm a gnat."

"Been parts of her missing for all her life," Phineas said as he sopped a piece of bread in a pool of reddish-brown liquid on his plate. "Redeye gravy. Try some." He pushed a bowl toward Dante. "Funny thing about those missing parts."

"What might that be?" Finding the potatoes palatable, Dante dipped his finger in the gravy and touched it to his tongue, then spooned some onto his plate.

"Seems those parts were inside her where none but herself could see them." Phineas drank deeply from his mug of coffee. "Seems to me she didn't recognize what she saw or know what to do with it."

"Could you define 'parts'?" Dante asked as he soaked up redeye with his bread.

"What makes a body feel anger, hurt, sadness, loneliness, fear, pleasure, joy, love . . . passion. The senses of the soul, her mother calls them. The missus and me, we knew when Betina be pulling 'em out and showing 'em for all to see. Till then twas like the missy's soul was blind."

Dante's fork clattered onto the table. *Blind.* It all came back to him—the lack of clear sight and sound, taste and smell . . . and texture. The inability to distinguish sour from sweet, bright from dull, heat from cold. His body had been blind and it had been the worst sort of hell, yet he had suffered anger, bitterness, resignation, sorrow . . . guilt. It had been better than nothing. He could not imagine what it would be like not to have the ability to feel a full measure of emotion.

And Phineas was saying that Betina, too, had been cursed. It only followed that she had not been sent back to him as a reward for his being a good little fellow all these years, but because she, too, had challenged the Fates. It made an odd kind of sense and explained why she seemed so like Bess, yet not like Bess at all. She was Bess as she might have been if she'd been less ethereal and more human.

"She be stumbling about now," Phineas said. "Tripping over her own self."

Oh, God, Betina was awakening to herself as he had awakened to life, only her pain was emotional rather than physical; her confusion was with what she was discovering within herself rather than with the world around her.

And she had not known *why,* as he had. Where Bess had been innocent in all things, Betina had simply been kept in ignorance and left to fend for herself as destiny presented itself to her in the form of incomprehensible circumstances.

He had lost his soul, but he had seen it and knew it well, while Betina had been blind to the nature of her own soul.

Dante's chair fell back against a cupboard as he abruptly rose and strode toward the back door.

"Have a care," Phineas called after him. "Mayhap the missy's soul was blind, but she never be weak or feeble in the head. A fine mind she has, and is smart enough to keep those from seeing it who wouldn't ken its workings."

Dante glanced at the old man over his shoulder. "I never thought otherwise," he said hoarsely.

"Haven't ye?" Phineas said softly as he scratched his head. "Then mayhap ye be knowing that those who take longer growing up oft times have a bucket or two more strength stored up than them who waste it all trying to get to tomorrow in a hurry.''

Recognizing it for the warning it was, Dante gathered his breath before responding in kind. ''Have a care, old man. Those who are in a rush to get *anywhere* often trample the ones who think to slow them down.'' He shoved open the door and let it slam shut behind him as he limped on his crutch down the road.

Tomorrow. He rolled the word around in his mind like something foreign he needed to translate into terms he could comprehend. For so long it had been a concept rather than actuality, as the days and years passed him by without touching him.

Of course he was in a hurry to reclaim his life and his future. Time would no longer slight him. Though only the silver streaks in his hair evidenced change in him, he'd become acutely aware that he would live and age and die as mortals were intended to do. He no longer had forever to contemplate his actions.

And tomorrow was no longer a day past forever.

It was like stepping from twilight into dawn as Dante left the gray gloom of the woods and left the road to hobble across the sun-gilded moor, searching for Betina. He had to find her, to be near her as she discovered those ''parts'' of herself Phineas spoke of.

The parts that were Bess, enclosed in a person who was growing apart from what she had been.

He blinked against the brightness, and his eyes burned with the shock of clear sight. Everything seemed to shoot out at him—the sharp blades of grass and twigged stems of bushes, the purple shades of heather and the false horizon of the nearby cliff edges against a blue sky draped with frothy ruched clouds—

an explosion of visual impressions he'd forgotten in his exile.

He paused to orient himself, to adjust to the shock of reality, and then to simply watch Betina as she paced a narrow track near the edge of cliffs that dropped into the sea with neither incline nor warning. Frowning, he stared hard at the strip of land separating her from the drop and finally judged it safe enough for now.

Her small figure moving at the edge of the moor seemed so fragile and alone against the land and sky and sea. As alone as he had been for a hundred years.

He closed the distance and eased himself down near the end of the path she'd worn in the grass. "It is said that when the wind blows, a body can be swept right over if it's too close to the edge."

She ignored him as she continued her pacing stroll from one end of the track to the other, the rear of her blue skirt bobbing up and down as a short train dragged the ground. A drapery affair of the same fabric was wrapped around her hips and gathered into an elaborate flounce, fitting the garment close to her figure in front and making her look impossibly deformed in back. A legion of buttons marched up the front of a fitted blue jacket with sleeves that were as layered as her skirts. Her extreme inward curve of waist suggested a corset that plumped her breasts while strangling her ribs. He could only imagine what undergarments she required to maintain such a silhouette.

Until now he'd only seen her in simple dresses of flowered or checked cotton, with a petticoat always drooping below her hem on one side or another. Her hair had always been down and tied with a ribbon at the nape of her neck, yet now it was pulled back and up into a froth of curls at the crown of her head, which seemed as flounced as the rest of her. All in all, he had never seen a woman so swaddled, stiffened, and hobbled. He far preferred her in her simple dresses that followed the lines of her body. Actually, he far preferred her nightdress that revealed the lines of her body and the dark curls between her legs.

He knew better than to comment, but couldn't contain his horror at having such beauty so distorted. "What in bloody hell have you got attached to your . . . ah . . . self?"

She squinted briefly as if she'd been focused on the distance and had to readjust her vision. "What? Oh . . . clothing," she said and resumed her pacing.

"Clothing," he repeated, annoyed by her continued preoccupation. "You are draped with more fabric than a mainmast. One wonders how you keep from listing aft."

Frowning, she twisted to look behind her. "It's a bustle of sorts, only it's done with ruffles and such rather than a cage."

A cage? "I see," he said dryly, determined to draw her thoughts from wherever they seemed to be wandering. "I take it that when Americans granted their women the vote, they dispensed with the cages as well."

"Um . . . not all of America. It's only in Wyoming that we have the vote, and I don't know who decides what we must wear . . . someone in Paris, I think."

"My mistake. . . . Will you please stop mincing about? The bob of your backside is giving me *mal de mer*."

She abruptly complied and remained rooted where she was, with her swathed and pleat-covered back facing him. "Tea with a little brandy and a hard biscuit helped my seasickness," she mused.

Annoyance gave way to fascination at such profound distraction. He'd witnessed brief episodes of it before, but not like this complete absorption. "Where on earth are you?" he asked.

Apparently she either didn't hear or she chose to disregard such an abstract question.

"I have seen peacocks with less of a tail," he commented, reasoning that no woman could disregard comments about her clothing—complimentary or otherwise—for long. "You are hung with more cloth than the King's drawing room."

"Queen."

"What?"

"Queen Victoria," she said vaguely. "Daughter of the Duchess of Kent. I believe she is in mourning for Prince Albert and wears nothing but black."

"Who in blazes is he?"

"Was," she corrected. "He was the Queen's consort before he died."

"Betina," he said patiently, "I far prefer seeing your unadorned face to your overburdened back. Will you please . . ."

She turned so quickly that her train could not catch up to her and wound around her like a shroud.

". . . turn around . . . don't move!"

His warning came too late as she took a step and promptly tripped on the train, pitched forward, then righted herself with waving arms and mincing footwork.

He averted his face to keep her from seeing the twitch of his lips.

"I don't mind if you laugh," she said with great seriousness. "It is funny."

"How reasonable of you. Most women would be awash in tears by now."

"Mama says that tears should not be wasted on unimportant things." She bent over and grasped the hem of her train and yanked it around to its proper place.

"Betina," he said softly as he held out his hand, "come sit beside me before your costume does you harm."

She eyed him warily.

He sighed. "I don't bite, though Phineas has assured me that you might if pressed too hard. I have no desire to add teeth marks to my collection of scars."

Evidently deciding that he spoke sincerely, she slung the tail of her skirt over her arm and approached him. An arm's length away, she lifted her hem a few inches and lowered herself to the ground, her "bustle of sorts" bunched beneath her.

"Raise up," he ordered and pulled the monstrosity free when she complied.

She plopped her bottom down again and stared out at the blurred horizon at the edge of the sea, saying nothing, lost within her thoughts once more.

Dante stretched out his legs and massaged the cramped muscles of his healing thigh, content to share the silence with her.

At his movement she glanced at him, then reached over and placed her hand on his thigh, brushing his away and kneading the muscle herself. It seemed to him an absent gesture, instinctive rather than thought-induced.

No matter what prompted her, it was a proprietary and intimate thing she did. The sort of thing lovers or mates did for one another as a matter of course.

Smiling, he lay back and folded his hands beneath his head. They were bound together, he and Betina, though he would not say it aloud. Not yet.

He knew when her mind took a particularly serious turn, for her hand stilled on his thigh, her brows drew together, her nose wrinkled, and her head tilted to the side. Her frown was endearing, like that of a child pondering the anatomy of a flower or the textures of a rock or the complexities of her own development.

Or a woman contemplating the nature of her own emotions.

She was trying to hide, as Phineas said she always tried to hide, within a soul that she hadn't grown into, as far away as she could get from people who tolerated her and loved her but couldn't understand her. Far away from the part of herself that she saw in her dreams yet didn't recognize.

"It won't go away, Betina, simply because you hide from it," he said softly, afraid to startle her too harshly from her thoughts. "You've already accepted the truth, impossible as it seems."

"I know," she said, and the wealth of misery in her voice was like a stone landing on his chest. "I dreamed of you for so long, riding up to me in the dark—always in the dark—and all I could see was your loneliness. You'd hold out your hand to me, and you'd touch my face and ask me to come with you to a new world."

He looked away from her and blinked hard as he remembered all the times he'd dreamed of the same thing. Memories happening again in the world of dreams, bringing them together though neither of them knew it. "Did you want to go with me?" he asked, needing to know that much at least.

"I did go away with you—every night," she said after a pause, and he thought she'd deliberately avoided relating her answer to Bess. "You took me up on your horse and we rode to magic places and we stopped to walk over moors like this one and then we'd lie in the heather and . . ."

"We held one another," he said, filling in what she did not say as he turned to his side and urged her down, angling his body over hers. "Like this."

"Yes," she said against his mouth as her body quivered and her hand wrapped around the back of his neck. She raised her head, her lips parted, reaching for him, opening wider for him, as he teased her with a light peck at a tipped-up corner of her lips, nibbled along the edges to the other side, then slipped his tongue into her mouth, exploring her texture and taste. She relaxed beneath him as her other hand gripped his waist, slid around to his back, fluttered restlessly along his spine.

She cried out in protest as he withdrew and lifted his head and he swept his hand over her bodice, freeing the top two buttons. "And like this."

She arched toward him as his fingers found the base of her neck, caressed the hollow in the center of her collarbone. "Yes . . . and more."

Covering her mouth with his, he plunged his tongue inside, forgetting restraint, knowing she wanted him by the little whimper she made every time he touched her, knowing by the way she thrust her chest upward. He deepened the kiss still more as his hand worked her buttons loose and spread her bodice open . . . traced the rise of her flesh along the line of her chemise, dipped inside to free her breasts, to circle them with his palm, to tease the puckered areolas between his fingers.

She caught her breath, held it, pressed closer to him.

Raising his head, he gazed down at her, seeing what he had only imagined—soft skin, sensuous fullness, pink-tinted buds swelling like roses before they bloom. He could not resist and took one into his mouth, explored it with his tongue, drew on it, and felt her swell.

And he grew and hardened and ached with need for her.

He released the last of the buttons and felt along her rib cage, her waist, her hips, searching for an opening, wanting to touch her, to find her. . . .

Her mouth followed his as he again lifted his head to sweep his gaze over the length of her body, seeing a white corset, stiff with stays and tight with lacings, a skirt caught beneath her and hobbled at the hem, the lace trim of a petticoat peeking out at her ankles.

He rested his forehead against hers. "You have armored yourself well against me," he said, his voice dry and raspy.

"What?"

"Your clothing vanquishes me, love." With a great, shuddering breath, he raised to a sitting position and tucked her breasts back into the gathered scoop neck of her chemise, lingering over the silken flesh and bending to kiss each nipple through the light fabric. It was torture to hear her moan in pleasure, to have her reach for him and hold his head to her breast as if she would never let him go. It was pain to straighten away from her again and feel the pull of denim over his swollen shaft.

Eyeing the row of buttons and loops, he flexed his fingers to still their trembling and began to fasten her bodice. "Did one of your suffragists design such a rig to thwart the passion of men?"

"I don't know who designed them," she said earnestly, though her voice quivered.

"Ah, Betina, I want you badly, but this is not the place." Reluctant to tuck her up completely, he left the top buttons open and ran his forefinger over the exposed wedge of flesh.

"No," she said, her voice shaking as she accepted his aid in sitting up again. "In my dreams the heather was soft as feathers, not prickly like this." She caressed a purple flower and sighed and plucked at her skirt, raising the fabric into stiff little peaks, then smoothing it out again. "Every night was like stepping into a fairy tale and you were the prince, so strong and sure of what you wanted when I wasn't sure of anything at all."

"I had the same dreams," he admitted as he lay back and met her gaze. "Memories haunting me. You, easing my solitude, and for a while each night I would believe that the roses bloomed because I saw you."

She trembled, and her breath shuddered as she released it. "But they never did."

"No. There was only existence without life."

Her hair tumbled and whipped about her head as she turned to him suddenly. "How did you bear it?" she asked, as if their earlier conversation had never been interrupted, as if it had been rolling about in her mind, separate from sensation and desire. "A hundred years alone with nothing growing, nothing changing."

Her voice was strained, impassioned. "And then to have it all change at once with no warning and no explanation. I would be very angry if I were you."

"I have grown weary of anger," he said and realized it was true. "I would not waste my life in such a way."

She brushed her hair away from her face with the back of her hand. "*Were* you angry?"

Puzzled by the direction of her conversation, he stared at her earnest expression, her troubled eyes, the flush burning high on her cheeks. "I was. But there was little else to do then, and even less with which to concern myself."

"*I* would have been concerned."

"There is little reason for it when one is a prisoner and has neither promise nor hope of escape, nor even a jailer to petition for mercy." He raised up on his elbows. "I knew exactly how and why my situation had come about, Betina. I passed sentence upon myself. You, however, did not bring about your own fate."

Her frown deepened as her hand found his thigh again and her fingers drew light circles over the denim fabric. "I've had other . . . dreams," she said, the words rushing out as she went on. "Only I don't think they were dreams. I saw her . . . me . . . except that my hair has a great deal of red, and the woman I saw had very black hair and her eyes were dark as coal, and mine have a bit of blue. . . . Still, I think it *was* me." She nodded as if satisfied with herself or with what she'd said.

Or perhaps because she'd said it at all.

"What did you see?" he asked.

"I saw a woman with black hair crying into the rose. I saw her talking to you from her window while you held on to the trellis and rested your hip on the sill. You were different too, with no silver in your hair—though that came after I found you in the yard, didn't it?—and you were very unreasonable and demanding, expecting her to fit her life to yours without question.'' She glared at him with accusation in her eyes and censure in her voice. ''That's why she was crying. She couldn't do it and you didn't understand. You didn't even try. How could she fit her life to yours when she couldn't even fit in with people who didn't expect anything from her?''

''How could I understand?'' he asked. ''She was of an age to marry. She showed me nothing but sweetness and love. Of course I expected that we should have a life of our own.''

''A life of *your* own, you mean,'' she said indignantly. ''She had a woman's body and a sweet face, and you thought to have yourself a docile wife who would never question or argue or assert herself in any way. You wanted her to love you enough to sacrifice all that was necessary to her happiness, with no thought to the consequences.'' She shifted to her knees and faced him with her hands planted on the ground as if she were about to attack him. ''Well, you got what you wanted, didn't you? She sacrificed everything for you.''

Every word she uttered was a knife opening another scar from the past, guilt and pain and emptiness reaching inside of him, tearing him apart. ''And I bloody well paid a high price for a sacrifice I did not want her to make,'' he lashed out, protecting himself with anger. ''I have paid for a full hundred years.''

As Betina rose to her feet, her gaze clouded in thought for a moment, then sharpened on him. ''Now that I think about it, a hundred years was not long at all. And as for your soul, maybe it left you because it didn't like you very much."

He inhaled sharply at the thrust, denying the pain and forcing himself to concentrate only on the present, on Betina and what could be. "Perhaps it was merely waiting as Bess's soul has been waiting," he said evenly, "until we had the strength and wisdom to live as we should have lived before."

Her eyes widened as if she, too, had been struck by an unexpected truth. Shaking her head, she pressed her lips together, then swept up her train and stalked away, stumbling over a hidden rock after three steps and glaring back at him as if it were his fault.

"You can't run away, Betina," he said softly. "You never could, for I was always there."

"I'm not running," she retorted. "I'm walking back to the inn."

"You can't escape your dreams."

"I doubt that I will have such dreams again now that I know heather is not soft and that my phantom *prince* is helpless against whalebone and laces."

Dante threw his arm over his eyes and sucked in his cheeks as she took off at a mincing trot across the moor. An involuntary chuckle escaped him at the absurdity of her final dig, erupting into unrestrained laughter as she disappeared into the gloom of the woodland.

How long since he had laughed? How long since he had felt the joy of a summer day, the richness of being in love, the pleasure of sharing thoughts with another, no matter how random and disordered and painful? How long since he had felt so alive with frustrated passion, with unreasonable anger and helpless amusement?

Had he ever shared such emotions with another . . . with Bess?

No, never with Bess. Only Betina gave him such freedom to display human frailty. Only Betina saw him as a man rather than a romantic hero.

He sobered abruptly and closed his eyes, seeing the memory of Betina's face, so earnest and distressed by turns as she plucked her thoughts from one place and then another and set them before him in neat rows of truth.

And truth, like dreams, were impossible to escape.

''Something is always waiting for each of us.''
—Etta Wells

17

She'd had enough. More than enough. Outside of enough.

Betina sat on the stairs, her chin in her hands as she concentrated all her energy on making some firm decisions. But she was too angry. More angry than she'd ever been in her life. Actually, she couldn't recall when or if she'd ever been really angry until she'd come here.

Until Dante de Vere. Just who did he think he was?

Glumly, she acknowledged that he knew who he was. It was her identity that was a source of confusion.

''I am Betina Marietta Wells,'' she said to the small wood spider dangling from the ceiling by a flimsy strand of silken floss. She never had figured out how such a small creature could produce so much thread. . . .

She forced the thought away. There were far more important things to think about than the wonders of nature. Like Dante and what he did to her. Dreams were one thing, but acting them out with such enthusiasm was quite another. How did he do it? Why did she let him?

Because you wanted to, a voice whispered in her mind.

She shook her head in denial. She couldn't possibly have wanted what had happened between herself and Dante, not once but several times, each more profound than the one before. No wonder Mama wanted time alone with Papa. Even the memory of it was enough to set her blood to flowing warm and slow in her veins and her heart to bumping in her chest.

He'd seen her breasts, touched them, and tasted them. He would have seen more if she hadn't been decked out in her "public clothes." She'd worn them because of him, because she thought she would feel more in control of herself, more confident. And she had, until he'd come to plague her and seduce her. Then she'd felt cumbersome and constricted and silly. One did not wear public clothing to wander around a deserted moor. Besides, she hated wearing so many layers. She always felt as if half of what the public saw was not her at all.

Dante hadn't cared for the current style. It had defeated him, he'd said.

She'd been disappointed and then oddly irritated. For one mad moment she'd considered tearing her clothes away from her body so he could see and touch and taste more of it.

Her face burned and she groaned as she buried her head in her arms crossed over her knees. She had to stop thinking about it. Decisions had to be made—about Dante, about her future. . . .

She groaned again as another thought crept into her mind.

Tim. How could she have forgotten her fiancé?

Because he does not make you want to tear your garments off, the meddling voice said.

"Oh, be quiet," Betina said peevishly as her face burned hotter and she imagined being naked with Dante . . . but not on the moor where the leaves of heather prickled and poked. In a bed . . . a soft featherbed with curtains hung around the canopy that could be drawn to shut out the world.

Gritting her teeth, she pushed Dante out of her mind . . . again.

It is not your mind where he dwells, but your heart.

"He will not be dwelling anywhere near me once he is fully healed," she replied to the disembodied voice. "As soon as I am certain he is well, I am leaving here."

She raised her head, startled by her declaration. How simple it was becoming to make decisions. All she'd needed was a little experience. In fact, it had been so simple that she decided there really was no need for her to have much contact with Dante at all, since he seemed to getting around quite well on his own.

And rather than question why she should wait to leave when Dante was getting around so well, she decided to make dinner so Phineas could spend his time with their patient. Smiling, she rose from her perch on the stairs and wandered toward the kitchen.

* * *

As he'd said on the moor, Dante was always there, in the background of her days, reminding her of his presence from a distance yet always within sight and sound of her, reminding her that she couldn't escape him. And at night, when she sought the peace and loneliness of her bedchamber, Betina discovered him in the corners of her thoughts, giving her no place to run to, no place to hide from him, even in sleep.

She would have preferred her old dreams, of a mystery lover come to carry her away, to the visions of a man whose hair was shot with silver and who walked with a limp brought on by a wound to his thigh. She could not pretend he was just a fantasy. The woman in his arms was undeniably herself. The memories were new ones that were hers alone.

Bess was gone.

The phantom was gone.

Only the present plagued her with confusion and doubt and restless dreams of passion . . . with Dante, his mouth on hers, his hands on her, his body inside hers. Often during the week she wished that Mama had never told her what it was like between a man and a woman. She might have found some peace then, for she sincerely doubted that even her imagination could have conjured such an act. In ignorance she might have found what had happened between them here in her bed, and later in his bed, and still later on the moor, frightening and awkward rather than a prelude to the pleasure Mama spoke of with a shine to her eyes and a flush on her cheeks.

She might have been able to ignore him altogether rather than merely pretending she paid him no notice.

He said little to her when they passed one another. If the space was confined, as it was on the rear staircase, he would press himself against the wall to avoid even the most innocent brushing of bodies. During meals he sat far away from her, out of reach of shifting feet beneath the table or an accidental graze of hands. Yet in spite of the distance between them, his manner seemed edged with a restless patience. She often caught him in a moment of complete stillness, watching her with a slant to his mouth and a sleepy-eyed gaze that held her equally still, feeling expectancy crackle in the air and magic beckon from the shadows, and she had the sense that he was waiting for her. That he knew she would come to him.

And then he would smile and arch his brows and turn away.

He spent his time with Phineas or walking outside, first on his crutch and then with the aid of a stout walking stick he'd carved for himself, spending two entire days shaping and smoothing it and rubbing it with oil until it had a rich matte luster.

Three days ago he'd shaved off his beard and let Phineas cut his hair into a shorter, more current style. She'd entered the kitchen seeking breakfast, and he was sitting at the table eating a large helping of fried potatoes and redeye gravy. It had stunned her to see his face bare of its whiskered mask, the grooves in his cheeks that deepened when he spoke or smiled, his squared-off chin with the small cleft in its center, the perfect shape of his wide mouth and hard angle of his jaw. He seemed a different person then, as he silently nodded to her then turned back to his plate and the chess game he and Phineas played between bites.

Two days ago he'd removed his shirt and begun to stretch and work his body, in carefully measured moves that did not overtax his healing wounds. Of course, she'd seen his body while she'd nursed him, and again when she'd stormed into his room to confront him about the dream she'd had. But a naked Dante lying unconscious did not seem as overwhelming as Dante moving with grace and ever-increasing power, his body hard and contoured with well-defined muscles and skin glistening with perspiration. He'd been within reach those other times, as he was not within reach now.

She admitted to herself then that, though she could avoid Dante, she couldn't escape him. He'd become a part of her, and she could no longer send her thoughts drifting away, no longer take refuge in the void she'd carried within herself. Her mind was no longer absent, but keenly aware of the world around her. Stunningly aware that Dante was a part of it whether she liked it or not.

Today she'd awakened to watery skies and complete silence—no muted sounds of footsteps or clanging of pots in the kitchen, no scrape of chairs being pushed back or closing of doors or creaks on the staircase. Only the aroma of fresh coffee wafting on the air assured her that she was not the only person in the world.

But the kitchen was empty, and a note propped up by a plate of biscuits occupied the table. Dante and Phineas had gone to retrieve Dante's clothing from his cottage.

She didn't even know where his cottage was.

She thought it would be nice to have the inn to herself, to not have to orchestrate her activities so that she wouldn't chance upon Dante, or be trapped in his gaze, or find herself watching him as he strengthened his body and provoked hers with his bare chest and strong calves showing beneath Phineas's Levi's that were too short for his long, sleek frame.

It had been nice at first, as she'd more closely examined the furnishings and collection of mementos in the inn, imagining who had chosen what and what had belonged to whom. She pictured the inn as it must have been when it was alive and filled with people, as it must have been in the quiet moments when no one was there but the family who owned it.

Bess and her father.

She didn't want to think about them. The images of them were too sharp in her mind—the father tall and robust and blessed with a mane of silver hair. She could have believed that she naturally supplied her own father's familiar countenance, if the man in her mind did not have dark eyes rather than Papa's light blue ones, or if the faces weren't different, the one being round and merry compared to Papa's lean and ruggedly chiseled features. In any case, there was no reason whatsoever for her to feel so uneasy. Bess and her father were, after all, her ancestors.

Somehow that knowledge added weight to her sense that she was again remembering people she couldn't possibly have known and moments she couldn't possibly have experienced.

She frowned as she trailed her finger along a sideboard in the private parlor. Something was wrong . . . different. Staring down at the wood, she studied the mark her finger had left behind in the dust—

Dust. She spun in a slow circle, glancing at every surface and each piece of bric-a-brac, all powdered with a layer of dust. The upholstery seemed to have faded a bit, and the curtains hung limply over the windows. . . .

Yet the inn had stood for a century without dust or decay, untouched by the years, abandoned by time.

Again she spun around, seeing it all, seeing yet more evidence to support Dante's claims that she had brought life with her to this slumbering place.

Covering her mouth with her hands to stifle her cry, she stood rooted in fear and panic. She did not want to be the one responsible for such changes. She wanted no part of enchantments and making past wrongs right again. She only wanted her own life, not a continuation of an old one.

She stumbled from the parlor and ran for the door, but it resisted her efforts to pull it open.

Suddenly, she staggered backward as the door opened with a hard push from outside. A strong hand shot out and grasped her arm, keeping her from falling. Lightning flashed in the sky and thunder crashed as the glare faded. She looked up at Dante and shook her head over and over again as tears rolled down her cheeks.

Rain began to fall in huge drops and the wind gusted suddenly, jerking the door from Phineas's hand and slamming it into the inside wall.

Her face was ashen pale and her eyes wide and desperate. Her mouth worked, but no sound escaped beyond the incoherent sobs that shook her body.

Dante knew fright when he saw it.

He guided her back inside and took her other arm, holding her at arm's length as his gaze swept first over her and then the entrance hall, through the open doorway into the parlor on his right, the staircase in front of him, and then into the common room on his left.

"Take care of the missy," Phineas said as he wrestled the door shut and pushed past Dante. "I'll see what's amiss."

Dante nodded and pulled her against him, enfolding her in his arms. Still she shook her head back and forth as if in denial, and still her breath came out in great gasping sobs. He held her head fast against his chest and felt her tears soak into the fabric of his shirt. "Betina, hush, love, hush. We're here. It's all right now."

"No!" she cried into his chest and tried to shake her head some more.

He winced in pain as he lifted her in his arms and carried her to the stairs, sitting on the third step and settling her in his lap to cradle and rock her like a child and smooth her hair away from her face as lightning cracked and thunder boomed.

Phineas barely spared them a glance as he crossed the hall and entered the common room, a fireplace poker in his hand.

Betina's sobs subsided to whimpering hiccups, and the flow of tears slowed to a trickle, though she trembled still.

"There now," he murmured in her ear. "Can you tell me what happened?"

"N-n-nothing."

"Did you have a nightmare?"

"N-no."

Tipping her face up with his finger under her chin, he met her gaze framed by black, spiky lashes. "You must have seen something to be so frightened."

"Dust," she said, and her chin quivered with the threat of more tears.

"Dust?"

She nodded. "It's everywhere."

"Dust," he repeated tonelessly.

"A-and a spider."

Now, *that* Dante could understand. He'd known grown men who were reduced to quaking in their boots at the sight of an insect. "Where is the little devil? I'll dispatch him for you."

"No. He's harmless, just a little wood spider."

"Then what—" Dante cut off his shout and inhaled and tried again in a softer voice. "Tell me—slowly and in detail—just what the bloody hell happened here."

"I told you—there's dust everywhere and I made a mark in it, and the heather was fresh in a vase when I arrived and now they're all dried and crumbling and . . . and . . ."

The tears flowed in earnest now, but thankfully without the shuddering hysteria that reduced *him* to a coward quaking in his boots. "Betina," he said patiently and then didn't know what to say.

Phineas appeared beneath the threshold of the common room, one hand scratching his head, the other holding the poker at his side. "Can't find a thing. Did she be telling ye what caused such a fret?"

"Unless housework strikes terror into her heart, I haven't the foggiest notion," Dante replied.

"Housework?" Phineas repeated. "The missy be helping her mama at the ranch since she was high enough to reach the tables and such. She always be a daydreaming through the chores. . . ." His voice trailed off as he walked back into the parlor, his footsteps changing timbre as he moved from bare floor to rug and onto wood again. He stepped back into the entrance, a thoughtful frown pleating his forehead. "Do ye be knowing what this place was like when we came?"

"As it is now," Dante said, losing his patience.

"No," she said and wrenched her chin from his hold.

"No," Phineas echoed. "There was no dust when we came."

"As if it had been left only moments before," Betina added, her face again buried against his chest.

Stunned, he leaned back against the stairs, feeling weak and disoriented as realization came with the sensation of chilly fingers skimming along his spine. Of course he'd known that the inn had been deserted by all earthly things like dust and insects and the passage of time, but he'd accepted it as he'd accepted everything else. He'd had no choice but to accept it. Yet now, hearing it with mortal ears, it struck him how queer it all really was.

"It's truly over," he said aloud and heard the shock and wonder of it in his voice. And against all reason, he, too, was frightened.

"It was what you wanted, mortal," a feminine voice sneered in his mind. *"Does it not please you to know that you, too, will age and cobwebs will someday fill your brain and you will wilt and fade with time, and insects will feed off your corpse?"*

He exhaled sharply at the harsh presentation of reality. He felt Betina's fingers clutching his shirt and the soft press of her body as she relaxed against him, her trembles easing as he absently stroked her back.

Yes, it was what he wanted. "Life as it is meant to be, rather than the sterile and unearthly existence without time or purpose or hope," he mused aloud and wondered who he spoke to—himself or the voice that taunted him.

"And so you have it, mortal," the voice said, but softly this time. *"A dubious gift whose wrappings can*

be cut at any moment if you do not treat it with respect and honor.''

His leg cramped beneath Betina's weight, punctuating his mortality.

Phineas turned to stare outside from the window bordering the front door, then looked back at Dante and Betina with bushy brows raised. ''I be thinking more's to come.''

Grimly, Dante nodded, not questioning what the old man meant or why he remained so calm in the face of such strange happenings. There was a quality to Phineas that defied description, an acceptance of whatever came his way, as if he considered anything he saw or heard or felt to be natural no matter how extraordinary it really was.

Like the woodland that still stood gray and stagnant, devoid of the rustlings and skitterings of animals but for the single bird that announced the coming of each day with a chirpy tune. And like the rosebush that would bloom only when touched by Betina's hands and the dew of her tears.

But she had not touched it since the night they'd lain by the side of the road and moonlight dappled their faces. She had not gone near it, but walked on the far edge of the road, averting her gaze.

''You understand, mortal,'' the voice came again, cold and challenging.

He angled his head to look down at Betina's face and found her sleeping against him like a child, with her hand curled beneath her cheek and her chest rising and her breath catching with the aftermath of sobs.

She had curled into him with trust, just as she had admitted that she knew the truth.

She knew, but she had not yet accepted what it meant.

He met Phineas's gaze, then looked beyond to the trees that did not drink from the drenched earth, the grasses and ferns that did not glisten with color darkened by the rain, but repelled all offers of renewal.

And he knew that it was far from over.

"We have little power over the human heart."
—Nemesis the Inevitable

18

Betina stretched and savored the last bit of darkness she'd enjoyed in her sleep. The darkness of fatigue, free of dreams and troubled thoughts. She felt rested and content and had no desire to question why.

Vaguely she recalled falling asleep in Dante's arms and the floating sensation of being carried up the stairs and laid upon her bed. And she remembered a kiss being pressed upon her brow and the counterpane being drawn over her.

She also recalled how frightened she had been and how hysterical she'd become and how Dante had held her and soothed her and made her feel safe, protected . . . cherished. Yet he had been exasperated and impatient with her too. He'd raised his voice to her.

No one had ever raised their voice to her before; she'd been treated as if her mind might shatter in the presence of shouting and anger. But she'd calmed when Dante had shouted. She'd felt stronger somehow because he had spoken to her and reacted to her as a normal person rather than a fragile bit of fluff.

But then, she reflected, he always had. And if memory served he'd been the same way with Bess, treating her like an adult, like a woman. It had frightened Bess.

It made Betina feel strong and capable and equal as a person.

It made her feel very, very good.

She stretched and yawned and smiled as her eyes fluttered open to sunlight and Dante sprawled in the chair in the corner. Not a phantom, but the flesh-and-blood man, dressed in black trousers, white full-sleeved shirt, and a brocaded waistcoat, both opened almost to his waist. He did look a proper rogue though, with stubble peppering his face and his hair tousled with a forelock falling over his brow. And he looked vulnerable, with his legs stretched out in front of him and one hand dangled over the side of the chair, the other massaging his wounded thigh as if it pained him even in sleep.

She pulled in her lips to keep from laughing at the way his head leaned into his shoulder at a cockeyed angle and his mouth hung open. He snored, just a little bit, and it sounded like the soft whuffles of a puppy or foal.

She liked him like this.

In the privacy of her mind she admitted that she liked him very, very much.

And the thought followed that she might even love him.

It should have startled her to have the word intrude so precipitously into her mind, but it had been there for a very long time, a part of her, waiting for her to recognize it, to admit its existence. And now, as she watched him sleeping in her chair and looking as vulnerable as she'd always felt, it was easy to accept the truth of it.

She loved him, and just then, with his face relaxed in sleep and his whuffling snores filling the room, it did not seem frightening at all.

Rolling to her side, she fought the tangle of petticoats and bedclothes and realized that he must have removed her dress. He could have removed more, but he hadn't.

I would never hurt you, he'd once said, and she knew it was true.

She sent the bedclothes to the floor with a hard kick and reached down to yank her petticoats out from under her, then raised up on one elbow and propped her head in her hands to watch Dante.

She liked waking up to the sight of him.

As if he sensed that he was being watched, he slowly opened his eyes to slits and peered about the room, not moving, though she noticed the way his muscles had tensed. She'd seen men do that at home, when they were in unfamiliar surroundings and alert for danger.

"You shouldn't have stopped snoring," she said quietly, careful not to startle him into sudden movement. "It's a dead giveaway that you're awake and ready to attack."

He sat up abruptly and winced as his head straightened. He slapped his hand to his neck and kneaded the cords that surely were cramping in protest. "How would you know that?'' he asked with a croak in his voice.

''I come from Wyoming, remember? They don't call it the Wild West for nothing. We have outlaws that would make the highwayman look like an unweaned child in comparison, not to mention Indians and bears and crazed moose and mountain lions and coyotes. . . .''

Her voice trailed off. From the way he studied her so intently, she had the impression that he wasn't really listening.

''You are well this morning?'' he asked.

''I should be, don't you think? I slept through most of yesterday and all night as well.''

''Are you well?'' he repeated patiently. ''As I recall, you were quite beside yourself over a bit of dust.''

''In the light of a clear day it seems like only dust and cobwebs rather than a musty gathering of magic and bad omens.''

''Sleep has a way of restoring and tempering our perceptions.'' He yawned and rolled his head from side to side, then back and forth.

''I don't know why I didn't notice it before,'' she said around an answering yawn.

''It is my experience that the bizarre becomes quite normal when that is all you see.''

''And the normal becomes bizarre,'' she added.

''Exactly so.'' He smiled, a quick flash of dimples alongside his mouth that disappeared before she could properly admire the shape of his mouth in such a pose. ''Then you are quite normal . . . as normal is defined at this given moment?''

''Yes.''

"I'm pleased to hear it," he said and shook his head as if to clear it. "Now pray enlighten me. I've heard of savages, but what are moose and coyotes?"

"Indians are not savages, Dante," she said, glad to accept the change of subject. "They are simply people whose customs and beliefs are different from ours. Mama says that there are times when she thinks they are far more civilized than we are."

"I stand corrected," he said wryly.

She nodded. "Moose are tall, four-legged creatures that look like knobby boxes set on stilts, and they have huge racks on their heads and jutting, blunt-tipped noses. Coyotes are sort of like wild dogs—or big foxes maybe—only not as well nourished," she said, answering his question. "We also have Bighorn sheep in the northern mountains, and they are nothing like your tame woollies here. They are large and strong and have horns that curl around themselves and can knock a strong man down with a single butt of a head."

He listened quietly and stared wistfully into the distance when she finished, his hand still rubbing his neck.

Swinging her legs over the side of the bed, she rose and walked over to brush his hand away and give his neck a proper massage. "You would like Wyoming," she said softly. "It is a good place for daring men and strong women."

"There are others like you?"

"No. We are all different I think." Her reply gave her pause. A few weeks ago she might have simply told him that *she* was different. For the first time in her life she didn't think of herself in that way. She didn't think of herself as being odd so much as an individual . . . unique. She chuckled suddenly.

"What can you possibly find so amusing at this hour of the morning?"

Again she chuckled, but this time at Dante. She had noticed over the past three and a half weeks that he did not awaken in the best of spirits. It must be the hours he kept, staying up most of the night—a hazard of his profession, she supposed. "I was just thinking that here where everything is so peculiar and mystical, I am probably so ordinary as to be considered different—a fate I am resigned to no matter where I go."

"Being normal?"

"Different," she said, distracted by the short hairs at the base of his neck. Broadening her strokes, she pulled his shirt back and kneaded his shoulders, liking how broad and hard they were, liking the smoothness of his sleep-warm flesh and the contours of tensile sinew beneath. "It's good that you are working your body. I've seen men go soft after too long a rest and never bother to regain their strength. Everything begins falling then—chest down to stomach and stomach overlapping their legs—sort of like an avalanche of useless flesh."

He leaned his head back against her midsection and looked up at her with a quirky smile. "Now there's a grisly picture." Reaching back, he grasped her hands and drew them downward over the plated muscles of his chest, holding them still over his flat nipples. "I assure you that I will not allow myself to go to ground, so to speak."

She felt the rhythm of his heartbeat and the rise and fall of his breathing. She felt his nipples pucker and harden, as hers were doing now. She felt the movement of his head on her midriff as he turned to press a kiss on the inside of one breast, then the other.

She felt incredibly hot.

"You shouldn't be walking about in your underpinnings," he said in a raspy whisper.

"You've seen me in less," she whispered back. "To pretend sudden modesty now would seem contrived."

His chest rose as he inhaled deeply and placed her hands back on his shoulders. "I like the way you think, Betina. Are all American women so sensible?"

Her hands slid from him as he rose and tottered on his feet, her fingers tingling from the remembered feel of him, the yearning to feel more. She stared at his wide back, at how it wedged into a narrow waist, at how even his buttocks were muscled and hard as they flexed with his efforts to steady himself. The thought occurred to her that he might be as unsteady as she with the beginnings of desire.

He took a step and pitched forward, landing hard facedown on the floor.

She skirted the chair and ran to him, dropping to her knees beside him, fearing that he had fainted in relapse of the fever that had kept him unconscious for the better part of two weeks.

His shoulders shook and she heard a rumble come from his chest, a strangled sound from his throat. "Oh, bloody damn. Bloody, bloody damn."

She sat on her heels and stared at his back, heaving with choked laughter. Either he was delirious or giddy with exhaustion. Placing her hand on the side of his cheek—all she could get to with his face flat against the floor—she felt his skin. He wasn't feverish.

He rolled carefully to his side, then to his back, his mouth curved in a rueful half-smile, half-frown. "Am I always to play the buffoon in your presence?"

he said as a flush colored his features an embarrassed red.

Bemused, she smiled back at him. "I hope so," she said, thinking that just then she liked him more than very, very much. "Shall I help you up?" she asked as she leaned forward to slide her arm beneath him.

"No! Not yet," he said.

She jerked back at the vehemence in his voice.

"My bloody leg is still asleep," he explained, then smiled wolfishly. "Why don't you join me down here instead?"

How tempted she was to accept his invitation. How tempting he was with his drowsy eyes and prone body, helpless against any exploration she might wish to make. "Um . . . no . . . I'm not dressed," she said inanely and licked her suddenly dry lips. "And I smell breakfast cooking. Phineas will be expecting us downstairs and . . . and I am ravenous."

"Yes," he said as his gaze roamed over her and his hand reached out, his fingers skimming her erect nipples, then up to trace the outline of her parted lips, to carry the taste of her to his own. "I see that you are . . . quite as famished . . . as I am."

She felt as if she'd received the deepest kiss, the most provocative caress, the most indecent proposal. She felt indecent, sitting on the floor in her camisole and petticoats, and with her breasts making a most shameful display of themselves.

She rather liked feeling indecent and shameful.

Her stomach grumbled.

Dante sighed heavily and rubbed the morning stubble on his face. "I suppose it would be too primitive of me to subject you to my attentions in such conditions." He raised up on his elbows and grinned. "All right, love. You may help me up so that I can leave you to your toilet."

In the end she helped him very little, as he seemed to find discomfort in her attempts to slide under his arm. She stood back and watched him slowly straighten, testing his leg, and then take a cautious step toward the door. "I'll see you downstairs."

"Yes," she said as she stared down at the floor, suddenly feeling shy.

He limped away from her.

From the corner of her eye she saw his cane laying beside the chair he'd occupied. She ran to pick it up. "Dante, wait." She caught up with him at the door. "Your cane," she said, breathless with rushing to catch him, breathless with the intimacy of waking up to him and taking care of his discomfort and bantering about subjects forbidden between unmarried men and women—and breathless, too, because it had all felt so right.

He took the cane and stared down at it as if he, too, felt awkward.

"Dante? You shouldn't have carried me up the stairs. It must have hurt you."

"I didn't want to let you go," he said. "You curled into me with such trust. . . ." He ducked his head lower and his thumb rubbed over the head of the cane. "A rather profound gift—trust."

Inexplicably she wanted to cry, for him and for the emptiness of the years, for Bess, who loved him enough to die for him yet not enough to live with him, for the trust he gave her by showing her his humility when most men disclaimed such an emotion. "You slept in the chair all night. Why?"

He smiled then, a small smile as he met her gaze. "To protect you from any dust or cobwebs that you might see in the dark."

"I only see phantom shadows in the dark," she said and placed her hand on top of his on the cane.

"The phantom is gone now, you know," he said. "As is the past. There is only myself and the present . . . and perchance a future." Raising his hand, and hers along with it, he kissed the backs of her fingers, then left her standing in the threshold, watching as he walked away.

Her fingers pressed to her lips, she shut the door with a soft click and backed into her chamber, shivering with a pervading sense of dread. She wanted to believe he was right, that there was only Dante and the present. But outside, the woodlands still brooded in gray and misty gloom.

And somehow she knew that the past still cast a shadow over them all.

"Here the natives lived as if 'now' was the past."

—Betina Marietta Wells

19

It was her phantom come to startling, arresting life.

Recognition shivered up Betina's spine and over her scalp as she rushed into the kitchen and stopped dead at the sight of him standing so casually before her with a biscuit dripping butter and preserves in his hand.

Attired in garments identical to those she'd cut from his body and discarded the night she'd found him, Dante leaned a hip against the sideboard and met her gaze with a grave one of his own. The claret velvet coat fit him to perfection, molding to his body like a glove. Black boots encased his muscular legs to the thigh, and tight-fitting buff pants emphasized their length and power. A French cocked hat plumed with a sweep of feathers dangled from a peg by the door. Rich lace adorned his stock and the cuffs of his stark white shirt.

"I've never seen a man wear lace before," she said, rattled at seeing the embodiment of a legend drinking a mug of coffee in her kitchen.

"Men do not wear lace?" he asked with a troubled frown that was almost comical.

"No. They wear suits, and their shirts have high collars and stiff cuffs that can be removed, or they wear buckskins or Levi's and calico shirts."

"I cannot imagine a proper Englishman wearing Levi's," he said, gazing at her—all elegance and masculine beauty in his outmoded finery that didn't seem dated at all.

"I don't think they do . . . except when in America and wanting to fit in."

"I'm reassured," he said with a smile. "I take it then that fine silks and brocades and velvets are reserved for the monstrosities women are forced to wear. Judging from your costume a week past, there would not be enough to drape both sexes . . . and speaking of clothing . . ." With arched brows he studied her form, his gaze lingering at the modest scoop of her blue frock, the fitted bodice embroidered with white silk threads, the feminine sweep of gathered skirt bordered with a deep, frothy ruffle edged in embroidery and deep scallops. "You look like the summer sky itself," he said grandly and held a chair for her. "I am gratified to see that couturiers have not completely lost their senses."

Phineas snorted as he splashed bacon grease over the tops of eggs frying in the pan.

"Oh, but they have," she replied, more concerned with buttering a biscuit than with what she said. "This is not mine . . . it was packed away in a trunk upstairs with an entire new wardrobe."

"I see," Dante said, his gaze sobering as it skimmed her form once more. "I'm sorry. I did not realize—"

It struck her then that seeing her in Bess's clothing might cause him pain as well as make her seem callous. "No, *I'm* sorry," she said in a rush. "The clothes in the trunk have never been worn, and I so prefer them to cages and padding and ruffles in unlikely places. And you didn't care for that either, so I—"

"You dressed for me?" he asked softly, his eyes speculative, his mouth quirked in a whimsical smile.

"Actually," she said as she munched on a small bite of biscuit, "I have no wish to listen to your constant grousing about my garments."

"It is rather shocking to see such changes in fashion," he said, then angled to look behind her. "I do like your coif. Very clever—allowing gentlemen to admire the beauty of your hair while keeping it out of your way."

"Thank you," she said and reached back to smooth her long hair, pulled simply away from her face and tied in a loose knot halfway down her back. She began to tell him that it was with lazy impatience that she had one day fashioned her hair this way rather than spend time and concentration on a more complicated and fashionable style. But why should she? Dante found it attractive, and laziness aside, it *was* rather clever.

Her face burned with a mixture of guilt and pleasure, yet she wasn't sure why she should feel either.

Heavens, what was the matter with her?

Her stomach grumbled as Phineas slid a filled plate across the table to her and another to Dante, added a third to his place, and thumped the coffeepot in the center.

"Eat. I don't be wanting to take all day with the meal when there's places to go."

Betina needed no urging and tucked into her food with haphazard glee, tasting one thing and then another as if it was all new to her. Her stomach filling rapidly, she sat back to drink her coffee. "Where are we going, and why?" she asked and picked the crumbs of her biscuit up with the pad of her finger.

"The village," Phineas answered with a scowl.

"Oh." Betina's spirits sank in disappointment. She licked the crumbs from her finger. "Well, then, if you two have business, I will change clothes and clean this place. It certainly needs it."

"I be telling ye the missy wouldn't go," Phineas mumbled.

"The cleaning can wait," Dante said.

She turned to him. "You meant for me to go?"

He gave her a rogue's smile. "I fancy a lark and suspect you do as well," he said.

"Going into the village is not a lark," she stated, remembering the humiliation and misery she'd experienced on her last visit to town.

Dante's eyes gleamed with mischief. "I promise you that it will be."

"Well, ye be dressed for it," Phineas said.

Betina kicked her old friend under the table. She had no desire to face the cold and superstitious villagers.

Phineas grunted with the blow. "They be wondering what ye be doing out here. Mayhap they need to see."

"See what?" she asked.

"That their legend is progressing quite nicely, of course," Dante said as he swept her plate out from under her nose and pushed away from the table to carry the dishes to the pan filled with hot, soapy water.

She stifled a giggle at the sight of such a grandly garbed man scraping food from plates and then washing them with quick, efficient motions. "You look as if you've done that before."

"I have lived alone for a long time. Do you think a mere gardener would have his own household staff to cosset him?" He dried the plates and turned to capture her within his gaze. "Shall we go?"

She went with him, against all reason and good sense and delicate sensibilities.

She sat in the luxurious comfort of the coach, with Dante occupying the seat across from her and Phineas decked out in his Sunday best acting as coachman.

What were they up to? she wondered, diverting her attention from Dante's knees pressing against hers, his booted feet on either side of hers on the floor. She had seen the twinkle in Phineas's eye as he handed her into the coach, the bounce to his step as he walked toward the driver's box and sprang lightly to his seat.

And Dante . . . Dante sat in brooding silence across from her, watching her, as if he expected her to bolt at any moment.

"This is important to you?" she asked.

"No. It is important to you," he said enigmatically.

"I assure you it is not." She refrained from telling him that she could suffer far kinder treatment from the people at home than she had been subjected to by the grim lot in the village.

"You believe, Betina, but you fear too much to accept the truth."

"I accept it," she said as she fought down a panic she could neither explain nor control. "I'm here, aren't I? I haven't called the authorities to cart you away to the nearest asylum."

"Your hands are cold and you have a pinched look about your mouth," he said and leaned forward to grasp both her hands in one of his, to skim his fingers across her lips then rest them at the side of her throat. "The pulse in your neck is fluttering like a wild thing." His touch lingered a moment before he released her and sat back once more. "Besides, you wouldn't be here if you weren't too curious to remain behind, cleaning away dust and cobwebs."

She opened her mouth then shut it again and directed her attention to the countryside gliding past her window. He was right, drat his perceptive soul. Annoyingly, disgustingly right. She was curious.

"Trust me, Betina," he said softly, his voice a gentle and reassuring caress.

"I do trust you," she said before she could talk herself out of it. "That's really why I'm here."

The entire village appeared to be turned out for what Betina realized was market day . . . or perhaps a county fair of sorts, since it seemed that only the locals were present. Stalls lined the walks, and farmers and drummers loudly hawked their wares. Women had stuck flowers and bits of heather in their caps and bonnets, and little girls swung their heads often to make their pretty new ribbons flutter in the air. Men strutted among horses and other livestock, their thumbs hooked into belts or braces as they argued the relative merits of one beast or another. The smithy's shed pumped volumes of smoke into the air, and a young boy played his flute badly as he hopped about in what she supposed was a dance.

She heard Phineas whistle a command to the horses, and they immediately slowed to a stately walk down the street, the cadence of their hoofbeats telling her that they were stepping high and proud though making little progress through the village. Her palms damp and her heart fluttering nervously, she peered outside.

Mouths fell open as Phineas guided the coach over the ridge that seemed to be the boundary between country road and village road. Every citizen down to the smallest child halted in their tracks to line the road and watch with avid interest. Even the hawkers fell silent.

"Good heavens," she said, forgetting her distress, "I feel as if I should raise my scepter and give them a royal wave . . . if I had a scepter."

Dante placed his French cocked hat on his head at a jaunty angle and sat forward, lifting his cane as if it were a scepter. "I'll show the scepter, you take care of the royal wave."

She glanced at him and saw that he indeed was brandishing the cane in a regal—and wholly condescending—fashion. Mechanically, she raised her hand and twisted it at the wrist in an equally regal wave, as a sense of unreality and the same euphoria with which she'd awakened that morning banished her misgivings and panic.

It wouldn't surprise her at all if the crowd broke into cheers.

But they did not. Instead, they stood still, forgetting the high spirits of bartering and haggling to watch in almost reverent silence as Phineas drove the coach to the end of the village thoroughfare and turned the horses for another walk along the other side of the road.

Halfway down, in the same spot they had left the coach the day they'd first arrived, Phineas stopped the horses and leapt down from the driver's box. With a flourish he opened the door and let down the steps, fitting an unlikely bow somewhere in between. As he straightened he flashed Dante a grin and Betina a wink.

Dante stepped down first and offered his hand to Betina, helping her descend with all the pomp and circumstance of the nobility. Phineas mumbled something about visiting with the smithy and crossed the street before she could protest his abandonment of her.

But Dante was there beside her, offering her his arm as he surveyed the crowd with lordly disdain. He lead her straight to the walkway fronting the shops, his cane preceding him as he walked with an exaggerated and rather dramatic limp.

The crowd parted.

"Tis her. I told you it was," a woman whispered to her companion in a high twitter.

"Didn't have any doubt, though she has changed a mite what with that red cast to her hair," the second woman said, her voice commanding in its depth.

Betina lowered her head to hide her flush. Never would she become accustomed to being whispered about behind her back.

"And how would you know if she looks the same or not?"

"She's the image of that poor girl."

''Oh, and you were there a century past to see her for yourself,'' the twitterer sniffed.

''No, but me grandmum was, and she was passing fair with charcoal and a bit of parchment. You've seen the pictures me Monty put under glass for me.''

''But this one is older.''

The deep-voiced one huffed. ''Then why is she with *him*?''

''Far be it from me to question the ways of nature, unnatural or not.''

''There, you see? If it's unnatural, then why can't she be older? It's been a century after all, and—''

Dante smiled and removed his hat.

A collective gasp rose from the crowd.

''Saints preserve us all, his hair!'' the twitterer cried. ''And look, he's leaning on his cane! He has a limp!''

''You noticing that only now?'' a third voice, blessedly moderate, broke in. ''Bert was on the moor the night *she* came—gathering heather, mind you—and he heard musket fire.''

''Oh mercy, mercy,'' the twitterer wailed. ''It's come to pass. He's found his soul and will be robbing us again.''

''Fool,'' the moderate one said. ''He never robbed us, nor those before us either. He stole from the collectors and paid our rents and taxes with the booty.''

''But the manor is empty these many years—the good squire chased off by *him*, and who'll he be robbing from now if not us?''

''The good squire,'' the moderate one said with forced patience, ''was a pig's hind end, who was glad enough to be rid of his contract to marry poor fey Bess after his fascination for her wore off. He hied himself off and wed the richest widow he could find.''

Dante chuckled as he fingered an apple, chose several more, and nodded to the farmer behind the stall. The poor man grabbed his wife's shopping basket and dumped the apples in before shoving them back at Dante. With a casual air Dante offered a coin, and when it was refused, dropped it among the produce and stepped away, all but dragging Betina toward the next display.

Digging in her heels, Betina frowned in concentration, not wanting to miss a word of the exchange taking place behind her.

''I think he looks even more grand with his silver-shot hair, and the cane suits him,'' the moderate one said. ''He could whistle at my window and I'd do more than let him kiss my hair.''

''Eliza! What would Bert say to hear you speaking so?'' the twitterer said.

''Why, I imagine he's got a stiff one just looking at how pretty our Bess has turned out. She has changed a bit and for the better, I say.''

''As *I* was saying,'' Deep Voice said with obvious satisfaction. ''After so many years who can guess what nature had in mind? Time touches us all, even the enchanted ones.''

''Well, this one ain't empty-headed,'' the moderate one said.

''How would you be knowing that?'' Deep Voice asked.

''The other one would never be seen in public with *him*, and if that ain't empty-headed I don't know what is.''

"He is fine," a fourth broke in. "And none is more fair than our Bess, then or now, no matter what's in her head."

The voices faded as Dante lead Betina farther along, pausing here and there to examine produce and trinkets and nod to cowering merchants.

"Heavens," Betina said. "They speak as if Bess and her highwayman belong to them . . . as if they're proud of us . . . them . . . whoever."

"We do, and they are," Dante said. "Smile, love, and sway your hips a bit."

"Why?"

"Because you are with me and you are happy to be alive . . . because we are here to show them that their patience has not been in vain."

"Patience? For what?"

"For taking care of their phantom while he awaited the return of his soul and his lady love." He made it sound as if they were one and the same.

"You?" she squeaked. "Me?"

"Exactly so. Without us they are simply an ordinary village populated with ordinary farmers and the like. Having their own bogeys makes them unique."

"I am not a bogey," she said indignantly. "I far prefer to be the princess in a fairy tale."

"A fairy tale," he said thoughtfully. "Yes, you're right of course. It's far more romantic."

"And you say they're proud of . . . us . . . even though you scare them witless?"

"A good fright is better than boredom. Why else would we celebrate All Hallows Eve or gather in mobs to watch a hanging?" He tested an array of pastries for freshness. "They are quite a proprietary lot, you see. We are a part of their culture."

"As the opera and theater are a part of culture?" she asked, trying to grasp the situation.

"An astute comparison," Dante said. "I have been the sole source of entertainment for them for a very long time. Then you arrived to add to the drama—the legend come to life again. Now you belong to them also."

"But they don't like me," she said. "They wouldn't allow me to lodge here."

"Of course they wouldn't. Your place is at the inn . . . near me. How can the curse be broken—or better yet, the legend enhanced—if you are lodged five miles away?"

"You have a horse," she said reasonably.

"If you were one of them, would you want the local shade riding into your village in the middle of the night?"

"I suppose not."

"The children would be up at their windows till all hours of the night watching us . . . and this is a love story, mind you. We wouldn't want the little buggers seeing what they shouldn't." He held up a small cake for her inspection.

Her mouth watered.

Grinning, he nodded to the baker, then adjusted the lace at his cuff. "I should have bought another ribbon and waited to crop my hair. They're accustomed to seeing Bess's ribbon tying my queue."

"The red one?" she asked, remembering the ribbon she'd laid on the bureau after untying it from his hair. "Do you have it?"

"No."

"But I put it on the dresser."

His expression seemed to become stone. "It looked faded the other day, so I picked it up and it shredded in my hands."

"Time touches us all, even the enchanted ones," she quoted sadly.

"Yes," he sighed. "That it does, in one way or another . . . but in this case for the better. Bess and the highwayman were both fools."

"They were young," she said, needing to defend them.

He halted in the middle of the walkway and gazed down at her, watching her closely. "Bess rarely ventured away from the inn, and she never would have allowed herself to be seen with me. And while you have her sweet and generous spirit, you are far more than she ever could have become. It is my good fortune to have become older and wiser in the past few weeks and able to see and appreciate the differences between you."

Pleasure blossomed in her chest, spreading through her until it filled her and she wanted to weep for the beauty of it. He did not see her as Bess. He saw her as she was here and now—a woman in her own right.

He kissed the tip of her nose, and murmurs of pleasure rose from the spectators. "Now give them a lighthearted sway of hip before they think we are discussing their doom," he instructed as they resumed their stroll.

Fascinated by Dante's view of the situation and fully in the spirit of the "drama," she minced a small step and swung her hips just a bit.

"Very nice, but perhaps a little more," he murmured.

"Absolutely not."

"No?"

"No," she affirmed. "Would you have them think I was reborn a tart rather than the sweet young girl they remember?" Her step faltered as she heard her own words, realized their meaning.

Reborn. They believed Bess had been reborn in her.

Dante had always believed it, though he saw her—Betina—beyond his memories of Bess, as if Bess were only a small part of her, brought to life to finish what they had begun so long ago.

God help her, but she believed it too.

"I don't believe it." Betina sighed as she untied her shoes and slipped them off to rest her feet next to Dante on the opposite seat of the carriage. "We spent the entire day playing ghosts come to life, listening openly to gossips who talked openly about us."

"And a fine performance it was," Dante said as he stretched out his legs and crossed his ankles on the seat next to her. "I have not been so entertained in years."

"I imagine not." She sobered then. "How did you stand it?"

"You asked me that once before." He rested his head back on the squabs and closed his eyes.

"You didn't answer."

"I have no answer, Betina. I had no choice as to whether I could bear it or not. It simply *was*."

"As I simply *am*—two very different parts of a whole?"

He opened his eyes to look at her. "Is that what you feel like?"

She nodded vigorously, anxious to say what she'd felt rather than understood until now. "Always. It was as if there was a part of me that was hidden, a part that sometimes replaced my thoughts with its own, a part that lived in my dreams. I could feel it inside, but I didn't know what it was . . . or why it was. I could only dream it."

"And you dreamed of me, yet they weren't *your* dreams."

"You understand."

"Yes."

Yes. "What a precious gift that small word is to me," she said thickly. "I never expected that anyone would understand me or know me or . . ."

"Love you as I love you?"

It stunned her to hear him say it so easily and earnestly. It burdened her to know he meant it, to know that she loved him too. Yet she questioned how she loved him: as Bess or as herself?

She clenched her hands in her lap and gathered the words she knew she had to say. "Many love me, Dante. Tim loves me for my quiet ways and easy manner." She ignored his snort of disbelief and continued. "Papa loves me as his little princess to be sheltered and protected and guided. Papa loves to guide everyone. Mama loves me and tries very hard to understand me, and maybe she succeeds a little." She shook her head against the futility of it. "I am something different in each of their eyes, yet none of them sees me as myself." *Even you,* she added silently. *You see enough of Bess in me that I wonder which of us will win out.*

She stared blindly out the window, wanting desperately to win, afraid that she would never know if

Dante would have loved her if Bess's spirit were not a part of her own.

Dante was right. She believed all of it—the legend and her part in it. Yet she did not accept the reality of the present. She was afraid to accept, when she loved so much, wanted so much.

Dante was a dream come true, and this was all a fairy tale that shouldn't be happening to mortals. How could it last?

She knew it might not. Dante would heal, and she would have to make yet more decisions. He had a second chance, free of obligations to anyone but himself. She still had her own life—one she'd fought hard for—and it would not go away or lie in wait as Dante had done for a hundred years.

But it would wait for a little while longer. Never had she felt so free to be herself, to indulge what she felt and wanted to feel rather than what was expected of her or what she was told she should feel and want. She would not have the outside world intrude upon her moments of discovery just yet. Not until she knew what place she wanted to take in that world. Not until she knew what to do about Tim.

She frowned and rubbed the bridge of her nose as she admitted to herself that she had already made a decision concerning Tim as well. He wanted so much from her, yet it was not what she wanted to give. He had such a wonderful life planned for them, yet it was not the life she wanted. Whatever the future held for her, she was certain Tim would not be a part of it.

Her life had changed drastically in the past two months since she'd left home. But it had changed by her hand. As for herself, she didn't think she had changed so much as become what she was meant to be. What she wanted to be.

For a little while at least she wanted very much to be the woman Dante loved, the woman who loved him without reservations. She wanted to live for the present and believe that whatever was meant to be in the future would come to pass.

She loved Dante, not because Bess had loved him, or because he was the embodiment of her phantom lover, or because she had dreamed of grand passion and Dante so easily brought her to that with even the most innocuous of touches. She loved him because he was no perfect fairy-tale prince, no dark and mysterious visitor in her dreams. He was simply Dante, with his humor and his torment, his gentleness and his urgency, his strength and his vulnerability.

He was a man. Just a man, who enchanted and charmed her and made her feel for the first time in her life like an ordinary person who had become special only because she was loved by him . . . Dante de Vere, a man who had silver threaded through his hair, who was beautiful to her with the scars that marred his magnificent body and the slight limp that interrupted his smooth and powerful gait. A man who had shared his fear and his anguish with her. A man who wanted more than a wife who simpered in the background of his life, more than a woman who could offer him nothing more than fondness. He was greedy. He wanted a woman who responded in conversation and in passion.

He wanted . . . everything.

She wanted to give him everything.

And she would, whether for a little while or forever.

She never would have thought she could be so very fatalistic, to love so completely yet acknowledge doubts and fears and the possibility of being hurt or disillusioned. But she also knew that ultimately she would have to face those fears. There were too many elements of the past interwoven in what she felt for Dante, what he felt for her. They had not begun fresh with a first meeting and only a future to look to. She would have to know what held the most power over Dante, and herself—yesterday or tomorrow.

She knew who he had been, but she also knew who he was now. She knew the difference between the highwayman, whom she would have abhorred for his reckless daring and cavalier ways, and the man who now accepted life as a gift and saw the world with both weariness and wonder. The man who seduced her with the same desperation and urgency with which she responded, and who teased her for her clothing but never for her preoccupations.

A man. Just a man who enchanted and charmed her. A man who loved her as she was a century ago and as she was now.

And for now she would accept his love and return it, and pray they would indeed build a bright future from such a grim past.

She didn't know if her decision was wise or right. She only knew that today was all anyone could count on. And today she wanted to experience the magic of loving her phantom before time caught up with them both.

"It's one part of ye telling the other part what might be. Ye just started listening sooner than most." —*Phineas*

20

Time again became Betina's friend, and the present world slipped away from her as easily as the coach rolled from moor to woodland. Mist crept along the ground and reflected the burning shades of sunset sneaking a little way into the gloom. Shadows hovered among the trees—magic waiting to have its way.

The silence, too, had been a friend as she and Dante had forsaken words for closeness. She'd taken his feet into her lap to massage away the cramps he suffered after a day of walking and posturing for the rapt villagers. He groaned in pleasure and wiggled his toes against her belly, and sensation awakened inside her, warm and expectant.

She leaned forward to knead his thigh and his hand found her hair, inching the skein upward until he could untie the loose knot and sift his fingers through the freed strands. Her breasts grazed his shins with every movement, and she nearly moaned in pleasure at the tightening of her nipples, the sweet teasing of such an innocent caress.

"Betina . . . enough," he said with a rasp in his voice.

She glanced up at him, and along the way her gaze caught on the place between his thighs . . . a swollen shaft straining beneath his tight doeskin breeches . . . then his chest rising and falling with carefully measured breaths . . . his face tight and controlled, half-light and half-shadow in the dying embers of daylight glimmering through the trees.

The coach lurched to a stop.

"I'll be getting supper on the table," Phineas called out, and then the door of the inn slammed shut.

She sat up and scooted back as Dante eased his feet from her lap.

"I don't know if I can get my boots on again," Dante said with a forced note of humor. "The carriage suddenly seems too small for such maneuverings."

"Then don't try," she replied. "I'm certainly not going to fumble around with mine." Opening the door of the coach, she jumped to the ground, thankful that her stockinged feet had not found a pebble. She peered back inside at Dante, at the way he sat so still and tense with his eyes closed. "Dante? Phineas is waiting."

"Phineas," he said. "A chaperone to set the most determined bounder to quailing in his stockings." He shifted in the seat as if to ease the restriction of his breeches. "You go on, love. I'll be along shortly."

"Dante?"

"Yes?" he said with an aggrieved sigh.

"Your costume is very dashing, but do you suppose the villagers would mind if you adopted a more modern and . . . um . . . less confining fashion?"

"You see too much, Betina," he said ruefully.

"It's becoming quite dark out here and I'm sure I see nothing at all," she said innocently and dashed for the inn.

Dante followed her a few painful moments later. It was becoming bloody difficult to exert control over a part of his body that seemed to have a mind of its own. He'd had no such problem with Bess. At least not to this extent. But then he doubted Bess had a carnal thought in her life. It hadn't occurred to him until recently, but he'd rarely had such thoughts about Bess. She'd had an untouchable quality that prompted men to want to protect her rather than ravish her.

Not so Betina, who apparently knew more about men than the chaste maidens of his day. He supposed that it was inevitable. America was the land of free speech, and women had the vote—he still couldn't reconcile himself to that—and such progress was not possible without open minds and a general enlightenment of the population. He'd noticed that while Betina blushed and stammered over certain intimacies, she accepted them without the fear and ignorance prevalent among women of the past.

He strode into the kitchen, his thoughts lingering on the differences between past and present, and nearly ran straight into the table.

"Come sit," Betina said, patting the chair beside her.

Phineas slapped a piece of ham between two thick slices of bread and bit into it without comment.

Dante sat.

Candles set at either end of the table cast a flickering glow on the table, enclosing them in a mellow circle of light. A bottle of wine from the cellar below served as centerpiece, surrounded by plates of ham and beef, cheese and the apples Dante had purchased in the village. Fragrant steam rose from a teapot on the cabinet. A wicked-looking knife sat at Phineas's elbow next to a loaf of freshly baked bread, also purchased in the village.

Betina leaned over to fill Dante's glass with wine, her breasts grazing his arm.

He reached for bread and piled meat—he didn't know which—onto it with a thick slice of cheese. "Shall we have a game of chess after our meal?" he asked Phineas, trying to ignore the rustle of her clothing as she moved.

Phineas glanced from him to Betina. "I be thinking of going to bed."

"So early, Phineas?" she asked. "It's not even completely dark yet. Are you ill?"

"I be well, missy. Rain's coming and it be good sleeping weather."

"I can't play chess very well," Betina said shyly. "But I am quite proficient at poker. I could teach you."

"I don't ken what your pap thought, teaching a young lady to gamble," Phineas grumbled.

"Poker? Gamble?" Dante said.

"It's just a game of cards," Betina said. "And Papa and I never played for more than bits of candy."

"A sweet tooth she has," Phineas explained. "So she paid close attention to the game. Now all the hands on the ranch be packing candy in their pockets on the chance of getting in a hand or two of poker."

"They indulge me, you see, for if I play Papa does too, and he has the most money." Her foot slid into his as she reached across the table for an apple wedge, cut it up, and popped a piece in her mouth.

He thought he should move his foot or better yet move his chair a distance away, but he didn't. He liked the feel of it, the intimacy of such an unlikely caress, and wondered what it would be like to sleep like this—with their feet pressed against one another for warmth and perhaps their fingers entwined beneath a pillow.

"Well? Would you like to learn poker?" she asked and refilled their wine glasses. "Or has Phineas scared you off? I know men have their pride in such things."

The grin she shot him was so smug that he placed his foot atop hers and grinned back. "A challenge I can't refuse," he replied. "Do you have cards?"

"Of course," she said happily. "What do you think we did on the train and then the ship during our journey here?"

He glanced at Phineas, who had suddenly found great interest in the bottom of his glass. "One wonders that you had room for clothing with all the candy you must have packed in your luggage. . . ." Tilting his head as Betina's words caught up with him, he searched for familiarity and found none. "Train?"

Betina sobered and reached for another apple wedge. "A locomotive . . . um . . . an engine driven by steam that pulls passenger or freight cars behind it on rails. The Indians call it an 'iron horse,' and the tracks run from coast to coast," she said proudly. "You have them here in England as well."

He tried to imagine such a thing and couldn't. "Cars?"

"Well, they call them that, though they're like boxes, longer than they are wide, with rows of seats in them for people to sit."

"You trust this?"

"Of course."

"Of course," he murmured, again overwhelmed by the thought of what he might find when he left this place. What seemed strange and perhaps even frightening to him—though he wouldn't admit to that—was taken for granted by a woman who barely reached his chin.

She laid her hand on his arm and moved it back and forth as if to soothe him. "It's quite new really, and there are many men who still ride their horses wherever they want to go, even if it's miles and miles away."

He barely heard her for the caress of her hand, for the earnest frown on her face showing so much concern for his confusion, for the way her knees alternated with his as she turned in her chair to face him.

"I was only eleven when they joined the transcontinental tracks at Promontory. Papa took me to see it, and it seemed like an ugly dragon belching smoke and growling." The words tumbled out of her mouth one after another, as if she were desperate to reassure him. She couldn't comprehend how overwhelming and intimidating it was to know that the world he faced was not the one he knew.

"But it was great fun riding in a private car and traveling at such great speed without having to worry about losing my seat in a saddle—"

He pressed his fingers on her lips, silencing her. Bleakness ate away at him with every new reminder she gave him that time had gone on without him, that life as he knew it had passed him by. That he no longer fit in.

She tilted her head and kissed his fingers and stared back at him with apology in her eyes. Grasping his wrist, she pulled his hand down, holding it in her lap and tracing each finger. "I find the world very frightening at times, Dante. I think everyone does."

The misery left him as he held her gaze and twined his fingers with hers. He felt her snuggle her other foot beneath his and wiggle her toes, as if she took comfort and shelter wherever she might find it, even under a table.

The scrape of chair legs on wood seemed far away as Phineas pushed back from the table and rose. "I be getting the cards," he said gruffly as he opened a drawer in the cupboard and slapped a deck of cards in front of them.

Betina didn't move, but continued to stare at Dante with wide eyes dark as night sprinkled with starlight, her hands unmoving in his, her lips parted.

"I be dealing," Phineas boomed. "The missy cheats when she can." Cards snapped as Phineas shuffled them and hit the table with muted clicks as he dealt them. "Ye be playing or not?"

Dante tore his gaze from Betina's and inhaled with a shudder. "I believe we should," he said as he drew his hand away from hers.

Her face flaming with a blush, she turned away abruptly, her feet sliding out from under his.

The floor felt suddenly very hard and very cold.

"Only two players, Phineas?" she said with a catch in her voice.

"I be showing him how to go on, or ye'll be gulling him into believing the rules change depending on what's in your hand." He took to his chair again and slid the one beside him out. "Ye sit here, where she can't be peeking at your cards."

Dante complied readily enough. Betina's scent of fresh air and roses seemed particularly heady at the moment, and the frequent nudge of her thigh seemed like the most provocative caress.

"What will we play for?" she asked, still subdued.

"Naught for now, while he be learning," Phineas said as he shoved the plates and remains of their meal aside. "Ye can fleece him later when he knows what he's about."

Steadier now that she was not so close, Dante picked up the cards dealt him and did his best to attend to Phineas's instructions—and failed completely to ignore Betina's feet tucking beneath his once more.

"Cards," Atropos mumbled. "A waste of precious time."

"What would you have them do," Lachesis asked, "when Phineas is hovering about?"

"I would have them get on with it," Atropos said. "I've had enough of these coy human games of seduction. Why can they not do what they want when it is so obvious they want to—"

"I must agree with Atropos," Ilithyia said. "They are torturing themselves and one another. And their bodies can burn only so long. They are both untried and—"

"Enough, sisters," Nemesis said as she rose from her chair. "They will join in their own time."

"But time is so very precious now, with Tim drawing closer to them every day." Clotho said. "And I

yearn to begin new skeins with different colors. I have been working with these for so very long."

"I know," Nemesis said as she wrapped her arm around Clotho's shoulders. "We all need respite. Shall we go to the pond and bathe?"

"Why not?" Atropos said. "It is clear Dante and Betina prefer gambling with nonexistent wealth to gambling with their emotions."

"You go on," Lachesis said. "I have no wish to tolerate the antics of the centaurs tonight."

"Nor I," Ilithyia said. "I will bathe in the morn when they are elsewhere and cannot steal my gown."

"They are harmless enough," Nemesis said, giving them a strange look. "But as you will . . . come, Atropos . . . Clotho."

Ilithyia and Lachesis stared into the fire long after their sisters had departed, watching the three humans bicker with good nature over their cards.

"Look at Dante," Lachesis whispered as if the humans might hear. "You can almost see his thoughts in his face."

"It is known that men are seldom able to think in such circumstances."

"But he is. He is thinking about her breasts and how they would peek out from her hair if it were unbound and she were unclothed."

"Yes, I know," Ilithyia said. "And she is thinking of what she saw beneath his breeches in the coach. Her mother taught her what it is for, and she is wondering how it would feel. . . ."

"See how their gazes meet and linger, then wander over one another's body? They imagine much, yet know so little."

"Dante concerns himself overmuch with his lack of experience," Ilithyia mused. "He has waited long and patiently for her and is now beset with misgivings."

"Patience should be rewarded."

The sisters looked at one another, then back into the fire.

"He suffers for want of her," Lachesis cried.

"Yes. And she yearns for him. See how she licks her lips, hungering for the taste of his mouth?"

"Yes."

Again, they looked one to the other.

"It should be magic the first time," Ilithyia said.

"Yes, for if it is not, they will hurt themselves in their urgency."

"And reap a poor memory of the experience."

They smiled and closed their eyes, directing their minds toward the inn, their lips moving with incantations forbidden by the elders. Incantations that drifted on the night wind and found entrance into human minds with every breath they took, filling them with thoughts of love and magic and the dance of star stuff on the air.

And then they studied the images in the fire once more.

"I am out of practice," Lachesis said.

"Shh, sister," Ilithyia breathed. "Their minds are open now and can hear us if we do not take care."

"Will it work?"

"I think so. Phineas's mind has always been open to us. He has heard us cast our spell and will honor it." Ilithyia smiled then for the memory of an old gardener who had died in England almost a century past and had become young again in her arms. Perhaps he

would be allowed to return to her in the somewhen of existence. . . .

Lachesis sighed wearily in the aftermath of stealing through mortal minds and sank to the floor to watch the mortals play coy games with their emotions.

"Oh," Betina pouted. "You won."

Phineas nodded in satisfaction as he chewed on the stem of his pipe, gathered up the cards, and set them in front of Dante. "Ye have the way of it right enough," he said and rose from his chair. "Since the horses still be hitched to the coach, I be using it to go for a game of chess with the blacksmith." Plates clinked against one another as he cleared the table and stacked the used china and silver in the wash pan. "Can't get a decent game here, what with talk of poker and trains, and I don't be having no sweets left," he grumbled.

"Isn't it late to be riding into the village?" Dante asked.

"Tis early yet," Phineas said. "And the smith is waiting for his mare to foal tonight. I be keeping him company and helping if need be." He took his jacket from a peg by the door and walked out onto the back stoop. "Don't be looking for me. The smith plays a slow game and the mare is a stubborn one."

Dante sat back and stretched his legs out on either side of Betina's feet. A mistake, for it seemed even more intimate somehow to have his calves against hers and the outsides of her feet rubbing the insides of his.

The door slammed and Phineas's footsteps faded toward the coach. A moment later the creaking of the wheels grew weaker as Phineas drove the coach down the road.

Night poured in the window with only a sliver of moon rising above the trees and stars dusting the sky. Tendrils of mist climbed the outside walls and over the window glass like curtains of gauze.

A robber's moon, Dante thought, and the greatest prize of all was within his reach. A woman such as no woman he had ever known, charming him with her mischievous play at cards and tormenting him with her ingenuous caresses and lingering stares. Did she not know what she did to him? Did she not know how his blood simmered in his veins and gathered in his groin with aching pressure?

This had to end.

"Now, what can we play for?" Betina said as she studied the room.

So innocent was her query. So unaware was her manner. Yet he saw the pulse flutter in her throat and the way she ran her tongue so nervously over her lips. He saw her nipples peak inside the light fabric of her dress and felt her feet stealthily withdraw to a safe distance.

Safe. Neither one of them was safe now, for a robber's moon ruled the night and the blood of a highwayman ruled him. He would have his prize or lose her on a gamble.

Either way his body would have relief from this torture.

"Dante? What do you wish to gamble?" she asked, and he heard her breathlessness.

"I have no sweets," he said casually.

"And we haven't enough matchsticks," she said.

"I have no more coin with me."

"Neither do I," she said, then her expression brightened. "Apples! We can cut them up and—"

"I think not."

"The flatware?"

"No."

"Bits of paper?"

He shook his head slowly as he kept his gaze on her, his eyelids lowered slightly in speculation. "How many garments are you wearing?" he asked and rubbed his forefinger over his chin.

"What?"

"I estimate two stockings and two petticoats and a chemise . . ." He held up his hands, folding each finger over as he named each article of clothing. ". . . your shoes and dress . . . are you wearing a corset?"

She nodded dumbly.

"Corset and cover," he finished. "Ten items then."

"Eleven," she squeaked as her gaze darted about the kitchen.

"Ah, yes, your pantalettes." He shifted in his chair, easing the growing discomfort of breeches that seemed to shrink by the moment. "And I have breeches and stockings . . ." He straightened his fingers to begin counting again. "Boots, shirt, waistcoat, stock, braces, handkerchief, stickpin, hat, fob, garters . . . and an undergarment."

She ran her tongue over her lips. "Fifteen."

"All right. We can forget the hat." It occurred to him that his hat was still in the coach.

"I have garters." Her squeak was becoming smaller.

Dante picked up the cards and shuffled. "Then I'll count the knot in your hair as a ribbon. Shall we play?" He shuffled again, taking his time.

"Dante?"

"Would you rather end it now?" he asked softly, not knowing whether he wanted her to say yes or no, but unable to resist a taunt. "Or are you confident enough in your skill?"

"We aren't wearing shoes."

The cards almost went flying as he fumbled to maintain his grip. She gave him a direct stare, and the flesh above the scooped neckline of her gown rose and fell at a rapid rate. She was going to do it.

Good lord, that meant he would have to do it too.

"As a gentleman I must warn you of the dangers—"

"Don't," she said, steadying her voice with a deep breath. "I . . . just don't warn me . . . please. I know what is happening. Mama told me—"

"Don't bring your mother into it," he grated.

"All right." She lowered her head.

Seeing her twist her hands in her lap and stare down at them so dejectedly, he felt like an ass for instigating such a situation. Still, it wasn't too late. He cleared his throat and forced himself to speak softly. "Betina, what do you think is happening?"

Her head jerked up and her eyes were wide and vague. "You are gambling that I will go to my room and lock my door against you. I am gambling that you are as . . . as . . . stimulated as I am." She nodded—once—as if she were satisfied with her statement.

Stimulated. He wanted to groan in agony. He wanted to shout at her in anger. He wanted to lock his door against her and her foolish courage.

But he wanted her more. And as she sat across from him, appearing so prim and proper and innocent, he knew that he wanted to see her completely abandoned and wildly reckless and thoroughly satiated.

As he dealt the cards Dante hoped that he could accomplish it without disgracing himself.

"There's a place away from there that is so large and uncluttered you can see tomorrow over the next rise."

—Dante de Vere

21

The mist had turned to fog, enclosing the inn, protecting it from the world. The kitchen was warm with the blaze Dante had built in the inglenook, and the walls seemed to dance with fire and shadow.

Dante's stockings were the first to be set on the table. Betina's garters and stockings lay next to his.

She swept her hair over her shoulder and untied the loose knot in her hair, letting the strands fall where they might over her shoulder and breast. "Your deal," she said quietly.

He shuffled and dealt, his gaze never leaving that fall of shining hair, the curled ends that brushed her waist like a crooked finger, beckoning him.

He studied his cards, kept them all and gave her three.

She folded and leaned over. A petticoat drifted onto the table.

Swallowing, he dealt again.

The second petticoat fell beside its mate.

She took the next hand, and his coat. And then his brocaded waistcoat, stock, and shirt joined the pile.

He began to cheat.

Her breasts pouted outward as she reached behind herself to unfasten her gown. The fabric slipped off one shoulder, then the other. She held it in place a moment and stared at him, at his neck, down to his shoulders, his chest, and it felt like a caress. Rising, she lowered her hands and allowed the gown to fall to her waist. She leaned over to step out of it, giving him a view of what lay beneath her scanty camisole. The gown fell to the planks of the table between them.

He lost his breeches and sighed in relief at the ease in pressure, then felt heat rush into his face as he caught her gaze on him rising within his smallclothes.

She began to tremble as she removed her corset cover.

He had the queen of hearts and nothing else in the next hand. It was enough.

Her corset laced in front, and as she worked the lacings free her nipples pushed against the thin cloth of her chemise, which was nipped in at the waist and dipped low over her chest, held in place by a single thin ribbon.

He winced as the corset hit the table.

The candles burned low and lower still, the circle of burnished gold light growing smaller as time tiptoed past, unnoticed.

He won the next play with a pair of kings—both black.

She hesitated over the ribbon. He arched his brows.

She pulled on one end and the bow came undone. The garment fell open to the first button farther down.

He held his breath as she slipped one button free . . . two . . . three . . . separated the edges . . . slid it down one arm . . . and the other . . . laid it atop the corset.

Her flesh glowed golden in the light, the areolae a soft rose, one barely visible through the fall of her hair.

He wanted to end it now, to take her breasts in his mouth, to bury himself in her. . . .

"Last hand," she whispered.

He shuffled; she cut; he dealt.

She spread her cards out—a king, a queen, five high.

He fanned out his cards—a king, a queen, six high.

She rose slowly . . . untied the drawstring of her pantalettes slowly . . . stepped out of them slowly . . . and straightened.

He'd dreamed of this, seen it a thousand—ten thousand—times in his fantasies, yet nothing prepared him for his first sight of a naked woman. Never had he envisioned the firmness of breasts quivering with each breath she took, their centers swollen and reaching outward toward him . . . the slant of rib cage into small waist, the small round shadow in the center of a slightly rounded belly . . . the curve of hips . . . the wedge of curls that gleamed burgundy and black . . . the slightly plump thighs . . . the taper of legs . . . the fair flesh that glistened as if sprinkled with star stuff.

Perhaps it had been.

Only magic could create such beauty. Only enchantment could bring him to his feet and carry him to the end of the table where she stood. Only a spell could hold him upright on liquid limbs as he reached out to touch the center of one breast . . . as he bent down to taste the softness . . . as he lowered to his knees before her and kissed the curls between her thighs . . . inhaled the scent of rosewater and woman . . . turned her slowly around, his hands molding the shape of her hips . . . tracing the cleft of her spine . . . fitting themselves to her waist and turning her back to him . . . sliding upward to cup her breasts and bring one to his mouth to nip gently . . . to taste . . . to draw on her.

Her breath caught. Her body trembled. Her hands cradled his head and held him to her breasts, one then the other.

He encircled her with his arms and pressed his cheek to her, his hands exploring her bottom, her thighs, the petal-smooth skin below her curls. He rose and held his breath as she slipped her fingers inside the waist of his smallclothes and pushed them down over his hips. They fell to the floor and he managed to step out of them without stumbling. Still, his hands never left her as they slid over the mist coating her, his belly and his chest sliding against hers, his manhood finding a place between her legs as he covered her mouth with his.

She cried out and wrapped her arms around his neck and opened her mouth, accepting the hard thrust of his tongue. Her hands framed his face. Her tongue moved with his. Her body pressed against his, urgent, frantic. . . .

He backed her toward the table and lifted her and stood between her legs. She looked down at him and touched him and enclosed him in her hands as their mouths met and parted and met again. Her legs opened and curved around his waist, and he felt the heat of her, the texture of her, smoother than silk, layered like the petals of a rose, moist like dew before sunrise.

He tried to control himself, to move slower.

Again she held his face, urging him downward to suckle her breasts, upward to take her mouth and steal her breath. She arched into him, and her nipples met his and their tongues mingled. She whimpered again; her hands were wild on him, caressing him frantically, stroking him insistently.

He could not wait. . . .

He began to lift her, wanting to carry her to a softer, gentler place, but she leaned back on her elbows and held him close with her legs.

He could not wait.

He tried to ease into her, but she arched and closed around him.

She cried out and he tried to pull away, but she shook her head from side to side and held out her arms, reaching for him as she moved her hips and—

Oh, damn, he could not wait.

He thrust once, twice, and she lifted her hips to follow him. He flattened his hand on her belly and held her still and thrust again and again and again.

She sobbed and gasped for air and fought his hold as she tightened her legs around him, drawing him into her until he felt as if he were drowning in her.

He held her hips and plunged into her once more, hard and fast. His muscles tightened and held him upright, and he felt as if his very soul spilled into her, becoming a part of her.

She sobbed and sobbed in her throat and arched into him once more. Her body tensed and didn't move, but held him tightly inside her, caressing him inside her with rapid little spasms of completion, drawing on him inside her, draining him as a profound sense of pleasure washed through him. He thought he could not survive if it didn't end.

He didn't want it to end.

He lowered her hips to the bed of their clothing and fell forward, his palms flat on the table, his arms locked to support his weight above her, unable to breathe or think or speak.

It didn't matter, for surely he had died again.

"I would think you'd have died from boredom by now," Atropos said as she entered the room with Clotho and Nemesis, all fresh from swimming in the pond outside their temple. "Surely you can find better things to do than watch those mortals sleep."

"They aren't sleeping," Ilithyia and Lachesis said in unison and gave one another a quick, guilty glance.

Suspiciously, Atropos peered into the fire. "Will wonders never cease," she exclaimed. "They did it . . . and in the kitchen. They are more inventive than I thought."

Nemesis and Clotho drew nearer and stared at the image of Betina lying on the table, her legs around Dante's waist as he stood before her, their bodies joined, their flesh glistening with the mists of passion, their movements arrested as if, for that brief moment, their hearts had ceased to beat and their thoughts flew among the stars.

"At last," Clotho breathed.

Nemesis smiled at the scene. "I assume it was rather spontaneous?"

"Yes," Lachesis sighed.

"Incredibly so," Ilithyia said.

"Well," Atropos snapped impatiently. "Was it good for them?"

"Yes," Lachesis said, "though Dante is riddled with misgivings about his prowess, and Betina has not come down from the clouds yet."

"His lack of experience no doubt," Nemesis said. "Still, it is good that he came to Betina as untouched as she came to him. It will have meaning for both of them."

"Well, it's about time they did something," Clotho said. "I would not have all my mending of their threads go to waste."

"Yes," Lachesis agreed. "All will be well now."

"Do not allow your idealism to get in the way of caution, sister," Nemesis warned. "There is still much to be resolved."

"I know," Lachesis said. "But for tonight I will forget that the past still lies between them and believe that they have only the future to settle."

Atropos snorted. "You know as well as the rest of us that the future cannot be until the past is done, and for them there is much yet to finish."

Sadly, the sisters trailed away to their own chambers, except for one, who stared into the fire and waited for the next drama to unfold.

Feeling began to return to Dante with a chill on his backside and a cramp in his thigh.

Betina opened her eyes to stare up at him, vague and unfocused.

"Heavens," she said breathlessly. "Poor Mama."

Mama? He looked away from her and swallowed, but the sudden lump in his throat wouldn't go down. She was thinking of her mother, and somehow that was worse than if she'd closed her eyes and thought of England or Wyoming or whatever. What had he expected? For her to swoon and declare that she had been as transported as he to some netherworld where only pleasure existed? Pleasure, hell, he corrected. It had been pure, undiluted ecstasy.

It had been worth waiting for.

And while he'd been taken by mist and magic, Betina had been thinking of her mother.

He straightened and eased away from her, out of her, not wanting to leave her yet needing to cover himself, to regain his balance . . . and his pride.

She said nothing as he donned his smallclothes—when had he shed them?—and breeches. In the silence and dim light cast by guttering candles, he felt more empty and alone than he'd ever felt in his life.

There was a rustle of cloth and a sigh, but he couldn't look at her, didn't want to see her fumble with her clothes as he was fumbling, didn't want to know that she was in a rush to cover herself, to hide herself from him in shame or regret.

The kitchen table. He'd taken her in the bloody kitchen on the bloody table. He'd had to play his game and torture himself in the process until he was wild and primitive, reduced to the basic elements of copulation.

He'd wanted to make love to her with slow skill and languid assurance.

Of course, he might have pulled it off if he'd actually been skilled and assured.

He headed for the back stairs, needing to find refuge in the solitude of his room, lick his wounds in total darkness, build enough courage to face her on the morrow. Barely past the opposite end of the table he cursed and halted and glared at the fire burning in the grate.

What kind of rotter was he to fail her and then think only of himself by walking away?

In desperation he grabbed the kettle, felt the weight and slosh of water inside, and hung it on the hook that swung over the fire. Adding wood to the grate, he watched the flames climb and lick at the sides of the kettle. Surely it would boil soon.

But it did not, and he abruptly turned toward Betina, spitting out the words that refused to be contained. "What about your mother?"

She hadn't dressed at all, but lay on her side on the plank table, their clothing strewn about her, a petticoat haphazardly dragged out from beneath her and barely covering her torso, a thoughtful frown on her face.

Heat climbed into his face. He wanted to hide it, but couldn't turn from the sight of her lying in such provocative innocence, her legs bare and one breast escaping her meager covering.

"I have to know, Betina," he said hoarsely, "why you think of your mother at such a time." God, but that sounded clownish. Did he look as absurd? Glancing down at himself, he saw an edge of his drawers bunched up above the waist of his doeskins, saw his bare calves and feet. He jerked his head up, startled by her voice. She was still frowning.

"Mama told me all about . . . this . . . what we did."

"She told you?" he asked, incredulous.

"Oh, yes, in accurate detail. She doesn't believe girls should be ignorant about the things they will encounter in life such as finances and doing man's work when the man is away and . . ." She lowered her gaze, and he wondered if the red in her cheeks was from the fire or from embarrassment.

"What we did," he supplied. He leaned his weight on his good leg and assumed an indolent pose. "And what we did was have sexual congress." *"Sexual congress?"* a voice said in his mind. A female voice, mocking him. *"Call it what it is, you fool, instead of sounding like a shy virgin. Bluff it out like a man."* He raked his hand through his hair as the dratted voice taunted him.

"Sexual congress?" Betina said. "I've not heard that term before. It sounds very cold . . . and political."

"What would you call it?" he asked.

"Well, Mama says that if a man pays for it, then it's fornication. If it is between a man and wife who do not have special feelings, one might consider it's simple copulation, like the animals do to procreate. But if their emotions are involved, then it's making love." She propped her head in her hand. "Mama said it was a lovely thing."

"Lovely?" he repeated dumbly. "She said that?"

"Yes. I saw her and Papa once, when I went to the kitchen for water. Papa was sitting in a chair and Mama was—"

"I can imagine," Dante said, amused in spite of himself. "What did you think?"

"I was older—fifteen or so—and Mama had already explained everything, so I was more curious than anything." She ducked her head and lowered her gaze. "I watched for a few moments, but it was so personal and they were making quite a bit of noise, so I ran back to bed."

"Did you think it was 'lovely'?"

"The look on Mama's face was . . . the water is boiling."

He turned to the kettle. It rattled on the hook and steam shot from the spout. "*Do* you think it is 'lovely'?" he asked, unable to look at her.

"No. Not lovely at all, but wild and magical and uncivilized. Mama didn't tell me that one forgets everything but sensation and goes beyond oneself and is truly free from the rules one has learned to live by." She traced the grain of the wood beneath her with her forefinger. "I wonder if she knows. I'd hate to think that she and Papa never went beyond lovely . . . are you making tea? I would love a cup."

Dante frowned at the kettle and reached for a china pot and the jar of tea. "You . . . ah . . ." He cleared his throat and made a clatter while brewing the tea. "You liked it then?"

"Yes," she said simply. "I wonder what it's like to make love in a bed?"

Dante squeezed his eyes shut for a moment and swallowed over and over again until he felt steady and tall and full of relief and pride. "Would you like to find out?" he asked quietly.

"I think that would be beyond lovely," she said, frowning down at the wood that held her interest. "That is if you want to . . . if you like it enough to—"

He abandoned the teapot and turned to her, sweeping her up and into his embrace, lowering her to stand on the floor, holding her fast as he kissed her hard, over and over again until he had to stop for air. He was swollen and painfully hard again and wanted to sit in a chair and lower her onto himself, feel her breasts against his chest as he rose into her and she tightened around him. He wanted to be uncivilized and make noise and find freedom in her arms.

But he eased her back instead and lowered her into the chair alone. "Tea," he said thickly. "And then we will discover what it is like to make love in a bed."

''You fill my world until there is little room for anyone else.''

—Bess to Dante, once upon a time

22

Betina discovered a trace of shyness in Dante as they sat across from one another at the table and drank their tea, she clothed only in his velvet coat and he wearing nothing but his drawers and breeches. He did not quite meet her gaze as he poured and served and spooned sugar into her cup. And he answered her compliments on his brewing skills with a noncommittal shrug of his shoulders and a slight flush creeping up his neck.

Oddly she did not feel shy at all, and wondered if she should.

But then why should she? She liked the way Dante looked at her body with a satyr's gleam in his eyes. She liked the feeling of her body responding to his gaze, the newness and anticipation of stomach flutters and her blood warming and knowing what might come next.

With Dante.

Betina discovered that he was a romantic as he tried to sweep her into his arms and carry her up the stairs. Having strained his healing wounds enough in carrying her upstairs the night before, he failed to do more than carry her a few steps before lowering her to the floor and shaking his head ruefully. It was enough that he tried.

And when she laughed at how absurd they must look, he laughed, too, and tried to take the coat away from her. She ran and dodged his grasping hands until he caught her in the pantry and wrestled with her for the coat.

His leg wedged between hers and her breathing quickened as they tussled, his thigh moving against her in a most provocative way. His hand brushed her breast on its way to her shoulder. She stilled and his hand hovered, then returned to cup her, his fingers skimming her nipple over and over again. He raised his free hand and did the same to her other breast. "Yield, or I will . . ." He glanced around the pantry and frowned at the crowded shelves, then brightened as he spied a bare one. "I will show you the improper use of a pantry."

"I will not yield," she said breathlessly as desire awakened and stretched within her. "The coat is mine. I won it."

"I won your stockings and garters and corset, but I am not wearing them," he said reasonably.

"But I won fairly and you cheated." Grasping his wrists, she held them for a sweet moment—only that—

as he opened his hands and her nipples swelled into his palms.

"I only now learned to play your game," he said with an expression of affront followed by a slow, lazy smile that suggested much about passion in the pantry. "How would I be skilled enough to cheat?" His knee moved closer between her thighs and he rolled her nipples between his fingers.

"You weren't skilled," she gasped as she lost control of a shuddering sigh. "I . . . knew what you . . . were doing the . . . entire time."

"You wound me far worse than any ball to suggest such a thing," he said, lowering his knee to press his hips into her, his erection hard on her belly. "I am simply a quick study."

"Hah!" She pushed his hands away and turned to dash for the stairs, taking advantage of his weariness and the weakness of his leg.

He caught up with her on the landing and advanced on her with lascivious menace, backing her against the wall, trapping her neatly with his arms on either side of her head as he nibbled at her ear, her neck, her lips, all the while easing the coat from her shoulders. "You would incite me to drastic action?" he said and thrust his tongue past her parted lips.

"What action?" she asked when he finally allowed her to breathe.

"To forget the bed and subject your back to yet another hard surface."

"And my . . . front as well," she said with an arch look at his groin. Taking advantage of his startlement at her brazen remark, she ducked beneath his arm and ran up to the second floor and down the hall to the inn's most luxurious corner bedchamber. She halted in the center of the room to wait for Dante to find her as he limped up the stairs, shouting threats to her person, each more outlandish than the one before.

And so she discovered that Dante knew how to play. She liked that too. There had been so many times in her life when she would hear squeals and laughter as her parents indulged in teasing games with one another. Now she understood the nature of those games, for if she came into view or someone else cleared their throat to announce their presence, her parents would stop abruptly, Mama with laughter sparkling in her eyes at Papa's sheepish expression. Inevitably at such times Mama and Papa retired early to their bedroom.

As she stood in the center of the room listening to his progress, Betina thought she could spend the rest of her life in such play.

Only with Dante.

She glanced around the room—at the canopied tester bed, high with a feather tick and elegant with a lacy counterpane and hangings yellowed with age, at the fainting couch upholstered in a slightly faded rose floral tapestry fabric, at the carved wardrobe and dressing table in cherry wood that was worn in spots and scratched in others. The signs of use and age seemed natural and likely a result of prolonged age and use rather than a sudden recognition of time passing. All in all, it was a lovely room in which to make love.

Perhaps she should build a fire. . . .

But no, she did not think she and Dante needed another source of warmth. Hugging herself, she remembered how it had been downstairs—so hot and frantic and . . . and . . . unbridled. She hadn't had time to think. She hadn't needed to really. Never in her life had she felt so free to be exactly as she was, without hesitation, without doubt, and without having to consider how she would be perceived or how her actions would be judged.

It struck her that she would not have felt so with anyone else, that it was Dante who gave her such freedom.

Only Dante . . .

She remained standing in the middle of the chamber, wondering what she should do while waiting for him to catch up to her. Fold back the bedclothes and climb between the sheets? Pose herself on the fainting couch with the lace counterpane draped seductively over her body? Sit in the chair by the fireplace? None seemed right.

Frowning, she realized that Dante had been silent for some time. Had he given up? Had he fallen and she'd been too preoccupied to hear?

But then she heard his uneven footsteps and it was too late to do anything but remain rooted to the worn carpet and meet his gaze as he pushed open the door and peered inside.

He walked inside carrying the pitcher and basin from his own quarters and pushed the door shut with his elbow, then stood as rooted as she, meeting her gaze in the moonlit room and nothing else.

She smiled tentatively, again feeling shy because he had changed into plain black trousers and she smelled soap and saw the smoothness of his face and his hair curling damply around his face and to the back of his neck.

He'd taken the time to wash and shave. For her.

Belatedly, she wished she, too, had cleaned up and donned a pretty nightgown and perhaps a ribbon in her hair. Lifting her hand, she tried to smooth down her hair, but it was wild around her and there was nothing to be done.

"Second thoughts?" he asked softly, and she thought he looked wary as he waited for her reply.

"No. It's just that I should have . . . um . . . made myself more presentable."

He seemed to relax then and walked over to the privacy screen in the corner to set the basin and pitcher down on the small stand in the corner. "I thought you might be uncomfortable . . . in places," he said haltingly and waved his hand at the stand. "You . . . bled . . . a bit."

"Oh!" She looked down at herself and felt embarrassment color her from head to toe. "Oh, yes. Thank you. . . ." Her voice trailed off as she turned one way and then another, not knowing what to do with herself. She certainly couldn't wash with him in the same room.

"I thought I'd get some brandy . . . or wine," he said in a rush and glanced away.

"Yes. Good idea. Wine would be lovely," she babbled.

He tossed her a wry smile and ducked out of the room.

Sighing in relief, she hurried over to the stand and pulled the privacy screen across the corner, feeling more the virgin now than she had earlier when she could honestly claim the distinction.

As she shrugged out of Dante's coat, she smiled and chuckled as she thought of how silly it was to want privacy to wash when she had made love with him on the kitchen table, then romped through the house with nothing to cover her nakedness but his coat and her own unruly mane of hair.

Anticipation began to build as she soaped and rinsed with a rough linen cloth over flesh sensitive with the knowledge of Dante's hands. Desire for him sharpened as her hands slowed and lingered on the places Dante had touched—her breasts, her ribs, between her thighs. . . .

Dante's footsteps echoed in the hall, loudly, as if he might be warning her of his approach.

Shivering with excitement, she scampered to the bed and slipped between the sheets, tucking them under her arms to keep them in place over her breasts.

"Foolish girl," a voice taunted, seeming to come from all around her. *"You sit in that bed all stiff and covered like a terrified virgin. Would you hinder him with concern for you? You were not so modest earlier."*

Heat radiated through her at the reminder, and without further thought, Betina pushed the sheet down with her feet, leaving herself covered only by airy lace and moonbeams.

Dante knocked on the door.

"Come in," she whispered and wondered if he heard her.

The door eased open and he stepped in, carrying a bottle from the cellar and two glasses. He paused halfway to the bed, his gaze covering her in a long sweep, then more leisurely as he exhaled slowly.

Her gaze fastened on the flesh exposed by his waistband, left unfastened at the top, and traveled down to the ridge becoming larger and more pronounced against the cloth.

He set the bottle and glasses down on the dressing table and traversed the distance between them at a stroll, his eyes drowsy and full of promises. At the side of the bed he released the fastenings of his trousers slowly, letting her see what lay beneath, then let them fall to the floor and stepped out of them. Still he stood before her, fully erect, seeming to reach for her with that one part of his body.

And she touched him with one finger, tracing the outline of him, feeling the strength and power of him. Her hand opened at the base of his shaft and enclosed him, and he threw his head back and breathed harshly in the silence. She moved her hand up over the length of him, then down again, and he groaned and grasped her wrist and held her hand away from him.

Her lips parted as he sat beside her, bent his head toward her, covered her mouth with his in an unhurried kiss that nibbled and explored and tasted until she grasped his shoulders and urged him closer . . . faster.

But he would not be rushed as he kissed her breasts through the lace, teasing her with light touches when she would have him take her into his mouth, touching her body with slow caresses, allowing the fabric to create friction against her flesh, driving her mad as his hands stroked her without uncovering her. And then his mouth followed the path of his hands, nudging aside the lace as his lips brushed each inch of flesh right down to her toes and back up again, pausing for a timeless moment as he urged her legs to part and slipped his fingers between, finding a place that seemed to be the center of all feeling, then entering her with one finger . . . two . . .

She wanted him to stop as his hand withdrew and he cupped her bottom and raised her hips, yet she couldn't find the words. As his mouth found her in a penetrating kiss, she writhed and thought she couldn't stand such tormenting pleasure, yet she wanted more.

She sobbed and thought there could be no more as he moved up her body slowly, so slowly, and he opened his mouth over her nipple and drew on her and bit gently and laved her with his tongue . . . and then did the same to the other.

She wanted him to take her hard and fast as his weight settled on her and he thrust inside her inch by inch, yet she savored the sensations of stretching to accept him, of closing around him and holding him tightly, of being filled by him. She wanted him to hurry as he withdrew slowly and then thrust deeply over and over again, yet she wanted it to go on forever as she arched to meet him and raised her hips to follow him as he retreated once more. She sobbed in frustration as his lips again found her breasts, her belly, and below, yet she twisted in pleasure at the heat of his mouth, the play of his tongue.

And she thought she would go mad as he rose above her and held her hips up and thrust into her hard and withdrew slowly, so slowly, and thrust again, deeper and faster until he groaned and stiffened and seemed to grow inside her. Heat filled her as his heartbeat seemed to become a part of hers, and the only air she needed was the breath of passion. She tightened around him and arched against him. Thought fled altogether as he plunged into her once more, then lay still, his hips cradled by hers, and all she knew was a pleasure that surrounded and consumed her.

She was dying, drifting free in a place as vast as forever, a place of darkness and mist and only the glimmer of star stuff to guide her back to awareness.

But in that first moment when time began again, she was aware of only Dante, seeming so vulnerable in her arms, yet trusting her to hold him. And she was aware that only with the man from her dreams would she know such magic.

Only with Dante would she know life and death and everything in between.

"At last you comprehend," Atropos said into the fire and chuckled at the way Betina searched the corners of the room for the source of the voice she heard. It had taken her a long while to perfect the art of amplifying her voice so that it came from all around the mortals rather than from inside their minds, but the stupefaction of their expressions when they heard her made the effort worthwhile. If they would play with unearthly powers, then they should know that unearthly powers would play with them in return. And it was rather amusing to nudge them this way and that and have them wonder if their actions were indeed inspired by their own thoughts.

She leaned forward and blew a bit of aurora dust into the flames. "You've dallied enough, girl. You are his and it is time for you to—"

"Atropos!" Lachesis cried as she ran into the room. "What are you doing?"

Atropos glanced at her sister in annoyance and cursed her lack of privacy.

"Yes, sister," Nemesis said as she entered behind Lachesis, with Clotho and Ilithyia behind her. "Tell us what you are doing."

"I am doing what must be done," Atropos said sourly. "I would end this thing so that we may go on to the lives of others."

"You are violating the laws set forth by the elders," Nemesis said.

"Your voice lacks true censure, Nemesis." Atropos narrowed her eyes on her staid and calm sister. "I wonder why." She smiled as she noticed that all her sisters suddenly found interest in furnishings they'd seen and used since the gods had reigned from Olympus. "It would appear that I may not be the only one guilty of interference."

Tears welled in Lachesis's gentle eyes.

Ilithyia lowered her head and plucked imaginary lint from her toga.

Clotho inspected a basket of fibers to be spun into thread.

Nemesis met Atropos's gaze. "I but gave Dante hope when he would have fallen into despair . . . and I was wrong to do so."

"I merely prompted Betina once or twice before Clotho wove filaments of memory into her thread," Lachesis admitted.

"I simply pointed out the obvious to them a time or two," Ilithyia said. "We are supposed to guide them, are we not?"

"And I simply nudged them when they seemed to be losing their way," Clotho said defiantly, though she did not look up from her task. "I have spent too much time mending and matching their threads to have them woven into lives in which they do not belong."

"And what were you doing, Atropos?" Nemesis asked as she settled in her favorite chair. "Besides indulging in voyeurism."

"I only made suggestions to them on the art of seduction." Atropos smoothed her girdle of gold inlaid with jewels. "They are both amateurs and stumbled too often into pride."

"I see," Nemesis murmured.

"Do you?" Atropos asked as she placed her hands on her hips. "Do you see how driven mortals are by useless emotions of pride and shame and guilt? Have you forgotten how they are ruled by their passions, both emotional and physical?"

"She is right, Nemesis," Ilithyia said. "A disappointing carnal experience can be a discouragement."

"Yes," Lachesis agreed. "You know how their minds flee in the face of desire."

"You give mortals too little credit," Nemesis admonished.

"Yes," Clotho added, "remember that their minds flee only if the mortals trust enough and love enough to allow it. In most instances it is a matter of free will and conscious choice."

"It is because of Dante's free will and Bess's conscious choice that we have a problem with them now, a hundred years after their souls should have begun anew," Atropos reminded them.

"The body is an instrument of the mind and the heart," Lachesis sighed, ignoring Atropos's comment, "especially in the case of Betina and Dante. Remember that he remained chaste for her. And remember that she is an enlightened female who knew what she was doing and why."

"Stop!" Nemesis rubbed her temples. "You give me a headache with your philosophizing. The issue is simple. We are forbidden to interfere."

Atropos snorted. "An outdated doctrine made by males too lofty to understand the nature of humans."

"Don't you see, Nemesis?" Lachesis said as she sat at her sister's feet. "We are the ones who were

not vigilant before. Clotho tried to spin Bess's thread with filaments too fine and fragile for human existence. The rest of us were too smug to keep good watch. Atropos has become too fond of using her shears—"

"I weary of this," Atropos cut in. "Much as I am loath to admit it, Lachesis is right. Because of our lack of interest in our tasks Bess bargained with death and Dante cheated it altogether. We have been compelled to interrupt time and tamper with the cycles of nature, as well as revive the sleeping forces of magic to ease our own consciences." She met the gazes of her sisters, each in turn. "At this point what is a little interference in the scheme of things?"

"Obviously I agree," Nemesis said, "or I would not be as guilty of whispering into mortal minds as the rest of you." She placed her hands on the high arms of her chair. "And Tim draws ever nearer to Betina and Dante."

"Yes," Clotho said. "And though I have woven his threads stronger than before and with far better clarity, I cannot give him more memory than he had a century ago."

"Meaning?" Atropos asked with arched brows.

"Meaning his threads were even more fragile than Bess's, and their color faded with the first touch of life. His mind was capable only of the simplest form of thought—"

"Emotion," Nemesis said.

"Yes, emotion," Clotho agreed. "He was capable of little else and certainly not of reason or regret. His memory was like a grain or two of sand in an empty jar. He is strong and intelligent now, but he

went completely mad after Bess's death, and I cannot give him more memory now than he had then.''

''In other words,'' Ilithyia said, ''though his former nature still dwells within his soul, it is like the woodland surrounding the inn.''

''Stagnant,'' Lachesis said sadly.

''And it may not awaken as Betina's has,'' Clotho added, ''for those filaments in his thread are so pale and weak that I can barely see them myself.'' She shook her head. ''They add nothing to the man he is now. If it weren't for those few pathetic strands carried over from his former life, I would say that he is again a new soul, rather than one strengthened and enhanced by the age and wisdom of renewed lives.''

''As Betina's are enhanced,'' Nemesis said.

''So,'' Atropos said as she glared at the fire, ''either Tim will finish the past, or it will haunt us all like a ghost that cannot find rest.''

''A proper analogy,'' Nemesis said.

''Can we not do anything more?'' Lachesis whispered.

''Of course we can,'' Atropos snapped. ''We can exercise our free will and make a conscious choice to meddle.''

''If we do, there can be no more whimsical indulgences on our parts,'' Nemesis cautioned. ''We must act together and face the possible consequences together.''

''And hope it is enough,'' Clotho said.

''Yes,'' Atropos said. ''By all means, let us hope it is enough.''

Part Three

Reckoning

"The past circling in on itself like a dog chasing its tail."

—Dante de Vere

23

It was like traveling from the present world into a past one—time rolling backward as Tim rode the final mile toward the village near Betina's property. Something didn't seem quite right, yet he couldn't identify what, other than the backward nature of the people and their farms and the general lack of traffic on the road.

For the third time in as many minutes he shifted uneasily in his saddle, feeling as if there was something he should know, yet didn't, feeling as if an emptiness were opening up inside him. An emptiness that could never be filled.

Shaking his head at such absurdity, he spurred his horse on, grateful that his love of all things equestrian had led him to learn from the Englishmen who frequented the Wishing Well Ranch. Otherwise their handkerchief-size saddles, high stirrups, and method of riding might have stalled his plans considerably. He had no wish to drive a carriage or to purchase a ride on a farmer's wagon. The sea voyage had been bad enough, with strange dreams visiting him in the night and a growing sense of unease plaguing him by day.

The captain of the ship had said it was the pitch and roll of the ship, but Tim knew better. He was neither squeamish nor given to illness of any kind. He had been riding horses since he was old enough to sit up straight and had even had a jaunt in a hot-air balloon once. And when he'd gone on a Grand Tour after graduating from university, he'd crossed the Atlantic and sailed the Mediterranean without suffering any ill effects.

He frowned, only now questioning why he had avoided England on his tour of Europe. At the time he'd told his father and Jacob that he saw enough of Englishmen in Wyoming and their homeland held no fascination for him. He'd known then how odd it sounded, when he should be interested in learning more about the country and culture of the very men whose patronage made the Wells Ranch such a success.

Yet he'd felt the same surge of panic when he'd stepped onto English soil that he'd experienced by simply discussing it. Only it was worse now, becoming stronger and more debilitating the closer he came to the village.

Still, what choice did he have? Etta had been right. Betina was his fiancée, and as such her future was his responsibility, or at the very least his concern. He was the logical choice to find her and take her home. God only knew what would have happened if Jacob had come as he'd threatened. The last time Jacob had blustered and boomed and tried to impose his control over Betina, she had defied him and crept away from the ranch like a thief in the night. He couldn't really blame her. Jacob had held her a pampered prisoner for far too long, limiting her vision of the world and keeping her to a slow walk through life when she wanted to run. Hell, even the most docile mare needed the freedom of a wide pasture or she would grow restive and intractable.

The last thing Tim wanted was a wife who dreamed of more than he could or was willing to give her. He loved Betina and planned to spend his life with her on the land he loved almost as much. And he had more faith in her than Jacob did, knowing that her mind could focus and concentrate when necessary. She read books and comprehended the layers of the stories far better than most, and she spent hours at a time studying one curiosity or another. Unfortunately Jacob did his best to see that she was dependent and under his control, and therefore safe from harm. To Tim's way of thinking, a year or so of separation from her was a small price to pay to have Jacob's hold on her weakened, not to mention the certainty that she would return subdued and ready—even thankful—to settle down with him in the simpler and more straightforward society of the western territories.

The road wound around a hillock and scaled another, and then the village lay before him in a shallow valley that could be better described as a dimple in the earth. His chest tightened as he stared at the houses and cottages and shops and the moor beyond. His breath came shallow and uneven as he heard the muted roar of the ocean crashing against the base of the cliffs. Cold sweat broke out on his forehead as his gaze fixed on the woodland that lay like a brooding shadow on the land in the distance.

He felt paralyzed as the horse plodded on, carrying him to a place he had never seen before yet suddenly, inexplicably feared.

The sound of hooves clattering on stone seemed distant and echoing as the dirt road gave way to a cobbled lane through the village. People paused to watch his progress with suspicious scrutiny and curious whispers among themselves.

His hands shook and his legs felt fluid rather than solid as he halted his mount to ask a woman for directions to the inn.

She studied him with narrowed eyes. "The inn ain't open for business."

"I know. I have business there," Tim said, supposing that small communities were the same everywhere, with each citizen believing it was an almost divine duty to be curious about and therefore protective of his neighbors. It was reassuring in a way. Betina would be safe here, and surely the nosiness of the citizens had begun to close in on her by now.

"Mmmm. Your business wouldn't be with the mistress, would it?" the deep-voiced woman asked.

"Since she is the owner, it follows that my business would be with her," he replied slowly, enunciating his words as if he spoke to a child.

"Might you be one of them solicitors that came through a year ago past?"

"As a matter of fact, I am a lawyer," Tim said. It felt rather good to acknowledge his status. At the ranch his law degree was secondary to his ability to manage the enterprise, and Jacob grew impatient when Tim took on an occasional case for a friend.

"So you came to settle matters at the inn."

"You might say that."

"All right then, I'll tell you how to get there. It's simple enough. . . ."

Tim could see it all as she described the way—the road that ran alongside and finally crossed the moor bordered by a sheer drop to the sea on one side and the forbidding woodland on the other, the road that led to the inn itself, the rosebush marking the dogleg turn just before reaching the yard. The vision was blurred and faded by mist, but it seemed familiar, as if he had been there many times before. He could smell the damned roses, and immediately his eyes watered and his nose burned. Roses always did that to him.

"Be wary, mind you," the woman said. "There's a curse on that place and the highwayman rides of a night, though he's been quiet this month past. May be that the girl will break the spell on him and the roses will bloom again."

"The girl? You mean Miss Wells?" he asked, yet felt no jolt of his heart as he usually did when Betina was mentioned.

"Aye. Wells is the name. And prettier than ever, she is. Saw her when she first came to claim the inn. That's the start of it, you know. May be that she will save the rogue from himself."

"What rogue?" he asked, knowing somehow that it was important.

"The highwayman, of course. Been riding that road for nigh on a century now, chasing the soul he lost when his Bess died and scaring the wits from good folk. Before that he just rode it to rob the gentry that passed by. Some has said he's caught it now and his hair is silver-shot and he walks with a limp. I wouldn't know since I was helping my sister with her confinement when him and Bess came to market. Caused a stir, they did."

The tale caused a stir in Tim's belly as well, twisting it up and wringing it out. He wanted information about Betina, but knew better than to jump off his horse and demand it. Even in Wyoming the citizens would have locked their jaws tight over such blatant intrusion from a stranger. He gathered his scattered wits and forced his voice to be calm, as if he were addressing an uneducated jury. "If he's such a nuisance why don't you call the authorities to stop him?"

"Ain't got no authorities to speak of," the woman replied.

"What of the army?"

"Don't want the likes of them around here. They killed our Bess sure enough, though it was her finger that pulled the trigger."

"Was this recent?"

"A hundred years, give or take." The woman sniffed. "*He's* been riding that road ever since."

A century. Good lord, he was dealing with a legend rather than actual fact. That meant that some opportunist had the foresight to exploit the local superstition for his own gain. And Betina, dreamer that she was, might be as easily taken in as the villagers. "Surely a group of your own men could chase him off."

"Why would they be doing that?" she asked, and Tim could swear she was horrified at the prospect.

"He is only one man, after all."

"Ain't a ordinary man. A legend, he is, and we're not of a mind to harry him."

"Why not, if he is terrorizing the area?"

"I told you—he's under an enchantment. No one knows what he might be capable of doing, and we ain't of a mind to find out."

"You said he walks with a limp," Tim said patiently, "and therefore he is vulnerable."

Again, the woman's eyes narrowed on him and Tim glanced away from her, shocked to find others walking toward them, some appearing belligerent and others merely curious. Oddly, it was the women who seemed the most hostile.

"The foreigner here thinks we ought to go after the phantom and chase him off . . . or finish him off," the woman said to the small crowd.

The wise thing, Tim knew, would be to ride on, but he couldn't. The fragmented tale the woman had told him held him in thrall. He had to know more, not out of fascination, but because of some deeper need . . . almost personal in nature. He told himself that it was Betina, of course, but failed to convince himself it was that simple.

"That so?" a man said and spat onto the ground. "Why should we do that?"

Tim frowned. Again something was wrong, out of place . . . or out of reason, more likely. "I simply suggested that if the man is a menace you should get rid of him.''

''You going out to the inn?'' another man asked.

''I am. Miss Wells is my fiancée,'' Tim said, deciding that he might get more information if he revealed his connection to Betina. People loved to gossip, and the dread overshadowing his thoughts prompted his need to know whatever he could find out about Betina and this highwayman.

''Oh!'' exclaimed another woman said with a high squeak in her voice. ''Tis trouble for sure.''

''Be silent, Prudie,'' a man wearing a blacksmith's apron said. ''Ain't no trouble at all.'' He stepped forward out of the crowd and looked up at Tim, his beefy arms crossed over a barrel chest. ''Do your business if you must, but be keeping in mind that we don't care for outsiders meddling in our concerns.''

''That's right enough,'' the woman who had given him directions said. ''*He's* one of us and you have no business with him.''

''You're confusing an old legend with a man who's obviously bamboozling you all.'' Tim knew it was a mistake the moment he said it, yet he felt reckless and disoriented for the foreboding that gripped him.

''Mayhap,'' Deep Voice said. ''But you mind that he's our legend and we take care of our own.''

Through the haze in his mind Tim recognized that the collection of villagers was fast becoming an angry mob, closing ranks around him and spooking his horse with their hostility. ''I understand,'' he said as calmly as he could and tipped the Stetson he wore even with the suits he'd worn since leaving the ship several days ago. He could imagine what the natives would think of Levi's and calico shirts. His hand-tooled boots with pointed toes and raised heels had received more than one stare during his trek across England. "And please keep in mind that I am here to take care of *my* own."

"Tim," a new voice said from the rear of the crowd. A voice Tim knew.

He searched the faces and found the timeworn and sun-dried features of a man who had been a part of his life for as long as he could remember. "Phineas," he said as he adjusted the angle of his hat. "Is Betina with you?"

"She be back at the inn cleaning away the dust and cobwebs, I'll warrant," Phineas said and ambled forward.

One woman gasped, and then another, and murmurs swept through the crowd.

"Dust!"

"Cobwebs!"

"After all this time!"

"Oh have mercy," The Squeaker cried, drowning out the others. "Tis true! Tis true!"

"Well, of course it's true, Prudie," Deep Voice said. "And time enough for things to be set right."

"We all knew it would come one day."

Suddenly the villagers drifted away in small groups, their heads shaking and nodding and bent close together as if they were telling secrets outsiders were forbidden to hear. Only Phineas and the blacksmith remained.

Disquiet swelled and pushed at Tim from the inside, yet he met Phineas's gaze. "I take it your arrival with Betina has caused quite a stir," he said evenly.

Phineas shrugged. ''Tis the nature of such things,'' he said enigmatically.

Tim had the feeling that Phineas spoke of ''things'' other than the villagers' superstitions. But it could be his imagination. Phineas was prone to speaking in riddles and mixing philosophy with tall tales to get a point across. He and Betina had learned more from Phineas's tales during their childhood than they did from their parents' dictates and stern lectures. ''I take it that since you are here, Betina is all right.'' If nothing else Tim knew that to be true. Phineas would never leave Betina alone if there was even a hint of danger.

''She be fine and there's naught to fret over,'' Phineas said. ''All's as it should be.''

''Good,'' Tim said and wondered why he suddenly had to fight for a deep breath, why he felt loneliness wash through him in a cold wave, why he felt smothered in grief.

''Ye might best be worrying about the loose shoe on your horse. He be coming up lame if ye don't let the smithy here take a look.''

''I'll see to it later,'' Tim said, wanting to escape this place, needing to outrun the panic that was like an illness inside him.

''Never known ye to be careless with your beasties, Tim,'' Phineas said.

The smith bent over and murmured to Tim's horse as he lifted its foreleg to examine the shoe. ''Tis loose, sure enough.'' He straightened and met Tim's gaze. ''The distance to the inn can be long and wearisome if you're afoot.''

"I be going back to the missy before the meat turns foul," Phineas said. "Smith will take care of the horse and ye can follow soon enough."

Before Tim could reply, Phineas was walking away and the blacksmith was leading his mount with Tim in the saddle toward his shop.

A coach rolled away onto the road in the direction of the inn, picking up speed as it clattered from cobblestones to dirt. Phineas sat high in the driver's box.

Tim stared at the cloud of dust all but obscuring the coach and wondered why Phineas hadn't offered him a ride. And why was he sitting atop his horse as if he were in a stupor while the smith led him wherever he might?

And then Phineas's assurance that "all is as it should be" seemed to take on ominous implications, as if Phineas's concept of what should be and his were not the same.

He dismounted in front of the smithy's and rubbed his hand down his face. This was insane—all of it. He had no reason to feel such panic and foreboding. He had a reputation for being calm and rational, and because of his ability to think on his feet he was also known to be an opponent to be avoided. Phineas of all people knew and respected him for those qualities.

He was tired, Tim told himself. He'd awakened long before dawn every morning to escape the dreams he didn't understand. Dreams of being helpless as he drifted in a dark void that swallowed every thought before it was fully formed, and the only constant was his love for Betina . . . his need to reach her before the darkness swallowed her too.

But they were just dreams and had no meaning.

Betina was safe, as Phineas said.

And Tim had no reason to doubt Phineas's word.

All would indeed be well as soon as he reached Betina.

"But when ye see things and feel them and think them, ye have to believe they might be true."
—Phineas

24

Tlot . . . tlot . . . tlot.

Betina stirred in Dante's arms as the sound of hoofbeats intruded into her dreams. She'd heard them many times before in her sleep—the sound of her phantom coming to her out of darkness and mist.

Tlot . . . tlot . . . tlot.

She frowned and nestled deeper into Dante's embrace as the sound grew louder, closer. The sound of not one horse, but several . . . and her phantom was lying naked beside her, his chest pressed against her back, his arms holding her close, his legs spooned into the curve of hers as he slept.

She opened her eyes and smiled at the warmth surrounding her, the sensual scent of Dante and passion in the air, the watery-gray light that was morning in this place filtering through the closed bed hangings of old lace. She remembered when Dante had drawn the curtains around the bed, enclosing them in a world where only she and Dante existed, where a mystical drift of mist mingled with their sighs of pleasure and touched their souls with a breath of magic.

Her smile widened at such whimsy, then faded as Dante shifted and his feet nestled more securely against hers.

Dante was here, no longer a phantom of the night, but her flesh and blood lover who did not leave her before dawn.

Dante's hand closed over her breast and his palm stroked her nipple in slow, tantalizing circles, as his other hand slipped beneath and around her to caress her at ribs and waist and lower.

Her body responded, her nipples swelling and moisture gathering between her thighs and her heart beating faster as she snuggled her bottom closer to him.

''Betina,'' Dante whispered against the back of her neck as his erection probed between her thighs. Finding her ready for him, he entered her slowly, his hand flattened on her belly, holding her still while he moved inside of her with small, maddening strokes.

As it always did when Dante was near, the world retreated, and she let it slip away. And she lay still, able only to feel as Dante caressed her breasts and teased her nipples, as he kissed the back of her neck and the lobe of her ear and the line of her jaw, as he moved inside her, slowly at first and then faster and deeper.

She couldn't see him and she couldn't move. Pleasure surrounded and consumed her as he withdrew and thrust once more with hard urgency, filling her, becoming a part of her for all time.

And then he, too, lay still, his body enfolding hers as she held him sheathed within her own embrace.

"Forever and a day would not be long enough to hold you like this, Betina."

She shivered as the weight of worldly concerns pressed on her heart, threatening to crush it. *Forever and a day.* Opening her eyes, she stared at the background of dreary gray light against lace curtains yellowed by time and knew that they would not have that long.

The bed curtains billowed slightly as the door opened. Dante tensed and held her fast.

"Ye be in there, missy?" Phineas called in a loud whisper.

She cleared her throat. "Yes, I'm here," she said.

"Trouble be coming soon. Thought you and Dante might want your clothes."

She wanted to sink into the mattress, disappear in it as she remembered their garments strewn over the kitchen table. They'd both forgotten that the world was always waiting to intrude and trouble always seemed to approach without warning.

Dante eased out of her and sat up. "What comes, Phineas?"

"Tim," Phineas said flatly. "He's in the village now, waiting for the blacksmith to fix a shoe that don't need fixing."

Again Dante tensed beside her.

Strangely, Betina felt resignation rather than panic at the news of Tim's arrival. It had only been a matter of time until someone came after her. And better Tim than Papa, since what came next was not her father's business. Unfortunately, it *was* Tim's. "Thank you, Phineas," she said.

"Weren't no trouble," Phineas said with a low chuckle. "The folk in town be rattling Tim so much he took my word about the shoe."

Resignation gave way to a sudden jolt of fear. "Did they tell Tim any . . . tales?"

"That they did, missy. That they did," Phineas replied with an odd note of satisfaction in his voice. "I be going to the kitchen to make some coffee now," he called as he pulled the door firmly shut behind him. "Don't be taking all day."

"Tim," Dante said without inflection as he sat on the side of bed, facing away from her. "Your fiancé."

"Yes." She sighed and sat up, her legs over the side of the bed, her back to Dante. So quickly magic disappeared, she thought. So harshly did life break enchantment. And now she and Dante could not even look at one another.

"You don't seem surprised that he's here."

"No."

"He's come to take you home."

"Most likely."

"And will you go?"

"I don't know what I will do." She squeezed her eyes shut, wishing that time would stop again as it had stopped for a century. That nothing would touch her and Dante and this place.

"I see."

"No." He didn't see at all, but her throat closed and she didn't know what to say to make him understand her fears and doubts. How could she make him see that she did not want to be trapped by his memories of Bess as he had been trapped here without his soul? That remaining with him without knowing whether he saw Bess or herself would be like losing her own soul? How could she explain that whatever part of Bess dwelled within her was only a part, the way the red cast in her hair was a part of her that came from her mother? How would she convince him that there was a world waiting for him that was far larger and more wondrous than the one he remembered? It all sounded like so much babble to her, and she would not babble to Dante.

She couldn't bear to sound foolish and flighty to Dante.

"I begged you once, Betina. I will not do so again."

She suddenly felt cold and numb. "You begged Bess, not me," she said and knew it was cruel. Pushing the curtains aside, she rose to escape the silence that descended like a thick and heavy fog, separating them, enclosing each of them in private thought and bittersweet memory.

"My mistake," Dante said as he, too, rose and strode for the clothing Phineas had left by the door. His gait was almost smooth, a sign that he was rested and healing well.

He did not need her any longer. His life had been renewed and he had found his soul again. He could go anywhere, do anything. He could pursue a new dream.

She had served her purpose. She could leave him now, without guilt or worry. . . .

But not without regret.

Betina bathed and dressed quickly and reached the kitchen just as Phineas poured three mugs of coffee and set them on the table. Dante was nowhere to be seen.

"Sit," Phineas said. "Ye'll be needing this before Tim comes."

Blindly, she sagged into the chair Phineas held out and reached for the mug in front of her, taking a quick, scalding sip. "Have you nothing else to say, Phineas?" she asked, wanting any confrontations between them to come now. She needed to feel something, even shame . . . or anger.

"There's naught to say, missy. Ye be a woman, and ye be knowing your own heart and mind. Ain't my place to be saying whether they be right or wrong." He sat across from her, then spooned sugar and poured cream into her mug.

"So you have no opinions?"

"Didn't say that."

"Tell me then," she said desperately.

"Seems to me that ye be getting enough opinions from other folk," he said and took a swallow of his coffee. "Ye have the courage to face your own convictions."

"My convictions are at odds right now," she said.

"Aye, true enough, I'll warrant. The past be like that—nosing in on the present and confusing folk."

"I am not Bess," she said vehemently, denying the doubt that haunted her thoughts.

"Mayhap. Mayhap not." He set his mug down and gave her a hard, level stare.

"You do believe it, don't you?" she said on a rising note of panic. "All of it. You think I'm Bess come back to life and that I belong with Dante."

"You're not Bess," he said matter-of-factly. "But she's a part of ye. The restless part that needs to be set free. Thought ye'd accept that by now."

"You believe, Betina, but you fear too much to accept the truth," Dante had said to her once. She knew now that he'd been half right. She did believe, how could she not? But the truth went beyond what had happened a hundred years ago, spilling into the present, confusing her. She could not accept the truth of what was happening now when she did not know what it was.

"Bess wants to be *free*." A short, hysterical laugh escaped her. "Free! I want to be *free*, too, Phineas. I came here to be *free,* yet I feel more bound than ever before. Tell me—how do I set us both *free*?"

"It'll come to ye." He cocked his head. "Tim be riding in now."

Angry and frustrated by Phineas's cryptic remarks, Betina swiped her hand across her eyes to dash away the tears that threatened to spill over. That made her more angry. She'd shed enough tears. She suspected that Bess had too.

"Betina, you have a guest," Dante said as he strolled into the kitchen, Tim behind him.

Startled, she jerked her gaze up to Tim's. His face seemed pale, and his jaw was clenched tight as it was when he controlled his temper to deal with a difficult guest or an inept employee.

"Your . . . friend let me in," he said and arched his brows in that way he had when he expected an explanation for slipshod work or a hangover on a morning other than Sunday.

"Um, Tim, I'd like you to meet Dante de Vere . . . Dante, this is Timothy Hawthorne, my father's manager."

"And Betina's fiancé," Tim said, scowling at her for the omission.

Dante nodded with an air of distraction as he studied Tim's blond hair, green eyes, and lanky build. "Hawthorne. I've heard a great deal about you."

"As I've heard about you," Tim said.

"It's gratifying to know that my fame endures."

"Infamy is more like it," Tim shot back. "Not only are you reputed to be a road agent, but a very old one as well."

"A road agent," Dante mused. "I like that. It sounds almost respectable."

"We hang outlaws in Wyoming," Tim said.

"As they do here, I assure you," Dante said with a mocking smile. "But at my 'advanced age' I no longer qualify for such an ignoble end. I have been retired for many years and now enjoy a solitary existence."

Betina doused her involuntary smile with a gulp of coffee.

"Coffee's on the table," Phineas cut in. "Ye be wanting a cup, Tim?"

"Yes, thank you, Phineas," Tim said as he edged past Dante and strode across the kitchen to lean over Betina and give her a peck on the cheek. "I've missed you."

His lips felt cool, almost clammy. She smiled weakly at him, yet her gaze sought Dante and remained on his form clad in black trousers, white shirt, and braces. He should look ordinary in such plain garb, but instead he seemed more dangerous than when he'd been decked out in his highwayman's costume. ''How are Mama and Papa?'' she asked, for want of anything better to say.

Tim straightened and picked up the mug Phineas slid across the table. ''Jacob is stomping around like his prize bull, and Etta is threatening to spit him and turn him over a fire if he doesn't calm down.''

''Papa sent you,'' she stated as she tore her gaze from Dante's.

''No. He was going to come himself. Your mother sent me instead.''

''Mama?''

Dante leaned his hip against the cabinet and listened without comment.

''She thought you would be happier to see me than your father.'' He raised his mug to his mouth, and Betina noticed then that his hands trembled slightly.

''Are you ill, Tim?'' she asked.

He raked his hand through his hair and sighed. ''I'm just tired. I've been riding almost constantly to make up for the time I lose answering the wires Jacob has waiting for me in every town that has a telegraph.''

''I've been a great deal of trouble,'' she said.

''No,'' Tim replied with a wry twist of his mouth. ''Jacob has been a great deal of trouble.''

''Wire?'' Dante said.

His softly voiced query caught her by surprise. She glanced up at him and instinctively gave him an explanation. "It's a means of communication—a code tapped out on a keypad and transmitted through wires strung between poles. There's a cable laid beneath the ocean connecting England and America." She watched him, knowing he was imagining it in his mind and marveling at yet another wonder of the modern world.

"You don't know what a telegraph is?" Tim asked.

"We are quite backward here," Dante said blandly. "Surely you noticed."

"I noticed." Tim sat down and leaned back in his chair. "The villagers are more preoccupied with old legends than with progress. They seem to think that Betina is responsible for your resurrection, so to speak." His stare hardened as it swept from Betina to Dante.

"Tim," she said quickly, "would you like something to eat—"

"Resurrection?" Dante interrupted. "Hardly appropriate, since I have not yet died and do not merit such divine privilege. I was, however, injured, and Betina was kind enough to offer me shelter here while Phineas nursed me back to health." He bowed toward Betina, then Phineas. "I understand that it is *de rigueur* in your country to play Samaritan to those in need."

His lips twitching, Phineas stared down at his mug.

"It's also *de rigueur* to have a revolver handy in case the one in need turns out to be a polecat."

Dante smiled broadly. "I assure you that Betina had not only a gun 'handy' but a wicked pair of shears as well." He pushed away from the cabinet. "If my hostess will excuse me, my own roof requires repair before the next rain."

"You're going to your cottage?" she asked dumbly. She hadn't thought of that, hadn't considered that he wouldn't stay here where she could see him, hear him, know he was near enough to touch.

"It is my home," he said as he picked up his cane from the corner where he'd left it the night before. And then he stood in front of her, lifting her hand to his lips and pressing a kiss to her fingers, a shockingly intimate and suggestive kiss that brought memories of other, more shocking intimacies they'd shared. It was all she could do not to snatch her hand away, to smile graciously and watch him turn and affect a subtle limp out the back door without another word.

Wood scraped against wood as Phineas pushed his chair back and rose. "I be going to feed the horses and clean the stable."

Betina watched him disappear out the door with mixed feelings of alarm and relief. As soon as she'd heard that Tim was on his way, she'd been anxious to talk to him, to settle things between them and set the course of her future. She was still anxious, yet she didn't relish the scene that would follow. Tim was a hard man, who knew what he wanted and usually got it. He loved her and wanted her and would not let her go easily.

"You're infatuated with him," Tim said bluntly.

She should have expected it. Tim had always preferred the direct approach and she knew that his banter with Dante was as subtle as Tim was ever likely to be. ''No, I'm not infatuated with him,'' she replied honestly.

''Surely you haven't deluded yourself into thinking you're in love with him.''

''It's not a delusion, Tim,'' she said, forcing herself to squarely meet his gaze. ''I'm sorry, I don't know a better way to tell you.''

Tim's face turned chalk-white and his mouth flattened. ''You don't know what you're saying.''

''You're wrong, Tim,'' she said, and suddenly she was angry. ''Contrary to the opinions of others, I always know what I'm saying.''

He inhaled deeply. ''All right,'' he said tightly. ''Then say it all. Tell me how you aren't going to marry me because you have an adolescent dream of living happily ever after with him in his *cottage*. Get it out of your system before I haul you out of this godforsaken place and talk some sense into you.''

Her chair fell back as she stood abruptly and faced him, her stomach churning and her fists clenched. ''I *do* love him. I am *not* dreaming of spending my life with him. I'm going to travel and make my own decisions and live my own life.''

''You love him, but you're not going to stay here with him,'' Tim intoned as she'd seen him do once in a courtroom. ''He's traveling with you then.'' He grasped her hand and she felt the clamminess of it, saw perspiration suddenly break out on his forehead. ''Dammit, Betina, don't you know that men like him feed off wealthy women?'' He shook his head. ''No, you wouldn't know. Jacob saw to that, keeping you like some princess in a tower.''

"Yes, Papa did," she said, "and when he wasn't around, Mama told me what I needed to know about life and marriage, and she told me about men who use women."

"Then you weren't listening," Tim replied reasonably, as if she were a child. "But since you claim to know so much, I'll be blunt. He'll use your body, spend your money, and leave you stranded."

"*You* aren't listening, Tim. Dante is not going with me anywhere. I'm going alone, except for Phineas if he wants, and I'll do just fine."

"You're coming home with me, Betina, or the next visitor you'll have will be your father."

"Is that supposed to frighten me? Do you think I can't say the same things to Papa that I'm saying to you?"

"You can say them, but Jacob won't give you the courtesy of listening. He'll just throw you over his shoulder and carry you home."

Betina glared at him, hating his calm voice, his calm expression, his calm pronouncements of truth. Papa would do exactly that, and the knowledge defeated her.

"I see you're beginning to think straight," he said, rising to his feet as he took her hand and twined his fingers with hers. He stood facing her, his other hand on her shoulder, caressing her gently as if to soothe her. "Jacob loves you and wants what's best for you. But he doesn't understand that he chased you away. Of course you want to see new places, try new things . . . even test your charm on a man—a stranger who hasn't loved you most of his life—"

She couldn't help it; she laughed wildly at the irony of what Tim said, what he believed. What would he say if she told him that Dante *had* loved her and waited for her for most of his life? A life that spanned more years than Tim could imagine. She clamped her hand over her mouth to stop herself from laughing, to keep from telling Tim what he wouldn't believe. To keep from convincing him that she indeed needed a keeper.

She reached up and skimmed his cheek with the back of her fingers, frowning at the clamminess of his skin, the tightness of his jaw. She had hurt him, and it had to end. Composing herself and her thoughts, she tried to ease the tension she saw in his face. "Tim, you've been many things to me—big brother, friend, protector. And you were my first love . . . maybe because of all those other things and the memories we share. I wish I could marry you, but I can't. I love you, but not enough. Not like I love Dante."

"You love him, but you're leaving him." Tim shook his head as if to clear it. "You'll have to do better than that, Betina." His voice seemed thick, his words a little slurred.

"All right, Tim," she said sadly, knowing she would be telling the truth, knowing, too, that once said out loud she wouldn't be able to call it back or convince herself that she might be wrong. "I'm leaving Dante because he loves someone else." She felt the misery of it opening wide inside her, threatening to swallow her. She lowered her hand and eased away from Tim, facing him with a steady gaze. "Her name is Bess, and he's waiting for her to come back to him." Brushing past him, she headed for the rear staircase, needing to escape this room that held so many reminders of a dream that couldn't come true.

"Betina," Tim called as she reached the first step.

She paused, but did not turn.

"I'm not giving up," he said firmly.

"I wish you would, Tim," she said and climbed the stairs to Bess's room.

Tim swayed on his feet as he lost sight of her, and it seemed as if she had faded away rather than merely climbed the stairs. He felt hot and cold at once, and he heard a *whoosh* in his ears, as if he were being sucked into a void. Sagging into the chair, he tried to catch his breath, to clear his vision, but he saw only hazy images he didn't recognize. Images that reflected pain and betrayal and blood . . . so much blood.

His head swam. He was falling, and then he was floating, with nothing above or below or around him. Nothing. He tried to think, but his mind was empty too, and all he knew was pain and betrayal and an instinct of sheer animal survival.

His eyes closed and trapped him in darkness.

"He remembers more than I expected," Nemesis said as she watched Tim slump over the table. "I had hoped otherwise."

"I too," Ilithyia said. "He suffered enough before with his mind almost empty, trapping his soul in the chaos of unreasoning emotion."

"And his heart feeling so much, needing so much," Lachesis added.

"Will it happen to him again?" Ilithyia asked.

"No, I think not," Clotho replied. "His threads are still strong and clear and vivid. It is only this one strand that influences him, and it is fragile."

"It is time to interfere," Ilithyia said with certainty.

"What do you suggest?" Lachesis asked.

"Phineas. He is wise, and his memories are complete and clear," Ilithyia replied.

"Yes," Nemesis agreed. "Speak to him, Ilithyia. His heart hears yours so easily. Tell him what must be done."

Ilithyia closed her eyes. Her body swayed as her lips moved, and her head tilted as if she were listening. She shuddered and opened her eyes and turned away to hide the quiver of her chin and the blush on her face. "It is done. Phineas knows what must be done. And he will do it well."

"Even so, this bodes trouble," Atropos said.

Nemesis nodded. "Yes. The time has come. Soon we will see if our charges find doom or redemption."

It wasn't over. . . . The knowledge was a beast in Dante's mind, feeding off him, devouring his belief that Betina was here for him, that she was his, would always be his. But the beast had come to the inn, with a congenial smile and firm handshake, and Betina had welcomed him with a familiarity that came from a lifetime of shared experiences.

The beast was Tim, an embodiment of the past.

Dante had felt unease before when Tim was mentioned, but he'd attributed it to Tim's position as Betina's fiancé. But then he'd recognized him, in spite of the obvious intelligence in Tim's eyes, the cultured and educated speech, the utter confidence of his bearing.

Tim, the ostler at the inn a century ago, a man in size, yet an infant in his mind. He and Tim had played together as children, and he had protected him when the squire's son tormented him with taunts and insults. And he and the estate gardener had seen to it that Tim always had fruit and decent clothing and simple activities to occupy him during the lonely hours. But Tim had died trying to warn him while Dante had gone on in the netherworld of existence while the years passed him by a hundred times.

Yet Tim's spirit, like Bess's, had somehow continued to exist.

But why? he wondered as he rode his horse through the woodland toward his cottage, the bundle of possessions he'd had at the inn tied to the saddle.

Why had Tim returned? Why was he such a prominent presence in Betina's life?

Dante feared the answer as he had never feared before.

"And truth, like dreams, is impossible to escape."

—Dante de Vere

25

The moor did not welcome Betina, but pushed her away with strong gusts of wind and the roar of an angry sea. The woodland, too, was inhospitable, with heavy mist that was impenetrable to the eye and damp, chill air that soaked into her bones. For two days in a row she'd left the inn, seeking escape from Bess's almost tangible presence in the third-floor bedroom, Tim's congenial and too loving manner, and Phineas's unsettling silence.

She wanted Tim gone and had told him so. If he was so understanding of why she needed distance between herself and her father, he was annoyingly obtuse about her need to be free of his gentleness and consideration, his small touches and reminders that he loved her. She'd told him about Bess in hopes that he would understand and respect her wishes. But he went on as if nothing had happened and their marriage would eventually take place.

Since he wouldn't leave she'd thought of packing up and going elsewhere, but Tim worried her. He looked ill with his paleness and hollowed eyes, and even his hair had lost its rich golden luster and lay on his head like bunches of straw. At times he seemed disoriented. Always he appeared troubled. Yet he protested otherwise, claiming that he was perfectly all right, and strangely, he would assure her that all would be well. He would see to it.

She needed Phineas, his wisdom and comfort, but that, too, was denied her as Phineas busied himself about the inn, saying little and offering nothing.

Dante was nowhere to be seen. When she'd gone upstairs after her confrontation with Tim, she'd found Dante's room empty, with not a single reminder that he'd been there for several weeks, befuddling her with his questions and logic, infuriating her with his insistence that she accept his role in her life both in the distant past and the present, and tormenting her with a love so vast and deep she felt she could not hold it. He'd awakened her to so many emotions and experiences, both her own and Bess's, that she couldn't sort through it all.

He'd awakened her to herself. And then he'd left her with nothing but doubts and regrets and memories. He'd left her free to do what she would.

She'd wanted freedom and she'd found it. Her life was truly her own now in spite of Tim's presence. Her mind was clear and open, yet loneliness was a thread that ran through her thoughts, stringing them together in a circle that held Dante in its endless embrace.

How she missed him.

Today she took refuge in the corner bedroom where she and Dante had created a world of their own for such a little while. She locked the door and kept silent as she wandered its boundaries and finally lay on the bed, hoping to find respite in a nap. But Dante surrounded her with his scent on the linens, and when her eyes drifted shut she dreamed of what they'd shared here. She felt it all—his presence beside her, his weight resting on her, his lips and hands caressing her . . . him, filling her and withdrawing, but always returning to her and muffling her cries with his mouth. She heard his voice as it had been in the aftermath. . . .

''Forever and a day would not be long enough to hold you like this, Betina.''

And then she saw his face, as if he really were in the room with her, and when she did not reply in kind she saw the emptiness he'd suffered for a hundred years in his eyes.

Her eyes snapped open and she sat upright, trembling at the force of the memories. She gasped at the sudden chill that came with the memory of the mockery in his expression and the bleakness in his eyes as he'd kissed her hand and left her.

''What did you expect?'' a voice snapped, and it filled and surrounded her. *''Your body received him, and then your heart turned him away. You gave him no explanation, no comprehension of why.''*

''He will always wonder,'' a different voice said, softer, more compassionate, yet censuring at the same

time. *"It will haunt him far more than Bess ever did."*

"You gave him a beginning, Betina," yet another voice said. *"But you have denied him an ending he can live with and accept."*

Her hands over her ears, she shook her head and bolted from the bed, from the room, from the inn. Her feet were bare, but she didn't notice the prick of twigs or the roughness of the ground. She swept her hair back from her face and ran into the woodland, and the mist closed around her, thinning in such a way that it seemed a path was opening in the air and closing behind her, guiding her, pushing her. Only the treetops were visible, rising above the mist, looming over her with hardened branches and brittle leaves like old wizards frozen in time. She did not know the way, yet she knew she would find Dante at the end of the path.

Dante sensed her approach as he always did when she was near—with a quickening in his mind, an awakening of his heart, a stirring in his soul. He heard her footsteps rapid on the ground, then silence as she halted. He gazed down at her from his perch on the roof, at her chest rising and falling with short, gasping breaths, at the way she stood so still beneath a tree with twigs and bits of leaves clinging to the deep ruffle of her simple blue dress, at her long, burgundy-black hair curling wild and free around her. She wore no shoes.

How barren time had been without her.

He'd waited for her, hoping she would come to him, knowing it could be no other way. He'd wanted to go to her, to make her accept, but he'd known how futile that was. He'd badgered Bess and made demands, and in the end he had lost her. Bess had been limited in the concept of love, the nobility and purity of emotion that dwelled in the most innocent of hearts. The kind of love one gave to God and country.

But he was just a man, too vulnerable to live without closeness and sharing and the bond forged when bodies expressed emotions impossible to define.

Bess had been as elusive and impossible to grasp as mist. She'd been his dream of magic and star stuff. Betina was the dream come to life, a woman of flesh and blood, heart and spirit appearing from the mist. She had a mind of her own and a heart made for giving and taking love in all its forms. That she loved him he was certain.

But she did not *want* to love him.

As she did not want to be here now. Her hair was wild and unbound and her gown was wrinkled, and he thought that she might have been dreaming again. That she had run to escape those dreams as she tried to escape him. Anger sparked and flared in him as he watched her standing tense and silent below him, poised to run.

He would not make it easy for her.

She looked up then and her lips parted as she saw him straddling the roof, his hair tousled from his labors, his chest bare and moist with perspiration, his legs exposed beneath the Levi's he'd cropped above the knees. He wished he'd known she was coming, wished he'd been bathed and properly clothed to receive her.

He wished he knew what to say.

Swinging his leg over the peak of the roof, he slid down the side and found purchase on the ladder propped against the outside wall. The work he'd done in the past two days had been good for him, loosening muscles bunched tight around his wounds. He barely felt the twinge of pain in his thigh as his feet hit the ground too hard in his haste to reach Betina.

He forced himself to walk slowly toward her, to stop at the well before she was within his reach, to wait for her to speak. But she only stood with her hand braced on the trunk of the tree, staring at him with a lost, confused look in her wide midnight eyes as the mist crept around her feet.

Turning, he lowered a bucket into the well, flinching at how loud it sounded when it hit the water below. He pulled it up again and dipped his hands in the cool water, splashed his cheeks and chest, reached for the sliver of soap he kept outside, then lathered and rinsed his face.

"I love you," she said.

He paused, controlling the shudder of relief that ran through him. He reached for the piece of linen he used for a towel and wiped it over his face and chest as he groped for words. "I know," he said, wanting to say so much more.

"You're a dream, Dante. A wonderful and dangerous and exciting dream. You've been with me forever. But—"

The anger burned hot in him at her words. He pivoted on his heel and strode toward her, reached for her, grasped her arms and jerked her to him, chest against chest, hip against hip. He didn't want to hear her "buts." He couldn't listen to her reasons for leaving him. And he knew—*he knew*—she planned to do just that.

He could not let her go.

Desperation drove him to hold her tightly, with one arm around her waist, and cover her mouth with his in a hard kiss that explored and claimed her with ruthless speed. He leaned back to look at her, to trap her gaze and hold it. ''Can you feel a dream, Betina?'' he asked as he swept his hand down her neck, released the ribbon that gathered the neckline of her bodice, slid it down her arms until only a thin camisole hid her from him.

She stared back at him without defiance, without protest.

Her silence maddened him. Her parted lips and panting breaths spurred him on. Tiny buttons gave way one by one until her breasts were bared to his touch. ''Does a dream do this to your body?'' he demanded as he stroked her nipples, feeling them harden and swell into his palm.

''No,'' she choked out and shook her head and arched into him as he bent to take her into his mouth. Her hands found his forearms and gripped him tightly, as if she would fall without him.

The mist rose around them as if it would shelter them from prying eyes, yet no one would be watching. No one had come here since the manor had been abandoned almost a century ago.

He straightened and reached for her skirt, dragging it up over her leg, then skimming her thigh and slipping his finger inside the opening of her pantalettes . . . inside her. ''Do you trust a dream to touch you like this?''

Her hands moved to his shoulders as she rocked her hips forward. "No," she said, and it was a whimper of need.

He caught her hand, and pulled it down, over his chest and waist and pressed it to his erection. "Can an illusion ache for you as I do? Can you hold it and feel the heat and want it inside you, knowing you *will* feel it hard and solid and *real*?"

"No," she whispered. "No," she cried. "N—"

He lowered his mouth to hers, biting her lips gently, laving them with his tongue, and she met him with her own as she stood on her tiptoes to get closer to his, to seal their mouths together in a slow, tormenting kiss that was like making love itself.

She stroked him, fumbled with the button at his waist, then all the others that held the Levi's closed over him, freeing him and taking him into her hand, wrapping her fingers around him in an urgent caress. She sobbed in frustration as his hand found her again, and she tried to get closer to him.

His hand probed more deeply, finding heat and moisture. She cried out against his mouth and sagged back against the tree, arching into him as he broke the kiss and nibbled his way down to her breasts, tasting one, then the other. He lifted her skirt and petticoats, and she closed her eyes and rolled her head from side to side as she drew him to her with her hands.

He stood poised to enter her, feeling her open to receive his thrust. "You shut me away from your sight, Betina," he said harshly. "Are you searching for your phantom?"

She bit her bottom lip and turned her head to the side, giving him her profile, showing him only a part of herself, the part that wanted to hide from the truth.

''Answer me,'' he said as he inched into her just enough to feel her tighten around him, straining to control himself, to keep from plunging into her completely, from taking her in any way she would accept.

''No,'' she said in a strangled whisper.

''Open your eyes, Betina. Look at *me.*''

She complied, showing him the desire in her eyes.

He pushed into her a little more. ''Can you feel a dream as you feel this?'' He thrust deeply, and she gasped and closed around him. ''Does a dream love you as well in the light of day as it does behind a veil of darkness?'' He cupped her breast and rubbed his thumb over the center.

''No,'' she replied as she grasped his waist and tried to pull him closer. ''It's you, Dante. Only you.''

Her answer inflamed him until he was blind with it. Too inflamed. Too blind. This was not what he had intended. Not like this. Nothing could be settled like this, in the heat and madness of passion.

He removed her hands from his waist and eased out of her and stepped back, clenching his teeth as her skirt brushed his shaft as it fell into place, covering her. ''Does your dream invade your sleep and take from you and leave you wanting more . . . like this?''

''Yes,'' she said, her voice subdued, her gaze still meeting his.

His breath caught and swelled in his throat at her honesty, at the love she displayed by making such a simple admission. ''Does a fantasy stand back and wait for you to accept him?'' he asked, hiding his fear behind a soft voice. Fear that she would leave him now, leave him with only a dream to hold. Deliberately he fastened the buttons of his Levi's, hating the pressure of unyielding cloth binding him, aching with it. "Does it vow not to touch you until you ask to be touched?"

"No, damn you," she said and pulled the edges of her camisole together, hiding herself from him.

"Tell me again that you love me, Betina," he said, struggling against the need to follow her, to take hold of her and never let her go. "Tell me, and then walk away."

"I love you," she shouted. "Heaven help me, but it grows inside me every day and it won't stop." Her chin quivered, but she didn't cry. "You should know that. But you don't, do you? You can't know how much love and trust it takes for a virgin to give so much, knowing . . . knowing that's all there will ever be."

"I do know," he said. "I thought I was waiting for Bess, never touching another woman, never really wanting one. But I wasn't waiting for her, Betina. I was waiting for you."

"No. Don't say such things. Don't make me believe what can't be true."

"I can't prove it," he said. "But it is true nonetheless." He smiled crookedly, mockingly. "I saved myself for the woman I love." He felt a flush rising up his neck into his face and looked down and nudged a pebble with his foot. "For you, Betina. It will always be you."

"I can't, Dante. I can't spend my life with Bess's shadow between us. I can't stop wondering who loves you the most—me or the part of me that is Bess. I'm changing, Dante, and I wonder if you will love me if I become less like her." Her thoughts tumbled out, one word on the heels of another. "It's magic here, but what of the outside world? What happens when the realities of living day to day replace the mist and rose petals and star stuff? You've lived in the past for a long time. What happens when you see the world and it is all new to you and you want to be new also? What happens if you decide you want to be free of the past?" She glanced around frantically, as if she needed to escape before she called back her words.

"Only the future will provide you with answers you can accept, Betina," he said, feeling calm, resigned, cold with the knowledge that she might not give him the chance to prove her fears wrong with a lifetime of sharing. "The path is to your left, Betina. It will lead you away from me . . . or toward me. It is—it always has been—your choice."

She turned and ran.

Unable to watch, he stared down at his hands, hands that could have held her, caressed her until she wanted to remain. He swallowed and blinked and raised his face to the sky, wanting to howl in the silence. . . .

Silence. No rustle of foliage. No footsteps fading away from him.

He gazed at the path, afraid to see the fog closing around her, taking her away from him, muffling even the sounds of her retreat.

She stood motionless, expressionless, her gaze riveted to a shadow among the trees.

"How very touching." A form separated from the shadows and the mist and walked toward them at a strolling pace, halting within close range of the Colt revolver in his hand.

Dante gazed at Tim with fatalistic calm as they stood in the clearing of the gardener's cottage—three points of a triangle, separate yet bound together. He'd known there had to be more. The past converging on the present, different yet the same—a cruel twist of irony to entertain the Fates.

He stared at Tim, at the hollow eyes and straw-colored hair spiking about his head as if he'd torn at it in a maddened frenzy. He looked like a scarecrow, mindless, driven only by emotion and love.

Tim . . . the instrument of reckoning.

Part Four

Redemption

". . . when a curse is broken, ye have a miracle."

—Phineas

26

"No. Oh, no. Not you too . . ." Betina moaned and covered her face with her hands. Her body shook and her teeth chattered as if she were freezing.

Dante saw the shock in her eyes, the knowledge of the past and Tim's place in it. "Betina," he said softly. "Go back to the inn, now, love."

"I think not," Tim said and swung the gun from Dante to Betina. "She will not slip through my fingers now."

"Aim your weapon at me, Hawthorne," Dante said.

Tim complied with a crazed smile. "You're quite right, de Vere. I would not have Betina hurt. You, on the other hand, have no purpose on this earth." His mouth twisted into a sneer. ''This is what you want, Betina? A tumbledown cottage on a crumbling estate? He has no occupation and lives off the fear of others.''

''Tim, listen to me,'' Betina said as she stepped forward, coming abreast of Dante.

''Listen to you?'' Tim said. ''Why? So you can lie to me again? He loves another, you said. Her name was Bess, you claimed.'' His voice became wild and shrill; his eyes bright with the fever of madness. ''Bess,'' he scoffed. ''You think I'm a half-wit to swallow such a tale? De Vere is not a man to love a woman who died over a century ago. A woman he cannot touch and scr—''

''Don't say it, Hawthorne,'' Dante warned.

''Why not? It's true enough,'' Tim shouted. ''I saw you, undressing her and fondling her as if she were a whore. And like a whore, she allowed it.'' He stared at Betina. ''Is that what you've been doing all this time, Betina? If I'd known you were so hot and ready for a man, I would have been happy to oblige you. I should have taken you anyway. Then you wouldn't have left me.''

''Tim, what's wrong with you?'' she asked.

''I've just witnessed my sweet and docile and *pure* fiancée opening her legs for another man; that's what's wrong with me,'' he snarled. ''I can forgive you though. It's Jacob's fault for keeping such a tight rein on you. And Etta's for filling your head with things you should have learned from me.''

She reached out to him. ''Tim, please take me back to the inn. We need to talk—''

''Not yet, Betina,'' Tim said and raised the gun, training the sights on Dante's chest. ''He treated you like a whore, and now it's time for him to pay. Isn't that right, de Vere?''

Betina moved swiftly then, lunging toward Dante, landing on her feet in front of him, shielding him. ''No, Tim,'' she said in a quiet, steady voice, cold with certainty. ''It can't end this way.''

''She be right, boy,'' Phineas said as he appeared from the side of the cottage. ''It can't end until ye make things right.''

''This has nothing to do with you, Phineas,'' Tim said.

''Hasn't it now?'' Phineas said as he sat on the brick wall of the well. ''Ye be holding a gun on the missy, and that be my business.''

''I won't hurt her, you know that,'' Tim said.

''I know lots of things, Tim.'' Phineas packed his pipe with tobacco, clamped it between his teeth, and calmly struck a match to light it. ''I know a story ye might like to hear.''

''You've grown senile,'' Tim said. ''And I'm not interested in one of your stories.''

''Mayhap ye ought to be interested.'' Leaning back against one of the wooden pillars supporting the well roof, Phineas raised his leg on the wall and propped his elbow on his knee. ''Ye can stand there and listen, boy. Won't take long.'' He looked up at the sky and the glow of a sinking sun burning red on the underside of gray clouds, then down at the mist that shimmered in subtle iridescent pastels as it grew thicker around their feet. ''Be night soon. That's when it all happened, ye know.''

''Goddammit!'' Tim shouted. ''I don't want to hear it.''

As if it were an afterthought of little importance, Phineas drew a revolver from the waist of his Levi's and propped it on his knee, the barrel aimed straight at Tim. "Ye be minding your manners, boy. Ye see, I'm closer to ye than ye are to them." He nodded toward Dante and Betina. "So ye just show some respect to an old man and his ramblings."

He gave Tim no chance to respond as he cocked the pistol and began to speak. "There was this old gardener who lived right here on this very place and tended to the manor grounds. And this boy was brought to him for learning a practical trade. He was fine and fit and had the ways of the gentry, and one day he brought home another boy what looked like a wet dog. The other boys had tried to drown him, y'see, because he be empty in the head and not good for much. But the first one, he took care of the half-wit and taught him what he could learn and made sure he was eating proper. Then there was the innkeeper's daughter, who was midnight and morning at the same time with her fair skin and black hair and dark eyes that looked like they had stars in them."

He puffed on his pipe as Tim glanced at Betina.

Dante didn't move, didn't react. He didn't have to. He knew the tale well enough.

"Now both these boys became men. The one—he was a gardener by day and a highwayman by night. The other had a way with animals, being close to a dumb animal himself, and he was hired by the innkeeper as ostler. Both loved the girl—the highwayman and the ostler—but neither knew the feelings of the other." Smoke billowed around Phineas's head and scented the air. "But one night the ostler saw his friend climbing the trellis to the girl's window and saw her greet him with a smile and saw him kiss the ends of her hair. Took the red ribbon right out of her braid, he did, and tied it around the hilt of his sword. "Look for me by moonlight,' he said. 'I'll come to ye by moonlight.' And then he rode away to do his night's work."

The sky above the trees to the west seemed to burst into flame as the sun reached the horizon.

Phineas nodded and smiled, as if he were paying a compliment. "Now the poor ostler couldn't think like other folk, but he felt more than most, his heart being bigger than his mind. He ran to the redcoats and told 'em about the highwayman and where they could find him. But the redcoats, knowing how slippery the highwayman was, went to the girl's room instead."

Tim trembled suddenly and had to support the revolver with both hands.

"They tied her up to her bed and stuck a musket beside her with the muzzle pointed at her chest, thinking it would keep her quiet, y'see. But they didn't know her. They didn't know that she was afraid of most everything, even the man she loved. So when she saw him through her window, riding to her as he promised, she got her finger down on that trigger and pulled it."

"He betrayed Bess?" Betina choked.

"No!" Tim screamed and covered his ears with his hands, the Colt dangling loosely from his forefinger. "I betrayed the highwayman. He was nice to me, and then I saw him climbing the trellis to her window." Tears streamed down his face and he swiped at them with his sleeve like a child.

Betina retreated until her back pressed against Dante's chest. He reached for her to set her out of harm's way, but she grasped his wrists and pulled his arms around her waist and held them there.

The light changed from gold to silver as twilight took possession of the sky and Phineas continued. "The ostler knew what he'd done and that the highwayman be riding into the same trap when he heard about the girl shattering her own heart to save him. Mayhap for the first time in his life the ostler had a clear thought." Phineas glanced from Betina to Dante and finally to Tim, his gaze steady on him. "He heard Dante riding back to the inn after he heard of what Bess did. Heard him and ran into the road to stop him . . . or to protect him . . . don't be knowing which. He died there, taking a ball meant for Dante."

"Making things right," Betina whispered.

"Twould appear so," Phineas said. "He were a good and gentle soul, caring for the animals and carving toys for the children. Dante taught him how and gave him a knife."

Tim reeled backward and righted himself. "I love her," he sobbed. "I love her!"

"That's what the ostler said to the old gardener after the girl died," Phineas said as he puffed on his pipe and watched Tim through the haze. "And the gardener told him that he didn't love her enough to want her happiness . . . but twasn't his fault, I be thinking. His mind was that of a babe's. He were birthed hard and were blue and still for a long while before he learned to breathe."

"She wasn't supposed to die for him!" Tim babbled. "They weren't supposed to kill anyone. They promised me they'd just take him far away. They promised."

Phineas tapped the bowl of his pipe on the heel of his boot. "Ye be moving away now, missy."

"No, Phineas," she said. "If it is to happen again, then Dante and I will be together this time."

"Get away, Bess," Tim said. "He deserves to die. He made you love him, and it was him that killed you. Him!"

Gently, Dante twisted his wrists from her hold and lowered her hands to her sides. Inhaling the rich rose scent of her, he pressed a kiss to her hair. "I asked for your love, Betina, not your life," he whispered and set her aside.

She ran to a point halfway between Dante and Tim, out of reach of both of them, yet still in the line of fire. Standing sideways, she glared at Dante. "How noble you are," she spat. "Or is it selfishness that prompts your martyrdom? Do you think you can find redemption by dying because of me?" Her hair whipped around her face as she turned her stare on Tim. "And you. I wouldn't have thought a man like you would give in so easily to the past, Tim. I wouldn't have thought you would give in to madness at all. Not when it isn't even *your* madness." Her chest heaved and anger burned red on her cheeks.

Tim cocked the pistol.

"Be ye mad, boy?" Phineas asked as he advanced on Tim. "Be ye mad enough to kill the missy?"

"I'm not insane," Tim said as his hand wavered and sweat rolled down his forehead and into his eyes. Again he used his sleeve to wipe away the moisture.

Dante took a long stride to Betina and shoved her roughly away as Tim tracked him with the gun.

She stumbled and fell to her knees. She looked like a dream just then, with the mist swirling around her to her waist and the approaching twilight softening her image, blurring it. She tried to get up and sobbed when she couldn't escape the mist, as if it were holding her, protecting her.

Dante smiled and stood with his feet braced wide apart, staring at the barrel of the pistol, knowing he couldn't move fast enough to disarm Tim, knowing that all he could do was wait for an end . . . or a beginning. Either way little would change, and Betina would have her life and her freedom.

"I'm not insane," Tim repeated and shook his head as if to clear it.

"Aye," Phineas said. "Ye not be insane, boy. Tis but a memory holding ye. Tis all of what's left of that other Tim, hanging on to ye, wanting ye to make things right for him."

"You can't know," Tim said. "How can you know?"

"I be knowing what I see and what I hear and what I feel," Phineas said. "I be knowing ye and Dante—" His brows descended in a frown as he abruptly clamped his mouth shut, then opened it again. "I be watching ye since ye were in leading strings. And I be grieving that ye want to harm another."

"Tim, it's me—Betina. Don't you know me?" Betina asked and tried again to rise to her feet. But still she failed and sank back onto her heels, waiting as Dante waited.

Dante closed his eyes as the memories came to him. Memories of a figure running into the road, running toward him and shouting incoherently. But then the shots had been fired—a dozen, a hundred shots—and the figure had fallen to the ground. So many lives lost to hopelessness. So much love sacrificed because of a reckless young highwayman who loved the thrill of the chase more than he valued life.

He walked toward Tim, steady and calm as Tim held the gun pointed at his chest. "Too much has been lost," he said. "I would end it now, Hawthorne . . . one way or another. Either kill me or put your weapon away."

Dazed, Tim squinted at Dante, then stared down at the gun as if he'd never seen it before. "Make things right," he slurred. "Didn't mean to kill anyone." He met Dante's gaze. "Thought they'd just take you away . . . dead . . . we're all dead."

"Tim," Betina called. "It's over. They're gone-all of them. We aren't them, Tim. Let them go. Come back to us. Please, Tim."

The pallor of Tim's flesh faded, replaced by a more healthy color, and his eyes cleared as he lowered his hand and the gun dangled at his side. He stared at each of them one by one, with an expression of confusion and horror. "Oh, God. What have I done?"

Betina gained her feet and walked toward them. "You haven't done anything, Tim. You're just angry with me, and we'll talk about it when we get back to the inn." Gently, slowly, she took the gun from his hand.

Phineas disappeared into the trees and returned leading Tim's horse.

Tim ran his hand over the back of his neck as he stared at the gun in Betina's hand. "Damned strange." He shook his head. "Couldn't hurt a fly, you know. I learned how to use that"—he nodded at the gun—"but never did—not on anything living. Won't even go hunting with Jacob."

"I know, Tim," Betina said.

"Damned strange. Don't know what hit me. . . ." Tim's voice trailed off and he pitched forward.

Dante caught him and lowered him to the ground as Betina fell to her knees beside him, checking his pulse and brushing his hair back. "He's unconscious."

"He weren't resting these past days, missy," Phineas said. "Sleep will fix him, I expect."

Alarm widened her eyes. "He won't come back, will he—that other Tim?"

"Ain't no other Tim that I can see, missy. Was just a jealous fit eating at him. Tis all done, and we needn't be dwelling on it."

"All done, Phineas?"

"Twas what I said," Phineas said.

Tim opened his eyes and focused on Betina. "It's all right, Betina. I'm just tired."

She pressed his hand to her cheek. "I'll take you back to the inn. You can rest now, Tim. I promise."

Phineas helped him to his feet and onto his horse. "Ye be sitting behind him, missy, to keep him from falling off." He lifted her up behind Tim and grasped the reins.

Betina turned to Dante, staring at him as Phineas led the horse into the woodland . . . into the mist.

He stood by the well, watching her until he couldn't see her any longer, and then he turned to rest his forehead on the wooden support, his shoulders heaving in grief for all the yesterdays that haunted them all, for all the tomorrows that lay in shadow before him.

He did not come in the dawning;
he did not come at noon . . .
The Highwayman—*Alfred Noyes*

27

Tlot . . . tlot . . . tlot . . .

Betina heard him riding toward the inn, but he always stopped at the bend in the road that turned into the yard. For three days and nights she waited for him to come to her, but he only sat atop his great dappled horse, staring at her window with the rosebush a shadow on the road beside him. And when she turned out her light, she heard a howl of anguish riding on the night wind as he rode away.

Last night she'd lit many candles in the corner bedroom and opened the curtains, letting him see her as she brushed her hair. He'd watched her as he sat so still in his saddle, as she stood so still in the window light with her hair swept over her shoulder, the ends curling at her waist like a crooked finger, beckoning him.

And he turned and rode away in silence like the phantom of her dreams.

The day passed slowly as she busied herself cleaning the inn and then wandering over the moor, picking fresh heather to scent the air and add a splash of color to the rooms.

The sun set and the moon rose new, a graceful crescent ship sailing in the indigo sky, casting a ribbon of silver light along the road. The trees stood as they always did, stooped in gray and black mourning with their leaves stiff and brittle on the branches, and mist lay on the ground in iridescent whorls that shifted with every breath of air that moved over the land.

She stood in the shadow of a tree behind the rosebush, waiting for Dante, knowing he would come again. A cloud drifted above her, cutting off the ribbon of moonlight at the base of the rosebush. She smiled, knowing it was magic.

Knowing that she had learned from the past and would use those lessons well to shape her own future.

Tlot . . . tlot . . . tlot . . .

Her heartbeat matched the rhythm of the horse's hooves as a familiar warmth flowed through her veins. She savored the sight of Dante approaching, a black cape spreading out from his shoulders and onto his ghostly horse, which pranced smartly and tossed its mane with impatience at such a slow pace.

Tlot . . . tlot . . . tlot . . .

The sound ended abruptly as Dante halted his mount and lifted his gaze to Bess's window, dark and empty and abandoned, then to the corner of the second floor, where a single candle cast golden light into the darkness. His head turned toward her suddenly and he stared at her, though she knew she was only a shadow among the trees.

She didn't know what to say to him. And then she couldn't speak as something stirred inside her, and it filled her and held her motionless. She felt it—sorrow and fear slipping away, helplessness and resignation fading out of her, then joy spreading like a smile inside her, rising in her, filling her until she thought she would burst with it. She pressed her lips together to contain her cry as it drifted away from her, leaving her only with the love she felt for Dante. *Her* love.

She stepped from the shadows and stood by the rosebush. "I love you," she said quietly.

"I know." He looked down at her with a brooding silver gaze. "And what of Tim?"

She should have expected that Dante wouldn't waste time waiting for answers. He'd waited too long already. "He left today. I will miss him."

"You will see him again when you return home."

"No. He's giving Papa his notice and then he's going to open a law practice . . . somewhere else."

He sighed and stared at the inn, at the light in the corner window. "He left you because of me."

"He left me because he wants me to be happy."

"In your independence," he said with a small smile.

"Yes, in my independence," she agreed. "I've waited a long time for the freedom to make my own decisions, to live my own life."

His shoulders heaved and his jaw bunched, and still he did not look at her. "I wish you well then." He adjusted the reins and tensed his leg and the horse began to turn.

"Dante, don't go," she said. "Please."

His gaze snapped to hers. ''Don't go? What do you want from me, Betina? What punishment is this? What new hell must I endure to gain *my* freedom?''

''We all are bound to something or someone, Dante. The only freedom we have is in being able to choose which path we will take into the future. I've made my choice.''

''And I made mine,'' he said flatly. ''A century ago. I chose to cheat death and curse the Fates, and I rode the same path night after night.'' He gave a harsh, bitter laugh. ''I am still riding the same path.''

''Why, Dante? Why do you ride the same path? Why are you here?''

''To see you,'' he said simply. ''To nourish the vain hope that you will see me apart from the past.''

''I see you, Dante,'' she said and knelt beside the rosebush. ''You're in every thought and every dream I have. You fill my world until there is little room for anyone else.''

''I have no wish to be in your bloody dreams.'' He swung his leg over the horse's neck and slid from the saddle, his expression hard and uncompromising, a dramatic study in silver light and midnight shadows. ''Dreams are for memories of the past and hopes for the future. I have no use for either. One day at a time is enough for me, Betina. One day of knowing I am alive, knowing that . . .'' He paused and cleared his throat, as if he felt awkward and unsure, as if perhaps the subject were too new for him and he had to fumble through the words. ''I want to be in your life, Betina. Without you I am nothing but a ghost wandering through visions of the past.''

''I know.'' She touched a stem on the bush, finding a stiff gray bud and cupping it with her hands. ''For years I felt as if I were dead inside, except when you came to me in my dreams. I won't become like that again.'' She met his gaze. ''I would have died *with* you the other day, Dante, because I couldn't imagine life without you. But I won't die *for* you, neither in body nor in spirit. I can't be a blind puppet anymore, seeing only phantoms and doing what others want without thought for what I want.''

''What are you saying, Betina?'' he asked as he knelt across from her, the bush between them. ''What do you want?''

She opened her hands around the bud and it was soft and full and blooming, the petals a silvered-rose color in the moonlight. One by one, the leaves on the stem lost their shriveled texture and became a rich, fertile green. She met his gaze and wanted to weep for the beauty in his face, the wonder, the hope he had forgotten how to feel. ''I want life, Dante. Real life, where the only dreams I have are of being loved and trusted and respected, of having children and living in my own home, of replacing the curtains in the parlor and buying a range for the kitchen . . . of how you will be beside me during the day and how you will make love to me at night.'' She smiled at the frown that passed over his face at the mention of a range. Later she would explain it to him—much, much later. Cupping another bud, she felt it open in her hands.

''Do you think I wanted anything else?'' He caught her hands in his across the rosebush.

''I don't know,'' she said honestly. ''You never told me what you wanted, except my body and my love.''

''They aren't enough, Betina,'' he said. ''They were never enough.'' He folded her hands over a third bud. "I want you to share your bright spirit and your passion, your sorrows and your needs with me." He smiled then. "And your suffragist opinions . . . and your body and your love."

"All right, Dante," she said as he opened her hands to reveal another blossom, another stem with leaves that were green and supple. "I can say that now. I am free to say it." She smiled at him and stroked his cheek. "Bess is dead."

"I didn't ask it of her, Betina."

"Dante," she said gently. "I saw it in a dream after I arrived at the inn—her life slipping away from her as she watched you turn your horse and ride away. She was smiling you know."

He squeezed his eyes shut and his mouth twisted. "I would have stopped her if I'd known. I wouldn't have ridden away." He jerked away from her and stared up at the sky, and she saw the glisten of moisture on his cheeks. "But . . . I . . . didn't . . . know."

Betina clenched her hands at her sides to keep from reaching out to him. She wanted to hold him and feel the tears he shed, but he held himself withdrawn from her as he struggled with his grief and guilt. "I felt her die, Dante, when you rode up to me and stared at my shadow in the trees. Inside, I felt her die and drift away. She is no longer even a small part of me. What I say to you comes from me. What I give you is mine to give. What I feel for you comes from me." She ran her finger over the soft petals of the rose. "I couldn't be sure of that until I knew she was gone."

He lurched to his feet, drawing her up with him, leaning across the bush to pull her into his arms. "She died so that I might continue with my life. I think . . . I think she knows that you are my life, and it has given her peace." His shoulders heaved and his body shuddered, and she held him tightly, felt his tears on her shoulder, and shed some of her own for a woman who loved so much and gave so much and waited so long for the ending of a dream she could not fulfill herself.

"Betina, you gave her peace, and you offer me love. I . . . oh, God . . . I never thought to know such love." He cradled her face with his hands, touched her lips with his, skimming them gently back and forth. "I search for the words, but there are none worthy of what I feel for you."

"Then show me, Dante," she replied as she chased his lips, teasing them with little nips and hoping to capture a deeper kiss. "Share what you feel with me."

"I would gladly," he said against her mouth. "If I did not fear that Phineas would come upon us again."

"Phineas is gone," she said into his ear, then bit the lobe gently over and over again. "He left with Tim. He has . . . decided he doesn't care . . . for retirement and wants to manage the ranch . . . until he can train another. He thought my husband might want . . . the . . . position."

He pulled back and held her at arm's length. "You're here alone?"

She drew up to her full and inconsiderable height. "I am an independent woman, who requires neither bodyguard nor chaperone." She pulled on the ribbon that gathered her neckline and slipped her dress down one shoulder. "My body, however, requires immediate attention . . . here . . ." She tugged on his hand and guided it to her breast and sighed as he swept her body with his other hand. ". . . and yes . . . there too."

Stepping around the rosebush, she unfastened his cloak and spread it on the ground in the same spot they'd lain before, then stood before him, waiting.

"Out here, Betina?" he asked, and his grin flashed white as he began to unbutton his black silk shirt.

"We both lost our virginity on a kitchen table, Dante, and then there was the tree." She lowered the bodice of her dress and it fell in a pool of blue around her feet.

"The tree." He sobered and paused in opening the cuffs that gathered in full, flowing sleeves, and she knew he was again groping for words.

She didn't want to hear them, didn't want the past to intrude on this night. "I think you must have been horribly bored doing nothing out here but riding about and chasing your soul. It's time you learned that there are other things to do in the moonlight." Her camisole fell open, revealing her breasts, and her nipples swelled and tightened into erect buds, reaching out for his touch.

He shrugged off his shirt and pulled her to him, held her close and tight against him. "I have found my soul, Betina. It came to me out of the mist after I felt it mingle with yours."

"And mine awakened when I saw you in your ridiculous highwayman costume." She slipped her hands into the waist of his black trousers and worked the fastenings free.

"Do you like this one better?" he asked as he loosened her petticoat and it, too, pooled at her feet.

"Mmmm. All black and very dramatic in design. The cloak is a nice touch." She worked his trousers and underdrawers down his legs together, following them until she was on her knees before him, her mouth tracing the thin line of silky hair down his belly, her tongue circling the tip of his erection.

He sucked in his breath and lifted her to her feet. "Betina, do not press me so. I would linger tonight."

Smiling, she stood obediently while he removed her pantalette and gasped as he followed them down, lingering along the way to lightly nip at her nipples until she held his head, urging him to do more than tease. He moved his mouth lower and lower, and his tongue circled a place that sent streaks of sensation through her body. She yanked on his hair. "Dante . . . I don't . . . think . . . I can . . . linger."

With a wolfish grin, he rose and turned to the bush beside them and plucked a flower.

"What are you doing?" she cried in dismay.

One by one he separated the petals from the stem, careful not to crush or tear them, and sprinkled them over his cloak. "I am making some magic of my own," he said.

Something grew within her chest—a pleasure of the heart, she thought, poignant and overwhelmingly sweet, filling her until there was no room for air, until there was room only for love. "Can you make mist as well?" she asked breathlessly.

"Alas, I cannot," he said. "But I would see you, Betina, clothed in moonlight and the flush of passion." He caught her mouth in a kiss, deep and potent and rich with tenderness. His hands found her breasts and her knees buckled. He lowered her to the bed he'd made with his cloak and followed her down.

The scent of roses drifted around them as her hands caressed his chest and her tongue bathed his small, flat nipples, as his mouth drew on hers and warmth became heat, as he kissed her again and again and his hands stroked the insides of her thighs then inside her, and his shaft pressed into her belly. . . .

She panted and sobbed beneath him and opened for him. "Dante, I can't wait."

He raised up above her, the tip of him poised against that tiny spot that drove her insane with wanting. "Can't you, love?" he murmured and thrust into her.

He was hard and solid and real—inside her, around her, above her. His head was thrown back as he plunged into her again and again and again, and his mouth descended on hers, his breath mingling with hers, his heart pounding against hers, harder and faster.

Ripples of pleasure became waves washing over her and she felt him tense, his body tight and rigid, his flesh as hot as hers. Silence fell over them. Hearts paused and breath hesitated and time stopped, and nothing existed but Dante filling her with life.

He buried his face in the hollow between her neck and shoulder, and she held him closely, her fingers grazing over his back and through his hair.

A shaft of moonlight fell through an opening in the trees and bathed the rosebush in ethereal light. "Dante," she whispered, awed at the beauty of it. "Look . . . the bush."

Raising his head, he followed her gaze, and she felt him tremble.

Every bud had come to life. Full, deep-pink blossoms opened. Dark, shiny green leaves smoothed out and glistened in the moonlight. The heady, intoxicating fragrance of roses filled the air.

"They are pink again," he mused, "and no longer tainted by the blood of the past." He eased away from her and sat beside her in profile, staring at the roses, his hands dangling between his raised knees. "I felt as if I were the only person on earth, even as I knew I was no longer a person.'' His voice was thick with emotion. ''I was empty, without a soul, without feeling or clear sight or taste or smell. I never suffered hunger, yet that was a hunger in itself—for food, for love and passion. I knew only anger and grief for a hundred years, and they fed off the spirit that was left me.'' His shoulders lifted and fell and his voice broke. ''I had no hope, Betina. I had died, and only my body survived. Like the roses and the woodland survived, without vitality and growth.''

Tears gathered in her eyes as she listened to him, to his voice shaking with the memory of so much pain and loneliness. Her heart twisted in anguish as his throat convulsed.

He turned toward her. ''I would do it again, Betina—for a hundred years or a thousand—if I knew that I would find you at the end of it.''

''I know,'' she said, and the tears spilled over and ran freely down her face as she looked up at him, at the shadow of stubble on his face, the scars that marred his flesh, and the silver threaded through his hair. She'd seen him as a highwayman, flamboyantly garbed in outmoded clothing and weapons that twinkled in the moonlight. He'd occupied the inn as an engaging rogue, who played with his shadow as if he were a baby discovering all the parts of himself. He'd come to her tonight looking like her phantom, dark and seductive in his black shirt and black trousers and flowing black cape. He'd terrified and charmed her, mocked and seduced her, infuriated and enchanted her. He'd appeared larger than life to her, yet he *was* her life.

He was Dante de Vere, a man—just a man—who trembled with the pleasure of sensation and wept openly in grief and guilt and regret. A man filled with the wonder of simply feeling, of realizing his dream of real love and honest sharing.

A man who even now dressed her against the chill and lay down with her on the ground, holding her as the moon sailed across the sky, speaking to her eloquently of love with murmured words and intimate caresses as they watched dew collect on the roses and glisten like star stuff reflecting the light of dawn.

"It's over," Betina sighed and nestled into his embrace. "Our long night is over, and tomorrow is here. . . ."

Dante kissed the top of her head resting on his shoulder and stroked her hair with his hand. "I have sat on this very spot and stared through the portal between wild moor and dormant woodland." He turned toward her, his face so close to hers, his voice a reverent whisper from his soul. "I have watched the light of the approaching sun spread ribbons of color across a sky still dark in the west—night mingling with day, yesterday joining with tomorrow . . . an end and a beginning."

"And it is ours," she sighed. "A gift to be shared."

"Always," he murmured, and his eyes drifted shut in sleep and in peace.

"Forever and a day," she whispered and pressed a light kiss to the corner of his mouth before, she, too, fell asleep to dream of the future.

Epilogue

"I could not ask for more," Ilithyia sighed as she watched Betina and Dante sleeping, their bodies entwined, Betina's hair spread around her and flowing around the roots of the rosebush.

"Nor I," Clotho said as she examined the threads she'd woven so carefully for so long.

Atropos smiled as she had not smiled in a millennium. "It makes me wish I was mortal . . . almost."

"Yes," Nemesis said. "To feel as they do, to discover as they have that magic dwells in the heart, in faith and trust and love. To dream and have the power to make those dreams come true."

Lachesis waved her hand over the flames, advancing time, seeing what Betina and Dante had yet to dis-

cover. "They will go to Wyoming and build a fine house."

Atropos raised her brows. "And Dante will finally get around to asking what a range is, and she will tell him and see the world through eyes that have not seen it before."

"Oh, look!" Ilithyia exclaimed. "They will return to the inn sometimes—just the two of them—and the villagers will whisper of legends as Dante and Betina ride over the road by moonlight and make love beside the rosebush."

"There," Clotho said as she carefully wound the threads into skeins. "They are finished and will be set aside until it is time for them to be cut."

"A pity," Atropos said. "I have grown fond of them and will miss them when their time is done."

"They will always be with us," Nemesis said. "For new life grows within Betina, and they will live on through their children and through the memories they leave behind."

Clotho nodded as she began spinning a new thread, thin and fragile with only a wisp of color, but it would be strengthened by new fibers as life was strengthened by time and experience. "And we will guide them as they choose which paths to follow."

"Guide, but not interfere," Nemesis warned.

"I rather enjoyed interfering," Atropos said. "And the occasion will rise again—of that I have no doubt. Humans are a foolhardy lot."

"What of Phineas?" Ilithyia asked with downcast eyes.

"He will come back to you," Nemesis replied. "For he is a part of us and will guide others who lose their way."

Ilithyia sighed and smiled, and a flush of anticipation spread through her.

"I had hoped the woodland would thrive," Lachesis said.

"The past cannot thrive, sister," Ilithyia said. "It can only stand as a reminder of itself."

"Have patience," Nemesis said. "In time new life will spring from the earth."

"It always does," Atropos murmured.

The five sisters of Fate fell silent as the images in the flames returned to the present—Dante and Betina awakening and rising from the ground and strolling hand in hand into the old inn. The flame of a single candle sputtered and died as they closed the door, shutting out the rest of the world for a little while longer.

Atropos knelt in front of the hearth, watching as sunlight brightened the sky. The trees stood dark and brooding like wizards frozen in time, their trunks bowed and bent as if they watched the roses bloom and gathered hope that, they, too, might come to life again. She turned to her sisters with tears brimming in her eyes. "It is a fitting end for a legend."

Nemesis rose from her chair and waved her hand over the flame, banishing the images as Dante and Betina stood in the window of the corner bedroom, their arms around one another, their mouths joined as their futures were joined. She wiped her eyes and smiled. "And they lived happily ever after," she mused. "A fitting ending indeed."

And still of a winter's night, they say, when the wind is in the trees,
When the moon is a ghostly galleon tossed upon cloudy seas,
When the road is a ribbon of moonlight over the purple moor,
A highwayman comes riding—
Riding—riding—
A highwayman comes riding, up to the old inn-door.

Over the cobbles he clatters and clangs in the dark inn-yard;
And he taps with his whip on the shutters, but all is locked and barred;
He whistles a tune to the window, and who should be waiting there
But the landlord's black-eyed daughter,
Bess, the landlord's daughter,
Plaiting a dark red love-knot into her long black hair.

The Highwayman—*Alfred Noyes*

Author's Note

Being a romantic, I have cried over the ending of Alfred Noyes's poem *The Highwayman* since I first read it many years ago. At that time, I wondered how Dante and Bess could have a happy ending and knew that someday, I would attempt to remain faithful to the poem I love so much and yet give Dante and Bess the ending they deserve. *Forever and a Day* is that attempt.

Because it is intended to be a kind of fairy tale, I felt free to play with history just a bit. Therefore Betina's father, Jacob Wells, founded the first dude ranch, though, in fact, such establishments did not come into being until the very end of the nineteenth century. My reasoning in adjusting time to suit myself? The culture already existed for such an enterprise. European noblemen and wealthy businessmen were going west—for the adventure and novelty and opportunity offered by the vast open spaces and resources of the territories. Some journeyed to Wyoming for what was reputed to be the cleanest air on earth. Others migrated out of greed arising from progress. Railroads and cattle ranches were springing up everywhere and making a privileged few rich beyond compare. Some lost their wealth with the toss of a card or the natural rise and fall of economic growth. Others increased their fortunes many times over by investing in the progress of the Industrial Revolution and the wonders of scientific discovery.

What an exciting and puzzling world Dante must find himself in when he at last ventures forth from the woodland that would forever remain in winter sleep. I leave it to you, the reader, to imagine his awe and wonder as he and Betina take their places in the world and build their own empire to pass on to their children.

Alfred Noyes penned *The Highwayman* some time after *Forever and a Day* takes place. I think that Dante and Betina read it and smiled with the knowledge that there are endings and then there are *endings.* In my imagination, the petrified woodland stands as a monument to past wrongs. Dante and Betina themselves remind us that hope is the second greatest resource in the souls of mankind.

As for the Five Sisters of Fate—they continue to bicker and meddle and fan the flames of human imagination. . . .

Sometime . . . somewhere.

I hope that your imagination will be captured by Dante and Betina as mine was so long ago.

Happy reading!
Connie Rinehold